D0556131

THE SHOGUN'S DAUGHTER

THE SHOGUN'S DAUGHTER

娘

Laura Joh Rowland

MINOTAUR BOOKS
NEW YORK

THE SHOGUN'S DAUGHTER. Copyright © 2013 by Laura Joh Rowland. All rights reserved. Printed in the United States of America. For information, address St. Martin's Press, 175 Fifth Avenue, New York, N.Y. 10010.

www.minotaurbooks.com

Library of Congress Cataloging-in-Publication Data

Rowland, Laura Joh.
    The Shogun's daughter : a novel of Feudal Japan / Laura Joh Rowland.—First edition.
        pages cm
    ISBN 978-1-250-02861-7 (hardcover)
    ISBN 978-1-250-02862-4 (e-book)
    1. Sano, Ichiro (Fictitious character)—Fiction.   2. Japan—History—Genroku period, 1688–1704—Fiction.   I. Title.
    PS3568.O934S34 2013
    813'.54—dc23

                                                                    2013013933

Minotaur books may be purchased for educational, business, or promotional use. For information on bulk purchases, please contact Macmillan Corporate and Premium Sales Department at 1-800-221-7945, extension 5442, or write specialmarkets@macmillan.com.

First Edition: September 2013

10   9   8   7   6   5   4   3   2   1

To my in-laws: Bob Rowland, Jim and Audrey Rowland,
Cynthia and Steve Gray, and Pam Rowland.
In memory of Jim and Wanda Rowland and John Rowland.
Thanks to all for love and support.

Historical Note

A STREAK OF misfortune began for Japan with the great earthquake of December 1703, which leveled most of Edo, caused a giant tsunami, and killed thousands of people. In a ritualistic attempt to usher in better times, the government changed the name of the era from Genroku to Hōei. It didn't help. In May 1704, the shogun's daughter, Tsuruhime, died at age twenty-seven. Her husband died a month later. Tsuruhime's death had serious ramifications for the future of the Tokugawa regime. She was the shogun's only child. It was unlikely that he would sire any others. Tsuruhime's death cost him the chance of a grandson to inherit the throne. Faced with his own mortality, he was under pressure to name a successor. Some historical sources say that Chamberlain Yanagisawa, the shogun's longtime advisor, tried to pass his son, Yoshisato, off as the shogun's son. Had he succeeded, Yoshisato would have become the next shogun, and Yanagisawa would have ruled Japan through him. Other sources debunk this story. If Yanagisawa did try such an audacious scheme to seize power, it didn't work. The shogun adopted his nephew, Tokugawa Ienobu, and designated him as the official heir and successor. However, the troubles continued. In July 1704 Lady Keisho-in, the shogun's mother, died at age seventy-eight. In 1707 another earthquake struck Japan, and Mount Fuji erupted. In 1709 the shogun died of measles, during an epidemic. Ienobu became shogun. *The Shogun's Daughter* is an episode in my story of what might have happened during those tumultuous times.

THE SHOGUN'S DAUGHTER

Prologue

Edo, Month 4, Hōei Year 1
(Tokyo, May 1704)

MOANS FILLED A chamber lit by a single dim lantern. On the bed, an emaciated young woman writhed under the quilt. Her face was an ugly mask of swollen pustules, covered by gray membranes, that clustered on her features, sealed her eyes shut, and preyed on her mouth like leeches. Pustules on her scalp oozed bloody fluid through her cropped hair onto her pillow. She whimpered in agony, fever, and delirium.

A nurse dressed in a blue cotton kimono, a white drape shrouding her face, knelt by the bed. She patted the sick young woman's hands, which wore mitts to prevent her from scratching the pustules, and murmured soothingly. On the tatami floor, one table held basins, soiled cloths, and ceramic jars of medicine; another supported an array of brass incense burners. The smoke from these saturated the air with bitter, astringent haze intended to banish the evil spirits of disease. On the walls, in murals of marsh scenes, herons, geese, and cranes peered avidly through the reeds, like carrion birds waiting for a fresh kill. Painted water lilies rotted in the stench of the young woman's decaying flesh.

A white gauze curtain hung over the doorway. Beyond this hovered two shadowy figures. Standing in the dark corridor outside the sickroom, they peered through the flimsy barrier that guarded them from contagion. One was a man dressed in sumptuously patterned silk kimono, surcoat, and flowing trousers. Short legs supported his long torso and

1

broad shoulders. The crown of his head was shaved in samurai style; his hair, worn in the customary topknot, gleamed with wintergreen oil. His companion was an old woman. Her modest gray robes clothed a figure as thin and fleshless as a skeleton. Silver-streaked black hair, knotted and anchored with lacquer combs, framed a narrow face whose right side was distorted, its muscles bunched together, the eye half closed as if in pain.

"Is there nothing more that can be done for her?" the man asked.

"There is not, according to the doctors." The woman's speech was precise, cultured. "They say that smallpox is not always fatal, but Tsuruhime has a bad case." She added in a waspish tone, "Which you would have heard, if you had been at home these past few days."

Annoyed and defensive, the man said, "I had important things to do."

"What could be more important than attending your wife on her deathbed?"

The man sucked air through his teeth. "At least it shouldn't be long now."

"You must be very pleased," the old woman said.

"I'm not thinking of myself," huffed the man. "I'm thinking of Tsuruhime. I don't want her to suffer anymore."

"What a pity you weren't so considerate of her when it might have made a difference."

The man cut an irate glance at the old woman. "Thank the gods I won't have to put up with an old busybody like you interfering in my affairs for much longer."

The woman stood as stiffly as a blighted tree in a storm. Her distorted face hardened with her determination to control her temper. "You should thank the gods if they don't punish you for your evils someday."

In the chamber, the sick young woman's movements stilled. Her whimpers faded to mewls, then ceased. The man and old woman watched in acrimonious silence. The young woman's breath rattled loudly, then quieted. Her chest rose and fell for the last time.

The old woman clasped her hand over her mouth. Tears spilled over her fingers. The man puffed his cheeks and blew out a sound that expressed more relief than regret.

The nurse picked up a chopstick wrapped with cotton on the end.

She dipped the cotton in a cup of water. She wetted the young woman's blistered lips, administering the *matsugo-no-mizu*—water of the last moment, the final attempt to revive a dead person. The young woman didn't swallow or move. The water trickled off her lips, gleaming in the lanternlight. The nurse looked toward the doorway and shook her head.

The two spectators stood united in apprehension. At least one of them knew this death was more complicated than it seemed. They both knew it would have serious repercussions. The old woman turned to the man. Her streaming eyes were so filled with grief that he couldn't meet them. She spoke in a challenging tone.

"Who wants to tell the shogun his daughter is dead?"

FIVE MONTHS AFTER the earthquake struck Edo, the castle was a giant construction site on its hill above the city. New stone-faced retaining walls braced the ascending tiers of leveled ground. Guard towers atop walls climbed skyward as masons repaired them. Buildings within the compounds on every tier wore grids of bamboo scaffolding in which workers swarmed. Animated by human activity, the castle seemed to move within the scaffolding, like a creature struggling to emerge from a cocoon. All across the sunlit city below rang the noise of saws and hammers—the birth cries of a city rising from the ruins at a furious, reckless pace.

Chamberlain Sano Ichirō led a procession of samurai officials toward the palace, at the heart of the castle, on its highest tier. Brown ceramic tile fresh from the kiln gleamed atop new, interconnected structures whose half-timbered walls wore a coat of dazzling white plaster. New saplings replaced trees uprooted during the earthquake or burned by the fires that came afterward. New white gravel covered the paths upon which Sano and his colleagues walked through the din from construction in other parts of the castle. The air scintillated with sawdust motes that settled on the men's black silk ceremonial robes emblazoned with gold family crests, on their shaved crowns and oiled topknots, on the two swords at each waist.

Ohgami Kaoru, member of the Council of Elders that constituted Japan's chief governing body, walked up beside Sano. "What's the reason for this emergency assembly?"

He'd aged fast since the earthquake, as had almost everyone else Sano knew. Sad wrinkles in his once youthful face matched the premature whiteness of his hair.

"Your guess is as good as mine." The earthquake effect hadn't spared Sano, either. At age forty-six he felt twice as old. Every morning when he looked in the mirror, he saw more gray streaks in his black hair, and his shaved crown had a silvery glint. He'd worked night and day, for five months, to rebuild the city and the wide outlying areas devastated by the earthquake.

"The shogun's second-in-command is as much in the dark as everybody else?" Ohgami said. "That's a bad sign."

The procession marched up the steps to the palace, past the sentries, and into the reception room. The sweet smells of fresh wood and tatami graced the air. A new mural adorned the wall behind the dais—purple irises blooming along a blue-and-silver river on a gilded background. More soldiers than usual lined the walls. General Isogai, commander of the Tokugawa army, stood by the dais. His physique was still stoutly muscled, his head bulbous on his thick neck, but his complexion was too red.

As men knelt in positions according to rank, murmurs arose. "Why all the extra troops? Is the shogun expecting violence to break out?" "It might, if this is about another round of promotions and demotions." "These are strange times. Even if you've performed admirably in your position for decades, you're apt to be dismissed in favor of a nobody who can bring in supplies from the provinces or pay extra taxes into the government's treasury." "How much more of this upheaval can everyone take?"

The earthquake had made and broken more careers than Sano cared to tally. He seated himself on the raised section of floor immediately below the dais. Ohgami and the other four old men from the Council of Elders sat in a row to his right. General Isogai came over and ponderously lowered himself to his knees on Sano's left. He wheezed and gripped his chest. The air filled with body heat and the odor of sweat. Sano's nerves vibrated with the tension that had built up in the atmosphere since the earthquake. Nonstop work had taxed his and his colleagues' endurance, had depleted their physical and mental reserves. He didn't know how much more they all could take, either.

The door behind the dais opened. Murmurs subsided as the shogun emerged. The shogun looked a decade older than his fifty-eight years, although Sano knew he'd done not a lick of work for the earthquake recovery. Frail shoulders stooped under his gold satin robes. The cylindrical black cap of his rank sat on a balding head with hardly enough hair to form a knot. The skin on his aristocratic face was like a crumpled, yellowish paper. He leaned on Sano's twelve-year-old son, Masahiro.

Masahiro settled the shogun on cushions on the dais, then knelt behind him. He wore his hair in a long forelock tied with a ribbon, in the style of samurai who haven't yet reached manhood at age fifteen. Tall and slender, strong from rigorous martial arts practice, he had intelligent eyes set in a mature, handsome face. Whenever Sano looked at his son, he ached with pride. Masahiro served as head of the shogun's private chambers, a post he'd won by proving himself capable after older, more qualified palace attendants had been killed by the earthquake.

The assembly bowed to the shogun. He raised his hand in a perfunctory greeting, then spoke. "We have had some, ahh, dark days since the earthquake. It was the worst natural disaster of my reign." A new tremor afflicted his reedy voice. "I hoped that changing the name of the era, from Genroku to Hōei, would help." Whenever a run of misfortune plagued Japan, the Emperor would proclaim a new era, in a ritualistic attempt to usher in better times. "But alas, it didn't. I'm afraid I have terrible news. My daughter, Tsuruhime, died of smallpox last night."

Sano and the other men in the room cast their gazes downward, troubled by the news of yet another death. More than a hundred thousand people had been crushed during the earthquake, burned in the fires, drowned in the tsunami, or succumbed to diseases afterward. Sano thought of Fukida, one of his favorite retainers, who had died. He felt lucky and guilty that his wife and two children were safe and well. He sensed caution in the air, like a veil of smoke.

No one here had personally known Tsuruhime; she'd lived in seclusion for her entire life. The officials were less concerned about her demise than about its effect on the shogun, whose whim commanded the power of life and death over everybody.

"It's unnatural to outlive one's child. How could it happen to me?" Anger lit a red blush spot in each of the shogun's sallow cheeks. "It's not fair!"

He'd apparently forgotten that many other parents had recently lost children during the disaster. Sano wasn't surprised that the shogun was more concerned about his own feelings than about his daughter, who'd died at the young age of twenty-seven. The shogun was the most selfish person Sano had ever known.

"I'm just glad I, ahh, stayed away from Tsuruhime when she took ill. Or I might have contracted the smallpox, too!" The shogun looked horrified at the idea rather than sorry he hadn't visited or said good-bye to her. "Her fate has made me more aware than ever of my own mortality. I, too, could be suddenly carried off by the evil spirit of death! And that is why . . ." He paused for suspenseful effect. "The time has come for me to, ahh, designate my successor."

Coughs among the audience disguised exclamations of awe. For many years Tokugawa clan members had vied to manipulate the shogun into bequeathing the regime to them or their children. Officials had backed the contenders in the hope of favors later. So had the *daimyo*—feudal lords who governed Japan's provinces. Now the speculation and competition were about to end. Dismay imploded within Sano.

He knew what was going to happen. He'd been fighting to prevent it, and he'd failed.

"For many years I put off naming a successor because I, ahh, didn't have a son," the shogun said. "I've been reluctant to adopt a relative as my heir." That was the usual custom for men of position who lacked sons, but the shogun desperately wished to be succeeded by the fruit of his own loins. "I prayed I would father a male child. I hoped Tsuruhime would, ahh, produce a grandson who would at least be my direct descendant. Well, that hope is gone. Thank the gods I don't need her anymore."

The relief in his voice offended Sano, who dearly loved his own young daughter, Akiko, and couldn't imagine valuing her solely as breeding stock.

"The gods have blessed me with a son, whose existence I was unaware of until recently. Now I present him to you as my official heir." The shogun clapped his hands. "Behold Tokugawa Yoshisato, my newfound son, the next ruler of Japan!"

A door at the side of the dais opened. A young samurai walked out and mounted the dais. Silk robes in shades of copper and gold clothed his compact, wiry build. He knelt at the shogun's right. His handsome face was wide with a rounded chin, his tilted eyes thoughtful and wary. The audience reacted to him with expressions that ranged from approval to caution to the horrified outrage that Sano felt.

General Isogai muttered, "If Yoshisato is really the shogun's son, then whales can fly."

It was common knowledge that the shogun preferred sex with men rather than women. That he'd sired a daughter was a miracle. Sano couldn't believe the shogun was Yoshisato's father by any stretch of imagination.

"Merciful gods," Elder Ohgami whispered. "It's really happening. The shogun is going to put a pretender at the head of the government!"

Yoshisato sat still and calm, with self-control impressive for a seventeen-year-old. Sano barely knew him but suspected he was smart enough to understand that although he had supporters who wanted him to inherit the regime, he also had many political enemies who would like to see him drop off the face of the earth, Sano and friends included.

Another man followed Yoshisato onto the dais. The shogun said, "And here is Yoshisato's adoptive father—my good friend Yanagisawa Yoshiyasu."

Yanagisawa was the only person Sano knew whose appearance had improved since the earthquake. The disaster had strengthened his tall, slender figure and enhanced his striking masculine beauty. His skin glowed with health; his dark, liquid eyes glistened.

Hatred boiled inside Sano as he watched Yanagisawa kneel at the shogun's left. He and Yanagisawa had been enemies for fifteen years, since Sano had entered the shogun's service. Yanagisawa, then chamberlain, had seen Sano as a rival. He'd done his best to destroy Sano, sabotaging his work, undermining his authority, criticizing him to the shogun. That was standard practice among officials jockeying for position, but Yanagisawa had also set assassins on Sano and attacked his family. While defending himself, his kin, and his honor, Sano had dealt Yanagisawa a few good blows. The rivalry between them was a constant cycle. One's fortunes rose while the other's fell. Now Yanagisawa smiled, with bla-tant triumph, straight at Sano.

Although Sano was currently chamberlain, the top dog in their feud, and Yanagisawa currently had no official position in the government, Yanagisawa was now the adoptive father of the shogun's official heir. He'd just won his biggest advantage over Sano: influence with the next shogun, a foothold in the future. And Sano knew he'd done it by sheer, outrageous fraud.

" 'Adoptive father,' my behind." General Isogai's face grew redder with anger.

"If he's not Yoshisato's real father, then I'm the emperor of China," Ohgami whispered.

The shogun beamed, trapped between Yanagisawa and Yoshisato. Everyone in the audience turned to Sano. Hostility narrowed the eyes of the men who'd decided to believe Yoshisato was the shogun's son and approved of his installation as heir. Sano felt hope pinned on him, like needles stuck in his skin, by his allies who didn't believe or approve.

General Isogai whispered to Sano, "This is your last chance to prevent your worst enemy and his spawn from taking over Japan."

"Give it your best shot," Ohgami urged in a low, fervent voice.

Sano was leader of the effort to disqualify Yoshisato. His allies were either too afraid or prudent to touch the job themselves. Sano didn't know whether his acceptance of it was more courageous or foolish, but he had to thwart Yanagisawa, or Yanagisawa would deprive him of his head as well as his place in the government. And it was his duty to protect his lord and the Tokugawa regime from Yanagisawa's plot to gain permanent power. That was Bushido, the Way of the Warrior, the samurai code of honor by which Sano lived.

Before Sano could speak, a man in the front row on the lower level of the floor reared up on his knees. He had a stunted figure and a hump on his back. It was Tokugawa Ienobu, son of the shogun's deceased older brother.

"Uncle, please excuse me." His tight voice seemed squeezed out of him. His upper teeth protruded above an abnormally small lower jaw. These deformities stemmed from a hereditary bone condition. "I must say this is the wrong time to designate your heir."

Yanagisawa's shoulders moved in a slight shrug: He'd expected an objection from Ienobu and he didn't fear him. Caution veiled Yoshisato's expression.

"I don't excuse you," the shogun snapped. "Why, pray tell, is this the wrong time?"

"You've just experienced the tragic loss of your daughter," Ienobu said. "Your emotions are affecting your judgment."

"His Excellency has realized the urgent importance of naming an heir," Yanagisawa interjected in a smooth, reasonable voice. "His son is his rightful successor."

"Why can't you be happy for me that I have the heir I always wanted?" the shogun whined at Ienobu. "Why do you want to spoil my, ahh, pleasure?"

"That's the last thing I want to do, Uncle," Ienobu said, as desperate to avert the shogun's wrath as he was to change his mind. "I just think you should consider the alternatives before you make such a serious decision about the future of the regime."

The shogun frowned in confusion. "What alternatives?"

"Honorable Father, perhaps Lord Ienobu wants to be named as your successor himself." Yoshisato spoke in a deferential tone while exposing his rival's base motives.

"Is that true, Nephew?" the shogun demanded. He disliked ambitious men who openly wangled favors from him.

"Not at all, Uncle," Ienobu hastened to say. But Sano knew Ienobu had worked hard to ingratiate himself with the shogun. Before Yoshisato had appeared on the scene, Ienobu had been the heir apparent. Ienobu's eagerness to get rid of Yoshisato and regain his former standing was obvious to everyone except the shogun.

"It's just that you learned about Yoshisato so recently . . . and the circumstances were so strange." Ienobu balked at declaring that he thought Yoshisato wasn't the shogun's child.

Sano jumped into the fire, although challenging the shogun's decision, even for his own good, meant walking a narrow path that bordered on treason. To impugn the shogun's newfound heir equaled courting death.

" 'Strange' is an understatement, Your Excellency." Sano repeated the story Yanagisawa had told when he'd sprung Yoshisato on the shogun: "Eighteen years ago, the court astronomer reads a prophecy in the constellations: You will father a son, but unless he's hidden away upon his birth, you'll be killed by an earthquake that's due to strike Edo in Genroku year sixteen."

Ienobu cast a thankful glance at Sano and continued the tale: "The astronomer confides the prophecy to Yanagisawa. Yanagisawa gives orders that any pregnancies in the palace women's quarters are to be reported to him and no one else. Soon thereafter, your concubine Lady Someko finds herself expecting your child. She tells Yanagisawa, who takes her into his home. Yoshisato is born."

"Yanagisawa adopts and raises Yoshisato as his own child," Sano went on. "He conceals Yoshisato's real parentage. Five months ago, the earthquake strikes, right on schedule. Your Excellency survives. The danger is past. Yanagisawa reveals the secret: Yoshisato is your son." Yanagisawa had plopped Yoshisato into first place in line for the succession, to guarantee that he—as Yoshisato's adoptive father—would be the power behind the next dictator.

The shogun smiled and nodded while he listened, like a child enjoying a favorite bedtime story. "Isn't it an extraordinary miracle?"

"It's so extraordinary that I don't think you should accept it without question," Sano said.

Vexation darkened the shogun's face. "Ahh, yes, you said as much when you first heard about Yoshisato. And I thought you had a good point."

"That's why I advised His Excellency to have you investigate Yoshisato's origins," Yanagisawa said suavely.

Sano suspected that Yanagisawa had suggested the investigation because he'd made sure Sano wouldn't find any evidence to debunk Yoshisato. "My investigation isn't finished."

"You've had four months," Yoshisato said. His youthful, masculine voice had an underlying edge of steel. "Have you proved that His Excellency isn't my father?"

"No," Sano admitted. He'd questioned officials, concubines, guards, and servants in the palace women's quarters, who'd lived or worked there when Yoshisato was conceived. Contrary to common knowledge that the shogun hardly ever bedded a female, the witnesses swore that he'd spent many amorous nights with Lady Someko. Sano suspected they'd been bribed or threatened by Yanagisawa. "But I also haven't proved that His Excellency is your father."

"My physician has analyzed Yoshisato's features and discovered, ahh, striking similarities to mine," the shogun said. Sano cast a dubious glance at Yoshisato. The youth was nothing like the shogun. "And Lady Someko can testify that I'm Yoshisato's father."

"Then why doesn't she?" Sano asked Yanagisawa, "Why are you keeping her locked inside your house instead of letting me interview her?"

"She's too delicate to be interrogated," Yanagisawa said.

"Is the astronomer too delicate? I haven't been able to interview him, either. He seems to have disappeared."

Yanagisawa smirked. "With all your detective expertise, you can't find him?"

He was alluding to Sano's past tenure as the shogun's *sōsakan-sama*— Most Honorable Investigator of Events, Situations, and People. Sano suspected that he couldn't find the astronomer because Yanagisawa had killed the man. "You are the only witness to the astronomer's prophesying about Yoshisato and the earthquake." He turned to the shogun. "Are you willing to accept Yoshisato's pedigree based on one witness's word?" Sano believed with all his heart that Yoshisato was Yanagisawa's own son, foisted off on the shogun.

The shogun tightened his weak mouth in defiance. "Yes. Yanagisawa is my old, dear friend. I trust him implicitly. He wants what's best for me. He wouldn't lie."

"If he wants what's best, then he should be glad to assist with my investigation." Sano said to Yanagisawa, "Why not advise His Excellency to grant me a little more time? And let me interview Lady Someko and the astronomer? Surely it's best that the question of Yoshisato's origin should be settled, so that nobody can dispute his right to rule Japan."

Rumbles of agreement came from the audience. Sano figured that his partisans thought there was still a chance he could prove Yoshisato a fake, and Yanagisawa's partisans believed Yoshisato's pedigree would be validated.

"Would Your Excellency rather risk putting a man who has none of your blood at the head of the Tokugawa dictatorship?" Sano asked.

The shogun shrank from this nightmare scenario. "Well . . ."

Elder Ohgami whispered to Sano, "Good shot."

Yoshisato touched the shogun's sleeve. "Please excuse me, but if there's even a slight chance that I'm not really your son, then I would rather go away than inherit a position I don't deserve." Sincerity permeated his manner.

The audience clamored in surprise. Few would turn down the chance to become shogun. Sano opened his mouth to call Yoshisato's bluff and tell the shogun to let Yoshisato go. So did Ienobu. Yanagisawa preempted them both.

"How selfless Yoshisato is," Yanagisawa said in a reverent voice. "He would sacrifice his right to rule Japan in order to err on the side of caution and protect Your Excellency."

General Isogai muttered, "How full of horse dung that bastard is!"

The shogun regarded Yoshisato with awe; he wiped a tear from his eye. Yanagisawa said, "The choice is clear, Your Excellency. Listen to Chamberlain Sano and drive Yoshisato away. Or accept Yoshisato as your son and be happy."

"Those aren't the only possible choices," Sano protested. "Your Excellency can allow the investigation to continue, and if it validates Yoshisato's pedigree, you can rest easy about naming him as your successor."

Ienobu jumped on the chance of reviving his hope of gaining the dictatorship. "If his pedigree is shown to be false, then you've saved yourself from making a terrible mistake."

The shogun vacillated. Nobody moved or made a sound. Suspense depleted the air supply. Sano could hardly breathe. The shogun studied Ienobu. Visibly repulsed by the physical defects of his nephew, his other choice of an heir, he grabbed Yoshisato's hand and declared, "Yoshisato is my son, my rightful heir and successor."

Amid pleased murmurs and resigned sighs, the assembly bowed to their future lord. Ienobu sank down, stricken. Yoshisato bowed in gratitude. Yanagisawa gave Sano a smug glance. No other battle Sano had fought with Yanagisawa had been as critical as this one he'd just lost.

"Now that that's settled, I have an announcement," Yanagisawa said. "There will be some changes within the government." The atmosphere turned noxious with panic as men realized that a purge was about to begin. Yanagisawa's gaze fixed on Ienobu. "You're no longer needed."

Ienobu's tiny jaw sagged. "What?" he croaked.

Yanagisawa smiled. "You heard me."

"Honorable Uncle—"

The shogun waved his hand as if shooing a fly. "You're dismissed. Go."

A picture of outrage and disbelief, Ienobu shuffled out of the room. Sano breathed the iron smell of blood in the air as everyone realized that if a Tokugawa relative could be thrown out of the court, no one was safe.

Yanagisawa said, "Ohgami-*san,* you are relieved of your seat on the Council of Elders."

Horror turned Ohgami's face as white as his hair. "But . . . but I've held it for twenty-five years!"

"Twenty-five years is long enough," Yanagisawa said.

Sano hated to see his friend's distress as much as he hated to lose his main ally on the Council. "Elder Ohgami is one of His Excellency's most competent advisors."

"Competence isn't the issue," Yanagisawa said. "Loyalty is. His Excellency wants to be sure he can count on his top officials to be loyal to Yoshisato. And he can't count on Ohgami-*san.*" He pointed toward the door.

Ohgami limped out like a wounded animal.

"General Isogai," Yanagisawa said, "You are demoted to captain at the army base in Ezogashima."

Ezogashima was the far northernmost island of Japan. General Isogai's flushed face turned purple. "No!" he roared, clenching his fists. "You can't do this to me! I won't go!"

"He's the army's best qualified commander," Sano protested. "You need him to protect the country."

"He can't be counted on to protect Yoshisato." Yanagisawa knew that General Isogai was among those who'd tried to block Yoshisato's installation. He beckoned to the soldiers. "You can go peacefully or not. But you will go."

Threatened with forcible ejection by his former troops, General Isogai hauled himself to his feet. He stalked out, muttering curses. Sano felt the coldness of the empty spaces on either side of him. And now Yanagisawa turned his predatory gaze on Sano.

"I'm taking over as chamberlain." Yanagisawa blazed with triumph; he'd wrested away from Sano the post they'd fought over for years, and he would probably hold it for his entire life, during the remainder of the shogun's reign and then Yoshisato's. "As for you . . ."

Sano knew there was no use arguing, blustering, or appealing to the shogun, whose gaze avoided him. He demonstrated stoic dignity as terror seized his heart. Yanagisawa wouldn't merely retire him or demote him. Too much bad blood existed between them. This was the end.

Yanagisawa smiled at Sano. After all these years as enemies they had an almost mystical bond; each could read the other's thoughts and emotions. Sano looked at his son, Masahiro, kneeling on the dais behind the shogun. Masahiro was too young to conceal his fear, but not too young to know that Yanagisawa would put Sano's entire family to death, so that nobody in it could avenge Sano. The assembly waited in hushed suspense to hear Sano's fate. Noise like a landslide of boulders came from the construction site outside.

"You will serve as Chief Rebuilding Magistrate," Yanagisawa said.

Shock rippled through the assembly. Masahiro gaped. Sano couldn't believe his ears. As Chief Rebuilding Magistrate, he would oversee the process of converting a pile of ruins to a new capital. Yanagisawa was letting him live, keeping him in the regime. Why?

Yanagisawa reeled off names, demotions, retirements, transfers, reassignments. Sano watched his allies leave the room. Most marched stoically with their heads high; others wept. An elderly minister fainted and the guards carried him out. Yanagisawa announced the names of the replacements, who filed into the chamber and knelt in the vacated spaces. In an instant the whole government had been reorganized. Sano sat alone amid Yanagisawa's cronies.

The shogun looked blank, unaware of the coup that had just occurred under his nose. Yoshisato's face was calm, controlled. Replete with pleasure, Yanagisawa said, "Oh, I almost forgot." He jerked his chin at Masahiro. "Get off the dais. You're no longer the head of the shogun's chambers. You'll be a castle page."

Obviously crushed by his demotion to his former rank, Masahiro stepped down from the dais, shamed in front of the whole assembly. Sano felt angrier for Masahiro than for himself. He knew how much pride the innocent boy had taken in the position he'd lost through no fault of his own. Sano could barely contain his urge to beat Yanagisawa to a bloody pulp.

The shogun had eyes only for Yoshisato. "Now I will install my son in the residence that is reserved for my heir and successor."

Yoshisato helped him descend from the dais. Yanagisawa followed. The officials rose and marched after the three men. Shinto priests in white robes appeared. Beating drums, they led the procession out the door. Troops waved banners emblazoned with the Tokugawa triple-hollyhock-leaf crest. Appalled by the festivity that had sprung from carnage, Sano and Masahiro trailed the procession outside. Musicians playing flutes and samisens materialized. A small crowd of men who'd been purged loitered by the palace entrance, too dazed to know what to do or too afraid to go home and tell their families what had happened. General Isogai and Elder Ohgami were among them. As Sano started toward his former allies, General Isogai's face turned gray. He clutched at his heart, moaned, and collapsed.

"Somebody fetch a doctor!" Sano called, kneeling beside the panting, groaning Isogai.

Ohgami knelt and drew his short sword. His face looked oddly flaccid, as if the blow to his honor had shattered the underlying bone. He plunged the sword into his stomach.

Sano realized with horror that his two friends had reached the limits of their fortitude. But he knew that his own were still to be tested.

娘

2

AT SANO'S ESTATE inside Edo Castle, carpenters built roofs on new, unfinished buildings grafted onto portions of the mansion that hadn't collapsed during the earthquake. They erected framework for barracks that would surround the mansion and house Sano's troops, who temporarily lived in tents on the grounds. Masons fitted new stone facings onto the earthen foundations of the walls around the compound. Work ceased only long enough for the men to bolt down food, to drink water and splash it on their sweating faces. Reconstruction of the castle was top priority, human fatigue no excuse for delay.

In the garden at the center of the private chambers, a little girl and boy ran across a bridge that arched over a pond to a pavilion in the middle. A white, orange, and black kitten chased a string that the boy dangled. The girl laughed gleefully. A canopy on wooden posts stood where the earthquake had shaken down the pavilion's roof. Under the canopy, Lady Reiko reclined on cushions. Her friend Midori knelt beside her, sewing as they watched their children play. Midori's baby lay asleep on a blanket. Reiko fanned her damp brow with a silk fan. She'd come outside to get some fresh air and escape the carpenters' hammering and sawing, but the weather was warm and she could still hear the noise. Being six months pregnant added to her discomfort.

"My other two pregnancies were so easy." Reiko clasped her round belly. She'd gained much more weight than previously, her legs were swollen, and occasional contractions made her nervous. "I don't know why this one is so difficult."

"You're a lot older this time," Midori said.

Piqued by this catty rejoinder, Reiko glanced sharply at Midori. "I'm only thirty-four." Then she saw Midori frowning fiercely as she jabbed the needle through the sash she was embroidering. Preoccupied with her own problems, she didn't realize what she'd said.

Shrieks came from the bridge. Midori's six-year-old son, Tatsuo, held the kitten by its shoulders. "Give it to me!" Reiko's five-year-old daughter, Akiko, pulled on its hind legs, crying, "Mine!" The kitten mewed frantically.

Midori jumped up, hurled down her sewing, and yelled, "Tatsuo! Akiko! Stop fighting over that cat, or I'm going to kill you!"

Startled, the children released the kitten. Midori's gaze searched the garden. "Taeko! Where are you?"

Her nine-year-old daughter ambled out from a bamboo grove. A slender girl with serious eyes in a round face and long, glossy black hair tied back with an orange ribbon, Taeko held a paintbrush. Her pale green, flowered kimono was stained with ink.

"Are you painting again?" Disapproval roughened Midori's voice. "Painting isn't for girls!" Taeko hung her head. "You're supposed to be watching your brother and Akiko." Midori pointed at the younger children. "Get over there!"

The baby woke up and started to cry. Taeko hurried onto the bridge, gathered the younger children, and took them into the house. The kitten scampered after them. Midori's temper dissolved into tears. "I shouldn't get so mad at the children." She sank to her knees, picked up the baby girl, and rocked her. "What's wrong with me?"

Reiko pushed herself upright and hugged her friend. "You're just upset about Hirata."

Hirata was Midori's husband and Sano's chief retainer. The two families were as close as blood kin, but lately their relations had been troubled, on account of Hirata.

Midori sobbed. "He's been gone for four months! I don't know where. I haven't heard a word from him!"

"There must be a good reason," Reiko said, trying to console her.

"It's his damned mystic martial arts!"

Nine years ago Hirata had begun studying the mystic martial arts with an itinerant priest. Since then he'd spent much time away from his family, taking lessons, practicing, and doing whatever else mystic martial artists did. Hirata's frequent, unexplained disappearances had strained his relationship with Sano as well as his marriage.

"He'll come back," Reiko assured Midori. "He always does."

"But maybe he's been in another fight. Maybe he's dead!"

Hirata had a reputation as one of the best martial artists in Japan. Other expert fighters were always challenging him to duels. Although no one had beaten him yet, Midori feared the day when someone would.

"He can take care of himself. Don't worry." They often had this conversation. Reiko said these same things over and over.

"How can I not worry? He's left us in such a mess." Midori's woe yielded to a new surge of anger. "He's never here when Sano-*san* needs him. Sano-*san* gives him a leave of absence to fix whatever problem is keeping him away from his duties, but instead of straightening himself out, my wonderful husband disappears again!"

Reiko was saddened by Midori's contempt toward the man she'd once loved.

"And when the shogun wants him, he isn't here." Hirata was the shogun's *sōsakan-sama,* a post he'd inherited from Sano when Sano became chamberlain. "So the shogun took away his post, his stipend, and his estate!" Midori wailed, "I don't have my husband, my children don't have their father, and we're poor and homeless!"

"You can stay with us for as long as you need to," Reiko said in a soothing voice.

Midori wept with gratitude. "You're so kind. We don't deserve it. Not when my husband has behaved so dishonorably toward yours. Sano will cast him off."

"No, he won't." But Reiko knew how displeased Sano was with Hirata. If Hirata didn't shape up, Sano would have to cast him off, never mind that they were old friends and Sano owed his life to Hirata. It was not only Sano's right as a master, but his duty to uphold Bushido, the Way of the Warrior. Hirata would become a *rōnin*—a masterless samurai; he and his family would have to fend for themselves with no place in society. Reiko didn't want to tell Midori that this was a definite possibility.

"It's those three friends of his!" Midori said angrily. "This is all their fault!"

Sano had told Reiko the little he knew: Hirata had met three martial artists, fellow disciples of his teacher Ozuno; they'd involved him in some secret business; Hirata wouldn't say what kind. Sano feared Hirata was in serious trouble.

"My husband wants to help," Reiko said. "But he can't unless Hirata tells him what's going on. And Hirata won't."

"He won't tell me, either!"

Reiko saw Hirata's behavior threatening her relationship with Midori as well as Hirata's samurai-master bond with Sano. The two couples had been close friends for more than ten years. Reiko would hate to see that end. Friendship was something rare that she cherished in this world of shifting political alliances.

The background noise changed. Drums, flutes, and samisens joined in the din of hammers and saws. This was the first music in the castle since the earthquake. Curious, Reiko positioned herself on her knees, then carefully stood. She saw Sano and Masahiro walking through the garden toward her, two dark figures in their black ceremonial robes.

"What's that music?" Reiko called. As they moved closer, she noticed Masahiro's bowed head and Sano's jaw set in anger. "What's wrong?"

"The music is from the procession accompanying Yoshisato to the heir's residence." Sano crossed the bridge and joined her in the pavilion. "The shogun just named Yoshisato as his successor."

"Oh, no." Reiko knew how hard Sano had worked to prove that Yoshisato wasn't the shogun's son. His failure distressed her as much as him. This was a far bigger problem than Hirata. Yanagisawa, her family's worst enemy, had won his bid for power.

Masahiro ran into the house. Reiko started to follow him, but Sano said, "He's upset. Let him go."

"There's more bad news, isn't there?" Dread skewered through Reiko.

Midori collected herself enough to realize that Reiko and Sano needed privacy. She picked up the baby and her sewing and went into the mansion. Reiko saw large red splotches on the white lapels of Sano's under-kimono.

"Is that blood?" She felt a stab of fear and a sudden contraction. "Are you hurt?"

"It's not mine."

The contraction subsided. "Then whose . . . ?"

"Elder Ohgami," Sano said, his voice tight. "He committed *seppuku* outside the palace. After he stabbed himself, I had to cut off his head to put him out of his misery." That was the usual procedure during ritual suicide.

"Merciful gods!" Reiko was as much bewildered as horrified. "Why did he do it?"

"He was demoted. So was General Isogai. He had a heart attack. The doctors don't know whether he'll live." Sano knelt beside Reiko and described the purge. "Yanagisawa is in control of the government. He's replaced his enemies with his cronies."

Reiko quickly grasped the dismaying implications. "That includes you and Masahiro?"

Sano nodded curtly.

Reiko burned with rage. She hated Yanagisawa as much as Sano did. Yanagisawa had once tried to kill Masahiro. And he now had unbridled authority. Reiko had a terrifying vision of her family cast out, disgraced, sentenced to death, executed.

"Masahiro has been demoted to page," Sano said. "I'm no longer chamberlain. Yanagisawa is. I'm the new Chief Rebuilding Magistrate."

Reiko was as astounded by the reprieve as she was glad of it. "Why didn't Yanagisawa kill you or throw you out of the government?"

"I wonder." Sano seemed equally confused.

"Do we have to move out of our home again?" That had happened the last time Yanagisawa had reclaimed the post of chamberlain from Sano.

"Yanagisawa didn't say he was taking back this estate. I suppose he doesn't want to live here while it's under construction. He has quarters in the palace guesthouse, near the shogun."

"Maybe your allies are protecting you," Reiko said.

"I don't have any left in the government who are in a position to protect me."

"What about the *daimyo*? You have friends among them."

"They have to go along with Yanagisawa. If they make things difficult for him, he could increase the tributes they have to pay the government or seize their fiefs."

"Then why is he keeping you around?"

Sano shook his head, mystified. "Only he knows."

Now that her initial shock was subsiding, now that Sano had survived the purge, Reiko said hopefully, "Maybe he's satisfied to demote you. Maybe he'll leave us alone from now on."

"Well, I'm not satisfied with meekly accepting a demotion." Angry resistance sharpened Sano's tone. "It's a blow to my honor and Masahiro's. I'm not letting Yoshisato become the next shogun, either. I have to fight back."

As much as Reiko suffered the blow herself, she longed for peace. "If the shogun wants Yoshisato for his heir, maybe it's your duty to accept it."

"Never! It's an assault on the regime I'm sworn to protect. Besides, Yanagisawa will never stop attacking us."

One of the sentries rushed into the garden, waving a lacquer scroll container. "Honorable Master! There's an army squadron at the gate. They brought you this."

Sano hurried to meet the sentry. He took the container, removed the scroll, and read it. The anger on his face intensified. "Yanagisawa is cutting my stipend in half. He's also commandeering most of my retainers. The troops are here to take them to their new posts in the provinces." Sano ran toward the gate.

Reiko followed, hampered by her pregnancy. They reached the front courtyard. Hundreds of troops swarmed in, outnumbering Sano's guards. They invaded the barracks and grounds; they called out the names of the men they were taking. The men yelled protests. The officer in charge said to Sano, "We have orders to kill anyone who won't go peacefully."

Furious but helpless, Sano told his men to cooperate. The troops marched them out the gate. Sano was left with some twenty retainers, not even enough to run the estate. Reiko was so upset that she felt faint. Sano helped her into the mansion. He sat her in the reception room and said, "See? What did I tell you? Yanagisawa is setting me up to take me down."

"You're right," Reiko said. "You can't just let things lie. There must be a way to thwart Yanagisawa and get your position and Masahiro's back. Can you talk to the shogun?"

"I'll try," Sano said without hope. "Yanagisawa controls access to the shogun. He also controls the Tokugawa army, now that General Isogai has been demoted."

Reiko posed her next suggestion carefully. "Suppose Yanagisawa were to die. It wouldn't require an army. And with him gone, Yoshisato won't last long."

Sano frowned at her hint that he should assassinate Yanagisawa. "I couldn't do it."

"Why not? Yanagisawa has tried to assassinate you, more times than I can count."

"Because Yanagisawa is my superior and a representative of the shogun. My loyalty to the shogun extends to Yanagisawa. Killing him would be dishonorable."

"Yanagisawa has never had any such qualms about you." Reiko understood that Sano was sworn to uphold Bushido, the strict code that dictated a samurai's behavior. She loved him for his honor. But her own code was different, despite the samurai blood that ran in her veins. She was a mother. Her children's welfare came before duty to Yanagisawa, who was their enemy, or to the shogun, whose capriciousness often put her family in danger. "But your loyalty to the shogun doesn't extend to Yoshisato."

Conflict troubled Sano's expression. "I don't think Yoshisato is the shogun's son. I believe he's Yanagisawa's. But because there's a chance that I'm wrong, I won't risk killing a child of my lord."

"Your honor will be the death of us!" Reiko exclaimed.

"Better an honorable death than a disgraceful life," Sano retorted. "I'll have to find another way to defeat Yanagisawa and prevent Yoshisato from becoming shogun."

No matter how much they loved each other, there were some things they would never agree on, Reiko had to acknowledge. And now, while they were stripped of resources and facing the challenge of a lifetime, they needed unity.

Masahiro ran into the room, his woe replaced by excitement. "Father! There's someone here to see you. It's the shogun's wife."

娘 3

"WHAT ON EARTH is Lady Nobuko doing here?" Reiko asked.

Sano was just as puzzled and surprised. "I've no idea." He'd seen the shogun's wife exactly once, at the end of an investigation into the kidnapping and rape of several women. "Let's find out." Sano helped Reiko to her feet. They followed Masahiro to the reception room.

In the place of honor nearest the alcove that held a calligraphy scroll and a porcelain vase of white azaleas were two women dressed in gray. The elder lay on her back, her sock-clad feet pointed at the ceiling and arms rigid at her sides, on the tatami floor. The younger woman knelt by her, pressing a cloth pad to her forehead. The pad was a poultice—a bundle of herbs that gave off a musty, medicinal odor. When Sano, Reiko, and Masahiro approached, the kneeling woman helped the prone one sit up. Sano and his family knelt and bowed to their guests.

"Greetings, Lady Nobuko," Sano said. "Your visit does us an honor."

"My apologies for behaving in this unseemly fashion." Pain tightened the older woman's crisp, elegant speech. Lying on the floor had disheveled her knot of silver-streaked hair. "My headache is especially bad today."

Although one of the most privileged women in Japan, she was as emaciated as beggars on the streets. Knobby shoulder joints protruded through her silk kimono. Tendons in her neck resembled flaccid ropes. Crimson rouge on her cheeks and lips gave her a flush of vitality, but the muscles around her right eye contracted in a spasm that distorted her narrow, sharp-boned face into a disconcerting mask of agony.

"I'm sorry you're not feeling well." Sano introduced Reiko and Masahiro.

Lady Nobuko's good eye studied them with shrewd interest. The other oozed involuntary tears. She seemed to approve; she nodded. "May I introduce Korika, my lady-in-waiting."

"I'm honored to make your acquaintance," Korika said in a sweet, breathless voice. In her late forties, she had a comfortably padded figure. Her hair, still mostly black, arranged in a round puff, emphasized the broadness of her face. Her forehead was so low that the eyebrows painted on it almost touched her hairline. Her wide smile, and eyes as black and shiny as berries, had an intense, eager-to-please expression.

"May I offer you refreshments?" Reiko asked.

"No, please." Lady Nobuko grimaced, as if nauseated by the mere thought of food and drink. "You must be wondering why I am here, so I will come right to the point. I must speak to you about Tsuruhime."

Her voice broke on a sob. Tears poured from both her eyes. Korika patted her hand consolingly. Although the shogun didn't mourn his daughter, his wife did.

"I'm so sorry," Reiko said with quiet compassion. "I understand that you and Tsuruhime were very close?"

Nodding, Lady Nobuko composed herself. "I was with her when she died. I'm only her stepmother, but I loved her as if she were my own child."

"Wasn't her own mother killed by the earthquake?" Sano recalled that Tsuruhime's mother had been one of the shogun's concubines.

"Yes, when part of the Large Interior collapsed," Lady Nobuko said. The Large Interior was the section of the palace that housed the shogun's female concubines, relatives, and their attendants and maids. "But even before then, Tsuruhime relied on me for guidance."

"Her own mother was a silly, flighty woman who had no business raising the shogun's daughter," Korika said.

"Don't speak ill of the dead," Lady Nobuko said, without rancor. Loud hammering came from the part of the house under construction. A wince further distorted her face.

Sano started to rise. "I'll tell the men to stop working."

"No." Lady Nobuko lifted a crabbed hand to forestall him. "The noise will prevent eavesdropping. I do not want anyone outside this room to hear what I have to say." She pitched her voice so that it was barely audible over the noise. "Tsuruhime was murdered."

Surprise jarred Sano and showed on Reiko's and Masahiro's faces. "I thought she died of smallpox," Sano said.

"Indeed she did," Lady Nobuko said, "but it was not a natural death."

"How do you know?" Sano asked.

Lady Nobuko turned to her lady-in-waiting. "Tell them what happened."

Nervous yet pleased to be the center of attention, Korika said, "It was a few days before Tsuruhime fell ill. My lady and I were visiting her. We decided to walk in the garden. Tsuruhime asked me to fetch her cloak from her room. As I was looking through the cabinet, I saw an old cotton bedsheet wadded up on a shelf among her kimonos. It was soiled with dried blood and yellowish stains." Repugnance wrinkled her nose. "I wondered what such a filthy sheet was doing there. I meant to tell the maid to throw it away, but I forgot. I didn't remember it until this morning. I looked for it, and it was gone."

"Korika told me about the sheet," Lady Nobuko said. "I think it belonged to someone else who'd had smallpox, and it was soiled with blood and pus from that person's sores. I believe it was put there to infect Tsuruhime."

"I've heard that soiled bedclothes can spread the disease to people who handle them," Sano said, intrigued yet doubtful. "But how can you be sure that this sheet was in fact contaminated with smallpox?"

"My intuition tells me," Lady Nobuko said.

Sano looked askance at her. Reiko frowned at him. She trusted in the veracity of female intuition; he was skeptical.

"Supposing the sheet was contaminated," Reiko said, "did anyone else in the household get smallpox?"

"No." Lady Nobuko sounded annoyed because logic discredited her belief.

"If Tsuruhime was deliberately infected," Reiko said, "then why?"

"To eliminate her without the appearance of foul play," Lady Nobuko said.

Korika spoke up, eager to support her mistress. "It was pure accident that I saw the sheet. If I hadn't, nobody would suspect she was murdered."

"Suppose you're right." Sano felt Lady Nobuko's certainty eroding his objectivity. "Then who killed Tsuruhime?"

"I am right," Lady Nobuko declared. "It was Yanagisawa."

The hammering stopped for a moment. In the sudden silence Sano felt shock course through him and Reiko and Masahiro. His heart began to pound.

"You think Yanagisawa planted a smallpox-infested sheet in Tsuruhime's room?" Reiko sounded astonished, dubious.

"No," Lady Nobuko said, "he wouldn't risk infecting himself or getting caught. But he was responsible. That's why I'm here. I want you to prove he's guilty."

Sano remembered that she had good reason for thinking Yanagisawa capable of a crime as evil as murdering his lord's daughter. She also had good reason to want to get him in trouble. And she wasn't alone in her wish.

"This is our chance to take Yanagisawa down!" Masahiro exclaimed.

"Evidence that he murdered the shogun's daughter would be a perfect weapon against him," Reiko agreed.

"Your wife and son are as intelligent as I've heard." The undistorted side of Lady Nobuko's mouth smiled. "They realize that our interests coincide, Honorable Chamberlain Sano. Or should I say, 'Honorable Chief Rebuilding Magistrate'?"

"So you know what happened today," Sano said, disconcerted.

"Yes. I employ people to keep me informed about what goes on at court. I also know that my husband has installed Yanagisawa's so-called adopted son as his heir and successor, and that you are far from pleased."

"That's right." Sano was tempted to leap at the opportunity to bring about Yanagisawa's downfall. Despite his hunger for vengeance, he tried to keep a level head. "But let's not get carried away before we examine your theory. Why would Yanagisawa want Tsuruhime dead?"

"Yanagisawa has fought an uphill battle to put Yoshisato in line to rule Japan," Lady Nobuko said. "Too many people aren't convinced he's the shogun's son. Yanagisawa can't keep down all the dissent forever. The last thing he needs is competition for Yoshisato. My husband isn't likely to father any more children." Lady Nobuko evidently knew his character despite the fact that their marriage was a political alliance between clans rather than an intimate union, and Sano knew they rarely even spoke. "If Tsuruhime had lived, she could have borne a son who would have been an undisputed descendant of the shogun."

No one had ever challenged her pedigree.

"A son of hers would have supplied a rallying point for people who don't think Yoshisato is a true Tokugawa and don't want Yanagisawa dominating the government for another term," Lady Nobuko went on. "Were that the case, what would happen after the shogun dies? Yanagisawa's opponents would start a war against Yoshisato, on behalf of Tsuruhime's son, and possibly seize control of the dictatorship. Yanagisawa understood that. He had Tsuruhime killed because she was a potential threat to his future."

"That's a strong reason for murder," Reiko said. Sano had to nod. "And Yanagisawa is ruthless enough to have had Tsuruhime murdered."

"She enjoyed perfect health all her life," Lady Nobuko said. "Doesn't it strike you as odd that she should contract smallpox a few months after Yoshisato made his appearance at court?"

Sano agreed but continued challenging the theory. "It could be a coincidence."

Reiko nodded reluctantly, but disdain twisted Lady Nobuko's mouth.

"Are you sure you're not reading too much into the situation because of what Yanagisawa did to you?" Sano asked. "Might you be snatching at a faint hope of revenge?"

"I was kidnapped and violated." Lady Nobuko's face grew pinched with anger at the memory of the suffering she'd endured. "I can't prove that Yanagisawa ordered it, but I know he did. I'm not imagining things this time, either."

Sano wondered if Yanagisawa's actions had pushed her to the point where she would invent a murder and frame Yanagisawa for it. He turned to her lady-in-waiting. "You're very devoted to Lady Nobuko, aren't you?"

"Yes," Korika said proudly. "I've served her for twenty-eight years."

"Did you really see a sheet soiled with blood and pus?"

Korika's broad face fell at his suggestion that she'd made up the whole story. Lady Nobuko said indignantly, "She wouldn't lie in order to please me."

"All right," Sano said, still reserving judgment. "But the sheet wouldn't necessarily have been Yanagisawa's doing. Who else might have wanted to kill Tsuruhime?"

"No one," Lady Nobuko said. "She was a sweet, harmless young woman. No one would have profited from her death except Yanagisawa."

"There's Yoshisato," Masahiro said.

Sano was proud of his son's astuteness. "With Tsuruhime dead, Yoshisato no longer needs to worry about a son of hers pushing him out of line for the succession."

"Yoshisato could have been an accomplice in the murder, but Yanagisawa was the instigator," Lady Nobuko declared.

"Father . . ." Masahiro seemed hesitant to voice a theory about which he didn't feel confident. "Even if Yanagisawa did kill Tsuruhime and you prove it, maybe he won't get in trouble. The shogun said that now that he has Yoshisato, he doesn't need her anymore. Would he care if she was murdered? Would he punish Yanagisawa for killing her?"

"You're a clever boy, but you don't know my husband as well as I do," Lady Nobuko said. "He doesn't care about Tsuruhime, but he will not tolerate anyone hurting anyone or anything that belongs to him." She said to Sano, "Your mother is proof of that."

Sano's mother had been accused of killing the shogun's cousin during Edo's other famous natural disaster, the Great Fire. The shogun had almost put her to death, even though he'd barely known his cousin, had assumed he'd died in the fire, and hadn't given him a thought until his remains turned up more than forty years later. Only a fluke of circumstance had saved her life.

"The shogun wouldn't let Yanagisawa or Yoshisato get away with killing his own daughter," Sano agreed. "If he were convinced they did it, he would disown Yoshisato and put them both to death."

"So," Lady Nobuko said, "are you going to investigate Tsuruhime's death or not?"

Sano felt as if he'd spent fifteen years trudging over the same terrain of his feud with Yanagisawa, and suddenly he'd happened on a new path. Maybe it would take him to vengeance, triumph, and a future without

Yoshisato as shogun and Yanagisawa ruling Japan through him. But the path was as dark and fraught with hazards as a jungle at midnight.

"An investigation could be dangerous if Yanagisawa hears of it," Sano said.

"I trust you to be discreet," Lady Nobuko said.

"Other inquiries of mine have become public despite my best efforts. And while you think your spies are good, they're nothing to Yanagisawa's. Should he learn that I'm investigating Tsuruhime's death and he's a murder suspect, he'll strike back without mercy."

Surprise lifted the brow over Lady Nobuko's good eye. "I thought you were the one man in Japan who's not afraid to stand up to Yanagisawa."

Sano frowned at her suggestion that he was a coward, the worst insult anyone could throw at a samurai. "It's not myself I'm worried about." He looked at Reiko and Masahiro. His family was more valuable to him than life itself. He would risk his own safety but not theirs.

"I'm not afraid," Masahiro said with the courage of a boy who'd already fought battles like a man, lived to tell, and thought he was immortal. "I want you to investigate. Don't you, Mother?"

"Yes," Reiko said. "This may be the only chance for you both to regain your posts and destroy Yanagisawa. After he's gone, it should be easy to disqualify Yoshisato and keep him from becoming shogun." But Sano could tell she was remembering that Yanagisawa had already halved his income and decimated his army today. They were in no shape for a war with Yanagisawa. They didn't even have adequate troops to guard the estate. Sano saw Reiko's fear for Masahiro and Akiko. Her hand clasped her pregnant belly.

"An investigation would be dangerous for you, too, if Yanagisawa finds out that you instigated it," Sano told Lady Nobuko.

"For a woman there's nothing worse than what he's already done to me." She donned the tragic air of a martyr. "And my life is so filled with suffering that I would gladly risk death for a chance to destroy Yanagisawa."

The force of his own hunger for revenge pushed Sano toward taking the first step on the dangerous path. But he said, "The evidence that Tsuruhime's death was murder is flimsy. A soiled sheet that was seen by one witness before it disappeared, that can't be traced to Yanagisawa. An investigation could endanger us all for nothing."

"I think it was murder. And I know you'll find evidence." Reiko's eyes shone with faith in Sano.

"I may find evidence that leads somewhere else than to Yanagisawa," Sano said. "If I do, I won't frame him and let the real killer go free."

"I am aware of your reputation for seeking truth and justice," Lady Nobuko said. "I won't ask you to compromise your honor. I want the truth about Tsuruhime's death. I want justice for her even if Yanagisawa comes out smelling like flowers."

"Very well." Sano didn't believe her. He thought her desire for revenge was blinding her to the possibility that someone other than Yanagisawa might be guilty. But Sano realized that he'd decided to conduct the investigation as soon as he'd heard her suspicion that the shogun's daughter had been murdered by Yanagisawa. He had additional reason besides keeping Yoshisato from inheriting the regime and securing his own family's future. He must avenge his friends whose lives Yanagisawa had destroyed. "I'll begin my inquiries at once."

Lady Nobuko looked satisfied, as if she'd never doubted Sano would cooperate. Korika smiled in relief. "Will you keep me informed as to your progress?" Lady Nobuko said as she and her lady-in-waiting rose.

"Yes." Sano wondered if he would regret his decision. Circumstances were pushing him along a dangerous course. "Remember, everyone: This must be kept strictly confidential."

But he was already committed to the investigation, and there was no turning back.

娘 4

THE FIRST POST station on the Tōkaidō—the main high-way leading to points west—was situated at the edge of Edo. There, a long line of travelers on foot, horseback, and riding in ox-drawn carts or palanquins and basket chairs carried by bearers inched toward a small building. From inside a window in the building, four officials questioned the travelers one by one.

"Name? Place of residence? Why are you coming to Edo?"

The officials recorded the information in ledgers. Clerks searched the travelers, their baggage, and their vehicles for hidden weapons, secret messages, and other contraband.

Hirata sat astride his horse, twentieth in line. Coarse dark stubble covered his face and his shaved crown. His wrinkled clothes were dirty. His fetid odor of sweat, urine, oily hair, and bad breath disgusted him. His skin itched from flea bites.

During his four months' absence from Edo, he'd been staying in cheap inns and camping in the woods. He hadn't bathed in days. He looked like the fugitive he was, and he felt the same anxiety, suspicion, and fear as every other man on the run.

Surveying the people ahead of him, Hirata saw four women decked out in gaudy kimonos and makeup. They flirted with the men near them—peasants driving oxcarts owned by the government and laden with wood, stone, and tiles, and the mounted army troops guarding the carts. Behind Hirata, peasants carried knapsacks; samurai bodyguards escorted merchants accompanied by porters lugging goods and cash boxes. Refugees from the villages destroyed by the tsunami numbered among the people flocking to Edo from all over Japan to make their fortune on the rebuilding boom. Edo was like an open sack, and people were stuffing it full of themselves, their muscle, their wealth, their ambitions, their diseases, and their vices. Hirata didn't see anyone he recognized. He cast his gaze over the surrounding area.

Beyond the post station rose the arched framework of a new bridge spanning the Nihonbashi River; the old bridge had collapsed during the earthquake. There, carpenters were busy at work. Ferrymen in small boats rowed passengers across the river. A new stable sheltered horses for rent. Porters, palanquin bearers, and basket chair carriers for hire sat in a campground, awaiting customers. New inns were under construction amid tents that served as temporary housing for travelers. When Hirata had left Edo, this area had been a complete ruin. Amazed at the progress made in a short time, he uneasily wondered what else had changed.

He concentrated his attention on the auras of the million people in the city, the energy that all living things emitted. His mystical powers allowed him to perceive the unique aura that each human possessed, that signaled his or her personality, health, and emotions. The landscape of Hirata's brain vibrated and sizzled with auras. Some belonged to people he knew. His mind shied away from those of his family and his master, whom he'd left on bad terms. Uncertain of his welcome, he yearned for them but dreaded seeing them again. He searched for one particular aura—the conjoined energy of the three men he'd fled Edo to escape.

He didn't find Tahara, Deguchi, and Kitano. But that didn't mean they weren't near. They, unlike most creatures, could turn their aura on and off at will.

The line moved forward. The gaudy women ahead of Hirata reached the post station. They told the officials, "We're maids looking for work."

It was obvious that they were prostitutes. The officials fondled them and made lewd remarks while searching them, then let them pass. Edo needed prostitutes to keep the merchants and workers happy.

Now came Hirata's turn. When he dismounted outside the window, he recognized the samurai official. "Arai?" It was his chief retainer. "What are you doing here?"

"Hirata-*san!*" Arai was just as surprised to see Hirata. "I work here."

"What are you talking about?" Hirata said, dismayed as well as puzzled. He hadn't wanted to meet anyone he knew while he was so dirty and ill-groomed. "Didn't I put you in charge of my detective corps before I left town?"

"Yes. But a lot of things have happened since then." Arai looked as if he hated to be the bearer of bad news. "The shogun got mad because you weren't around when he wanted you. He took away your post. You're not his *sōsakan-sama* anymore."

Hirata was horrified, even though he'd expected it and knew it was no worse than he deserved. "What am I?"

"You're still Chamberlain Sano's chief retainer. Except that Sano isn't chamberlain anymore. Yanagisawa is. He got the shogun to name Yoshisato as his heir. And he demoted a lot of other people besides Sano."

"When was this?" Hirata said, appalled.

"Today."

"What happened to Sano?"

"He's Chief Rebuilding Magistrate," Arai said.

"And my detective corps?"

"Disbanded. Your stipend was revoked, and there was no money to support us. A friend of mine got me this post. Other men weren't so lucky. There are many government positions open because people died during the earthquake, but the regime can't afford to fill them all. Some of our men are working as laborers and living in the tent camps."

"Why didn't they stay at my estate?"

"Your estate was taken away, too."

Panic seized Hirata. "Where are my wife and children?"

"Sano-*san* took them in," Arai said.

Guilt increased Hirata's dread of seeing his family and Sano. Midori was probably furious because he'd left her and the children homeless. And Hirata had not only forsaken his duty to Sano, he'd stuck Sano with the responsibility for his family. Hirata was tempted to turn around and leave town again, but he couldn't. Along with scores to settle, he had apologies and amends to make. He might as well start now.

"I'm sorry," he said to Arai. "I didn't mean for this to happen."

"You don't need to apologize," Arai said with prompt sincerity.

Hirata could see that although Arai was unhappy with the situation, he bore Hirata no grudge. A master could do whatever he liked, and his retainers must accept it without complaint. That was Bushido. Hirata felt even guiltier: Arai was a better samurai than he.

"May I ask where you've been?" Arai asked.

"Traveling around the country." Hirata couldn't say, *I've been running from three men who pretended to be my friends. I discovered they were thieves and murderers. Wherever I went, Tahara, Deguchi, and Kitano tracked my aura and followed me. I've barely managed to stay one step ahead of them. And I'm terrified because their combat skills are better than mine and I know they'll find me sooner or later.*

Arai frowned, puzzled. "Why did you leave?"

Hirata couldn't say, *Tahara, Deguchi, and Kitano tricked me into joining their secret society.* They'd sworn him to secrecy about it. *They said its purpose was to do magic rituals and fulfill a cosmic destiny for the world. But they lied. Our rituals evoked the ghost of a warlord who promised us supernatural powers. The price we pay for them is helping him destroy his enemy. And his enemy is the Tokugawa regime. I ran away rather than commit treason with Tahara, Deguchi, Kitano, and the ghost.* The penalty for treason was death for the traitor, his family, and all his close associates. And Tahara, Deguchi, and Kitano would kill Hirata, his family, and Sano if he talked, or if he opposed them. They wanted to bring him back into the fold, against his will.

"I had business to attend to," Hirata said.

After an uncomfortable silence, Arai said, "I apologize for prying." Bushido decreed that a master didn't owe his retainers explanations, but Hirata saw that Arai was hurt by his evasiveness. "Well," Arai said, "I'd better not keep the other people waiting." He dipped his writing brush in ink and wrote Hirata's name in his ledger. The precious bond between master and retainer was severed during that moment. "Why are you coming to Edo?"

Because nowhere is safe from Tahara, Deguchi, and Kitano. There's no use running anymore. It's time to face the consequences of what I've done and make things right with my master. "Official business," Hirata said.

Arai wrote the answer in his ledger and started to gesture Hirata toward a gate built across the highway, where guards eyed the travelers who passed through the open portals into town. "Wait. I just remembered. A

samurai who came through yesterday asked about you. His name was—"
Arai paged backward through his ledger. "Tahara."

Dread mounted so high and fast in Hirata that it dizzied him. Tahara was already here. Deguchi and Kitano couldn't be far away. "Oh? What did this Tahara say?" Hirata asked, trying to sound casual, as if he didn't know the man.

"He wanted to know if you'd entered Edo. He asked all the officials. We said no."

But the men had guessed that he would return. They were waiting for him. He had to shut down the secret society and banish the ghost to the netherworld forever before they could make good on their threats, but he didn't know how. Hirata walked through the gate as if through a portal to hell.

5

AS SOON AS Lady Nobuko and her lady-in-waiting left the mansion, Reiko turned to Sano and Masahiro. "This could be our most important investigation ever. Where shall we begin?"

Sano saw excitement sparkle in her eyes. He felt a stab of consternation.

Reiko had helped him investigate crimes since they were first married fourteen years ago. No ordinary wife, she was the only child of one of Edo's two magistrates, and her widowed father had given her the education usually reserved for sons. She'd learned martial arts along with reading, writing, history, literature, and arithmetic. She'd practically grown up in his Court of Justice, listening to the trials he conducted. Sano's investigations had often benefited from her talent for detective work, but this time he must manage without her help.

"*We* aren't beginning this investigation," Sano said. "Not with you in your condition."

"Oh," Reiko said, taken aback, as if she'd forgotten her pregnancy.

"It's not safe. You're supposed to rest," Sano said.

"That's right, Mother," Masahiro said. "You can't go out."

"You're a child. You can't tell me what to do," Reiko protested.

Sano smiled a half amused, half worried smile. "Our child is grown up enough to be protective toward you. You should listen to him." It was nice to have another man on his side, but the last thing he needed was discord within his family.

"But there may be women who need to be questioned." Reiko's

strength as a detective was eliciting information from women who might withhold it from a male investigator, exploring their private world and discovering clues hidden from Sano.

Sano couldn't help bristling at her implication that he couldn't handle the investigation. "I'll cope."

"Aren't you supposed to start your new job as Chief Rebuilding Magistrate?"

"Yes." Sano concealed how daunted he was by the responsibility. "But I'll make time to investigate Lady Nobuko's allegations."

"I can look for clues," Masahiro said eagerly. "Pages can go everywhere and nobody notices them."

"That's good." Sano was glad to see Masahiro find something positive about his demotion. But Masahiro, for all his intelligence, was still only twelve years old. Sano must not expect too much from him, even though he'd performed impressively during past crises.

The same misgivings clouded Reiko's eyes: She didn't want to put Masahiro in a situation a child couldn't handle. "Who else do you have to help?"

There was no use trying to hide the truth. "My former allies might be willing to help, but bringing them in on the investigation would make it harder to keep it secret." Seeing Reiko's and Masahiro's worried faces, Sano tried to look on the bright side. "I still have Detective Marume." Marume served as his chief retainer in Hirata's absence. "He and Masahiro and I can manage the investigation by ourselves."

Masahiro nodded, pleased to be included as an equal with the men. Reiko twisted her hands together, fraught with her desire not to be left out. "Can I help if I don't leave home?"

"What can you do at home?" Sano was skeptical.

"I can talk to witnesses. They can come to me."

"Maybe, if they're women. But it could still be dangerous. It's not always easy to tell the difference between witnesses and murderers. And you've been attacked by women before."

"You still have enough troops to protect me." Reiko seized Sano's arm. "I can't sit idle while Yanagisawa and his son are set to rule Japan and our family's future is at stake!"

She'd helped him solve difficult cases before. Sano couldn't forego the slightest advantage this time. "Very well," he said, although reluctant to put his wife and unborn child at the slightest risk. "But you have to promise: You don't leave this house. Witnesses and clues have to come to you. And my troops are with you every moment you question anyone."

Reiko rewarded him with a brilliant smile. "I promise."

TAEKO SAT AGAINST the lattice-and-paper wall in the corridor outside the reception room. The shogun's wife and her lady-in-waiting had left a short while ago. Taeko listened to Sano, Reiko, and Masahiro talking as she leafed through a book she'd made of small rectangular sheets of rice paper tied with black ribbon through two holes. On the pages were paintings she'd done, of the kitten, a pine tree, a butterfly, a spray of cherry blossoms. They didn't look enough like the subjects or as good as the pictures of them in her mind. Taeko wished she could paint like real artists. But her mother said she couldn't have art lessons as her brother did.

Taeko couldn't grasp the meaning of everything she'd heard, but she understood that the shogun's daughter had been murdered by Yanagisawa, the bad man who was always causing problems for Masahiro's family. She understood that Masahiro and his father were in trouble and proving that Yanagisawa had killed the shogun's daughter would get them out of it. Interesting things seemed about to happen.

Masahiro rushed out of the room. Taeko felt her heart begin to sing and dance. She smiled. For as long as she could remember she'd liked Masahiro more than anyone else.

"Masahiro!" she called, tucking her book under her sash.

He paused and turned. "What?"

Taeko suddenly felt shy even though she'd known him all her life. He was so tall and strong and handsome! "Where are you going?"

"To do some investigating."

Taeko scrambled to her feet. "Can I go, too?"

"No."

"Why not?"

"You're too young, and you're a girl," Masahiro said bluntly.

Taeko knew that Masahiro didn't feel the same about her as she did about him. To him she was like his little sister—a playmate when he wanted one and a nuisance when he didn't. Hurt by the knowledge, Taeko turned away from Masahiro.

"Hey," Masahiro said, impatient but concerned. "What's the matter?"

Taeko shook her head. If she tried to speak, she would cry, and if she cried, he would think she was even more of a baby than he already did.

"You're unhappy because you can't come with me," Masahiro said, as if pleased to figure it out yet distressed because his rejection had hurt her. "But it could be dangerous where I'm going. Why do you want to go so badly?"

Taeko couldn't admit that she wanted to be with him, to share in whatever he was doing, because she liked him. "I want to help," she managed to say.

Masahiro laughed. It was a friendly laugh, but Taeko cringed with shame. "Well, there isn't anything you can do. So you'd better stay home."

As he walked away down the corridor, Taeko felt a spurt of the same stubbornness that made her keep painting even when her pictures weren't any good and her mother told her to stop. Masahiro could tell her what to do, but she didn't have to listen, did she? Maybe, if she followed him, she could find a way to help him with his investigation. If she did manage to help him, he might feel differently toward her, mightn't he?

Nothing else she'd done had changed his mind about her. She had to try something new.

Taeko hurried after Masahiro.

6

SANO RODE OUT the castle gate with Detective Marume and two troops, all he could take from home while leaving enough to guard his family. The avenue across the moat was crowded with beggars loudly soliciting alms. Nuns, priests, and monks vied with homeless refugees driven into the cities by the tsunami that had flooded their coastal villages. Sano noticed a family camped out on a blanket, surrounded by their few possessions. It was a woman, little boy and girl, and a man with bandaged stubs for legs. Sano felt a stab of pity and had to look away.

He and Marume crossed the avenue and rode through the *daimyo* district, past new buildings that had sprung up at estates flattened by the earthquake. The streets were choked with oxcarts hauling timbers and stone. Wheels dug deep ruts; flies swarmed over manure that reeked under the hot sun. Porters lugged rice bales, water casks, and bundles of food for the peasants who hammered, sawed, plastered, and tiled. In the estates that belonged to minor *daimyo* who governed small provinces, gaps in unrepaired walls exposed framework on bare foundations. In those owned by powerful lords of large, wealthy domains, nearly completed barracks surrounded stately new mansions. Lord Tsunanori, *daimyo* of Kii Province—also the husband of Tsuruhime and the son-in-law of the shogun—was in that fortunate category. But his stronghold was an enclave of gloomy quiet. Black mourning drapery hung over the double-roofed gate where Sano and his men dismounted from their horses.

"Where are the relatives, friends, and neighbors?" Marume asked.

"Shouldn't they be coming to pay their respects to the shogun's dead daughter?"

"This house has been visited by smallpox." Sano was glad that Marume was recovering from the loss of Fukida, his partner, who'd died during the earthquake. The two men had been like brothers. Lately Marume had begun to regain his robust physique and talk more. "People don't want to risk infection."

"What's a little smallpox between friends?" Marume said with a touch of his old humor. "I'll risk it with you anytime."

"I'm glad I still have you for company."

"I wonder why Yanagisawa let you keep me. Probably because he knew I would make too much trouble for him if he tried to take me away."

Sano approached the two sentries at the gate, introduced himself, and said, "I'm here to see Lord Kii Tsunanori."

A servant escorted Sano and Marume through the estate, to the martial arts practice ground. Straw archery targets stood at one end. Raucous laughter came from the other end, where a crowd was gathered around two people batting a shuttlecock back and forth with wooden paddles. The paddles were brightly painted with portraits of Kabuki actors, the shuttlecock fashioned from a hard, round soapberry and red feathers. Sano recognized the game as *hanetsuki,* traditionally played by girls at the New Year. But these players were a broad-shouldered samurai with a long upper body and short legs, dressed only in a loincloth, and a pretty young woman in a white under-kimono. The woman missed a shot.

"Take it off!" yelled the audience, comprised of other samurai and young women.

Giggling, the woman dropped her robe. She flaunted her naked breasts and shaved pubis. The audience roared. The usual penalty for missing a shot during *hanetsuki* was an ink mark on the face, but this couple had perverted the innocent game: Their penalty was removal of an item of clothing.

"It looks like they're getting near the end of the game," Marume said. "All that's left to go is her socks and his loincloth."

The male player hooted and pumped his fist in the air. The female didn't seem to mind exposing herself. Her shaved pubis identified her as a prostitute; she was probably accustomed to such bawdy entertainment.

Sano cleared his throat and said, "Lord Kii Tsunanori?"

The audience quieted. The male player turned. Sano recognized Lord Tsunanori; they'd met a few times. Lord Tsunanori's arrogant stance bespoke his pride in himself. Sano knew he was an excellent swordsman who often competed in, and won, tournaments. But his head didn't match his strong physique. It had a squat shape with a roll of fat at the back of his neck. His regular features had an odd slackness. The skin drooped around his large, bold eyes.

"Chamberlain Sano?" Lord Tsunanori's mouth was loose, as if the muscles didn't have enough tone to hold the full lips closed. They gaped now, in dismay, because Sano had caught him in behavior inappropriate for a widower on the morning after his wife's death. He pretended that the scene Sano had just witnessed had never happened. "Welcome. Let's go inside."

Sano didn't tell Lord Tsunanori about his demotion. He let Lord Tsunanori think he was still the shogun's second-in-command, backed by the full authority of the government. Lord Tsunanori led Sano and Marume toward the mansion. The naked woman tossed him his robe, and he put it on. It was heavy silk, printed in clashing red, orange, and purple, typical for rich, fashionable *daimyo*. Sano smelled sweat, alcohol, and wintergreen hair oil on him. They went into a reception room. A funeral altar held offerings of fruit, flowers, and wine, and a portrait of Tsuruhime. She'd been a plain woman; she had the shogun's weak chin. She looked lonely.

Sano introduced Detective Marume, then said, "We've come to offer you our condolences."

"Not many other people have come." Lord Tsunanori sounded resentful. "They're afraid to set foot here, and we're not having the usual funeral rites." Those included a wake, with the body present in a closed coffin. "The remains were cremated last night." Corpses of smallpox victims were burned immediately, to prevent contagion.

Lord Tsunanori glanced at a tray stand that held decanters and cups. "I've forgotten my manners. Sorry. Would you like a drink?"

Sano and Marume politely refused. Lord Tsunanori said, "Of course.

Nobody wants to drink or eat anything here. I guess I'll just have one by myself." Lord Tsunanori knelt, poured a cup of sake, and downed it. Sano noticed his flushed face and awkward movements; he was already drunk. "Customs have gone out the window because Tsuruhime died of smallpox."

Sano saw an opening to begin his inquiries. "How did she get smallpox? It's not that common." It mostly afflicted the poorer classes, who lived in crowded, unsanitary conditions.

"There's all kinds of diseases going around everywhere since the earthquake," Lord Tsunanori said. "I hear there's smallpox in the tent camps. She must have brushed up against somebody in town."

"Had she been out of the house much during the days before she became ill?" Sano couldn't believe she had; ladies had mostly stayed home since the earthquake. Conditions in Edo were unpleasant due to the debris and construction work, and crime had increased because impoverished, desperate citizens had resorted to attacking and robbing the rich.

"I don't know. You'd have to ask her servants."

Sano planned to. "Has anyone else in the household come down with smallpox?"

"No, thank the gods."

"Why only Tsuruhime?"

"She was just unlucky, I guess," Lord Tsunanori said. "As soon as she broke out in sores, I had her isolated."

"Who took care of her?" Sano asked.

"Her nurse."

"Why didn't she get smallpox?"

"She had it when she was young."

People who'd survived smallpox were safe from a recurrence. "Who had access to Tsuruhime's room?"

"Her ladies-in-waiting, the servants."

"Could anyone else have handled her things?"

"Handled, how?" Lord Tsunanori looked puzzled, then alarmed. "Do you mean, put something in with them that was contaminated with smallpox?"

Sano and Marume shared a surprised glance. How quickly Lord Tsunanori had jumped to the notion that his wife had contracted smallpox from a contaminated item placed among her possessions. "I just wondered," Sano said. "I've heard it's possible to get smallpox from touching things used by someone who had the disease."

"Are you suggesting that somebody deliberately tried to make my wife sick?" Lord Tsunanori demanded.

How quickly he'd jumped to the idea that her death had involved foul play. "Assassination is always a possibility when an important person dies suddenly from an unusual cause," Sano said. "Do you think someone killed your wife?"

"Do I think someone killed my wife?" Lord Tsunanori spoke in a hushed tone. He frowned, stammered, then said, "No. I never thought of it at all." His loose mouth dropped. "You think *I* infected her with smallpox. That's what you're getting at."

"Did you?" Sano asked.

Lord Tsunanori reacted with the same tone, frown, and stammers as before. "No! I would never! What gave you that ridiculous idea?"

Behind his back, Marume held up one finger, then two, then three, counting the denials. Sano noted how quickly Lord Tsunanori had interpreted his question as an accusation. Keeping his pact with Lady Nobuko confidential, Sano started to say he'd heard a rumor.

Lord Tsunanori cut him off with an angry exclamation. "It must have been Lady Nobuko."

"Why do you think it was her?" Sano said, startled.

"She hates me. She thought I was a bad husband." Lord Tsunanori's voice took on a whiny, aggrieved note. "I gave my wife every luxury she could have wanted. But Lady Nobuko expected me to worship the ground Tsuruhime walked on. Lady Nobuko was always criticizing me. To please her, I would have had to rub my nose against Tsuruhime's behind, just to show how grateful I was to be married to the shogun's daughter."

"It sounds as if you weren't grateful at all," Sano said.

"No man in his right mind would have been. I paid dearly for the privilege. I had to give huge tributes to the government." Lord Tsunanori quaffed another drink, wiped his mouth on his sleeve. His eyes had a glassy look. "After the earthquake, I was the first *daimyo* that the shogun came to for money to fix Edo." He held out his palm, which was calloused from sword-fighting practice, and wiggled his fingers. "Because I was his son-in-law."

Disturbed by what he was hearing, Sano said, "Didn't Tsuruhime bring you a big dowry?"

"It was chicken dung compared to what I've spent on account of her. Things didn't turn out the way I expected when I agreed to the marriage. Tsuruhime was supposed to bear me the shogun's grandson. I was supposed to have a chance to be the father of the next shogun. But she never conceived. After a few years of trying, I quit sleeping with her. The bitch!"

Sano was shocked to hear even a garrulous drunk malign his dead wife so crudely. He pitied Tsuruhime, even though she was beyond caring. "It wasn't her fault that you lost money on her." Or that she hadn't borne him a child. Sano knew that Lord Tsunanori had no illegitimate offspring, despite the fact that he had concubines. The wife usually took the blame for infertility. The husband didn't want to admit he was responsible. It was the same with the shogun. His failure to produce an heir had been blamed on his wife, his concubines, his preference for men, and sins committed in a past life, but woe betide anyone who suggested that his seed was defective. Sano had had a hell of a time discrediting Yoshisato, partly because the shogun welcomed Yoshisato as proof of his virility.

"Tsuruhime made the situation worse," Lord Tsunanori said. "She treated me like dirt. And she wasn't even pretty." Anger at her turned to disgust. "Lady Nobuko spoiled Tsuruhime. She taught her that because she was the shogun's daughter, she should expect people to treat her like a goddess and punish them if they didn't. Her servants were afraid of her. She beat them with a hairbrush. I had to pay them exorbitant wages to work for her. Hell, *I* was afraid of her. She kept threatening to tell her father that I was a bad husband. The shogun could have granted her a divorce, but you'd better believe he'd have charged me a fortune to get rid of her!"

"Thanks to the smallpox, you got rid of her for free," Marume said.

"Hey, I don't like your attitude." Then Lord Tsunanori realized that his own wasn't so respectable. "I shouldn't speak ill of Tsuruhime. But I'm glad not to be married to her anymore."

"Did Lady Nobuko know how you felt about Tsuruhime?" Sano asked.

"Yes. Whenever she lectured me about what I owed Tsuruhime for the honor of being her husband, I gave her a piece of my mind."

Sano expelled his breath in consternation. He'd come to prove Yanagisawa was responsible for Tsuruhime's death, but here was another suspect. And Lady Nobuko knew Lord Tsunanori had strong reason for killing Tsuruhime, but she'd kept quiet about it. She'd set Sano on a dangerous campaign against Yanagisawa while aware that he could be innocent and that if Sano pursued the investigation he might run afoul of Lord Tsunanori, who was a powerful *daimyo* and the shogun's son-in-law. But Sano couldn't stop the investigation just because it might not incriminate Yanagisawa or because it would make him new enemies.

"I'd like to talk to the members of your household," Sano said.

Surprised by the change of subject, Lord Tsunanori drew back from Sano with appalled realization. "You didn't come here to offer condolences, did you? That was just a pretense. You think Tsuruhime was murdered, and you're out to get me for it!"

"You've given me reason to think you're guilty." Sano could easily imagine Lord Tsunanori getting fed up with Tsuruhime and feeling driven to kill her as a last resort. "I've no choice but to investigate." He had a duty to obtain justice for his lord's daughter, no matter if it wasn't Yanagisawa he brought down. Sano rose; so did Marume. "I'm going to talk to your household members. I'm also going to inspect Tsuruhime's room."

Lord Tsunanori stood, swayed, pointed his finger at Sano, and shouted, "Get out of my house, or I'll throw you out."

His men rushed in. Gathering around him, they glared at Sano and Marume. Sano smelled nerves burning alcohol out of them. Lord Tsunanori's face flushed and muscles engorged with combat lust. Samurai instinct urged Sano to fight, but a brawl with Lord Tsunanori was too dangerous for another reason besides the fact that he had a huge army at his disposal. The other *daimyo* already resented the government for draining their treasuries to pay for rebuilding Edo. Sano had barely managed to stave off one rebellion since the earthquake. The *daimyo* might seize on his clash with Lord Tsunanori as a pretext to launch another.

To defuse the conflict, Sano spoke in a mild tone. "If you're innocent, you should be glad to cooperate with my investigation. If you don't cooperate, that would mean you have something to hide."

Lord Tsunanori shifted his weight as contradictory emotions pulled at him. His eyes flashed with anger because Sano had saddled him with a dilemma, but he wasn't drunk enough or stupid enough not to foresee the serious consequences of violence against a government official. The cash-strapped regime would welcome the excuse to confiscate his wealth.

"Very well." Glad to avoid a fight while saving face in front of his men, Lord Tsunanori gestured as if tossing garbage at Sano's feet. "Interrogate my household. Search my wife's room. You won't find any evidence against me." He spoke with such confidence that Sano wondered if he was really innocent or really sure he'd covered his tracks. He told his men, "Go collect everybody for Chamberlain Sano to talk to."

They departed. Aggression flared in Lord Tsunanori's eyes again. "If you go around saying my wife was murdered and I'm under suspicion, you'll be sorry." He wasn't drunk or stupid enough not to recognize how dangerous the suspicion could be to him, or not to know the trouble that he and the other *daimyo* could cause Sano and the Tokugawa regime.

"Good enough." Sano pretended grudging concession, hid his relief that he could count on Lord Tsunanori to keep quiet about the investigation.

It was the only bright spot in his investigation, which was already going wrong, leading away from Yanagisawa.

娘 7

THE SHOGUN'S HEIR'S residence was isolated in the west-
ern fortress of Edo Castle, on the tier of the hill just below the palace.
Enclosed by stone walls topped by covered corridors and a guard tower,
the residence was a miniature version of the palace. Damage from the
earthquake had been repaired. The residence was a safe nest from which
the new dictator of Japan would eventually hatch.

Yanagisawa strode through the chambers, sliding open the partitions
between them, admiring the gilded landscape murals, smelling the fresh,
sweetly scented tatami, and exulting in the territory he'd won in this
round of his battle for power.

"I've done it. We're here at last, set to rule Japan!"

At the opposite end of the building, Yoshisato stood in his new
room. He rearranged books and clothes that the servants had unpacked.
"What do you mean, *we*? *I'm* the one who will inherit the dictatorship."

Stung by his ungraciousness, Yanagisawa said, "You couldn't have
gotten here by yourself." He moved toward Yoshisato. "Whose idea was
it to pass you off as the shogun's son?"

"Yours," Yoshisato admitted grudgingly. He rammed books onto
shelves.

"Well, then." Yanagisawa prided himself on the brilliant scheme he'd
dreamed up after he'd lost his favorite son, after Ienobu had devised a
plot to banish him from court. Yoshisato, one of his other four sons, was
his salvation. "Don't forget how hard I've worked to convince the

shogun, his clan members, and his top officials that you are indeed his son. Don't forget how much money I've paid in bribes to persuade people to support your bid for the succession."

"Don't forget that it wasn't your money. It came from my allowance from the shogun."

"Without me you wouldn't have that allowance. So you shouldn't mind if I celebrate *our* accomplishment."

"Do it by yourself. Now that I'm the shogun's heir, I don't need you anymore."

Fear stabbed Yanagisawa. He'd known that the day he put Yoshisato in line to become the next dictator could be the day he outlived his usefulness to Yoshisato. They'd been at odds during their four-month collaboration. It was a miracle that they'd come this far together.

"You do need me." Yanagisawa had to convince Yoshisato. One bad word from him, and the shogun would throw Yanagisawa out of the regime. Yanagisawa's enemies would descend on him like a pack of wolves. "I'm the one with a lifetime of experience in politics. You're just a seventeen-year-old boy. Without me, you'd be eaten alive."

"I won't be seventeen forever," Yoshisato said, irritated because Yanagisawa was right. He meticulously folded clothes into drawers. "And I've learned a lot."

"With my tutoring," Yanagisawa reminded him. "And I got rid of witnesses who could have testified that your mother never slept with the shogun." He'd scoured the city clean of officials and servants who'd worked in the castle at the time Lady Someko was purported to have been the shogun's concubine. He'd also cleared out people in his own household who knew she'd been sharing his bed at the time Yoshisato was conceived. He'd bribed the witnesses to keep quiet, threatened them, sent them to faraway places, and had the most dangerous ones assassinated. "You couldn't have done that for yourself. And you need me to deal with the false witnesses who are sure to crop up." How he resented having to justify his worth to this insolent young man!

Yoshisato glowered, resentful of his own need. "All right. You can stay until the shogun dies and I take over. Then you go."

That the dictatorship would someday be entirely in Yoshisato's hands! Yanagisawa forced a scornful laugh. "If you think you'll be fine on your own once you're shogun, then you're a fool. There are many Tokugawa relatives who would like to rule Japan themselves. When the shogun's not around to protect you, they'll rise up against you. I'm the one who has powerful allies to back you with their armies."

"You also have powerful enemies. As long as you're with me, they're my enemies, too. When I dump you, they'll accept me as their lord."

"I've heard your lame political theories before: Get rid of me, and my enemies will be so grateful, they'll let you rule happily ever after. What you don't understand is that bad blood runs deep. My enemies won't forget that you're my protégé. They'll destroy you as revenge on me. And Sano will lead the charge. You shouldn't have insisted on keeping him in the regime."

"That's the price you pay for my cooperating with your plot," Yoshisato said with a grin. "Let Sano stay, or I tell the shogun I'm not his son and you made me pretend to be."

Yanagisawa fumed at the ultimatum. "You won't tell the shogun now."

"Try me. Kill Sano. See what happens."

Yanagisawa glared at Yoshisato, whose smirk widened to a nasty grin. He didn't dare call Yoshisato's bluff. He didn't trust Yoshisato not to jeopardize them both for the sake of a victory in their private war. The boy was as ruthless as he was. The same blood flowed in their veins. Yanagisawa knew it, no matter that he'd convinced half the world that Yoshisato belonged to the shogun.

"You're asking for trouble by keeping Sano around just to spite me," Yanagisawa said. "If he can't prove you're not the shogun's blood heir, he'll wait until the shogun is dead, and he'll assassinate you before you've ruled Japan for one day."

"He won't," Yoshisato said with confidence. "Sano's not like that."

Incredulous and disdainful, Yanagisawa said, "I've known Sano a lot longer than you have. He will. That's what I would do."

Yoshisato regarded Yanagisawa with sardonic amusement. "Your trouble is that you judge Sano, and me, and everyone else by your own measure. It blinds you to reality."

Yanagisawa grimaced. There was no use arguing. He and Yoshisato were equally stubborn. Like father, like son. "Very well. Keep Sano at court as if you're a little boy with a pet viper in a basket. Someday you'll see that I'm right."

Yoshisato laughed. "If Sano does assassinate me, it would be worth it, having him beat you in the end."

The magnitude of his antipathy hurt Yanagisawa; he loved his son even though he detested the youth's attitude. "Why do you hate me so much?"

Yoshisato gazed at him with fierce, hard eyes. "Don't flatter yourself. I wouldn't waste that much emotion on you."

"Fine." Yanagisawa pretended indifference, but he longed for Yoshisato to love him in return. He'd been terribly lonely since his favorite son, Yoritomo, died. He missed having someone who cared about him. He cursed himself for craving more from Yoshisato than Yoshisato was willing or able to give. "So why can't we be friends? It would make things easier for both of us."

"Excuse me for not feeling particularly friendly toward you. You ignore me for my whole life, and then my half brother dies and you need a new political pawn, so you come sucking up to me. What a wonderful basis for friendship."

Yanagisawa knew that Yoshisato was hurt because Yanagisawa had, in effect, disowned him by positioning him as the shogun's son. "So I didn't fuss over you like a mother hen while you were growing up. Not many fathers would have." Yanagisawa's own father had been a cold, ambitious man who'd introduced Yanagisawa to the shogun as soon as Yanagisawa was old enough to tempt the shogun's sexual appetite. Yanagisawa's longtime affair with the shogun had resulted in many political and economic benefits for his family. "But I've given you something worth far more than my attention—the chance to rule Japan. And I'm here now. Can we put the past behind us and make a fresh start?"

Longing, pain, and confusion mixed in Yoshisato's gaze. It was clear that he cared more about Yanagisawa than he wanted to admit. Then his face hardened. "It's too late. I'm not your son anymore. I'm the shogun's. And you're not going to stick around when I'm head of the regime. You might stab me in the back like you've done to other people who've crossed you."

Yanagisawa felt as if he were pushing a wild horse up a mountain while it bit, thrashed, and tried to kick him down. Too furious to apologize for his past sins and grovel, he grabbed Yoshisato by the front of his robes, shook him, and yelled, "You ungrateful, stubborn, foolhardy wretch! You won't deprive me of my rightful share in ruling Japan!"

"Yes, I will!" Yoshisato grabbed Yanagisawa's wrists. "Take your hands off me!"

A quavering voice called, "Hello?"

Yanagisawa and Yoshisato froze. They both knew they mustn't fight in front of anyone, especially the shogun. They kept their battles private.

The shogun tiptoed into the room, as hesitant and nervous as if he were a trespasser instead of the lord over everything he saw. "Am I, ahh, intruding?"

"Not at all, Your Excellency." Yanagisawa smoothed Yoshisato's robes with a fond gesture before unhanding the young man. "Please join us."

He'd already wiped his expression clean of his inner turmoil and donned a relaxed, serene pose. Yoshisato wasn't yet as adept at concealing his emotions. Anxiety showed through his artificial calmness like bare flesh through inexpertly laced armor.

The shogun wandered through the quarters while Yanagisawa and Yoshisato followed. "Ahh, this place looks different than I remember. But I only lived here a short time, when my older brother was shogun. He suddenly took ill and named me as his successor. A few days later he died. I became shogun." Worry deepened the lines in his forehead. "My brother waited until his end was near before he designated his heir. Perhaps I should have chosen to do the same."

Yanagisawa and Yoshisato exchanged alarmed glances. They'd thought Yoshisato safely installed, but now the shogun was having second thoughts. "Your brother waited because he knew the dictatorship would pass to you whether or not he officially designated you as his heir," Yanagisawa said. "You and he were both sons of the previous shogun." Yanagisawa suspected the older brother had hoped the younger would die first and his son, Ienobu, could inherit the regime. Ienobu would have liked that. "Your installation was a formality he put off. But there's no need for you to wait until you're on your deathbed to install your son as your heir, with all the ceremony, honor, and pleasure you both deserve." Yanagisawa extended his arms to draw Yoshisato and the shogun together.

Shying away from Yoshisato, the shogun said, "The problem is . . . Lately I've, ahh, begun to wonder if you're, ahh, really my son."

"Of course I'm your son!" Yoshisato looked so anxious that Yanagisawa winced. Fearful of being punished for his deceit, Yoshisato had reverted from Yanagisawa's brilliant protégé to the inexperienced seventeen-year-old he was.

Yanagisawa needed to get at the root of the shogun's belated misgivings and dig it out, fast. He spoke loudly, to draw the shogun's attention away from Yoshisato. "Why on earth should you wonder, at this late date, if Yoshisato is really your son?"

The shogun pivoted, as if he were a Bunraku theater puppet and Yanagisawa had jerked the poles that controlled his body. "Last night I woke up to hear two men whispering outside my bedchamber. They said I'm not Yoshisato's father." A red, angry spot of blush colored each of his cheeks. "They said you are."

Yanagisawa cursed inwardly. He'd given orders, backed by threats, that no one was to talk about Yoshisato's parentage near the shogun. He and Yoshisato tried to make sure that one of them was with the shogun at all times, to discourage gossip. But lately the shogun had insomnia; he couldn't fall asleep unless he was alone in his chamber. He'd evidently heard someone whispering, through the thin walls.

"Who was it?" Yanagisawa said, disguising his consternation with outrage. "Who dared to voice the blasphemous suggestion that I'm your son's father?"

Sheepishness weakened the shogun's anger. "Ahh, I didn't recognize their voices."

They were probably his guards or personal attendants, the only people allowed near the shogun while he was sleeping. "It was just idle speculation," Yanagisawa said in a consoling, condescending tone. "You should ignore it."

"But I can't!" The shogun flapped his hands. "It's been happening every night for months." He whispered loudly, " 'Yoshisato is Yanagisawa's son. He's not the shogun's. Yanagisawa is Yoshisato's father.' " Shamefaced, he added, "I didn't mention it earlier because I was afraid to, ahh, have to take it seriously."

Yanagisawa realized that something more sinister was at play than careless gossip. The whispering represented a deliberate attempt to make the shogun believe that Yoshisato was a fraud. And Yanagisawa could guess who was responsible.

"Those are just ignorant dolts talking," Yoshisato scoffed. "Don't listen, Honorable Father."

The shogun turned on him. "Don't call me 'Father' when I'm not certain you have the right to do so!"

Yoshisato stared, aghast. The shogun scowled at Yanagisawa, pointed at Yoshisato. "I want the truth: Is he my son, or have you put a cuckoo's egg into my nest?"

Yanagisawa deployed the wisdom, skill, and instinct gleaned from his long relationship with the shogun. He arranged his features into an expression of concern and sympathy. "The truth is that there seems to be a problem with your health."

"My health?" Always easily distracted by the mention of his favorite topic, always terrified of illness, the shogun gasped. "What sort of problem?"

"Well, let me see," Yanagisawa said. "You've been having insomnia, is that correct?"

The shogun nodded, his clasped hands extended toward Yanagisawa, dreading yet eager for bad news.

"And headaches?"

"Very often."

"What about dizziness?"

Yoshisato frowned, trying to figure out what Yanagisawa was doing.

". . . No," the shogun said. Always vulnerable to suggestion, he changed his mind. "A little."

"Blurred vision?" Yanagisawa asked.

The shogun's pale complexion turned stark white. He nodded, convinced that he had blurred vision, whether he really did or not.

"And you've started hearing strange voices." Yanagisawa tapped his chin with his fingertip and nodded sagely, as he'd seen physicians do while considering a patient's symptoms. "Hmm." The sudden enlightenment on Yoshisato's face was so comical that Yanagisawa almost laughed. "Taking your other symptoms into account, I would say the voices are hallucinations. The problem is just as I suspected."

"Merciful gods!" The shogun clutched at Yanagisawa. "What is wrong with me, pray tell?"

"Nothing serious." Yanagisawa's tone belied his words. "You have a blockage of the energy flow to your brain."

The shogun's eyes bulged with terror. "What should I do?"

"Go immediately to your physician. He'll set you right."

"Yes, yes." The shogun hurried out of the room.

"You made that up," Yoshisato said scornfully.

"I got us out of a tough spot," Yanagisawa said. "You only made things worse."

Yoshisato regarded him with offense and disbelief. "How is the doctor supposed to treat the shogun for his imaginary illness?"

"Oh, he'll give him a harmless potion. That's what he always does when the shogun fancies he's sick."

"But those voices are real. How can a potion make the shogun stop hearing them?"

"It can't, but I can. The shogun will have a new set of guards and attendants before the day is over. They'll be my people, who will prevent anyone from saying a word outside the shogun's chamber. I'll stop this campaign to poison the shogun's mind against you."

Yoshisato's ire turned to dismay. "The whispering is part of a campaign? Not just idle gossip?"

"That should be obvious to you, if you've learned anything about the ways of the court."

"Who's behind it? Ienobu?"

Yanagisawa pointed his finger at Yoshisato. "Very astute of you, if a little slow. If you're discredited, Ienobu will inherit the dictatorship. He'll put both of us to death before the ink on the succession document is dry."

Realizing that his rival was craftier than he'd thought, Yoshisato looked younger and more vulnerable than he had moments ago. "What are we going to do about Ienobu?"

"What do you mean, *we*?" Yanagisawa said with a sarcastic smile. "Are you admitting that you need me after all and you want me to stay?"

The same anger, frustration, and helplessness that Yanagisawa had felt earlier now showed in Yoshisato's expression. Yoshisato squared his shoulders and tightened his jaw, striving for dignity. "Yes." His tone boasted that he was smart enough to recognize that he was in over his head and to accept help from a father he hated rather than perish on his own.

Yanagisawa's heart swelled with pride in Yoshisato. What a marvelous son! Would that the shogun never believed that Yoshisato's fine qualities came from someone other than himself. Hiding his thoughts behind a patronizing smile, Yanagisawa said, "I'm glad that's understood."

He anticipated an eventual clash with Ienobu. Thank the gods that the shogun didn't have other, closer relatives to contend for the succession! Yanagisawa foresaw more struggles with Yoshisato, but at least he had one consolation.

The shogun's daughter was safely dead. She couldn't produce a rival for Yoshisato.

娘

8

"MY WIFE'S CHAMBER is this way." Stiff with reluctance, Lord Tsunanori led Sano and Marume along a corridor through the women's quarters of his estate.

A powerful smell of incense and lye soap filled the air. Sano's eyes watered. Marume coughed and said, "I'm glad the place has been disinfected, but they overdid it a little."

Lord Tsunanori opened a door in the lattice-and-paper wall, stood aside, and said, "This is where Tsuruhime died."

Crossing the threshold, Sano tried not to breathe. He felt queasy even though he'd witnessed death so many times that he'd lost count and there was no corpse here. He couldn't help fearing contagion even though no spirits of disease could possibly withstand such thorough cleansing. The room was empty of furniture, the cabinet doors open to reveal vacant shelves and drawers, the floor bare. A damp, caustic-smelling patch darkened the wooden planks where the sickbed had been.

"There's nothing to see, but look as much as you want." Lord Tsunanori sounded spitefully pleased to disappoint Sano. He waited in the doorway.

Sano glanced into the cabinets. No soiled linens materialized. Nothing except the lavish mural of marsh scenes indicated that a wealthy, privileged woman had once lived here.

"I had to have everything burned." Lord Tsunanori spoke with more regret than he'd expressed about his wife's death. "Her robes alone were worth a fortune. But they might have been contaminated with the smallpox, so they had to go."

"Are you finished?" Marume asked Sano, his voice muffled by the hand he held over his nose and mouth. The stout-hearted detective feared smallpox as much as Sano did.

"Yes." As Sano exited the chamber, his own relief was strong.

Lord Tsunanori led the way to the outer portion of the mansion. "You said you wanted to talk to my people." He ushered Sano and Marume into a vast room created by opening the partitions between three adjacent reception chambers. "Well, here they are."

A huge crowd overflowed out the open doors, onto the verandas, and into the garden. *Daimyo* estates could contain more than a thousand people. The lords had even bigger estates and retinues in their provinces. In Edo they kept only enough people to provide security, to maintain their property, and to wait on them when they were in town for the half of each year that Tokugawa law required, and to care for their women and children, whom the law required to stay year-round as hostages to their good behavior. Sano gazed at the troops mingled with servants, at officials crammed alongside women in silk kimonos. It was a truly impressive, huge pool of witnesses.

"I'll start with your wife's personal attendants," Sano said. "Detective Marume and I will question each one individually, in private."

Displeasure darkened Lord Tsunanori's face. "I have a right to be present when you talk to them."

"It's not your right by law," Sano said. "It's a courtesy that I can allow you or not. And I choose not to have you present."

As Lord Tsunanori started to bluster, a samurai official in the front row of the crowd beckoned him. Lord Tsunanori leaned down. The official whispered in his ear. Lord Tsunanori turned back to Sano with a smug, vindictive smile and said, "It seems you're not the shogun's second-in-command anymore. My man here tells me you've been demoted to Chief Rebuilding Magistrate. Funny, you didn't mention the fact that you're out of favor at court."

Sano felt the hot sting of humiliation as his heart sank. The bad news had caught up with him at a most unfortunate time. "My position doesn't matter," he retorted.

"Oh, it does. You've lost the authority to tell me what to do." Lord Tsunanori smirked. "Actually, I've changed my mind about letting you to talk to my people at all."

"In that case, I'll change my mind about keeping my inquiries confidential," Sano said. "I'll tell the shogun my suspicions about Tsuruhime's death."

Lord Tsunanori bit his flaccid lips as he vacillated between his fear of being implicated in the murder of the shogun's daughter and his desire to best Sano. "All right," he said sullenly. "You can talk to them. But only in my presence."

"Fine," Sano said, thankful that Lord Tsunanori hadn't called his bluff. He couldn't afford to let Yanagisawa hear of his investigation when it had barely begun.

Lord Tsunanori gathered Tsuruhime's personal retinue from among the crowd. There were six guards, two palanquin bearers, and ten female attendants. Three of the women sported elaborate hairstyles and fashionable silk garments; they were ladies-in-waiting. Cotton garments marked the other seven females as servants. One of these wore a white drape that covered her head and cast a shadow over her face. Lord Tsunanori took the attendants and Sano and Marume to a smaller audience chamber. He seated Sano and Marume on the dais. His retainers organized the attendants in a line on the floor below, then stationed themselves by the door. Lord Tsunanori knelt beside Sano and said, "Go ahead."

Sano beckoned the first witness, a maid with a ruddy complexion. She came forward and bowed. "Did you ever see a stained old sheet among the things in your mistress's cabinet?" Sano asked.

Lord Tsunanori shook his head. The maid said, "No."

"Stop influencing her," Sano said.

"I'm not."

Sano stifled a sigh; he turned back to the maid. "Have you ever seen anyone acting strangely while handling your mistress's clothes or bedding?"

"No," the maid said.

"Do you know of anyone besides your mistress who'd recently had smallpox?"

"No." She sounded more eager to provide the answer Lord Tsunanori would deem acceptable than to tell the truth. He rewarded her with a smiling nod.

Marume rolled his eyes. Sano said, "That will be all." He called the next person in line, a stout guard. "Did you escort your lord's wife when she went out of the estate?"

"Yes," the guard said.

"Did she go out often during the ten days or so before she got small-pox?"

The guard glanced at Lord Tsunanori, who nodded vigorously. "Yes, all the time."

Sano had difficulty envisioning Tsuruhime as a gadabout in the earthquake-ravaged city. "Did she go anyplace where there might have been people with smallpox?"

"Yes, I think we went by the tent camps. In fact, I'm sure we did."

Sano thought the guard would probably swear that Tsuruhime had wallowed in the cesspools. He dismissed the man. As the interrogation continued in this fashion, Lord Tsunanori's retainers wandered out of the room, probably to tell the other household members the questions Sano was asking and the answers Lord Tsunanori wanted them to give. Then came the woman with the white head drape. Her brown-and-lavender flowered kimono was made of cotton but finer than the usual indigo garb worn by servants. Walking up to the dais, she carried her slim, curved figure with a dignity unusual for a commoner.

"What is your name?" Sano asked.

"Namiji." The woman bowed.

Sano saw what the shadow cast by the white drape partially hid. Round scars stippled with pits marred her complexion. They disfigured the visible half of her mouth and nose, although the eye on that side of her face was clear and well shaped, its expression intelligent. This was the woman who'd had smallpox during her youth, who'd been Tsuruhime's nurse. Instinct told Sano that she was the most important witness here and he must not let Lord Tsunanori meddle during her interrogation.

He rose and said, "I'm arresting this woman."

Lord Tsunanori's loose mouth dropped. "Why?" The woman shrank from Sano, pulling the drape tighter around her face.

"She's wanted by the law, for suspicion of thievery," Sano improvised. "I recognized her name and description."

He stepped off the dais, seized her arm. She recoiled, protesting, "I've done nothing wrong!" Her voice was husky, as though the smallpox had scarred her throat.

"You're making that up." Caught between disbelief and offense, Lord Tsunanori said, "You can't go around taking people's servants."

"Watch me," Sano said.

Marume took the nurse's other arm and helped Sano pull her toward the door. Lord Tsunanori and his retainers hurried after them. Sano was afraid they would use force to stop him and then would come the fight he wanted to avoid, that could provoke the entire *daimyo* class into rebellion. But he had to secure his witness.

Lord Tsunanori pushed past Sano and Marume in the corridor, flung out his arms to block their passage, and sputtered, "I won't let you do this!"

"Why are you so afraid?" Sano countered. "What is it you think she'll say when she's not under your control?"

Lord Tsunanori rolled his tongue under his lips. His gaze moved from Sano to the nurse. Then he spoke with his usual arrogant confidence. "Go ahead, take her. See if I care."

Sano and Marume escorted the nurse from the mansion. She went without resisting. Lord Tsunanori didn't follow them outside. His sentries watched Sano and Marume join their troops in the street. Sano saw two bearers carrying a palanquin for hire. He waved them over. When they set the black wooden sedan chair on the ground, he told Namiji, "Get in."

Still holding the drape over her face, she settled herself in the shadowed interior of the palanquin. Sano spoke to his two troops, in a low voice that she wouldn't hear. "Take her to my estate. Tell my wife that she's Namiji, the nurse who took care of the shogun's daughter. My wife will know what to do with her." Reiko would be happy to question her and find out what she knew about the murder. "Don't tell her where you're taking her or why."

The troops rode off, escorting the bearers and palanquin toward the castle. Sano and Marume mounted their horses.

"Where are we going?" Marume asked.

"To begin my work as Chief Rebuilding Magistrate. Better to let Yanagisawa think I'm bowing to his authority than let him suspect I'm working against him behind his back."

As they rode around a team of oxcarts laden with stones, Marume said, "A fat lot we learned from that disgusting Lord Tsunanori."

"On the contrary," Sano said. "He told us that he had reason to kill his wife. And who would have had better opportunity than him, the lord of the estate?"

"But we came up empty as far as Yanagisawa is concerned."

Sano nodded with regret. "I would have liked to ask Lord Tsunanori if Yanagisawa or any of his people had been in the estate shortly before Tsuruhime took ill. But Lord Tsunanori would have guessed that I'm trying to connect Yanagisawa with her death."

"He would have run straight to Yanagisawa and told him," Marume agreed. "Then the investigation wouldn't be a secret any longer."

"And Lord Tsunanori wouldn't have to worry that it might hurt him, because I would be too busy fighting Yanagisawa for my life." Sano mulled over his encounter with Lord Tsunanori. "We also learned that Lord Tsunanori is hiding something. Why else would he have interfered while I questioned his people?"

"Yes, and he was pretty quick to jump to the conclusion that his wife had been murdered and he's a suspect," Marume said. "That looked like a guilty conscience. When Lady Nobuko came to see you, did she mention that he hated his wife and wanted to be rid of her?"

"No." Sano felt a surge of anger toward Lady Nobuko. Not only did he not have evidence against Yanagisawa; he had an accomplice who lied to him.

"Why didn't she?"

"That's a good question," Sano said.

9

娘

"THERE'S A VISITOR here for you, Lady Reiko," the maid said.

"Who is it?" Reiko knelt in the bath chamber, washing her daughter Akiko's hair.

Bent over a basin of water, Akiko wriggled as Reiko scrubbed her scalp. "Mama, you're getting soap in my eyes!"

"Hold still!" Reiko said.

Akiko shrieked and flailed her arms. "I don't like my hair washed!"

"It's a woman named Namiji." The maid backed out of the doorway to avoid splashes.

"You wouldn't need it washed if you hadn't been playing in the stables. How many times have I told you not to?" Reiko struggled to hold onto her daughter and her temper. She asked the maid, "Who is this Namiji?"

"But I like the horses," Akiko protested.

Reiko had liked them, too, when she'd been a child and her grand-mother had told her to stay away from them because they were dangerous. Akiko was a young version of herself—brave, adventuresome, rebellious.

"The horses could bite you or trample you," Reiko said. "You're lucky that you only fell in manure and got it in your hair. Now stop fighting me!"

"She's a nurse," the maid said.

"We don't need a nurse," Reiko said. "Nobody is sick." Akiko's fist hit her stomach. "Ouch! Stop! Don't do that! You're going to hurt your baby brother or sister!"

"I don't want a baby brother or sister." Akiko began to cry.

Reiko realized that Akiko was already jealous of the new child. She and Akiko had a difficult relationship, and not only because they were so much alike. Akiko seemed to crave Reiko's love while spurning it and doing her best to anger Reiko. She'd refused to let the maids wash her hair; she'd insisted that Reiko do the dirty work. She must sense that a baby would steal attention from her mother, which she wanted for herself.

"The nurse took care of Tsuruhime, the shogun's daughter," the maid said. "Your husband sent her. He said you would know what to do."

Now Reiko understood that Sano had sent a witness for her to question. Elated because she now had a chance to help save her family, she wrapped a towel around Akiko's clean, wet head and rose.

"Don't go!" Akiko wailed.

"I'll be back soon." Reiko pulled away from Akiko's clinging hands. It seemed she was always leaving Akiko, and Akiko always felt abandoned. Reiko recalled the time when Masahiro had been kidnapped and Reiko and Sano had left home to rescue him. Akiko had been too young to remember; yet on some level she knew her mother had deserted her and she'd not forgotten. But there was nothing to do about it now. Reiko hurried to the reception room.

Near the alcove knelt a woman dressed in a brown cotton kimono printed with lavender bush clover. A large white scarf shrouded her hair and draped diagonally across her face, the end wound around her neck. Two of Sano's troops stood against the wall inside the door. Reiko approached the woman, who tensed visibly.

"Welcome, Namiji-*san*," Reiko said, kneeling opposite her guest.

The woman bowed, her courtesy automatic yet graceful. "Who are you?" Her husky voice, muffled by her scarf, blended seductiveness with coarseness. Reiko could see only her right eye. Its flower-petal shape and long lashes hinted at beauty.

"My name is Reiko. I'm Sano-*san*'s wife. I believe you met him at Lord Tsunanori's estate?"

". . . Yes. Why was I brought here?"

Reiko deduced that Sano hadn't told the nurse that Reiko was supposed to question her about her mistress's death. He must have wanted

Reiko to take her by surprise. "To meet me," Reiko said. "May I offer you some refreshments?"

Namiji skipped the customary polite response. "Am I under arrest?"

"No."

"Then I'll be going." Namiji started to rise.

"Not until we've talked," Reiko said. The troops moved in front of the door.

Namiji sank to her knees again. A sigh puffed out the smooth white fabric of her scarf. "Talked about what?"

"An important matter that would be better to discuss face-to-face." In order to gauge the woman's veracity, Reiko needed to see more of her. "Would you please remove your scarf?"

Namiji's hand flew to the scarf, as though she feared Reiko would tear it off her head. She wore cotton gloves the color of bare skin. Her visible eye narrowed with cunning. "I had smallpox when I was seventeen. I haven't been contagious since then, but who knows? If I take off my scarf, I might infect you—and your baby."

Reiko felt a visceral stab of fear that brought on a contraction. Although it was unlikely that she could catch smallpox from somebody who'd had the disease years ago, she realized that this investigation posed threats to her even if she never left home. "All right, leave your scarf on," she said, angry because she knew Namiji was taunting her. She tried to sympathize with this woman, who must have endured terrible suffering. "I'm sorry you had smallpox."

"You're just glad it wasn't you."

Reiko saw that sympathy wouldn't induce cooperation from Namiji. She matched frankness with frankness. "You're right. I am glad. Just as you must be glad that the smallpox killed your mistress but not you."

Surprise at Reiko's remark dilated the dark pupil in Namiji's visible eye. "So you think I should be glad to be alive? Well, you don't know what it's like."

"No, I don't." Curious, and wanting to form a rapport with Namiji after a bad start, Reiko said, "Would you like to tell me?"

Namiji laughed, a sound coarser than her voice. "Where shall I start? With the children who throw stones at me in the street? The women who whisper and giggle behind my back? The men who yell insults? Or the fact that no one will ever marry me?"

Reiko had seen how badly people treated those with physical or mental defects. It must be more hurtful than she'd thought. She felt guilty because she'd never tried to stop the tormenting. Nobody else did; it wasn't the custom.

"Is that why I'm here?" Namiji asked. "For you to pick at my wounds? Did your husband send me here as a toy for you?"

"Certainly not." Offended by the accusation, Reiko said, "He sent you here for me to ask you about Tsuruhime."

"Ah." Mockery glinted in the nurse's eye. "He couldn't do it himself because Lord Tsunanori was getting in the way."

Reiko began to understand what must have happened at the estate. Lord Tsunanori had interfered with Sano's investigation. The reason must be that he was afraid of it. Had he, not Yanagisawa, killed his wife?

Namiji regarded Reiko with amusement and curiosity. "I've heard about you—you help your husband solve crimes. Your husband must think Tsuruhime was murdered. He must want you to find out if I know anything about it."

"Do you?"

"If I did, I wouldn't tell you." Namiji added primly, "Lord Tsunanori doesn't like his people to talk about his business."

"You're not leaving here until you answer my questions," Reiko said. "Did you like Tsuruhime?"

"Yes. She was friendly and kind and not demanding." Namiji's manner suddenly turned gentle and sweet. "I shall miss her very much."

The act might have fooled Reiko if Namiji hadn't already shown her true, unpleasant self. "You're lying."

"All right, I admit it," Namiji snapped, unable or unwilling to keep up the act. "I didn't like Tsuruhime. When she married Lord Tsunanori, she refused to let me wait on her, even though my family has served his for generations. She said my scars were so ugly, they made her sick." Namiji's gloved hands clenched. "She wouldn't allow me in the women's quarters, where I'd worked all my life. She wanted me thrown out so she wouldn't have to see me."

Lady Nobuko had described Tsuruhime as a sweet, harmless woman. Now Reiko glimpsed a different side of the shogun's daughter. Maybe she'd been a victim murdered for her own cruelty, not just political gain. And maybe Yanagisawa wasn't the culprit. Reiko's heart sank as she realized that the nurse had had good reason to want Tsuruhime dead and her first inquiry was leading her in the wrong direction.

"But Lord Tsunanori wouldn't let her," Namiji said smugly. "I had to work in the kitchen, and live in the servants' quarters, and stay out of her sight, but he kept me on."

"Why did he?" Reiko was surprised that Lord Tsunanori would side with a servant instead of his wife.

"There's always a shortage of trustworthy servants, in case you haven't noticed."

"If Tsuruhime wouldn't let you near her, then how did you come to be her nurse?"

"Because she got smallpox. I was the only person at the estate who could go near her without catching it." Namiji laughed her coarse laugh. "She ended up with the same disease that made me so disgusting to her. And every time she looked up at me sitting by her bed, she saw what she would look like if she survived. Which she didn't. Isn't that funny?"

Reiko thought it more suspicious than coincidental. "Do you know of anyone who had smallpox shortly before Tsuruhime took ill?"

"No."

"Did you see a stained sheet among Tsuruhime's things?"

"Stained with what?"

"Pus and blood, from someone else's smallpox sores."

"Why? Was there one?"

Reiko analyzed Namiji's puzzled, innocent manner. She couldn't tell if it was genuine. Although Namiji had talked freely to her own detriment, she might be better at concealing knowledge than she seemed. "You tell me."

"I don't know anything to tell you. Is that how she got smallpox, from someone else's infected sheet?"

"Suppose it is," Reiko said. "You hated her. You're obviously pleased by her death. Did you put the sheet in with her things?"

"I couldn't have." Namiji spoke as if the accusation were stupid as well as unjust. "I told you, Tsuruhime didn't allow me in her quarters until she took ill and she didn't have a choice."

"Then who could have done it? Lord Tsunanori?"

"Not him," Namiji declared.

"Then why did he interfere with my husband's inquiries?"

Namiji ignored the question. "If I tell you who might have done it, will you let me go?"

Reiko was taken aback to learn that while she'd been trying to coax Namiji into incriminating herself, the nurse had been hiding a card with which to bargain for her freedom—the identity of a new suspect. Namiji had figured out that this was a murder investigation when Sano had started asking questions at Lord Tsunanori's estate. But maybe she'd known beforehand that Tsuruhime had been murdered, and she'd squirreled away a tidbit of information in case she fell under suspicion and needed to protect herself.

"Who might have done it?" Reiko asked.

"Will you let me go after I tell you?"

"How do I know whether this person really could have infected Tsuruhime or if you're going to feed me a lie to divert my suspicion from you?"

Namiji chuckled. "You don't."

Although she distrusted Namiji and was vexed by her insolence, Reiko needed any clue she could get. "All right. But you'd better convince me that your information is good. If I think you're just pointing the finger at someone you don't like, then I'll tell my husband that I think you killed Tsuruhime. He'll send you to trial for murder."

Everyone knew that virtually all trials ended with guilty verdicts and the punishment for murder was death by decapitation.

"Oh, it's good," Namiji said confidently. "Eight days before Tsuruhime took ill, she had a visitor. I saw him. It was the shogun's new son."

Surprise jolted Reiko. The child inside her rolled. This was the first clue that connected Yoshisato—and Yanagisawa—with Tsuruhime. Hiding her excitement, Reiko said, "Go on."

"Yoshisato came to the estate. Tsuruhime received him in her chambers. She didn't ordinarily let men in there, but he was her half brother. He brought her a fancy chest full of presents. They were together for almost an hour. Alone." Namiji put a gloved finger to her temple, as if an idea had just occurred to her. "I wonder if there was a stained sheet inside that chest. And if he sneaked it in with her things while she wasn't looking."

Reiko couldn't wait to tell Sano what she'd heard. But he would want to check Namiji's story. "Can anyone vouch for what you've just told me?"

"Tsuruhime's servants and ladies-in-waiting. They saw him, too. Can I go now?"

Honor-bound to keep her part of the bargain, Reiko told the guards, "Take her back to Lord Tsunanori's estate."

"In case you're thinking of bringing me back for another chat—" Namiji leaned close to Reiko, whipped her scarf away from her mouth, and coughed in Reiko's face.

Reiko cried out in horror as she recoiled from Namiji's moist, sour breath. Terrified despite knowing that Namiji wasn't contagious, Reiko scrubbed her face with her sleeve.

Namiji burst into malicious laughter. "That will teach you to stay away from me!"

The guards seized her and dragged her away from Reiko. Reiko heard her laughing all the way down the corridor.

10

MASAHIRO HURRIED THROUGH Edo Castle, on his way to help his father with the most important investigation of their lives. He wore a leather shoulder pouch and a pole attached to his back that flew a banner printed with the Tokugawa triple-hollyhock-leaf crest—his page's uniform. An official stopped him, said, "Take this message to the north army command post," and pushed a scroll container into his hands.

Unable to refuse because his position in the regime was already shaky, Masahiro delivered the scroll. Afterward, he met two fellow pages. They blocked his way down the passage.

"What have we here?" said one of them, a surly, thickset boy named Ukyo.

"It's the great Masahiro, who used to be head of the shogun's private chambers," said Gizaemon, the other boy. His little black eyes glinted with mean pleasure in a face like a rat's. "But he got kicked out of the palace today."

These boys and others had resented him because the shogun had chosen Masahiro to serve as head of his chambers and bypassed them. Masahiro stood his ground even though Ukyo and Gizaemon were two years older, taller, and stronger than he. "Get out of my way."

" 'Get out of my way,' " Ukyo mocked him in a girlish falsetto.

Gizaemon snickered. "Say 'please.' "

Masahiro knew he could beat them in a sword fight. He'd done so at martial arts practice, another reason they were tickled by his downfall.

But drawing a weapon inside Edo Castle was against the law, punishable by death.

" 'Please,' " Masahiro said through gritted teeth.

The two boys stood aside. As he passed them, they grabbed him. They wrestled him onto the ground, seized his hair, and banged his face against the paving stones. Then they released him and walked away, laughing.

Masahiro stood up. He wiped his face with his hand, which came away bloody from a cut on his nose. He burned with shame and anger. Remembering how he'd been demoted in front of the assembly at the palace, he blinked back tears. That, and seeing his father brought down by Yanagisawa, had been the worst experience of his life. And this attack was only a taste of trouble to come, Masahiro knew. Yanagisawa would never leave his family in peace. Masahiro held his head high while he strode through the castle, avoiding the gazes of the people he passed. As he exited the castle gate, he swore to solve the murder of the shogun's daughter and prove Yanagisawa was guilty.

By the time he reached the crowded, bustling *daimyo* district, the temple bells began tolling noon. The sun shone with a force that promised a hot summer. Laborers repairing the estates had stripped down to their loincloths. Their naked legs and torsos gleamed with sweat. Sawdust choked the air. Masahiro loitered near Lord Tsunanori's gate and pondered what to do.

The sentries wouldn't just let him walk in and start asking people, "Did you see Yanagisawa kill the shogun's daughter?" Masahiro reached in his bag, took out a scroll container, and approached the sentries. "I have a message for Lord Tsunanori, from the shogun."

"Thanks, I'll give it to him," one of the men said.

"My instructions were to put it into his hands myself," Masahiro lied.

"I'll see that he gets it." The man snatched the scroll from Masahiro.

Masahiro wondered what Lord Tsunanori would think when he opened the empty container. He walked around the estate, peering up at the surrounding barracks, until he reached the back gate. It was open and unguarded. A group of carpenters sauntered in, carrying boards over their shoulders. Masahiro followed.

Although repairs had been finished on the lord's mansion and the parts of the estate visible from the outside, new stables and servants' quarters were still under construction, amid hammering and sawing. Smoke billowed from hearths under a huge tent where cooks prepared food for the *daimyo*'s entourage. Oxcarts, workbenches, piles of lumber and stones, and trash heaps took up much of the grounds. Masahiro saw shaved crowns and topknots on many workers. There weren't enough peasants to rebuild Edo. Samurai who normally spent their time loafing now had to work for their stipends. As Masahiro looked around, wondering where to start his inquiries, he heard shouts, then a loud shattering noise.

Four samurai stood atop a building. They'd been affixing ceramic tiles on the roof. Below them a box lay on the ground amid broken tiles. Two of the samurai cursed angrily. A third yelled, "Look what you did, you clumsy fool! It's a good thing nobody was standing down there. Go pick those tiles up!"

The fourth man, who'd knocked the box off the roof, climbed down a ladder. He was younger than the others, in his early twenties. While they had strong, tough muscles and faces, he had a slender build and handsome, sensitive features.

"Save the unbroken ones," a man on the roof ordered. "There's a shortage of tiles."

Masahiro hurried over to help. "Thank you," the young man muttered as he and Masahiro sorted good tiles into the box and threw fragments onto a trash heap.

The other men sat on the roof and watched. Disgruntled because they were forced to do menial labor, they took out their anger on their comrade, talking about him as if he weren't there. "I never saw anybody so careless." "He doesn't pay attention to what he's doing." The young man's sensitive mouth tightened as he sorted tiles. "His head has been in the clouds." "Do you think it's because of the mistress?" The men chuckled.

Masahiro's attention perked up. The mistress—that must mean Lord Tsunanori's wife, Tsuruhime. He studied the man he was helping. Could he have something to do with the shogun's daughter and her murder?

The young man flung the last good tile into the box. His cheeks were bright red. With quick, angry movements he lifted the box onto a wooden platform and cranked a pulley. The men on the roof grasped the box and guided it onto the roof. They continued their conversation.

"All those afternoons he spent alone with her in her room before she got sick." "Did he think the master wouldn't find out?" "Now that she's dead, he's really lost his wits."

"Shut up!" the young man burst out, glaring up at his comrades. "Just shut the hell up!"

They guffawed. One said, "Jinnosuke is in a bad mood." Another said, "His little balls must be aching because he's not getting any pussy!"

Masahiro had overheard enough conversation at Edo Castle to understand that these men were talking about sex. Their remarks implied that the young man had had an affair with Tsuruhime. Masahiro was excited because it might have a bearing on her murder.

Jinnosuke stalked toward the gate, his eyes shiny with angry tears. The other men called, "Hey, come back here and get to work!"

Masahiro hurried after Jinnosuke. Outside the gate he bumped into a little girl in a green kimono. "Taeko?" Startled, he said, "What are you doing here?"

"I came to see you." She looked timid and anxious.

"How did you know where I was?"

"I followed you."

"You followed me?" Masahiro said, taken aback. "All the way from the house?"

Taeko nodded. She hunched her shoulders.

Masahiro was upset because he hadn't noticed her. If he couldn't spot a little girl on his trail, what would have happened if someone dangerous had been stalking him? He would be dead. And Taeko must have seen the other pages bullying him. His face burned with fresh shame.

"I thought I told you to stay home," he said.

She looked at the ground. "I wanted to help you investigate."

Masahiro looked up the street. Jinnosuke was nowhere in sight. Masahiro ran to the intersection, looked left, then right. All he saw were porters, oxcarts, mounted troops, and pedestrians. He ran back to Taeko.

"I lost my witness!" All the anger and frustration that had built up inside him today spilled over. "It's your fault."

Taeko stared up at him with alarm. "I'm sorry. I didn't mean to—"

"That's why I didn't want you to come," Masahiro said, venting the emotions he'd struggled to hide from other people. "Because you would get in the way! And now I have to put off my investigation to take you home!"

Tears welled in Taeko's eyes. "I'm sorry. I won't bother you any-more." She turned and ran down the street.

Now Masahiro was sorry he'd scolded her. She didn't understand what he was going through. He'd done the same thing those samurai had—taken out his anger on an innocent person. And Taeko was his friend. How he regretted hurting her feelings!

"Wait, Taeko," he called.

She was gone.

娘 *11*

IN THE HIBIYA administrative district south of Edo Castle, the regime's high officials had once lived and worked in stately mansions enclosed by high walls. The earthquake and fires had destroyed most of the district, but as Sano rode through it with Marume, he noticed porters lugging trunks and streets blocked by oxcarts filled with furniture. Residents were moving back into their repaired homes. Still, glaring signs of the disaster remained. Barricades made of scrap wood and other debris substituted for walls not yet rebuilt. Beyond these rose the tents where many residents still lived.

Sano and Marume dismounted outside a new gate. The sentry admitted them to a mansion whose wood structure smelled pungently of fresh cedar resin. The plaster on the half-timbered walls looked fresh enough that Sano could leave his handprint in it if he wanted.

"Didn't the chief tax collector used to live here?" Marume asked.

"He committed suicide," Sano said. The earthquake had begotten a flood of suicides that was only just tapering off. Many people, driven to despair because they'd lost relatives and friends, their homes, work, and income, had chosen to die rather than face a future that seemed so bleak. Sano thought of Elder Ohgami. "It's now headquarters for the rebuilding magistrates."

Inside the mansion, chambers were filled with clerks who sat at desks piled with ledgers and scrolls. Maps and architectural diagrams covered the walls. The clerks argued about deadlines, roadwork projects, and new bridges. They negotiated prices for labor, supplies, and loans with merchants who added sums on the beads of *soroban*. Sano and Marume met a samurai in the hall. He had a smile so bright and a complexion so shiny that his face seemed to glow. It dimmed a little when he recognized Sano.

"Greetings, Sano-*san*," he said, and bowed. "I'm Moriwaki, one of the rebuilding magistrates. The four others are out in the field. I heard you would be coming."

"Greetings." Sano could tell that Moriwaki wasn't pleased to have a new chief put over him. He introduced Marume. The men exchanged bows.

"Are you ready to start learning your new job?" Moriwaki asked.

"Yes." After fourteen years in regime's top inner circle, Sano found himself in the position of being trained by a subordinate. It dealt another humiliating blow to his samurai pride.

"Come right this way." Walking with energetic speed, Moriwaki led Sano and Marume to an office furnished with iron trunks for documents and money, ledgers on shelves, and new lacquer cabinets. He knelt behind the desk in the raised study niche.

"You look familiar," Sano said as he and Marume knelt on the floor. "Weren't you once a checkpoint guard at the castle?"

"Yes." Moriwaki laughed at his former modest rank. "After the earthquake, I organized brigades to clean up debris inside the castle. I went on to supervise rebuilding the roads and canals around town. My superiors were impressed. That's how I got this job." He beamed at Sano. "I never thought I'd be sitting with you like this."

Sano had a distasteful sense that he and Moriwaki were passing each other—Moriwaki on his way up, Sano on his way down. Sano thought again of his colleagues who'd killed themselves. How much more could he endure?

Moriwaki showed Sano maps and building plans, budgets and schedules, explaining at top speed. Detective Marume put on the drowsy, vacant expression of a dull-witted pupil at school. Sano's head spun with technical details for which his past experience had ill equipped him. He felt in danger of becoming a mere figurehead, the kind of official he'd always scorned.

"There's lots of government money pouring into the earthquake re-covery, and lots of people skimming it off," Moriwaki said. "We have spies watching out for corruption. We investigate tips, and we conduct trials of people who are caught stealing or cheating."

Finally Sano saw something he was qualified to handle. "I'll take that over."

"One thing to keep in mind: When Chamberlain Yanagisawa helps himself to the relief funds, we have orders to look the other way." Mori-waki grinned. "I don't need to tell you what he's capable of doing when he's crossed, do I?"

Anger flamed suddenly and ferociously in Sano. Not even the earth-quake could stop Yanagisawa from robbing the government. Sano thought of the refugee family camped outside the castle. Money slated to help them and other suffering people would go toward buying political sup-port for Yanagisawa and Yoshisato. That was more reason why Sano couldn't let them take over Japan.

Moriwaki gave Sano a ledger. "Here's a list of the spies, the tips that need to be investigated, and the trials scheduled. We also investigate construction accidents."

A clerk put his head in the doorway. "There's been an accident at the Ryōgoku Bridge."

Sano had to get away before he exploded. "I'll go investigate."

RIDING THROUGH THE Nihonbashi merchant quarter, past buildings repaired, under construction, or still in ruins, Sano and Marume encountered news-sellers hawking broadsheets filled with sto-ries of brawls between gangs from rival villages, who'd come to Edo since the tsunami. Business flourished in moneylending shops; the merchants raked in strings of coins and drove borrowers into debt. A refugee couple tried to sell Sano their daughter, a common practice these days. Canals were jammed with boats waiting to unload at the fish market. People made desperate by food shortages clamored to buy directly from the boats. Sano felt the fragile city bursting its seams, nearing the lim-its of how many people it could hold. Along the river were new ware-houses from which supplies went out as fast as they came in. New docks accommodated barges, houseboats, and ferries. Ahead Sano saw the Ryōgoku Bridge, the site of one of the earthquake's worst disasters.

People trying to escape the wreckage and fires in the city had jammed the bridge, which had collapsed under their weight. Hundreds of people had drowned in the Sumida River, which had been heated almost to a boil by debris from burning warehouses. Where the bridge had collapsed, now tall wooden supports rose, reinforced by crossed beams. Three new spans arched high above the river, reaching toward Honjo district on the opposite bank. Chattering crowds flocked along the path, on a pier, and around the massive stone base where the bridge originated. Fishermen stood in boats gathered beneath the bridge's last span, gazing down at the water.

"What happened?" Sano called as he and Marume dismounted on the path.

"They just put up another section of the bridge," an old peasant man said. "It collapsed. Five men died. They're looking for the other."

"Accidents are too common these days," Marume said. "How many men have been injured or killed?"

"Hundreds. I've lost count," Sano said. "With the push to restore the city, the engineers and workers are taking shortcuts and sacrificing safety. Not just in town, but at the castle."

Marume nodded. "I wonder how solid some of those new walls and towers are."

Splashes came from the water near the boats as divers surfaced. They cried, "He's pinned under the pilings! We can't move them—they're too heavy!"

At least an hour must have passed since the accident. Sano doubted that the lost worker could still be alive. Marume nudged Sano and said, "Look at what the wind just blew in."

Hirata jostled his way along the pier. Sano stared, surprised to see his chief retainer after five months. Hirata looked like a tramp with his shaggy hair and beard. At the end of the pier, he dropped his swords. He dove into the river and disappeared. The water under the bridge roiled. Sano, Marume, and the crowd watched in hushed anticipation.

"How can he hold his breath for so long?" Marume muttered.

Hirata broke the surface, gasping for air. He held the inert body of a man. The crowd cheered. The divers looked dumbfounded. Fishermen hauled the man into a boat. They pounded his chest, tried to push water out of his lungs. Giving up, they shook their heads.

Moans of disappointment rose from the crowd. Hirata swam to the pier. People in the crowd pulled him up, handed him his swords, and patted his back as he staggered to the riverbank. Obviously upset because he'd failed to save the injured man, he headed straight to Sano and Marume as if he'd known all along that they were there.

"Where have you been?" Marume demanded.

Sano knew Marume was angry with Hirata for his absence. When Marume looked at Hirata, he didn't see an old friend; he saw the fellow samurai who'd deserted their master.

Panting from exertion, Hirata slicked water off his face with his hand. His gaze, filled with shame and anguish, met Sano's.

"Do you think you can just stroll into town and expect Sano-*san* to take you back as if nothing had happened?" Marume said, infuriated because Hirata was ignoring him.

"I owe you an explanation," Hirata said to Sano.

Sano studied Hirata with distrust, wondering if Hirata meant to tell the truth or fabricate an excuse.

"This ought to be good," Marume said.

"Can I talk to you alone?" Hirata asked Sano.

"All right." Sano wanted to give Hirata a chance to regain his trust. Maybe Hirata had a valid reason for desertion. Maybe the bond between retainer and master could be repaired.

Marume shook his head in disapproval. Leaving him, Sano and Hirata walked along the river. They stood side by side on the stone embankment, gazing across the water.

"I'm listening," Sano said.

Hirata described how Tahara, Deguchi, and Kitano, his teacher's other disciples, had lured him into their secret society. He told Sano about the demonstration Tahara had performed, that had convinced Hirata to join, that had caused the death of Yanagisawa's son Yoritomo.

Sano turned to gape at Hirata, incredulous. "They killed Yoritomo? By doing such a little thing?"

"You don't believe me." Hirata's expression was both defensive and mournful.

Sano decided Hirata wasn't lying. Hirata was a terrible liar; he could withhold information, as he'd done for so long, but he couldn't hide dishonesty. Hirata believed what he was saying. Sano faced the river again, thinking back to that awful scene fifteen months ago, when his investigation of a scandalous murder had led to Yoritomo's death. It had seemed straightforward at the time. Events had spun out of everyone's control. Fate had taken its own, inexplicable course.

Or had it?

Sano remembered an uneasy feeling he'd had since then—a suspicion that there was more going on than he could see, hear, or logically deduce. He knew that the mystic martial artists of legend could command supernatural forces. Why not modern-day ones? Sano let himself consider the possibility that Hirata's friends had somehow caused Yoritomo's death. If they had, then Sano wasn't to blame. He could stop feeling guilty.

"Go on," Sano said.

Hirata told about a magic spell book, a ritual, and a ghost warrior who'd appeared to him in a trance and burned a message onto his arm. He described how the message had vanished after he'd done its bidding.

Rage thunderstruck Sano. "You set Masahiro up?" At the time Sano had thought there was something strange about a run-in that Masahiro had had with Lord Ienobu. Hirata had pulled the strings behind the scenes. "You put my son in danger!"

"I didn't mean to," Hirata said, defensive but contrite. "I didn't know what was going to happen."

Reining in his temper, Sano said, "Tell me more about this ghost warrior."

"My friends say he's the spirit of a warlord who was killed during the Battle of Sekigahara."

Sano knew that the veil between the human world and the spirit realm was thin. He'd once met a ghost himself. "Tell me more about these friends of yours."

"Tahara is a retainer to the *daimyo* of Iga Province. He does security work for the government. Kitano is a soldier in Lord Satake's army. Deguchi is a Buddhist priest in the Zōjō Temple district."

"And the ghost died heroically on the battlefield. They're all fine, upstanding citizens. What else?"

Hirata pressed his trembling lips together. His eyes contained an anguish so black that they seemed to drain light from the day. Sano had seen that look on men on their way to the execution ground. "They murdered Ozuno. They stole the magic spell book. The ghost fought against Tokugawa Ieyasu and lost. He wants to avenge his death by destroying the Tokugawa regime. He enlisted Tahara, Kitano, and Deguchi to help him, because he's just disembodied energy and he can't act by himself. They enlisted me." Hirata gulped, as if the words he had to say nauseated him. "Destroying the regime is the purpose of our society."

Here, at last, was the reason for Hirata's secrecy, the nature of his trouble. Sano's outrage was so powerful it exploded. "You involved yourself in a treasonous conspiracy!" Grabbing Hirata by the shoulders, Sano shouted, "What were you thinking?"

Hirata bit his lips and blinked. Sano had never raised a hand to his men, but Hirata's offense pushed him past the point where mere words could adequately express his anger. Sano punched Hirata on the cheek. Hirata staggered; he didn't hit Sano back. A samurai didn't strike his master.

"Have you no loyalty to our lord?" Sano punched Hirata's face again and again. "Have you lost all your respect for your own honor?"

Blood trickled from Hirata's nose and mouth. Tears mixed with it while he let Sano punish him. Sano was horrified that their friendship had come to this. His urge for violence died. As sapped of energy as if he'd gone ten rounds in combat practice and lost every one, Sano sat down on the embankment. Hirata sat a few paces away. He held his sleeve to his bleeding mouth and nose. Sano looked at his hand. His knuckles were bruised, nicked by Hirata's teeth, and bloody. His anger turned hard and cold.

"When did you find out the purpose of the secret society?" he asked.

"Four months ago," Hirata said in a muffled voice.

"Meaning, you didn't know what the society was all about before you joined."

Hirata nodded miserably. "If I had, I never would have gone along with Tahara and Kitano and Deguchi."

The excuse thawed Sano's anger only a little. "Shouldn't you have taken the trouble to find out before you got mixed up with them?"

"I guess I trusted them," Hirata said sheepishly.

Even as Sano deplored Hirata's judgment, he realized the error in his own. Studying the mystic martial arts hadn't changed Hirata as much as Sano had thought. It had given Hirata expert combat skills and deep spiritual experiences and knowledge of the supernatural world, and Sano had misinterpreted that as wisdom and maturity. But underneath, Hirata was the same simple, naïve, impulsive youth he'd been when he'd entered Sano's service fourteen years ago.

"How could you be so stupid?" Sano shook his head, regretting his mistake as well as Hirata's. He should have known that the mystic martial arts, and the opportunities and temptations that came with them, were too much for Hirata to handle.

"I knew Tahara, Kitano, and Deguchi were dangerous. I thought that if I joined their society I would have some control over it." Hirata paused, then admitted, "I wanted the knowledge they were offering."

Sano had to admit that his own motives weren't so noble. He hadn't complained when Hirata had gone off with Ozuno to study the mystic martial arts. He'd been glad Hirata had found hope after he'd been crippled by a terrible injury when he'd taken a blade meant for Sano. Beset by guilt over Hirata's suffering, Sano hadn't wanted to think about whether the mystic martial arts would really be good for Hirata. He'd only been glad when they'd made Hirata stronger than ever and he didn't have to feel guilty anymore. As a master, Sano didn't owe his retainers anything, but as a friend, he should have tried to protect Hirata.

"Why did this ghost want you to meddle with Ienobu?" Sano asked.

"I don't know," Hirata said, "but he wants Ienobu to be the next shogun."

Sano wondered what Ienobu would think if he knew a ghost was working on his behalf. "How would making Ienobu the next shogun destroy the Tokugawa regime? And how would pitting Masahiro against him help?"

Hirata shook his head, ashamed and bewildered. "The ghost didn't explain."

"Why didn't you tell me all this earlier?"

"Because Tahara, Deguchi, and Kitano threatened to kill me if I talked."

Sano threw Hirata a disbelieving glance. "Why did that scare you? You can beat any three men at once. I've seen you."

"Not these three." Hirata spoke with certainty and despair. "They also threatened to kill you."

"Don't make me your excuse for treason," Sano said. "I can take care of myself."

"No, you can't. Tahara has gotten close enough to you to have killed you if he'd wanted to, and you didn't even notice." Hirata added, "That's why I left town—not just to save myself, but to make them chase me instead of attacking you."

"Why are you telling me all this now?"

"Because I can't keep secrets from you anymore." The passion in Hirata's voice reminded Sano of a young man pleading, fourteen years ago, for the privilege of serving as his retainer. "It's wrong."

"I won't argue with that." Sano asked, "Why did you come back?"

"It's time to face up to my mistakes," Hirata said. "It's time to make things right."

"Good," Sano said. "How?"

They turned toward each other. Hirata said, "I'll help you fight Yanagisawa."

"No. I'll deal with him myself." Sano could certainly use the help, but he didn't trust Hirata enough to bring him in on the murder investigation. "What are you going to do about your friends?" The confusion and unhappiness in Hirata's expression made Sano's heart sink. "You don't know, do you?"

"I'll figure it out," Hirata said bravely.

The breath gusted from Sano. "I'm afraid things have gone too far for that. You've entered into a plot against the regime." He stood and spoke words he'd never thought he would have to say. "I must arrest you and your friends and charge you with treason."

"No!" Hirata jumped to his feet, thrust out his arms to forestall Sano. "I don't care if you arrest me and put me to death, I deserve it, but don't go after my friends! They'll kill you!"

He seemed truly more concerned about Sano than himself. Sano hated to send Hirata to a trial that would surely end in a guilty verdict and a death sentence, and he had doubts about the wisdom of confronting three men Hirata thought were so dangerous, but he said, "You've confessed that you and your friends are parties to treason. My duty is to protect the Tokugawa regime. I have to take action against all of you."

"Just give me some time," Hirata begged. "I'll shut the secret society down. I'll eliminate Tahara, Deguchi, Kitano, and the ghost. Then I'll turn myself in." He clasped his hands. "I promise!"

Sano inhaled a deep breath, facing a dilemma. Bushido required him to uphold the law. Fourteen years of friendship and his huge debt to Hirata demanded mercy. "How much time?"

Hirata exhaled with relief. "A few days. Maybe five?" He sounded as if he would like to ask for more but didn't dare.

"All right." Sano thought of the occasions when the shogun had given him a time limit for finishing an investigation. Now he was the one handing down the ultimatum. "Five days."

12

TAEKO PRESSED HER back against the wall of a *daimyo* estate and peeked around the corner. She watched Masahiro run up and down the street, searching for her among the crowds. The temple bells had rung the hour twice since she'd run away from him. This was like playing hide-and-seek, but he didn't look like he was having fun. He looked angry. Tagging after him had only made him like her less.

Eventually he got tired of looking for her. He muttered to himself and stomped away. Taeko didn't follow him. If she did, he would scold her some more. Then she was sorry she'd let him go. She wasn't supposed to leave the estate by herself. As long as she'd been following Masahiro she wasn't exactly disobeying, but she would have to go home alone. Her mother would be furious. Taeko glumly wandered the streets until she neared the gate where she'd met Masahiro.

It was still open, but a soldier loitered outside. What was in there that Masahiro thought was so important? What had he meant when he said he'd lost his witness?

Seven children gathered at the gate. The four girls were about the same age as Taeko, the boys a little older. Curious, Taeko stole up behind them. They were skinny, with tangled hair and dirty faces. Their clothes were ragged, their feet bare. They were orphans, Taeko guessed. There were a lot more orphans since the earthquake. They lived on the streets and begged and did whatever else they could to earn money.

"We're looking for work," one of the boys said.

"Come on in." The sentry called to someone inside the estate, "Take these kids to the housekeeper."

As they walked in through the gate, Taeko had a bright idea. If she could find a witness for Masahiro, maybe he wouldn't be mad at her anymore. She followed the children. The guard paid her no attention; he thought she was with them. Once inside the estate, Taeko felt uncertain and afraid. It had buildings under construction, and tents, and workers, and noise, just like at home, but it was so much bigger. And what was a witness? Taeko hoped that if she saw one she would recognize it.

A manservant herded the children to a woman who wore her gray hair scraped into a tight knot and a white apron over an indigo kimono. The housekeeper lined up the children in a row, Taeko at the end. She walked down the row, studying each one. Her chin jutted up toward her nose, which curved down in a hook.

"This lot is worse than the last," she grumbled to the manservant. "But with the shortage of help since the earthquake, and so much work to be done, I have to take whatever I can get." She came to Taeko. Taeko bowed; the other children hadn't. "Have you ever worked in a rich samurai's house before, little girl?"

Taeko nodded. She helped take care of her little brother and sister. That should count.

"Well, this one has some manners, and she looks clean," the housekeeper said. "She'll do. Get rid of the rest." The manservant led the other children away. The housekeeper said to Taeko, "Come with me."

Resisting the urge to run, Taeko meekly obeyed. Despite her fear, she wanted to impress Masahiro. This was her chance.

The housekeeper led her into a big tent. Peasant women and girls were washing clothes and linens in huge tubs of boiling-hot water. Mountains of more dirty laundry waited. Steam filled the air, which smelled of lye soap that made Taeko's eyes burn.

"Wash those." The housekeeper pointed to baskets ranged around a tub.

The baskets contained men's loincloths. The long strips of white cotton fabric were soiled and rank. Taeko's stomach turned. She gingerly picked up some cloths, dropped them in the steamy water, and didn't know what to do next. At home the maids did the laundry.

"They're not going to wash themselves, idiot!" The housekeeper picked up a ceramic jar, poured soap into the tub, and hit Taeko hard on the back of her head. She shoved a washboard into Taeko's hands. "Start scrubbing!"

Taeko gasped with pain and shock. Nobody had ever hit her before, except her brother when they were playing. The other women laughed. Taeko wanted to tell her father that the housekeeper had hit her. He was the best fighter in Edo; he would teach the mean old woman a lesson. But her father was away. And Taeko must help Masahiro.

Swallowing her pride and distaste, she thrust her hand into the hot, caustic water, picked up a dirty loincloth, and began scrubbing.

AS HIRATA RODE away from the Ryōgoku Bridge, his cheek and mouth hurt where Sano had hit him. He wished Sano had hit him harder; he was so angry at himself. He'd managed to make things worse! Belatedly he realized he shouldn't have approached Sano until after he'd dealt with Tahara, Deguchi, and Kitano. He cursed his mistake.

And here they came. Their aura pulsed faintly, like a whispered taunt, in the distance. Hirata wanted to gallop his horse in the opposite direction. But he'd promised Sano, and himself, that he would set things right.

He had five days.

The aura's rhythmic cadence boomed more distinctly, thrumming along his nerves. Hirata followed the aura through the Nihonbashi merchant quarter. The men were leading him on, to a location they'd chosen for this first encounter in the four months since he'd told them he knew the truth about them and wanted to quit the secret society.

In a poor neighborhood that hadn't yet been rebuilt, the aura magnified to such an intensity that the landscape of Hirata's mind shivered with every boom. Colored lightning veined his vision. He could barely see the piled ruins that still lined the streets or hear the construction noises from other parts of the city. At the end of the street, where the neighborhood gate was crushed under two collapsed houses, wind spun up from the ground. A funnel cloud of debris formed. Hirata halted his mount. The aura shut off suddenly. The whirlwind dissipated. The debris settled around three men standing side by side.

Panic constricted Hirata's lungs; he could hardly breathe. His horse reared and whinnied. As Hirata calmed the horse, Tahara, Deguchi, and Kitano strolled toward him as casually as if they'd just stepped out of a teahouse. Hirata dismounted and walked to meet them. It took every bit of courage he could muster.

"Hello, stranger," said Tahara, the leader of the society, who walked between his two comrades. His voice was simultaneously smooth and rough, like rapids flowing over jagged boulders. A black surcoat with broad epaulets, a flowing bronze silk kimono, and wide trousers clothed his athletic physique. A twinkle in his deep black eyes, and a left eyebrow that was higher than the right, gave his strong, regular features a rakish charm.

"Look what the wind blew in." Hirata echoed the words he'd heard Marume say about him earlier.

Deguchi, the priest with the shaved head, dressed in a saffron-dyed robe, smiled. He never spoke; he was mute. When he and Tahara and Kitano had tried to steal the magic spell book from Ozuno the first time, Ozuno had tried to strangle Deguchi and damaged his vocal cords. His ageless oval face had an eerie, radiant beauty despite the fact that it was plain, with a flat nose and pursed mouth. His heavily lidded eyes glowed with sweetness and menace.

"You led us on a merry chase," Kitano said. In his fifties, gray-haired but robust, he wore the iron helmet and armor tunic of a soldier. A smile crinkled his eyes, but the rest of his face was an immobile mesh of scars. During the battle, Ozuno had cut Kitano's face, severing the nerves. "A lot of good it did you, though. Here you are, back in the fold with us."

"No, I'm not," Hirata said as the three men surrounded him. They were clean, neatly groomed, and fresh. During the chase across Japan they'd probably slept in nice inns and eaten well while they let him tire himself out. Furious at them for playing with him, he said, "I'm only with you for as long as it takes to tell you this: I quit. I'm dissolving the secret society."

"Oh, please." Tahara grimaced. "Not this foolishness again."

"Haven't you gotten it through your head yet?" Kitano said. "Once you're in the society, you can't quit."

90

Deguchi drew his index finger across his smooth throat. Hirata felt his own neck muscles contract as he imagined the cold graze of a blade. The second time the men had tried to steal the spell book, they'd succeeded, and they'd killed Ozuno. They could kill Hirata. But he knew of one person who'd quit the society and lived to tell, an itinerant monk he'd met via a tip from a friend. Hirata clung to the hope that he, too, could walk away from them and survive.

"I'm changing the rule," Hirata said.

"How?" Tahara said, scornful and amused.

"Your lord would be interested to know what you're up to." Hirata moved his gaze to Kitano. "So would yours." He told Deguchi, "And so would the authorities at Zōjō Temple. Unless you all agree to dissolve the society and never summon the ghost again, I'm going to tell your masters. They won't like you putting them in trouble with the regime." If Tahara, Deguchi, and Kitano's conspiracy were exposed, their masters would be reprimanded and heavily fined, if not put to death for harboring traitors. "They'll kill you to protect themselves."

"Oh, come now," Kitano said impatiently. "There's not an army that can stand up to us. If you report us, it will only force us to kill a lot of innocent people."

"Sano-*san* among them," Tahara said. Deguchi nodded.

The threat to Sano was the trio's strongest hold on Hirata.

"Enough of your silly threats," Kitano said. "It's time for another ritual."

Frantic, Hirata said, "No." He could think of nothing else to do except fight them. If he were dead, killing Sano would serve them no purpose. Despite the anguishing thought of his family, Hirata reached for his sword.

An invisible energy wave issued from the three men. It hit Hirata with a solid, numbing force. His hand stopped short of his weapon. He struggled to move it but couldn't. The numbness spread up his arm and through his nerves, paralyzing him. The force exerted by Tahara's, Kitano's, and Deguchi's will reduced Hirata's whole body to a heavy, inert mass of flesh. The only movable parts were his eyes. They rolled wildly with terror. He tried to speak but couldn't.

The other men watched him with amusement. Tahara said, "I think he wants to say something. Shall we let him?"

"Why not?" Kitano said.

Their energy waned slightly. The numbness left Hirata's throat, lips, and tongue. He said, "If you have the power to do things like this, why do you need me? Why can't you do whatever the ghost wants by yourselves?"

"The ghost has special plans for you." Tahara sounded as if he begrudged Hirata the privilege. "In the meantime, you're doing the ritual."

Hirata tried to protest, but the numbness silenced him again.

"Get on your horse," Tahara said.

Animation suddenly returned to Hirata's muscles. His legs walked him to his horse. His foot placed itself in the stirrup; his hands pulled him onto the horse; his rear end sat in the saddle. Tahara grasped the reins. He and Deguchi and Kitano led the horse, with Hirata their captive rider, through the ruined streets toward the hills outside town.

13

A GENTLE SPRING twilight descended on the city as Sano
and Marume rode up to Edo Castle. The sky was radiant in shades of pink,
gold, and lavender. The noise from hammers and saws ceased. Dust
settled out of the cooling air.

"Peace at last," Marume said with relief.

Sano thought Edo was holding its breath, waiting for tomorrow's onslaught of rebuilding. Nearing the gate, he looked for the family he'd seen
that morning. He saw human shapes huddled along the avenue, but he
couldn't tell which were theirs. Inside the castle he heard the ordinary
sounds of evening—footsteps and horses' hooves on stone pavement, talk
and laughter from sentries in the covered corridors and watchtowers along
the walls. Patrol guards carrying lanterns passed. Everything had a sem-
blance of normalcy. At Sano's estate, shadows softened the irregular lines
of walls and buildings still under reconstruction. Sentries by the recently
finished guardhouse let Sano and Marume in the new gate. Sano and
Marume left their horses with a stable boy. As Sano walked through the
inner precinct, birds trilled. After the earthquake, birds had been scarce,
as if most of them had sensed the earthquake coming and flown away. Any
that had stayed had been devoured by starving citizens, in spite of the Buddhist prohibition against eating meat and the Tokugawa law against hunting. But the canals and highways were now clear of earthquake debris, and
transport of food into the city had resumed. The birds had returned to
nest in Edo Castle. It was a good omen, Sano hoped.

Flames in stone lanterns lit his path to his mansion. Repairs to its front section, where he conducted business, had been completed. Reiko, Masahiro, and Akiko appeared on the veranda. They called excitedly to Sano. He smiled, thankful for them. That his family had survived the earthquake was a miracle. He could savor their togetherness despite the tribulations of politics.

"Masahiro and I have a lot to tell you," Reiko said as Sano climbed the steps.

"I have a lot to tell you," Sano said.

Akiko said, "Papa!" and held up her arms to him.

She always brightened his spirits. He picked her up, hugged her, and set her down. "You're getting so big. Pretty soon I won't be able to lift you anymore."

They went into the house. As Sano removed his shoes and hung his swords on the rack in the entryway, Reiko asked, "Where have you been all day?"

"Working at my new job, mostly." Sano told her about the accident. "The engineer is under a lot of pressure to finish the bridge. The supports weren't installed properly. He's to blame for six deaths. I had to arrest him for negligence." Sano didn't mention his disturbing encounter with Hirata. "Let's have dinner while we talk about our investigation."

They went to the private chambers, which weren't quite refinished; some rooms still needed floors varnished and tatami mats laid. The parlor still contained displaced furniture and trunks of clothes. Sano and his family ate rice, grilled seafood, and soup made with tofu and spring greens.

"I'm glad it's not dried fish and seaweed and pickles anymore," Akiko said, referring to the preserved edibles they'd relied on for months. "I'm sick of earthquake food."

Sano smiled at her innocent pleasure in the return of good meals to their table.

"Did you find evidence that Yanagisawa murdered the shogun's daughter?" Reiko asked.

"Not exactly." Sano described his visit to Lord Tsunanori's estate. "If I didn't want to believe Yanagisawa killed her, Lord Tsunanori would be my favorite suspect." He swallowed a mouthful of tea. "Did you talk to that nurse I sent you?"

"I did. What a nasty woman! She deliberately coughed in my face, and she taunted me about giving me smallpox!" Reiko scrubbed her face with a napkin. "She hated Tsuruhime. And she's had smallpox. She could have gone to the tent camps, found someone with smallpox, then brought back their soiled bedsheet and put it in with Tsuruhime's things without any harm to herself. If *I* didn't want to believe Yanagisawa is guilty, she would be *my* favorite suspect." Reiko thought a moment. "Tsuruhime is starting to sound not very nice. If everybody hated her, it will be hard to figure out who killed her. But someone inside her house would have had an easier time killing her than someone from outside."

"Not everybody hated her." Masahiro told Sano, "I got inside Lord Tsunanori's estate today." He described the young samurai whom the others had teased. "It sounded as if he liked her too much."

"If there was an affair between him and Tsuruhime, that adds new complications," Sano said, interested. "What else did you find out?"

"Nothing." Masahiro's eyes clouded, as if with a troubling memory. "When he ran out of the estate, I lost him. I can go back tomorrow and talk to him."

"All right." Sano would give Masahiro a chance to pursue the lead he'd found.

"The nurse did tell me something that implicates Yanagisawa," Reiko said. "Yoshisato came to call on Tsuruhime shortly before she took ill."

Sano felt a stir of excitement followed by trepidation.

"That means Yoshisato had a chance to put the infected sheet in her room," Masahiro said. "Yanagisawa could have told him to. Aren't you glad?"

"Yes, because this could be construed as evidence against Yanagisawa. No, because it's also evidence against the shogun's heir. We have to be careful with it." Sano turned to Reiko. "Do you believe the nurse's story?"

"She said Tsuruhime's servants and ladies-in-waiting can confirm it."

Although it connected Yanagisawa with Tsuruhime's death, Sano had mixed feelings. Was Yoshisato a willing participant in Yanagisawa's plan to seize power? Or had Yanagisawa forced him to pose as the shogun's long-lost son? Sano thought of Yanagisawa's elder son, Yoritomo, and recalled what Hirata had told him today. Even if the secret society were to blame for Yoritomo's death, Sano still felt responsible for creating the circumstances for it to occur. Sano hated to destroy another young life. But he'd undertaken this investigation with full knowledge of where it might lead. If he brought down Yanagisawa, then Yoshisato would probably go down, too. And Yoshisato might be far from an innocent pawn. He might be guilty of murdering Tsuruhime as well as becoming her father's heir by fraud.

"Well. Since we haven't been able to incriminate Yanagisawa, we'll go after Yoshisato." That said, Sano couldn't entirely quell his misgivings.

A maid came to the door. "Excuse me, but Lady Nobuko is here to see you."

Reiko and Masahiro started to rise, but Sano said, "I'll see her by myself." He had a bone to pick with Lady Nobuko.

Lady Nobuko and her lady-in-waiting were in the reception room. Her face had relaxed a little, as if the prospect of revenge against her enemy had eased her headache. Korika smiled eagerly. Lady Nobuko barely greeted Sano before she demanded, "What did you discover?"

Short-tempered from too many acrimonious confrontations, Sano said, "I discovered that you lied to me this morning."

Lady Nobuko blinked at his tactless manner. "What are you talking about?"

"I asked you who else besides Yanagisawa might have wanted to kill Tsuruhime. You said no one. Then I went to see Lord Tsunanori. He made it patently clear that he hated her and wanted to be rid of her. He said you knew."

"Yes, I knew." Lady Nobuko sounded annoyed, as if Sano was frivolously wasting her time. "So what?"

"So why didn't you tell me the truth?"

"Lord Tsunanori didn't kill Tsuruhime."

"How do you know?"

"He hasn't the intelligence or the imagination to think of infecting her with smallpox."

"Oh, well, I'm glad to hear such definitive proof that he's innocent," Sano retorted. "Did you know that Tsuruhime's nurse had had smallpox?"

"Yes. Why does it matter?"

Sano didn't bother answering; he could tell that Lady Nobuko knew exactly why it mattered. "Why didn't you tell me about the nurse or about Lord Tsunanori?"

Korika cringed from Sano's anger. Lady Nobuko sighed in exasperation. "Because if I had told you that they could have murdered Tsuruhime, you might not have believed it was Yanagisawa. You might not have agreed to investigate her death."

"If you'd told me she was murdered, it would have been my duty to investigate regardless of who you think killed her."

"Your duty? Yes. Your top priority?" She gave a dry chuckle. "Not unless there was something special in it for you, such as a chance to destroy Yanagisawa."

She was right, but that didn't make Sano feel any friendlier toward her. "Because you lied to me, I spent today finding out things you already knew."

The muscles on the right side of Lady Nobuko's face contracted tighter. She regarded Sano with disappointment. "Didn't you find any evidence that Yanagisawa is guilty?"

She was so focused on her single objective that she didn't care about anything or anyone else, Sano thought. "Actually, I did."

"What kind of evidence?" She leaned toward him, avid as a raptor.

"Before I tell you, I want two things from you," Sano said. "First, answer this question, and answer honestly: Is there anything else you're not telling me?"

"No," she said, irate.

"Second, promise that from now on you'll never withhold information from me again."

Lady Nobuko looked as offended and disgusted as if he'd asked her to give him her underwear. "All right. Now stop wasting my time. What have you learned?"

It was dangerous information to give a person he still didn't trust, but Sano owed it to Lady Nobuko. Her lady-in-waiting's story about the bedsheet had presented his best opportunity for bringing Yanagisawa down. "There's a witness at Lord Tsunanori's estate who claims that Yoshisato visited Tsuruhime there shortly before she got smallpox."

Lady Nobuko said triumphantly, "I told you so!" Korika smiled with relief because her mistress's humor had been restored. "Yanagisawa murdered Tsuruhime, and he sent Yoshisato to do the dirty work."

"I haven't had a chance to substantiate the story," Sano said. "Don't jump to conclusions."

"Don't be so quick to discount it," Lady Nobuko said. "It's our first big step toward destroying Yanagisawa and preventing Yoshisato from becoming the next shogun." She and Korika rose to leave. "You'll see that I'm right."

LATER THAT NIGHT Reiko sat in her bedchamber, brushing her hair. Sano came into the room, fresh from his bath. He removed his robe and hung it on the clothes stand. The light from the lantern made his body gleam. Reiko admired his firm muscles. His skin was marked with scars from battles he'd fought, like badges of honor. She smiled. After more than fourteen years of marriage, while six months pregnant, she desired her husband as much as when she'd been a new bride. She was glad their quarters had been rebuilt and they didn't have to sleep with the children. Now they could make love in private.

In bed together, she and Sano embraced. Moonlight filtered in through the open window. A light quilt shielded them from the cool spring breeze. But Reiko sensed absent-mindedness in Sano's caresses. His thoughts were far away.

"What's the matter?" she asked.

He rolled away from her and lay on his back. Studying him in the moonlight, Reiko saw the tense, unhappy set of his profile. "Are you still upset because of Lady Nobuko?" He'd told her about the woman's lie.

"It's not that." Sano said reluctantly, "I ran into Hirata today."

"Oh! He's back?" Glad and excited, Reiko said, "I should go tell Midori."

"No." Sano caught her hand.

"Why not?" Reiko said, puzzled now. "Why didn't Hirata come home with you? Has something bad happened to him?"

"Something has happened. 'Bad' doesn't begin to describe it." Sano reluctantly told Hirata's story. Reiko listened in disbelief. When he'd finished, they gazed at the ceiling while she absorbed what she'd heard.

"Magic rituals and a ghost! A plot to destroy the Tokugawa regime! I never imagined Hirata becoming involved in anything of the sort." Reiko thought about Hirata and recalled things Midori had said. "But I understand how he could have fallen in with the secret society. He's not a good judge of people, and he doesn't think enough before he acts."

Sano chuckled wryly. "You know him better than I did." He thumped his fist on the bed. "The fool! Dishonoring himself! Putting me in this position!"

"You're not really going to arrest him and charge him with treason?" Reiko was horrified by the very idea. Even if Hirata deserved it, his family didn't.

"I gave him five days to put an end to the society and the conspiracy," Sano said. "In the meantime, don't tell Midori. There's nothing she can do. She'll only worry."

A frantic knocking shook the door. "Sano-*san*? Reiko-*san*? Are you awake?" It was Midori, breathless and panicky. "I need your help. Taeko is missing!"

"What? Oh, no." Alarmed, Reiko crawled out of bed, threw on her robe.

Sano was already up and dressed. Reiko opened the door. Midori fell into her arms and began to cry. "I thought she was painting somewhere. But it started getting dark, and when she didn't come in for dinner, I went looking for her. I can't find her anywhere! No one's seen her since this morning!"

Reiko remembered her horror when Masahiro had been kidnapped. She tried to soothe Midori. "I'm sure Taeko is just fine."

"I'll send out search parties." Sano headed for the barracks.

Midori thanked him and sobbed. Reiko hugged her friend. "Hush, or you'll wake the other children." She silently prayed that Hirata would get himself out of trouble and Midori would never have to know what he'd done.

娘 *14*

IN THE WOODED hills high above the city, at a place where the ground leveled onto a plateau, tall cedar trees surrounded a clearing. The circle of treetops framed a crescent moon that smiled down upon a wide, flat rock below. Footsteps crunched on dry leaves along a path that led to the clearing. Insects shrilled. An owl hooted and took flight with a flutter of wings.

Light from the lanterns they carried preceded Tahara, Deguchi, and Kitano into the clearing. Hirata followed mutely, obediently, under their spell. Kitano swept leaves off the rock and set out a ceramic flask and a metal incense burner he'd brought in his knapsack. He lit the burner while Deguchi placed and lit oil lamps around the perimeter of the clearing. Hirata waited, an inert lump of flesh and misery. Purplish smoke and golden sparks issued from the burner, which was filled with a mixture of herbs from China, a recipe from the magic spell book. The other three men leaned over the burner and inhaled deeply.

"You, too," Tahara ordered.

Resisting with all his might, Hirata obeyed. The smoke burned into his lungs, spread through his veins, and clouded his mind. Unnatural light colored the forest as vibrantly green as in daytime. Noises amplified. Small animals in the underbrush sounded like bulls charging. The moon's smile enlarged and shrank with the throbbing of his heart.

Tahara, Deguchi, and Kitano began to chant a spell in ancient Chinese. "Don't just stand there," Kitano said. "Chant."

Hirata helplessly recited the foreign, melodic syllables he'd memorized without understanding them. Tahara took a swig from the flask, then offered it to Hirata. "Drink up," he said, his white smile flashing.

Hirata's hand lifted, closed around the flask, and poured the contents into his mouth. His throat muscles swallowed the potion he wanted to gag on and spit out. The potion tasted different every time. This time it seemed less a liquid than a sensation of jasmine-flavored ice splinters that vaporized before they reached his stomach. Tahara, Deguchi, and Kitano chanted louder, faster. Their images swam around Hirata. His voice kept pace with theirs. He felt a familiar, terrifying burn in his muscles, nerves, and bones.

He was going into a trance.

One moment he was in the clearing with Tahara, Deguchi, and Kitano. The next, he was alone at a crossroads in the middle of a vast field. Afternoon sunlight dazzled his eyes. The air was chilly, damp. He could move again. On both sides of the field rose mountains, the woods on them vivid with crimson, orange, and gold autumn foliage. He breathed the iron-and-salt smell of blood, the foul odors of death.

The field was littered with men's corpses. They wore armor tunics and leg guards, and metal helmets. Some had banners printed with clan insignias on poles attached to their backs. Some still clutched swords, spears, or arquebuses. They lay on grass that was red with their spilled blood. As Hirata gazed in horror at the carnage, vultures flocked amidst it. The air resounded with the buzzing of flies. A figure came trudging toward him, backlit by the sun, along the muddy road. He recognized the tall silhouette—the helmet crowned with horns shaped like an upended crescent moon, the flared ear guards and armor tunic, the jutting swords. Panic assailed Hirata. It was the ghost.

The ghost accelerated his pace so fast that he cut a fiery streak across the landscape. He was standing within arm's length of Hirata before Hirata could flee. Although his heart thudded with fear, curiosity immobilized Hirata. He took his first good look at the ghost by daylight. The ghost's armor was made of small metal plates covered with black leather and laced together with blue silk cord. A circular crest with two crossed feathers in the center adorned his black lacquer breastplate. Chain mail encased his arms; leather gloves with metal backs protected his hands. His face was hidden by the brim and face shield of his helmet.

"Who are you?" Hirata asked.

"My name was Otani Yoshitsugu." The ghost's voice, echoing inside his helmet, had the resonant, booming cadence Hirata recalled. He removed the helmet. His head was bald, his face a raw, red sore that had eaten away at his nose. Filmy eyes stared from lidless sockets.

Hirata shouted and recoiled.

Otani burst out laughing. "I had leprosy when I was alive." The sore suddenly healed. Eroded flesh grew back; new skin spread over sinews; hair sprouted into a sleek black topknot. "It no longer afflicts me now that I'm dead." Otani had the face of a man some forty years old, with the mark of strong character in his slanted brows, shrewd eyes, and broad, firm mouth.

"What is this place?" Hirata recovered enough to ask.

Otani swept his gaze around the field. "This is where I died."

The valley was the site of the famous Battle of Sekigahara, in which Tokugawa Ieyasu—the shogun's ancestor—had defeated his rivals, including Otani. The battle had apparently just ended. The trance had sent Hirata to the past.

"When my side began losing the battle, I committed *seppuku* rather than be captured and executed. My retainer cut off my head." Otani gestured toward the ground near Hirata.

There Hirata saw Otani lying in the mud. His head was severed; it lay beside him. Its raw, disfigured face grimaced in agony. Then the vision dissolved. Beyond shock, Hirata looked up at Otani. "Why did you bring me here?"

"To show you what I suffered at the hands of the ancestor of your lord. To show you why I seek revenge."

Hirata knew that the ghost was trying to break down his resistance. He couldn't help admiring Otani, a samurai who'd followed the Way of the Warrior to the ultimate degree. But Hirata was also furious at Otani for leading him astray from his own honor.

"To hell with your problems," he said. "I'm not doing anything else for you."

He turned and ran down the road. Otani's image stayed in front of him. Hirata ran until he was gasping for breath, but he couldn't escape the ghost. The corpse-strewn valley stretched ahead farther than he could see. Hirata shook his head, pressed his hands against his temples, and screamed, but he couldn't break his trance.

"I will let you go back to your world after I have told you what to do and you have promised to do it," Otani said.

Hirata collapsed, panting, to his knees in the mud. Bitter wind cooled the sweat on his face. "Damn you!"

Otani said, "Kill Deguchi."

Rage gave way to shocked disbelief. "But . . . Deguchi is one of us. Why do you want me to kill him?"

"Suffice it to say that he must die."

"How is his death supposed to help you destroy the Tokugawa regime?"

"That's none of your business."

"It is my business, when you're telling me to commit murder!" Hirata pushed himself to his feet. "How am I supposed to kill Deguchi anyway? He's a better martial artist than I am."

"Not by much." Otani added, "Don't tell Tahara or Kitano what I want you to do."

"They'll want to know what you said. What am I supposed to tell them?"

"Anything but the truth. Until you promise to kill Deguchi, you'll stay here with me."

Hirata smelled the bloody corpses, saw the carrion birds feeding. He thought of his family and Sano. The ghost apparently had the power to keep him from ever returning to them. He weighed that against the prospect of killing a man for whom he had no love.

"I promise," he said.

"Good," Otani said, as if he'd never expected Hirata to do otherwise. "I'm granting you a new talent in exchange for your cooperation. You can levitate objects using mental energy. When your task is finished, we will meet again."

Hirata abruptly found himself back in the clearing.

The darkness of the mild spring night engulfed the forest. His mind echoed with the parting words from Otani: "If you renege on your promise, I will kill you during your next trance. Die in a trance, and you die for real."

Hirata stood by the altar with Tahara, Deguchi, and Kitano, paralyzed again.

"What happened?" Tahara asked. The men had never accompanied Hirata into a trance. They had their trances with the ghost at other times.

"I'll tell you after you set me free," Hirata said.

Tahara looked to Deguchi and Kitano. They nodded. The paralysis left Hirata so abruptly that he fell against the altar stone. Regaining his feet, he flexed his stiff muscles. "I went to the site of the battle of Sekigahara. The ghost introduced himself. His name is Otani Yoshitsugu."

"We know that," Kitano said impatiently. "What did General Otani say?"

"He gave me the power of levitation." Hirata stalled, trying to think of a good lie.

Surprise lifted Tahara's eyebrow. The other men had greater powers than Hirata, and they liked it that way. "What does he want us to do?"

Hirata avoided looking at Deguchi. "He said to clear the earthquake debris out of the tributary canal in Kanda tomorrow."

"What for?" Kitano asked.

"He didn't say."

Tahara and Kitano shrugged. The ghost often told them to do menial work that had no apparent purpose. "What else happened?" Tahara asked.

Hirata forced himself to meet the men's gazes. "Nothing."

"Well," Tahara said, "I guess we'll clear the canal and wait to see the results."

Hirata could tell that the three didn't trust him any more than he trusted them. He inwardly cringed from the suspicion in Deguchi's glowing eyes. He spoke with all the nonchalance he could muster. "I'll see you tomorrow at the canal, then."

"Tomorrow," Kitano said. "You'd better be there."

Walking down the trail to his horse, Hirata felt shaken to the bone. He hadn't thought that things could get worse, but they had. If he tried to kill Deguchi but wasn't strong enough, then Deguchi would kill him. If he succeeded in killing Deguchi, then Tahara and Kitano would kill him because he'd betrayed the secret society; they would never believe the ghost had told him to do it. If he didn't kill Deguchi, the ghost would kill him the next time the men forced him to participate in a ritual.

What in heaven should he do?

15

SHORTLY AFTER DAYBREAK, Sano stepped out of his mansion. The sky was a pale, luminous blue, but the sun hadn't risen high enough to chase away the shadows that filled the grounds. The guard Sano had assigned to lead the search party walked in through the gate and said, "We finished searching the castle. We didn't find the little girl."

On the veranda Midori began crying. Reiko tried to comfort her. They'd sat up all night, waiting for news of Taeko.

"Search outside the castle," Sano said, disturbed because Taeko had been missing for almost an entire day and the city was dangerous. "She can't have gone far," he added, to console Midori. "I'm sure she'll be brought home soon."

"Yes, master." The guard bowed and hurried away.

The women went back in the house. Masahiro ambled onto the veranda, dressed in his white martial arts practice uniform. Yawning, he said, "What's going on?"

For the past few months Masahiro had been sleeping so soundly that almost nothing could rouse him and he had trouble getting up in the morning. Sano supposed he was growing so fast that he needed extra rest. He'd slept through the excitement last night. When Sano told him about Taeko, his eyes opened wide with dismay.

"She's missing?" Still not fully awake, Masahiro said, "I'll help look for her."

"No, there are enough people searching already," Sano said. "You have your martial arts lesson, then school with your tutor, then your work." That was Masahiro's routine, which the earthquake had disrupted for several months. Sano had to be strict about maintaining the routine, or Masahiro wouldn't get a proper education, and Masahiro couldn't shirk his page duties. "If you go delivering messages around the city later, you can keep an eye out for Taeko."

Masahiro started to object, but Sano said, "No excuses. You have your duties. Other things will have to wait."

And Masahiro wasn't the only one with duties. Sano had his work as Chief Rebuilding Magistrate and the murder investigation to finish.

"HEY, YOU!"

The loud call startled Taeko awake. At first she didn't know where she was. Lying on a hard surface, underneath a scratchy blanket, she heard strange noises and many people moving around. This wasn't her room at home. Bolting upright, Taeko saw women rising from the thin mattresses they'd slept on amid washtubs. Sunlight filtered through a ceiling made of oiled canvas. She smelled lye soap. She was in the laundry tent at Lord Tsunanori's estate.

Yesterday, after she'd worked until sundown, the housekeeper had given her a mattress and blanket and told her to sleep wherever she could find space. Miserable and homesick, she'd thought she wouldn't be able to sleep in such a cold, uncomfortable place with so many strangers. But she'd been so tired, she'd fallen asleep immediately. Her heart sank. By now her mother must have discovered she wasn't at home. Her mother must be terribly worried.

"You'd better get up if you want something to eat," said the girl beside her, who'd wakened her. The girl had a round, sullen face; her name was Kiku.

Taeko scrambled out of bed, shivering in the cold, wearing the wrinkled clothes she'd slept in. She and the other maids hung their mattresses and blankets on a line outside to air. Then they lined up to use the few privies. By the time her turn came, Taeko was pressing her legs together, trying desperately not to wet herself. Then she waited in line to strip and wash in a basin in another tent. The housekeeper inspected the girls to make sure they were clean enough. Taeko was self-conscious because she'd never undressed in front of strangers. Since she had no fresh clothes, the housekeeper gave her a rough blue cotton kimono and white head kerchief. Joining the line for breakfast, Taeko felt like a different person.

Breakfast was a cup of tea and a bowl of noodles with dried fish and pickled vegetables. The girls crouched in the yard to eat. The tea was lukewarm and bitter, the gruel watery, the fish and pickles too sour. Taeko could barely eat although she was starved. She missed her mother so much that tears fell into her tea.

But she couldn't go home yet. She had to find Masahiro a witness—whatever that was.

A ROOM IN the rebuilding magistrates' headquarters served as a makeshift court of justice for the new sort of criminals that the earthquake had spawned.

Sano knelt on the dais, flanked by a secretary who sat at a portable desk, and an assistant with a ledger of the cases on the docket. On the floor below him a tray of gravel substituted for the *shirasu*—the white sand symbolizing truth, normally spread on the floor under a mat on which defendants sat. White sand, like many other items, was scarce in post-earthquake Edo. Criminals were not. The room was jammed with people.

"Honorable Chief Rebuilding Magistrate Sano will hear the first case," said his assistant, a tired-looking older samurai. "Nagasaka Daiemon, Deputy Custodian of Military Stores at Edo Castle, come forward."

A man in the front row stood. The last time Sano had met Custodian Nagasaka had been the day after the earthquake, when he'd inspected the damage to the castle. Nagasaka had shown him collapsed arsenal buildings, crushed arquebuses, and gunpowder spoiled by water used to prevent fire and explosions. Sano barely recognized Nagasaka; the man looked so sick and ashen. Nagasaka avoided Sano's gaze as he knelt by the tray of gravel.

"You are charged with misappropriating government funds." The assistant called the witnesses, two young spies from the *metsuke*, the Tokugawa intelligence service.

Kneeling near Custodian Nagasaka, they testified. "We posed as clerks at the arsenal." "I saw him buy eight hundred guns from the gun maker." "He wrote in the inventory that a thousand new guns were purchased." "He kept the rest of the money."

Nagasaka listened in wordless shame. There seemed little need for a trial; the spies had caught him in the act, and he was so obviously guilty. But Sano must follow court procedure. He said, "You may speak in your own defense."

"I needed to fix my house. The money was there. I couldn't resist." Nagasaka began to weep. "I confess."

"Then I pronounce you guilty." Sano hated condemning a man who'd faithfully served the regime for years, who'd rashly stolen from it during his time of need. "I sentence you to death by decapitation."

Guards escorted Nagasaka from the courtroom in shackles. Sano didn't think the amount of money involved was worth a man's life, but it exceeded the threshold between petty theft and serious embezzlement. Since the earthquake, the law was even harsher than usual. Samurai who misused relief funds couldn't redeem their honor by committing *seppuku*. They had to be executed like common criminals.

All except Yanagisawa.

Remembering the family camped outside Edo Castle, Sano was more determined than ever to rid the world of Yanagisawa. But he also had his new job to do. Since the earthquake, desertion of one's post was also a capital crime.

"Next case," he said.

"Your next case will have to wait," said a voice from the back of the courtroom.

Sano looked across the audience. As if summoned by Sano's thoughts about him, Yanagisawa stood in the doorway, backed by a squadron of troops.

Anger seethed in Sano. "You can't just walk in and interrupt the trials."

"I beg to differ." Yanagisawa's face was smooth, but Sano read animosity behind it. "Everybody leave, so I can have a private talk with Sano-san." His troops cleared the room.

Sano rose as Yanagisawa strode across the room to meet him. "What do you want?"

Yanagisawa's smooth façade transformed into a scowl. "What do you think you're doing?"

"I'm doing the job you assigned to me." Sano knew that the thing he'd wanted to avoid had happened: Yanagisawa had learned about his investigation.

"Don't play innocent." A harsh rasp edged Yanagisawa's suave voice. "Why have you been sniffing around Lord Tsunanori's estate?"

Sano had hoped Yanagisawa's spies wouldn't get around to reporting his movements until after he'd finished the investigation. "Why have you been stealing earthquake relief money? To buy political support?"

Yanagisawa ignored the questions. He didn't seem to care whether anyone knew about his embezzlement. He probably thought nobody could hold him accountable. "Answer me."

"Lord Tsunanori's wife died. I went to pay my condolences to him."

"Don't play games." Yanagisawa moved threateningly closer. "Nobody else has set foot in that house. Everybody is afraid of catching smallpox. You wouldn't have gone, either, except for one reason."

Sano saw new, tight lines of strain etched into Yanagisawa's handsome face. "Why are you so on edge?" He took a step toward Yanagisawa, counterattacking to give himself time to think of how to find out whether Yanagisawa was guilty of the murder without letting him know that he and Yoshisato were suspects. "Can't you relax now that you're the adopted father of the shogun's heir?" He took a stab in the dark. "Or isn't it working out as well as you expected?"

Either the stab missed, or Yanagisawa hid his flinch. "You think Tsuruhime's death wasn't natural. You think someone deliberately infected her with smallpox."

"Murder by disease?" Sano feigned surprise. "That's an interesting theory."

"Don't act as if this is the first you've heard of it. Who put it in your mind? Was it Lady Nobuko? She paid you a visit yesterday."

There was no use denying it; Yanagisawa's spies were as effective as Sano had warned Lady Nobuko. "Unless you've taught flies to eavesdrop on my conversations for you, you don't know what Lady Nobuko and I discussed. Why would you jump to the conclusion that she thinks

Tsuruhime's death was murder and she put me up to investigating it?" Yanagisawa had jumped as fast as Lord Tsunanori had, Sano thought.

Yanagisawa's liquid eyes glinted. "Because I know the old bitch. She has it in for me. And I know you, too." He pointed a finger at Sano's heart. "Stop this investigation. Keep your nose out of Tsuruhime's death."

"Maybe I should investigate it, now that you've raised the possibility that she was murdered. Why would you want me not to?" Sano said.

"Because you're doing it to attack me," Yanagisawa said. "You can't stand the fact that I have you beaten." The odor of sweat and turbulent emotions wafted from him. "You've cooked up a crime where there was none. You're plotting with Lady Nobuko to frame me and Yoshisato and turn the shogun against us."

"Tsuruhime was the shogun's daughter. If she was murdered, it's my duty to find out who killed her and yours to back me." Sano added, "Tsuruhime was also Yoshisato's half sister. If indeed Yoshisato is really the shogun's son."

The glint in Yanagisawa's eyes ignited. He grabbed for Sano's neck. Sano seized Yanagisawa's wrists.

"You've been causing me trouble for fourteen years! You killed my son!" Yanagisawa shouted, trying to pull free of Sano. "I'm not going to let you ruin everything for me this time!"

Sano was startled that Yanagisawa had lost his self-control so fast. If he'd been so quick to lash out physically every time someone crossed him, he would never have climbed so high in the regime. Success in politics required discipline. His elder son's death had wreaked havoc with his mental state, and the earthquake had quickened tempers all around. Sano was no exception.

Fed up with Yanagisawa's insults, sabotage, and attacks on his family, he flung his weight at Yanagisawa, propelling him across the room, and slammed him against the wall. "I'm sorry for what happened to Yoritomo, but it's not my fault he's dead! It's yours!" Sano's talk with Hirata had put Yoritomo's death in a new light. "If you hadn't made a political pawn of him, he wouldn't have been at the palace with the shogun that day. He would still be alive!"

"Don't you put the blame on me!" Yanagisawa shouted. His guards grabbed Sano and tried to yank him off Yanagisawa.

Holding on, Sano yelled into Yanagisawa's face, "I'm going to talk some sense into you whether you like it or not!"

Yanagisawa thrust his head forward. It banged Sano's. The jarring impact and the pain momentarily blinded Sano. He lost his grip on Yanagisawa and reeled backward, taking the guards with him. The guards stumbled, then held him steady. Sano regained his senses. Yanagisawa breathed hard as he struggled to compose himself. He rubbed his wrists. The flesh where Sano had held them was reddish-purple with bruises.

"If you don't quit your investigation——" His words issued from between clamped teeth.

"You'll what? Put me to death?" A burst of sarcastic laughter escaped Sano. "Why didn't you do it yesterday? It would have made a nice climax for the big purge."

Yanagisawa didn't answer. Sano felt the quality of his foe's anger change for a moment, as if its heat were aimed toward someone other than Sano.

"What's the real reason you don't want me investigating Tsuruhime's death?" Sano asked. "Is it because you or Yoshisato killed her and you're afraid I might find enough evidence that I wouldn't need to frame you to take you both down?"

"Only in your fantasies!"

Before Sano could mention that he knew Yoshisato had visited Tsuruhime shortly before she got smallpox, Yanagisawa said, "By the way, isn't it terrible what happened to Lady Nobuko three years ago? Kidnapped and raped, poor thing." Yanagisawa gave Sano a tantalizing smile. "Wouldn't it be even more terrible for it to happen to your wife?"

Sano stared, speechless with horrified rage. Yanagisawa was as good as saying he was responsible for the assault on Lady Nobuko and would have the same done to Reiko if Sano didn't cease his investigation. Yanagisawa knew that his family was Sano's most vulnerable spot. And with his army reduced, Sano couldn't prevent Yanagisawa from invading his estate and taking Reiko any time.

Yanagisawa added, "I hear Lady Reiko is pregnant," then stalked out of the room with his guards.

Alone in the courtroom, Sano sat on the dais, letting his temper cool before his next trial, thinking about what had just happened. If Yanagi-sawa hadn't killed Tsuruhime, would he be so desperate to stop the investigation? His own behavior was good evidence of his guilt.

Something else good had come of the altercation with Yanagisawa. Yanagisawa knew about the investigation. There was no need to keep it secret anymore.

Shaken by Yanagisawa's parting words, Sano massaged his sore fore-head. Yanagisawa wasn't the only one who needed to discipline his emotions. Sano looked at his hand, bruised from his assault on Hirata. This was his second physical altercation in two days.

This time he'd goaded Yanagisawa into threatening Reiko.

16

AFTER HIS LESSONS, Masahiro ran to the *daimyo* district before anyone could give him a message to deliver. He had to look for Taeko. Yesterday, he should have kept looking, but he'd been mad at her for getting in the way of his investigation, and he'd thought she'd gone home. Now he'd made another mistake by not telling his father that she'd followed him to Lord Tsunanori's estate yesterday. But he'd been so sleepy this morning, he hadn't thought of it until after the search parties had left. If something terrible had happened to Taeko, it was his fault.

Outside Lord Tsunanori's estate, Masahiro didn't see her among the water sellers and food peddlers, the servants going about their errands, the troops patrolling. He searched the nearby streets. There was still no sign of her. Masahiro reached a neighborhood gate that led to the Nihonbashi merchant quarter. He hoped Taeko hadn't wandered there. Masahiro would never admit it to anyone, but since the earthquake he was afraid to go into the city. But he had to find Taeko. He took a deep breath, put on his most confident air, and strode through the portals.

Nihonbashi five months after the earthquake was a chaotic mix of buildings under reconstruction and still in ruins. Masahiro walked cautiously along the narrow alleys where peasants crowded around merchants who sold food from temporary stalls. Beggars accosted Masahiro, pleading for alms. The ground was muddy, still black with soot from the fires. He covered his nose to block the powerful stench. Night soil collection had resumed, but waste accumulated after the earthquake still fouled Edo. Stray dogs foraged in the garbage heaps. They growled and snapped at Masahiro. Walking faster, he came upon tattooed gangsters fighting. Down another alley lined with the black shells of burned houses, a brutish, gaudily dressed man and two samurai bodyguards led a group of little girls. Masahiro had heard about merchants rounding up girls orphaned by the earthquake and selling them to brothels. One of these girls was about nine years old and wore a green kimono.

"Taeko!" Masahiro ran to the girl and grabbed her arm.

She turned her plain, surprised face to him. She wasn't Taeko. A bodyguard yanked Masahiro away from her, kicked him in the behind, and sent him flying into a garbage heap. He stood up, dusted himself off, and looked around in despair.

He was standing outside a teahouse, the only intact building on this block. It was an open storefront screened by a blue curtain that hung from the eaves and extended halfway down to the raised plank floor. Customers sat inside; the proprietor served them drinks. Sunlight shone on them through holes in the roof. Five men were peasants in a group, the other a samurai sitting alone. The samurai was Jinnosuke, the young soldier from Lord Tsunanori's estate.

Masahiro couldn't believe his good luck. If he hadn't been looking for Taeko, he might never have found the soldier again. She had, in a way, helped him with his investigation.

SUNLIGHT SPARKLED ON the Sumida River as Yanagisawa and three bodyguards rode across it in a ferryboat. The fresh breeze cooled Yanagisawa's face, which was still hot from his clash with Sano. The ferryman carefully plied his oar, navigating around barges piled high with wood, rice bales, produce, bamboo, roof tiles, and other goods to supply Edo's rebuilding boom. Merchant vessels, guarded by Tokugawa navy ships, sailed up the river.

Yanagisawa and his bodyguards disembarked at the dock on the eastern bank of the river, in the Honjo district. They walked across the wide strip of land along the waterfront. This was a firebreak, where permanent structures were banned to reduce crowding and prevent fires from spreading. Here a large outdoor entertainment district had flourished before the earthquake had knocked down most of the canopy-covered stalls. Many had risen anew. Customers flocked to sample the refreshments, play games, and see the acrobats, jugglers, storytellers, menageries, and freak shows. Edo wanted to have fun again.

In the Honjo district, smoke drifted from kilns in the northern sector, where ceramic tiles were produced. Vegetable markets had once lined the many canals. The larger canals had been cleared of earthquake debris, but smaller ones were still clogged with the remains of houses that had flooded when the earthquake pushed water from the Sumida River inland. Townspeople were busy rebuilding their houses along stagnant, mosquito-infested waterways. Yanagisawa was relieved to enter the samurai enclave. Here, rich members of the government had suburban villas where they could go to escape the political hotbed of Edo proper. Other samurai lived here permanently. The only estate completely repaired was the two-story mansion at which Yanagisawa and his men arrived.

"I'm here to see Lord Ienobu," Yanagisawa said to the sentry in the guardhouse.

"You aren't welcome," the sentry said. "Lord Ienobu's orders."

"Unless he wants me to bring the army to invade his house, you'll let us in."

The sentry shrugged and opened the gate. He knew better than to defy a threat from the shogun's second-in-command for the sake of obeying the shogun's cast-off nephew.

Once inside the estate and past the barracks, Yanagisawa and his men came upon a garden planted with new shrubs, saplings, and flowerbeds. Thinking of his own estate, still in ruins, because he'd been too busy with political maneuvering and too short on cash to fix it, Yanagisawa felt a pang of resentment. Ienobu's estate was like spit in the eye. Inside the mansion, Ienobu sat on the dais in the reception room. With his hunched back, and his skinny arms and legs jutting at odd angles, he looked like a molted, hollow shell of a cicada.

"I had a bet with myself that you would barge in on me today," he said. "And here you are, right on schedule."

Although Yanagisawa knew Ienobu must be furious at him, Ienobu's mocking manner was placid. Yanagisawa tethered his own unruly emotions. In a battle of wits, they would put him at a disadvantage. "Then you must know why I'm here."

"You're not satisfied with throwing me out of the court. You wanted to see me living in squalid ruins. Sorry to disappoint you."

Yanagisawa figured that Ienobu had rushed to rebuild his estate the moment Yoshisato had appeared at court as the shogun's son. Ienobu had wanted somewhere to go to ground if Yanagisawa ran him off. This spoke volumes about Ienobu: He thought ahead, planned for all possible contingencies. Now he had a secure, comfortable base from which to operate.

"Guess again," Yanagisawa said.

"You want to rub salt in my wounds?"

"Far be it from me to indulge in such a cheap thrill."

"May I offer you some refreshments?"

"Never mind." Far be it from Yanagisawa to eat or drink anything in Ienobu's house. It would surely be poisoned.

"I give up, then." Ienobu's expression proclaimed that although he'd lost a major battle to Yanagisawa, he wasn't quitting the war.

"I came to talk about a little problem the shogun has been having," Yanagisawa said. "He's complained about noise outside his bedchamber."

Caution hooded Ienobu's bulging eyes. "What sort of noise?"

Yanagisawa knew that Ienobu knew exactly what sort. "People whispering at night. They've been disturbing his sleep. Have you anything to do with it?"

"Far be it from me to disturb my honorable uncle."

Yanagisawa knew Ienobu was lying through his big teeth. "You'll be glad to know the problem has been solved."

Ienobu feigned mild curiosity. "Oh? How?" Air whistled through his nostrils as alarm quickened his breathing. He feared that Yanagisawa had arrested his henchmen who'd been telling the shogun that Yoshisato wasn't really his son and they'd confessed that Ienobu had put them up to it.

"Let's just say I've put a stop to the chatter," Yanagisawa said.

"Good." Ienobu tried to sound enthusiastic, but his voice was flat.

Yanagisawa smiled. "I'm glad we had this talk. If the chatter should start again, your uncle and I know who not to blame." His warning gaze told Ienobu that if he tried any more funny business, there were worse fates than being dismissed from court. Even the shogun's nephew could have a fatal "accident."

Ienobu shifted position, scrambling for a rejoinder. "*I* just thought of a problem I'd like to bring to *your* attention. Would you like to guess what it is?"

Apprehension stiffened Yanagisawa's smile. "I doubt that I'll have to guess." But he already had. "Because you're going to tell me anyway."

"My sources say the shogun's daughter was murdered. Did you have anything to do with that?"

"Of course not." Yanagisawa spoke in an amused, disdainful tone, but his heartbeat skipped. He'd hoped that even if Lady Nobuko and Sano had gotten the idea that Tsuruhime's death was murder, nobody else would, especially not Ienobu. "Your sources are blowing smoke up your bony rear end. Tsuruhime died of smallpox."

Ienobu grinned; he knew he had the upper hand. "Not all cases of smallpox are natural. A sheet stained with blood and pus was found in Tsuruhime's room before she took ill. It came from the bed of another smallpox victim."

Yanagisawa's heart sank. There was evidence that Tsuruhime had been deliberately infected. Ienobu's spies had heard about it; Yanagisawa's own hadn't.

"You can't really believe that story," Yanagisawa scoffed. "You've been putting your ear to the rumor mill so hard, you must have ground it off." He leaned from side to side, pretending to check on whether Ienobu had both ears.

"I'm not the only one who thinks it's true," Ienobu said smugly. "Your friend Sano-*san* does, or he wouldn't be investigating Tsuruhime's death."

Yanagisawa was all the more disturbed to hear that Ienobu knew about Sano's investigation. "Then where is the sheet?" Yanagisawa had to get hold of it and destroy it before it could be used against him.

"If you don't think it exists, then why should you care where it is? What I'd also like to know is, how did the sheet get into Tsuruhime's room?" Ienobu's eyes were bright with suspicion and malice. "Perhaps you can tell me?"

"Perhaps *you* can tell *me*. You're so convinced that Tsuruhime was murdered; it's probably because you killed her yourself."

"Not I," Ienobu said with pious conviction. "Tsuruhime's death doesn't help me. You're the one who wants Yoshisato to be the next shogun. If Tsuruhime had lived to bear a son whose pedigree was indisputable, she could have knocked Yoshisato out of the succession." Ienobu pretended to have a sudden, bright idea. "But wait—you're not the only one with a motive. Yoshisato's is stronger. After all, the dictatorship is his to lose."

If Yoshisato were implicated in the murder of the shogun's daughter, he could lose more than his right to rule Japan. He could be put to death. Yanagisawa was more worried about Yoshisato's safety than his own. His love for Yoshisato made him vulnerable. Losing one son had almost destroyed him. He couldn't lose another. But Ienobu didn't seem to have anyone he cared about more than his repulsive self.

"You're speaking of the shogun's heir. Be careful," Yanagisawa said, his voice hushed with menace. "Or you could find yourself brought up on charges of treason."

"No, you're the one who should be careful. You're playing a danger-ous game, passing your son off as the shogun's. I'm offering you a chance to get out of it with your head still attached to your body. Tell the sho-gun the astrologer made a mistake: Yoshisato isn't his son."

"You'd like that," Yanagisawa said, astounded by Ienobu's nerve. "That would put you back in line to inherit the regime. But if you think I'll do it, you're insane."

"If you don't, I'll help Sano prove that you and Yoshisato murdered Tsuruhime. My uncle will put you both to death for treason. And I'll be the next shogun."

Although upset by the idea of Ienobu and Sano joining forces, Yana-gisawa said, "Go ahead, make friends with Sano. It will make things more convenient for me: I can destroy you both at once."

"I have to give you credit," Ienobu said with mocking admiration. "No one else bluffs as well as you. You should really take my advice, though. If you don't, we'll just see which one of us comes out on top. And I have a bet with myself that it will be me."

"That's a wise bet," Yanagisawa retorted. "When you lose, you can still collect from yourself."

Ienobu smirked, as if he saw the anxiety Yanagisawa was trying to hide. "Here are my troops to escort you out. They've timed it just right. Our conversation is finished."

Furious because he'd been intimidated by Ienobu, then rudely dismissed, Yanagisawa rose. Coming here had been a mistake. Instead of subduing Ienobu, he'd escalated the strife between them. Ienobu was an even craftier and more ruthless adversary than he'd thought. Ienobu was trouble that wouldn't go away even if Yanagisawa managed to avoid being blamed for Tsuruhime's murder.

Ienobu uttered a dry laugh, like cicada wings rubbing together. As Yanagisawa walked out of the room, he called, "I'm so glad we had this talk."

娘 **17**

MASAHIRO STEPPED INTO the teahouse. The proprietor and peasants bowed. Jinnosuke ignored him. The young samurai slouched morosely over the table that held his sake cup. Masahiro walked over, knelt opposite Jinnosuke, and said, "Hello. Do you remember me?"

"No. Should I?"

"I was at Lord Tsunanori's estate yesterday. My name is Masahiro. I helped you pick up the tiles."

"Oh. Yes. Thanks." Recognition glimmered in Jinnosuke's bleary eyes. He was drunk, Masahiro realized. He motioned to the proprietor. "A drink for my friend, and another for me."

The proprietor set a cup in front of Masahiro. Masahiro bravely downed the sake. He'd only had a few drinks in his life. This time he managed not to cough; the liquor was watery, cheap. He sought to start a conversation about Tsuruhime's murder.

"Those men you were working with yesterday," he began.

"Those bullies! They're always picking on me!" Jinnosuke burst out. "They don't understand what it's like to lose someone you love." His voice broke. He gulped his sake.

"Who did you love and lose?" Masahiro prompted.

Jinnosuke shook his head, pressed his trembling lips together.

"Was it Lord Tsunanori's wife?"

"Shh!" Jinnosuke glanced nervously at the other customers. He asked in a low voice, "How did you know?"

"I guessed," Masahiro said, "from what the bullies said."

"They won't keep their mouths shut. I'm going to get in trouble for sure." Jinnosuke dropped his head in his hands and groaned. "I never meant to fall in love with Tsuruhime! When she was alive, I didn't care what happened to me. She was all that mattered. But now that she's gone—" His thin shoulders heaved with a sob.

"How did it happen?" Masahiro thought that falling in love with his master's wife was a stupid thing for a samurai to do.

"I was one of her bodyguards." Jinnosuke wiped his eyes with his sleeve. "Whenever she went out, I rode alongside her palanquin and we talked about the weather, the things we saw, anything to pass the time. One day there was a beautiful cloud in the sky. It was shaped like a swan. I made up a poem about it and recited it to her. We discovered that we both liked poetry. We started writing poems and passing them to each other at home. It was fun, a secret game.

"But the poems got more and more personal. And one night there was a moon-viewing party. We went for a walk in the woods, and I told her I was in love with her. She said she was in love with me. And, well, one thing led to another."

Masahiro had been to moon-viewing parties and knew that other things went on there besides looking at the moon. He'd heard the whispers, scuffles, and giggling in the darkness.

"It was my first time," Jinnosuke said. "She was so passionate, as if she was starved for lovemaking. We couldn't get enough of each other. When her husband was away, we would meet in her chamber. We thought people wouldn't notice. But pretty soon the fellows started making remarks, and the maids giggled when they saw me. It wasn't smart of us, I know."

Masahiro thought it wasn't smart to get drunk and blab to a stranger. He remembered Detective Marume telling him, *People are stupid. That's a real advantage for a detective.*

"Then Tsuruhime got smallpox." Tears welled in Jinnosuke's eyes. "Nobody was allowed to go near her except her nurse. I couldn't even send her letters. I didn't trust the nurse not to tell Lord Tsunanori." He choked on a sob. "I couldn't even say good-bye."

Masahiro felt sorry for Jinnosuke, but he remembered Detective

Marume saying, *You can't allow sympathy to get in the way when you're interrogating a witness.*

"Did Lord Tsunanori find out about you and Tsuruhime?" Masahiro asked.

"I don't think so. If he did, he would have killed me. But maybe somebody told him. He's been giving me dirty looks. Or maybe I'm just imagining it." Jinnosuke pressed his hands over his temples. "Merciful gods, I'm so confused! I don't want to go home. I can't take any more stares or jokes, and I'm scared of Lord Tsunanori."

You have to keep on them even if it makes you feel bad, Detective Marume's voice said in Masahiro's memory. "If Lord Tsunanori did know, what would he have done to Tsuruhime?"

Jinnosuke looked up in surprise. "Nothing. What could he have done? She was the shogun's daughter. You don't divorce the shogun's daughter, shave her head, or send her to work as a prostitute in the Yoshiwara pleasure quarter."

Those were the usual punishments for women who committed adultery, Masahiro knew. But maybe Lord Tsunanori had punished Tsuruhime in a way that no one, including the shogun, would know he'd done it. Maybe he'd infected her with smallpox so that her death would seem natural. Masahiro remembered what his father had said last night: *If I didn't want to believe Yanagisawa killed her, Lord Tsunanori would be my favorite suspect.* Now Masahiro was beginning to think that Lord Tsunanori was indeed guilty.

He wished he hadn't found Jinnosuke, hadn't gone to Lord Tsunanori's estate. All he'd accomplished was to lose Taeko and find more evidence that pointed away from Yanagisawa.

A GUESTHOUSE STOOD near the palace, secluded within stone walls, amid pine trees. Yanagisawa strode into the house, which the shogun had lent him because his estate wasn't rebuilt yet. Still fuming from his clashes with Sano and Ienobu, he kicked off his shoes in the entryway and threw his swords onto the rack. On his way to his private chambers, he heard noises in the adjacent room. That was where Yoshisato had lived before moving to the heir's residence. Yanagisawa looked in and saw Yoshisato standing by the cabinets built into one wall.

"Why aren't you at the palace?" Yanagisawa demanded. "Didn't we agree that one of us should be with the shogun at all times?"

"He's reading documents in the privy. He'll be there for a good hour. Rather than stand outside the door and smell his farts, I came to get some things I forgot to pack when I moved." Yoshisato held up a stack of clothes. He eyed Yanagisawa curiously. "Why the bad mood?"

"I just had words with Sano and Ienobu."

Yoshisato cast his gaze up at the ceiling. "Why am I not surprised? What happened?"

"Sano is investigating the death of the shogun's daughter, just as I suspected. He refused to stop. He and Ienobu both accused me of infecting her with smallpox by planting a contaminated bedsheet in her room. Ienobu practically admitted he's responsible for the whispering campaign, and he's certainly not going to give up trying to discredit you. So excuse me if my mood isn't more cheerful."

Surprise lifted Yoshisato's brows. He seemed not to have known there was any doubt that the shogun's daughter had died a natural death or that Sano was investigating it. "I suppose you gave Sano and Ienobu as good as you got. You really know how to fan a fire."

"Don't." Yanagisawa held up his hand. "I've had enough for one day. I'm not going to listen to criticism from you."

"You will listen," Yoshisato said, his eyes hot. "Because it isn't just your future that will be affected by your actions. Mine is at stake, too."

"All right," Yanagisawa said, exasperated. "What do you, in your infinite wisdom, think I should have done?"

"You should never have started a feud with Sano. You should have been so nice to him that he would be licking your shoes now. You should have befriended Ienobu instead of ignoring him until he started to be a problem and then pushing him out of the court."

"Oh, well, I'll just travel back in time and change the course of history!"

"Since you can't, you should go to Sano and Ienobu and apologize."

That Yanagisawa should apologize to his enemies! "Have you lost your mind?"

"I'm trying to help you find yours. Offer them anything they want in exchange for supporting me as the shogun's heir. Tell Sano he can be chamberlain and you step down. Promise him and Ienobu their own provinces to rule when I'm shogun. Convert them from enemies to allies who will help me control the regime when I'm shogun."

Yanagisawa slashed the air with his hand. "I won't put up with Sano for another term. I won't share power with him and Ienobu."

"You will," Yoshisato said, deadly earnest. "Because it's how I want to handle them. And because you have to stop creating enemies and strife everywhere you go, or neither of us will live long enough for me to become shogun."

The nerve of this brat! "I've controlled the regime for the greater part of twenty years! I know what I'm doing! Whereas you have no political experience. We have to crush Sano and Ienobu and our other enemies before they can crush us!"

"Your old-fashioned ways aren't working. It's time for a fresh approach."

"You're insane!"

"I'm the shogun's heir. You're not."

They must sound like two little boys fighting in the nursery, Yanagisawa thought. "You already admitted that you can't function without me."

"I've changed my mind. I'm going to give you a choice: Either you cooperate with me, or your days at court are over." Yoshisato looked scared to be alone but seemed braced by his convictions. He stalked out of the house.

Yanagisawa gazed after him, furious at the ultimatum, helpless because Yoshisato had the power to make it stick.

"You should listen to him," said a husky female voice. "He's right."

A woman dressed in a brown kimono stood in the doorway. It was Lady Someko, Yoshisato's mother.

"What are you doing here?" Yanagisawa demanded.

"I live here, remember?" She had the same wide face, rounded chin, and tilted, sparkling eyes as Yoshisato. At age forty-three, she was as beautiful as the day she and Yanagisawa had first met. She gave a laugh that was at once seductive and unpleasant. "You moved me in with you the day you revealed Yoshisato as the shogun's son." She stepped into the room and flung out her arms. Her long sleeves spread like wings; the silk glinted with orange lights like flames. Gold ornaments shimmered in her upswept hair, which was still glossy black. "So here I am."

Yoshisato had also inherited her wits, sharp tongue, and impertinence, Yanagisawa regretted. While Yoshisato would never forgive Yanagisawa for ignoring him most of his life, Lady Someko would never forgive Yanagisawa for stealing her from the husband she'd loved and making her his concubine. She'd nursed a grudge against him for more than eighteen years.

"You were eavesdropping," Yanagisawa accused.

Lady Someko shrugged. "I'm borrowing a page from your book: Spy on your enemies, so you'll know what they're up to."

Yanagisawa's anger at Yoshisato expanded to include her. "Don't ever do it again."

"If you don't like having me here, let me go home," Lady Someko retorted. She and Yoshisato had once lived in their own villa and, after the earthquake, had shared a house with Yanagisawa's three other sons and their mothers. "Oh, but you can't let me go, can you? You have to keep me under control so I don't do anything to spoil your plans."

She was the only person who knew for sure that she'd never slept with the shogun, the only person who knew Yoshisato was really Yanagisawa's son.

"You shouldn't be too eager to spoil my plans for your son to be the next shogun," Yanagisawa said. "Keep your mouth shut, and you'll be secure for the rest of your life. Talk, and you'll be put to death for fraud. So will Yoshisato."

"And so will you." Her tone and expression were vicious. "I would almost be willing to sacrifice myself and Yoshisato, just to spite you."

"Almost," Yanagisawa said. That was his hold on her—the fact that if she compromised him, the son she dearly loved would suffer. "Don't be difficult. I've positioned Yoshisato to rule Japan. You should thank me."

Lady Someko gave an unladylike snort. "Oh, and I should thank you for making my son a target for everyone who hates you." She paced around him; her fiery skirts swirled. "Every day I hear rumors that you've finally gone too far. Do you know what I think? That you can't pull off this plot. That Sano or Ienobu or one of your other enemies is going to bring you down."

Her voice had the ominous resonance of a curse. "Shut up!" Yanagi-sawa ordered. "Never say that!"

"You can shut me up but not change what I think."

Yanagisawa felt the same sensation of his self-control slipping, his temper consuming him, as during his confrontations with Sano and Ienobu. "Let's see what you think about this." He grabbed her wrist.

Fear widened her eyes as she laughed. "What are you going to do?" Her wrist felt small and delicate in his grasp. "Beat me?"

Yanagisawa wanted to pummel her face into a pulp so she couldn't speak and he wouldn't have to see the mockery in her eyes. "I hate you!" He wanted to vent his anger on her. But a sudden rush of desire flushed heat through his body. He jerked Lady Someko close to him.

"Hah!" she exclaimed. "You hate me, but you want me!" A triumphant grin bared her sharp teeth. "Doesn't that make you feel like a fool?"

He was a fool, enslaved by her power to arouse him; yet he savored the urgency of his arousal. When he'd first made Lady Someko his concubine, he'd tolerated her viciousness because it added excitement to the sex, like an aphrodisiac poison. Recently they'd come together again. In the interim Yanagisawa had had so many lovers that he'd lost count. Women, men, pubescent boys and girls—his desire respected few boundaries, except that he usually preferred his lovers to be young. But when Lady Someko goaded him into such a fever as this, he wanted her more than he'd ever wanted anyone else.

Yanagisawa locked his arm around Lady Someko's waist. He pressed his erection against her. She laughed scornfully.

"Is that as big and hard as you can get? You're pitiful!" She rubbed herself against him. Her lips shone with saliva.

She wanted him as badly as he wanted her. The aphrodisiac worked both ways. Yanagisawa squeezed her breasts. Her nipples were hard under her smooth silk garments. He dragged her down onto the floor, threw himself on top of her. She kicked and screamed. He pulled her skirts above her waist. One of Lady Someko's hands tore open his robes, jerked at the loincloth wound around his crotch. The other punched his head. He fended off her blows while he pried her legs apart with his knees. Her legs were slender and smooth. Her pubis was shaved, in the fashion of prostitutes. Yanagisawa had never asked why; he didn't care. It whetted his excitement. As she freed his penis, he thought he would climax before he could take her. She jerked it so savagely that he cried out in pain. He reached down and tore her hand off him. He shoved his fingers between her legs.

She moaned. She was wet, ready. He plunged into her. The pleasure was almost unbearable. As he began thrusting, Lady Someko clawed at his face. He grabbed her hand before she could scratch his eyes. Her fingernails raked his cheek. This was part of her allure—that if he let down his guard, she would hurt him. She arched her back to meet his thrusts. She dug her nails into his back, leaving sore gouges on scars from their previous couplings. Yanagisawa pinned her arms alongside her head. She bucked frantically, then stiffened and wailed as she climaxed.

Yanagisawa thrust faster, pounding her against the floor. He climaxed in a burst of ecstasy that seemed to launch him out of his body, into some black, dreadful void. He yelled while he emptied himself into Lady Someko. His body shuddered with its release.

Lady Someko collapsed under him. Their ragged breaths mingled as his body calmed and his wits returned. Now Yanagisawa couldn't stand being close to Lady Someko. Drenched with sweat, he rolled off her, covering his limp penis with his kimono. He reclined, propped on his elbows. He heard silk rustle as she pulled down her skirts, then a whimper.

He looked at her lying beside him. Her hair was disheveled; gold ornaments had scattered across the floor. She turned her head away from him. He saw a glistening trail on her cheek. She was crying.

"Damn you," she whispered.

She was ashamed of her desire for him, Yanagisawa knew. She felt defeated every time she succumbed to the pleasure he gave her. She sat up, rearranged her hair, collected the ornaments, and reinserted them with trembling fingers. Her makeup was tear-streaked, but she had dignity even as she rose on unsteady legs. She smoothed the brown folds of her kimono, which glinted with their fiery sheen.

Hobbling out of the room, she called over her shoulder, "You should do as Yoshisato says. Placate your enemies. Get them on your side. Or you'll be sorry."

IN THE LAUNDRY tent at Lord Tsunanori's estate, Taeko pushed a hot iron along a damp kimono spread on a board. The air was steamy from the water in the tubs. Her arm ached from lifting the heavy iron off the charcoal brazier. Her fingers were blistered with burns. The other women chattered gaily as they worked, but she was homesick and miserable.

"Hey, you," said Kiku, the sullen girl who'd wakened her that morning. "Help me carry these quilts to the house."

Eager to escape the hot tent, anxious to look for a witness, Taeko set down the iron. Carrying quilts, she followed Kiku into the mansion, through the women's quarters. Lord Tsunanori's concubines, female relatives, and their attendants sat in their chambers. Their high voices filled the air, which was stale with perfumed hair oil and tobacco smoke. A loud shriek pierced the din.

Taeko paused to look inside the room from which it had come. Kiku went on without her. A maid in a blue kimono and white head kerchief knelt, a comb in her hand, behind a sour-faced, richly dressed woman. The woman shouted, "You pulled my hair again!"

"I'm sorry." The maid cringed. She was perhaps ten or eleven years old.

The woman snatched up a hairbrush, hit the girl on her face, and yelled, "Get out!"

The girl hurried from the room, her hand over her left eye. She ran down the corridor past Taeko. Taeko was horrified by the woman's cruelty. Her parents, and Masahiro's, didn't let anybody hit the servants. Taeko went after the girl, followed her outside to the garden. Ladies sat in a pavilion, feeding carp in a pond. The girl ran to a bent willow tree and ducked under its hanging boughs. When Taeko caught up with her, she saw the girl curled in the green, sun-dappled shade, sobbing.

Taeko crawled under the boughs and dropped her stack of quilts. "Are you hurt?"

Holding her hand over her eye, the girl sat up. Her oval face was lovely despite the tears that blotched her ivory skin, the ragged kerchief. Taeko would have liked to draw her someday.

"What are you doing here?" The girl's voice was a fearful whimper.

"I came to help you," Taeko said.

The girl's smooth brow wrinkled. She seemed puzzled by the idea that anyone should want to help her. "You'd better go back to work, or you'll get in trouble."

She also seemed more concerned about Taeko than herself. Taeko warmed to her. "It's all right. Let me look at your eye."

The girl slowly lowered her hand. Her eye was red, swollen.

"Can you see out of it?" Taeko asked. The girl nodded. Relieved, Taeko noticed that her cheek had taken the worst of the blow. It was bruised around broken skin. "Your face is bleeding." Taeko dabbed her sleeve against the girl's cheek.

"I haven't seen you before," the girl said. "Are you new?"

"I started working in the laundry yesterday. My name is Taeko. What's yours?"

"Emi."

"Does that lady hit you often?"

Emi nodded sadly. "They all do."

"Well, they shouldn't. They're mean and stupid." Taeko knew that some ladies didn't like servants who were prettier than themselves. "And jealous."

Emi smiled. It was like the sun coming out after the rain. "You're the only person here who's ever been kind to me. If there's anything I can do for you . . ."

Taeko didn't like to take advantage of a poor, lonely, picked-on girl, but she needed help. "Maybe there is. I'm looking for a witness. Can you tell me where to find one?"

Confusion pursed Emi's delicate mouth. "A witness to what?"

"I don't know," Taeko confessed. "I don't even know what a witness is."

"I think it's someone who saw or heard something," Emi said. "There were two samurai here yesterday. They were asking questions. I heard Lord Tsunanori's men say they were looking for witnesses."

The two samurai must have been Masahiro's father and Detective Marume, Taeko realized. They'd come to investigate the murder of the shogun's daughter, who'd been Lord Tsunanori's wife. A witness must be a person who knew something about the murder. That was what Masahiro wanted!

"Do you know anything about Lord Tsunanori's wife?" Taeko asked hopefully.

Apprehension clouded Emi's lovely features. "We're not supposed to talk about the mistress."

Taeko felt a stir of excitement. She sensed that Emi knew something important. "I promise not to tell."

Emi peeked through the willow branches to make sure no one was eavesdropping. "It was the night before Lady Tsuruhime got sick. She gave me a coin and a folded piece of paper and told me to take them to a pharmacy shop the next morning. She said to give them to the man there and bring her back what he gave me. I was surprised because I didn't usually work for her. Whenever she wanted something, she usually asked her own maids. And she ordered me not to tell anybody."

This didn't sound related to murder, but Taeko liked secrets and she wanted to hear the rest of the story. "Did you do what she asked?"

"Yes. I went to the shop. There was an old man. I gave him the paper and the coin. He gave me a bag of herbs."

"What were they?"

"I don't know."

"What was on the paper?"

Emi shook her head. "I can't read."

"What happened to it?"

"The man threw it away."

"What else happened?"

"I took the bag home. But when I got here, the women were all upset because Lady Tsuruhime had smallpox. Nobody was allowed to go near her except her nurse. So I couldn't give her the bag. And I couldn't give it to anybody else because it was supposed to be a secret."

"Where is the bag now?" Taeko scarcely dared to hope.

Emi chewed her lip, torn between obedience and her desire to help Taeko.

"Tsuruhime is dead," Taeko said. "It doesn't matter to her."

Sighing, Emi reached inside her kimono and pulled out a small cloth pouch that had been tied around her waist with a string. "I didn't know what to do with it. I was afraid to throw it away."

Taeko extended her open hand. Emi dropped the bag in it, seeming glad to pass it to someone she trusted. She frowned as if she had another secret she wondered whether to share.

"What is it?" Taeko asked eagerly.

The willow boughs rustled. Kiku thrust her head between them. Emi gasped. Taeko shoved the herb bag inside her kimono.

"Hah, there you are!" Kiku said to Taeko. "Come out!"

Taeko and Emi scrambled from beneath the willow. Kiku said, "What were you doing?"

"Nothing," Taeko said.

"Hiding from work, is more like it," Kiku said. "I'm going to tell the housekeeper. You're going to get in trouble."

"It's my fault," Emi said. "I hurt my eye. She was just trying to help me."

Kiku pointed at the front of Taeko's kimono. "What have you got in there?"

"Nothing." Taeko folded her arms.

"You're lying." Kiku thrust her open hand at Taeko. "Give it to me."

Taeko ran. Kiku chased her and shouted, "When I catch you, you're going to be sorry!"

BY SUNDOWN SANO had conducted twelve more trials. He'd condemned two more men, sentenced seven to beatings, imposed hefty fines on three, and acquitted none. His close view of the rampant corruption outraged him, yet he deplored his own role as a judge who served up death and suffering along with justice. By the time he and Marume rode up to Edo Castle, he was as exhausted as if he'd fought a battle all day, and he still had urgent business to do.

Sano knew where to find the shogun; therefore, he also knew where to find Yoshisato, who rarely left the shogun's side. After leaving Marume and his horse at home, he walked to the martial arts practice ground. A tournament had been scheduled. The tournaments were designed to give the warrior class a reprieve from earthquake problems, vent their frustration, and raise morale. They ran until after dark. The shogun never missed one.

On the practice ground, shadows cloaked the archery targets and horse-racing track. A pond for water battles reflected the orange light of the setting sun. Lanterns hanging from strings tied between poles illuminated a crowd of cheering, clapping men who sat in wooden stands. Sano walked between the stands, to the edge of the arena.

In the middle, two men armed with wooden swords, dressed in white jackets and trousers, circled each other. One was Yoshisato, the other an instructor from the Tokugawa army. The men lunged and slashed, their blades clacking. Yoshisato was athletic, graceful, and well trained. Sano knew the instructor was going easy on him—no one in his right mind would risk injuring the shogun's heir—but Yoshisato fought hard. The match ended with his blade against his opponent's neck. The spectators applauded. The shogun laughed in vicarious delight, cheering his heir. As Yoshisato walked off the field, Sano moved toward him. A palace guard intercepted Sano and said, "Don't get any closer."

"It's all right," Yoshisato said. The guard retreated. Sano knew without looking that Yanagisawa was absent. If he were here, he'd have rushed to separate Sano and Yoshisato.

"What do you want?" Yoshisato said, his tone carefully neutral. He sounded just like Yanagisawa when Yanagisawa was plotting mayhem. Either he really was Yanagisawa's son, or he'd taken to imitating his adoptive father.

"Just to talk," Sano said.

"Why don't we talk while we have a match?" Yoshisato said with a challenging smile.

"Are you serious?" It wasn't a good idea for two men to spar when they were on opposite sides of a feud. Sano had seen fights like that end in death.

"It's our only chance for a private conversation."

Sano glanced at the audience. Men craned their necks, trying to eavesdrop. A samurai didn't refuse a challenge unless he wanted to look like a coward. "All right."

Someone tossed Sano a wooden sword. As he inspected it, he hoped he wasn't making a mistake. He'd won many real fights, but he was almost thirty years older than Yoshisato, and although he was adept at controlling his weapon during practice matches, so as not to hurt his opponent, an accident was always possible.

Yoshisato walked confidently to the center of the field. Sano followed. They faced each other, swords in hand. The audience rumbled with anticipation. Yoshisato lifted an eyebrow, waiting for Sano to speak or move first.

He was so like Yanagisawa, in his mannerisms if not his looks.

"I'm investigating the murder of the shogun's daughter," Sano said.

"I know. You think somebody infected her with smallpox."

"Who told you? Your father?"

Yoshisato smiled briefly, letting Sano know that he knew Sano didn't mean the shogun. "My adoptive father."

Sano bowed, ceding their first round to Yoshisato while formally opening the match. Yoshisato bowed to Sano. They flexed their knees in combat stance, raised their swords. The cheers from the men in the audience had a rawer edge of excitement than was usual during tournaments. They knew this was a match between real enemies. They expected to see blood.

"I've been told that you went to visit Tsuruhime shortly before she got smallpox," Sano said as he and Yoshisato circled each other. His muscles felt stiff, rusty. Since the earthquake he'd not had much time for martial arts practice. "Is it true?"

"Yes." Maybe Yoshisato realized there was no use lying; maybe he felt he had nothing to hide. He lunged, slicing at Sano.

Sano easily dodged. He could tell that Yoshisato was testing his skill, not attacking him in earnest yet. "Why did you visit her?" Sano wielded his blade, carving the air near Yoshisato. A few mocking cheers rose from the audience.

Yoshisato deflected each cut with a grace that hid the effort. His supporters roared. "She was my half sister." He wasn't even winded from his previous match. But Sano knew, with the instinct of a veteran fighter, that Yoshisato had never fought a real battle. "I wanted to meet her and pay my respects to her."

"How did you like her?" Sano asked as he and Yoshisato charged, slashed, and parried. He was breathing faster.

"I didn't." Yoshisato was having the harder time concentrating on both the fight and the conversation. "She was an awful braggart. 'This is the most expensive tea.' 'My cook made these cakes. He's the best in Edo.' 'This kimono I'm wearing is made of the finest Chinese silk. It was a present from our father. He's the most important man in Japan, and he thinks nothing is too good for his daughter.' All the while, she flirted with me, giggling and batting her eyelashes behind her fan," Yoshisato said in disgust. "As if she thought I would be impressed by her beauty and her charm. But she didn't have any."

This jibed with Lord Tsunanori's description of his wife, Sano thought. "You brought her a chest of gifts. What was in it?"

"Boxes of sweets, some vases, and a bolt of silk." Yoshisato ducked as Sano's sword whistled over his head. "Not a smallpox-contaminated bedsheet. I'll save you the trouble of asking me if I killed her. I didn't."

He charged and lashed at Sano. When Sano parried, Yoshisato's sword hit his with a resounding clack that rattled his arm bones. The audience cheered louder.

"You were in her room," Sano said. "You could have had the sheet tucked inside the silk." He feinted at Yoshisato's left side. While Yoshisato moved to block the cut, Sano made another that whacked Yoshisato's right hip. "You could have sneaked it in among her things."

Boos from the audience drowned out the cheers. Yoshisato looked alarmed: The cut would have been fatal if Sano's blade were steel. "How could I? She was there the whole time. She'd have seen. I suppose I could have said, 'Excuse me while I put this sheet with your underwear and give you smallpox.'"

His voice dripped with sarcasm, like Yanagisawa's. He launched a series of cuts that Sano had to work hard to fend off. One rapped his thigh. Sano tried not to gasp with pain. "I didn't. Have anything. To do. With Tsuruhime's death." Yoshisato punctuated each phrase with a slash of his sword.

Sano was rapidly tiring. "You admit you didn't like her."

"I felt sorry for her." Compassion softened Yoshisato's voice while his blade relentlessly battered Sano's. "She didn't know our father at all. Her presents were sent by his secretary. He couldn't have cared less about her." Yoshisato attacked Sano with increased vigor. "She wasn't nice, but she didn't deserve to die."

Sano's heartbeat was speeding; he could hardly talk and breathe at the same time. "She could have interfered with your becoming the next shogun, if she'd lived to bear the shogun a grandson."

"For the last time, I didn't kill her." Yoshisato whacked viciously at Sano, who shook the dripping sweat out of his eyes as he defended himself. "If I had to resort to murder to be the next shogun, then I would rather not be the next shogun at all."

His words were spoken with such ardent sincerity that shock froze Sano. Had this been a real fight, Sano would be a dead man.

The crowd shouted for Yoshisato to finish him off. Instead, Yoshisato retreated and began circling Sano, giving Sano time to recover. Confusion rippled through the audience. "You misjudge me," Yoshisato said. "You think I'm like Yanagisawa-*san*. But I'm not."

"I'm beginning to see that," Sano said.

"You've been having this feud with Yanagisawa-*san* for almost as long as I've been alive. Well, I want none of it." His breaths came faster now as he and Sano resumed fighting. "I want you and me to be allies, not enemies."

Shock upon shock stunned Sano. He almost missed parrying a blow to his ribs. "If this is a joke, it's not funny."

"It's no joke." Not a glimpse of humor, or malice, showed on Yoshisato's solemn face. "Why do you think you're still alive? Yanagisawa-*san* wanted you killed. If not for me, we wouldn't be having this conversation."

"*You* protected me?" At last Sano knew the reason he'd been spared. "Why?"

"Because you're an honorable samurai. I want to build a coalition within the regime, and I want you to be part of it because you try to do what's right rather than what's in your own selfish interest."

Astonished and skeptical, Sano lashed his sword at Yoshisato's feet. "How do you know that about me? This is the first time we've met."

"I've talked to lots of people." Yoshisato jumped Sano's blade. "Your friends, and even some of your enemies, have good things to say about you."

Sano was impressed that Yoshisato hadn't blindly accepted Yanagisawa's judgment. "Why do you want this coalition?"

"Because I hate all the corruption, and incompetence, and political warfare I've seen since I've been at court! I want to bring people together, so that there can be peace, and progress, when I'm shogun. But I can't do it alone. I need men like you to help."

They were both fighting in order to continue their conversation rather than to win. Now Sano realized that Yoshisato was genuine. He was decent, idealistic, and touchingly naïve, the exact opposite of Yanagisawa. His dream of a harmonious rule had a strong appeal for Sano, who gained a new respect for him. That such a young man, from such a background, should have the vision to create a better world without the strife his elders considered normal!

"Does Yanagisawa-san know about your plans for a coalition?" Sano asked.

"Not yet."

"He'll never go along with it, especially if it includes me."

"Don't worry. I'll handle him."

Sano almost believed Yoshisato could. "Do you believe you're the shogun's son?"

"The shogun has named me as his heir," Yoshisato said as they circled, attacked, counterattacked, and retreated. "That's proof enough for me."

"Well, I say you're not," Sano said. "You shouldn't inherit the regime. I can't ally with a fraud."

"Why not accept the fact that I'll be your lord someday and work with me instead of fighting me?"

They were both breathless now, from sparring verbally as well as physically. Sano admitted to himself that Yoshisato's proposition was tempting. A peaceful partnership with the next shogun, a better government, and security for his family—these weren't advantages to be easily rejected.

"Will you at least promise to consider it?" Yoshisato asked.

He sounded as young as Masahiro. His face was alight with hope, zeal, and pleading. Sano couldn't say no. "I promise," Sano said.

Yoshisato's smile expressed relief and gratitude. "That's all I ask."

They backed away from each other, ending their combat in a draw, and bowed. The audience's cheers faded into discontented, puzzled murmurs: There wouldn't be blood spilled tonight. Sano and Yoshisato bowed to the shogun, who squinted at them. Everyone sensed that something unusual had happened, even if they didn't know what.

Sano had come to interrogate a murder suspect and wound up liking Yoshisato, his enemy's pawn.

娘

19

"I CAN'T STAND this anymore!" Midori cried, pacing the parlor floor. "What if Taeko never comes home?"

"She will," Reiko said soothingly. She knelt at the table and removed the lids from the dishes on their dinner trays. "Just be patient."

"But maybe she's been kidnapped!" Midori mopped her tear-drenched face with a handkerchief. "Or maybe she's lying dead somewhere!"

"Don't even think that!" Reiko, too, had begun losing hope that Taeko would be found safe after an entire night and day. Now another night was upon them. "You should eat. Look—it's your favorite, grilled oysters."

"I can't. If only Taeko would come back, I'll never scold her again. She can paint all day if she wants!"

Sano came into the room. The women looked up eagerly. He said, "Has there been any news of Taeko?"

Her hopes dashed, Midori buried her face in her hands and sobbed.

"No," Reiko said unhappily. "The search parties are still looking."

"I can't find her, either," Masahiro said, entering the room. "And I went all around Lord Tsunanori's estate."

"Why on earth would she be there?" Reiko asked.

"She followed me yesterday, when I went to investigate the murder."

"You didn't tell us," Sano said.

"You should have!" Midori cried. "What was she doing there?"

"I know." Chastened, Masahiro said, "She wanted to help me with the investigation. I said no. I thought she went home. I didn't know she was missing until this morning."

Midori uttered a sound of woeful disgust. "She never would have left the castle if not for you. You're a bad influence on her. And you shouldn't have left her in the city by herself!"

"I'm sorry," Masahiro said, clearly hurt by the rebuke and upset because Taeko's disappearance was at least partially his fault. "I've been looking for her all over Nihonbashi."

"You went into Nihonbashi by yourself?" Reiko exclaimed. "You know I don't like you doing that unless you have to deliver messages. It's too dangerous since the earthquake. All we need is another missing child."

"I'm not a child," Masahiro protested.

"You've acted like one," Reiko said. "You have to learn to be more responsible."

Then she remembered that Masahiro was only twelve. She and Sano tended to treat him like an adult and expected too much from him. No matter how precocious he was, his mind wasn't finished growing.

Detective Marume's voice said, "Cheer up, everybody. Here's something you lost."

Reiko, Sano, Masahiro, and Midori looked toward the doorway. There stood Marume with Taeko. She wore a dirty blue cotton kimono and white head kerchief. Her face was streaked with grime.

"Taeko!" Midori ran to her daughter. Her joy quickly passed. She grabbed Taeko's shoulders. "You naughty girl! I've been worried sick about you!"

TIRED, HUNGRY, AND shaken by her adventures, Taeko said in a small voice, "I'm sorry, Mama."

"Where did you find her?" Sano asked Marume.

"She just walked in the gate. I'll leave her to you." Marume departed.

Midori patted her hands over Taeko, checking for broken bones or other damage. "What's this you're wearing? What happened to your own clothes? Where have you been?"

"Why did you run away from me yesterday?" Masahiro demanded.

"Why didn't you come home? Now I'm in trouble because I didn't take care of you!"

Taeko looked at him through tears that welled in her eyes. He was mad at her, just as she'd been afraid he would be. It was too much.

"Don't scold her," Reiko said, taking pity on her. "Let's just be glad she's safe."

Midori knelt before Taeko, hugged her tight, and wept. "Thank the gods!"

Taeko wanted to lean against her mother and forget everything that had happened, but she had to tell it. "I was inside Lord Tsunanori's estate."

"Inside?" Masahiro said. "What were you doing there?"

"Working." Takeo described how she'd gotten a job in the laundry.

Midori released her. "Why would you do such a thing?"

"I had to look for a witness." Taeko said to Masahiro, "Because I made you lose yours. I wanted to find you another one."

Masahiro groaned. "That was so stupid!"

"No, it wasn't." Hurt by his criticism and driven to defend herself, she said, "I found a witness. Her name is Emi. She's a maid. She told me something about Lady Tsuruhime."

Her mother and Reiko looked surprised. "What was it?" Sano and Masahiro asked together.

"Don't encourage her!" Midori snapped. "She'll think she can get away with doing whatever she likes."

"I need to know," Sano said in a stern voice. "This investigation is important to our families. If Taeko has learned something that could help it, she must be allowed to tell us." Midori reluctantly nodded. Sano said to Taeko, "Go ahead."

Shy yet pleased to be taken seriously by him, Taeko said, "Lady Tsuruhime sent Emi to buy something at a pharmacy shop. It was supposed to be a secret. But Lady Tsuruhime got sick and died before Emi could give it to her. So she gave it to me." Taeko reached inside her kimono and pulled out the cloth pouch. "Here it is."

"This could be an important clue," Reiko said, taking the pouch from Taeko. She opened the drawstring and displayed the dried leaves, flowers, wood chips, and root fragments inside.

"We need to find out what they are," Sano said. "Masahiro, go get a physician."

Masahiro gave Taeko a dirty look as he left. He hadn't forgiven her. Instead he seemed upset because she'd found the clue and he hadn't.

"I'm going to give you a bath, then feed you, then put you to bed," Midori said, and pushed Taeko out of the room.

REIKO AND SANO looked at each other, stunned by the turn of events. All that Reiko could immediately think of to say was, "Are you hungry?"

Sano began eating the dinner Midori hadn't touched. "I had a skirmish with Yanagisawa. He knows about the murder investigation."

"Oh, no." A knot of fear tightened around the baby inside Reiko.

After eating in silence for a moment, Sano said, "The good news is, we don't need to hide the investigation from him any longer. Which meant that I was able to question Yoshisato."

Reiko sensed he wasn't telling her everything that had happened with Yanagisawa. Not much relieved, she said, "What did you find out?"

"That Yoshisato protected me from Yanagisawa. That's why Yanagisawa hasn't killed me. I have Yoshisato to thank for my life."

Now Reiko was even more astounded. "What else?"

"That Yoshisato is an excellent swordfighter, but I can hold my own against him, at least when we're not really trying to kill each other." Sano described the tournament. "That he did visit Tsuruhime, but he claims he didn't infect her with smallpox."

"Do you believe him?"

Sano nodded; he ate an oyster out of its shell.

"Why?"

"Because he's not what I expected. I still think he's Yanagisawa's son, but he's a far better person." Sano chuckled, as if at a joke on himself. "He wants to form a coalition to improve the government. He asked me to be in it, as his ally."

Reiko sat back in astonishment. "What did you tell him?"

"I promised to think about it."

"How could you?" Reiko couldn't imagine Sano allying with

Yanagisawa's son, the boy who stood to inherit the dictatorship by fraud. "To protect our family?"

Conflict shadowed Sano's features. "That's the biggest reason, yes. But he has the makings of a good shogun."

How ironic that a fake should be better qualified to be dictator than the current shogun, Reiko thought.

Masahiro came back with the physician, a nice old man who wore the dark blue coat of his profession. Sano gave him the pouch and said, "Can you tell us what these are?"

The physician poured the herbs onto his palm and examined them. "Pennyroyal, cotton root bark, and *dong quai*." He frowned at Reiko. "You haven't taken this, have you?"

"No," Reiko said.

"Good," the physician said. "It causes the womb to contract and the opening to relax. You shouldn't take it unless you want to induce an abortion."

Reiko felt suddenly faint. The musty smell of the herbs nauseated her. Abortion was legal and common, but she couldn't bear thinking about it. "Get it away from me, please!"

Sano sent Masahiro to lock the herbs in the safe in his office. The physician left. As her faintness and sickness abated, Reiko recognized the implications of the herbs. "Tsuruhime wanted medicine that causes abortions. That means she must have been pregnant."

Sano nodded. "With a child she didn't want."

They were both silent, shocked by their discovery. Had she not died, the shogun's daughter could have borne a child and complicated the battle over the succession.

"It couldn't have been Lord Tsunanori's," Sano said. "Not if he was telling the truth when he said he hadn't slept with her in years, and I think he was."

"Then who was the father?" Reiko asked.

Masahiro returned. "It must be Jinnosuke the soldier. I saw him today. He said he and Tsuruhime were, uh, lovers." Masahiro blushed as he described his talk with Jinnosuke.

Reiko smiled. He was shy about sex, at least when discussing it with his parents. She was proud of him for interviewing a witness all by himself and finding a clue. "Suppose Jinnosuke was the father. Maybe Tsuruhime was afraid her husband would be angry because he would know the baby wasn't his." That seemed a logical reason for her to want an abortion.

Sano shook his head. "Lord Tsunanori might have been angry at her for committing adultery, but not necessarily about the baby, especially if it was male. He wanted to be the father of the shogun's grandson. He'd have been glad to claim it. Even if it was female, he could have used it to make a marriage alliance with another powerful clan."

"Tsuruhime must have known that if she didn't want the child, she couldn't let Lord Tsunanori find out about it," Reiko said. "That must be why she swore Emi to secrecy."

"Jinnosuke thinks Lord Tsunanori knows about him and Tsuruhime," Masahiro said. "He's afraid Lord Tsunanori will kill him. Maybe Tsuruhime wanted to protect him by getting rid of the baby."

Reiko was disturbed because Masahiro was learning about adultery, illegitimate pregnancies, and abortions at such a young age, but she was proud of his skill at reasoning. "That seems a likely explanation."

"It seems likely that Tsuruhime was infected with smallpox because she was pregnant," Sano said.

"And if Lord Tsunanori didn't do it, then we're back where we started," Reiko said.

"With Yanagisawa as the best suspect," Sano agreed.

"Along with Yoshisato," Reiko said.

Sano nodded, looking troubled. "I hope it's not Yoshisato."

"You're always telling me to be objective during investigations," Reiko reminded Sano. "You warn me against favoring suspects who are people I like."

"I know." Sano seemed irritated because she'd thrown his own words back at him, and uncomfortable because he wasn't following his own rule. "Yanagisawa may be responsible for Tsuruhime's death, but I don't think Yoshisato was in on the crime."

"If Yoshisato was, you can't let him off the hook," Masahiro said.

"I won't." Now Sano sounded on edge because his son thought he might be so unfair.

Reiko felt an anxiety that verged on panic. At times she and Sano had disagreed during investigations. She prayed that this wasn't one of those times. They had enough problems already.

"I have to obtain justice for the shogun's daughter," Sano said curtly. "I will, no matter who the killer is." He headed toward the door.

"Where are you going?" Reiko asked.

"To see Lady Nobuko. I want to hear what she has to say about this latest development."

SANO WALKED UPHILL along the stone-walled passage that led to the palace. Chilly night steeped Edo Castle in darkness relieved only by the lanterns at checkpoints and torches carried by patrol guards. Only scattered, distant footsteps, the rattle of night soil carts heading out of the city, and occasional voices calling interrupted the quiet. Sano welcomed privacy and peace. Tension from the acrimonious day seeped from his muscles, but his mind was still on edge. He needed to adjust to the news of Tsuruhime's pregnancy and its implications. He also had to consider Yoshisato's proposition. How could he balance his need to protect his family with his responsibility to protect a youth who was associated with his worst enemy yet might be innocent of the murder? He loved his wife and son, but right now he couldn't listen to them challenging his judgment. Sano walked slowly, wanting time alone to think.

The palace was deserted except for the sentries at the entrances. Stars glittered above the curved peaks and gables of its roof. Flames flickering in stone lanterns lit Sano's way to a separate wing of the women's quarters. There Lady Nobuko lived in a little house attached to the main building by a covered corridor and surrounded by a narrow garden whose earthen wall and bamboo thickets excluded noise. Korika, her lady-in-waiting, opened the door.

"I want to see Lady Nobuko," Sano said.

A worried expression came over Korika's broad, pleasant face. "I'm sorry, but Lady Nobuko has gone to bed. She had a bad day."

Sano was about to make it worse. "Wake her up. This is important."

"Very well." Korika ushered him into a small parlor, lit a lantern, and left.

Sano knelt. He waited for a long while before she returned with Lady Nobuko.

"You had better have a good reason for calling at this hour." Lady Nobuko wore her usual drab, dignified robes, but her silver-streaked hair hung in a thin braid, and she hadn't put on any makeup. Deep wrinkles on her face, usually filled in with thick white rice powder, made the muscle spasm around her right eye even more apparent.

"I do. I just learned that Tsuruhime was pregnant."

Lady Nobuko's muscle spasm tightened, wrenching her face diagonally. Korika put her hands to her full cheeks. Moaning in pain, Lady Nobuko curled up on the floor.

"You didn't know, then." Sano's statement confirmed the obvious.

"She didn't tell me," Lady Nobuko said weakly, while Korika massaged her temples. "She confided in me about everything . . . except that."

"Merciful gods," Korika whispered. "The grandchild the shogun had always hoped for. It died with our poor Tsuruhime."

Lady Nobuko looked up at Sano, angling her neck and moving her eyes carefully to avoid worse pain. "How do you know she was pregnant?"

Sano told her about the maid, the herbs, and Tsuruhime's romance with the soldier.

Lady Nobuko closed her eyes; tears spilled. "I had no idea about this affair. But I do know that Tsuruhime was terribly afraid of childbirth. When she was eight, her nursemaid became pregnant out of wedlock. The maid hid her condition until she went into labor in the room where she slept beside Tsuruhime's bed. Tsuruhime was awakened by screams in the night. The maid's bed was drenched with blood. The servants took Tsuruhime away, but not before she'd seen the baby's arm sticking out from between the maid's legs. The baby was dead. The physician cut it out of the maid. She screamed all the while. Then she bled to death. The story was all over the women's quarters the next day. Little girls have big ears."

Sano could only imagine the horror of what Tsuruhime had seen. It was indeed a reason for her to have wanted to avoid having a baby, regardless of who the father was, no matter that it was the grandchild of the shogun.

Recovered from her shock, Lady Nobuko pushed herself upright. "As much as your news hurts me, I see some good in it. Tsuruhime's pregnancy is evidence that Yanagisawa murdered her. He would have wanted to prevent her from bearing the child, to ensure that the shogun wouldn't choose it as his heir instead of Yoshisato. Killing her was the only way."

"If he knew about her pregnancy," Sano said. "I haven't had a chance to determine whether he did."

"Oh, he must have known. Once you prove it, you can destroy him." Lady Nobuko's eyes shone with unholy glee. "But destroying Yanagisawa isn't enough. You must destroy his bastard, too." Her hatred of Yanagisawa spilled over onto Yoshisato. "You have to prove they both murdered Tsuruhime."

Conflict wrenched Sano's innards. His new liking for Yoshisato vied with his obligation to Lady Nobuko. "If they're both guilty, I'll prove it and make them pay." Before he'd met Yoshisato he'd looked forward to destroying Yanagisawa's pawn. Now he said, "If Yoshisato isn't guilty, I won't take him down along with Yanagisawa."

"You must!" Lady Nobuko clutched Sano's arm. Her hand was a gnarled claw that dug into his flesh. "I don't want Yanagisawa's bastard inheriting the regime." She was so intent on taking revenge on Yanagisawa that she didn't care whether an innocent young man suffered.

"When I agreed to investigate Tsuruhime's death, I told you that I would be looking for the truth. If the truth is that Yoshisato is innocent, then he shouldn't be punished for the murder." Sano firmly withdrew from her grasp.

"But if Yoshisato lives to become the next shogun, Yanagisawa will win!" The spasm in Lady Nobuko's face tightened. Groaning in pain, she lay down again.

That was a dilemma for Sano. Meeting Yoshisato hadn't only put him at odds with Reiko, Masahiro, and Lady Nobuko; it was interfering with his quest for revenge on Yanagisawa.

"Please, you'd better go," Korika said to Sano.

As he stepped off the veranda stairs into the fresh air and darkness of the garden, Korika came running after him, calling, "Wait!"

She stood in the doorway, silhouetted by the light within. "Can't you give Lady Nobuko what she wants?" Her voice was pleading, anxious. "She's an old, sick woman. It would mean so much to her."

"I understand," Sano said with honest sympathy. "And I commend your devotion to her." Korika seemed to love her mistress even though waiting on Lady Nobuko must be a chore. "But I can't frame someone who's innocent."

"Yoshisato doesn't deserve to be shogun!" Korika wrung her hands. "He's a fraud!"

Sano remembered Yoshisato asking him to join a coalition for the good of Japan. "I won't destroy him just to make Lady Nobuko happy."

Or to fulfill his own duty to prevent a fraud from inheriting the regime.

Meeting Yoshisato had also put Sano at odds with his own honor.

Korika's plump bosom swelled, then deflated as she sighed. She turned and went into the house. Before the door closed, the light gilded her profile. Her expression was so hard that for a moment Sano thought he was looking at a stranger.

20

THE SUN ROSE over Zōjō Temple like a red pearl dissolving in milk. Crimson light bled onto the roofs of worship halls, shrines, and pagodas. Hammering and sawing announced the day's construction work. The temple was no haven from the rebuilding boom. Gongs tolled. Monks, priests, and nuns headed for town, a parade of people with heads shaved and begging bowls in hands, the nuns and monks in plain hemp robes, the priests in brilliant saffron.

Hirata crouched under the bridge that spanned the Sakuragawa Canal. The parade crossed the bridge with a soft thunder of straw sandals on wood planks. When the echo of the last footstep faded, he scrambled up the bank and followed the parade. Far ahead, up the highway that ran between wooded hills, Deguchi walked with his brethren. His aura made him as obvious to Hirata as if a giant red arrow were pointing down at him. Hirata hoped Deguchi wouldn't notice he was being followed, recognize Hirata, and perceive his intentions.

Hirata meant to kill Deguchi.

Everything in him abhorred the idea. Murder was against his code of honor. He didn't want to be a slave to a ghost. But unless he did General Otani's bidding, Otani would kill him the next time the secret society forced him into a trance. And Hirata had promised Sano that he would make things right. The only way he could think of to dissolve the secret society was to kill the other members. He might as well start with Deguchi.

The nuns, monks, and priests entered the Nihonbashi merchant district. They fanned out through the alleys, begging alms at the shops that were open, at the market stalls. Deguchi walked east, alone. Hirata kept a safe distance from him and watched for an opportunity to kill him. It had to be someplace where no one would see. It had to be fast. One try was all Hirata would get.

Deguchi kept to the main streets, which were filled with people. He looked straight ahead; he didn't seem to notice that he was being followed. He didn't stop to beg. Hirata wondered where he was going.

They reached the Sumida River. The water was leaden beneath an overcast sky. Deguchi climbed into a ferryboat. Hirata stood on the embankment until Deguchi was halfway across the river. Then he hired another ferryman to row him to the opposite shore. There, he tracked Deguchi's aura through the crowds in the Honjo entertainment district. Deguchi hurried through the quarter where townspeople were building new houses along canals. His aura crackled with impatient energy. Hirata caught up with him in an enclave where samurai officials lived in suburban villas. Deguchi slowed his pace, holding out his begging bowl to officials in palanquins and troops on horseback. Hirata followed him past estates under construction. Deguchi came to one that appeared to be finished. He circled the estate twice, not looking directly at it. The second time he neared the gate, he crossed the street. The villa there was enclosed by two-story barracks, its gate open. Trees overhung the repaired buildings to the left of the gate. Carpenters were installing new roof beams on the barracks to the right. Deguchi strolled in through the gate. Hirata waited a few moments, then followed.

Inside the estate, more carpenters were busy at work on a villa. Hirata hid behind a pile of timber and watched Deguchi stroll up to the barracks. Deguchi stood gazing up at the rooftop near the gate. Its eaves were at least twice as high as he was tall. He set his bowl on the ground, raised his arms, flexed his knees, and jumped. His fingers caught the eaves. He pulled himself up, climbed the slope of the roof, and disappeared into the trees. Hirata ran alongside the barracks and stopped some twenty paces past the spot where Deguchi had jumped. He performed the same move, less expertly. As he pulled himself onto the roof, he made loud, scuffling sounds. Crawling up it, he kicked a tile loose. It fell and shattered. Hammering covered the noise. When he was safe under the tree branches, he knelt and looked to his left.

Almost hidden by the leaves, Deguchi sat on the roof ridge, gazing across the street. He and Hirata had a good view inside the estate that Deguchi had walked around. Its barracks enclosed a garden where flowerbeds bloomed amid grasses and shrubs. Gravel paths led to a two-story mansion. Hirata turned back to Deguchi. Deguchi hadn't moved. If he knew Hirata was near, he gave no sign. He waited patiently. Curious, Hirata delayed attacking Deguchi, although this might be his only chance.

What was Deguchi up to?

TAEKO SAT ALONE on the floor of the room she shared with her little brother and Akiko. Her mother had taken away her painting things and the other children's toys. She had nothing to occupy her. She couldn't even look outside. Her mother had shut the doors to the veranda. She could only eavesdrop on conversations.

"Locking her inside her room for three days seems a little extreme," Reiko's voice said.

"It won't hurt her," Midori answered crossly. "She has to learn her lesson."

Akiko's voice said, "Can I play with Taeko?"

"No," Midori said. "She's being punished."

Soon Taeko heard thumps, scuffling, and giggles beneath the floor. Akiko and Tatsuo were playing in the crawl space under the house, between the foundation posts. She remembered the times she'd wanted to be alone to paint, but she longed to join them now.

"Akiko! Tatsuo!" Midori yelled. "Come out! Didn't Reiko and I tell you not to play under the house because of the poisonous spiders?"

A long, loud spate of hammering interrupted Taeko's eavesdropping. ". . . have to find out if Yanagisawa and Yoshisato knew." Sano's voice.

"How?" Reiko.

Akiko and Tatsuo began stomping and whooping through the house. Midori yelled at them to be quiet.

". . . wonder what she knows." Reiko again. "I can write to her and ask her to visit me."

"He'll never let her."

"It can't hurt to try."

Taeko wondered who they were talking about. She heard Sano leave the house. She listened for Masahiro. He didn't seem to be home. She hadn't meant to get him in trouble. How could she make him forgive her? Locked in her room, Taeko sighed.

It was going to be a long three days.

AFTER CONDUCTING TRIALS until noon, Sano rode with Detective Marume to the Nihonbashi merchant district. Now he sat alone in the private back room of a teahouse. Through the barred window he could see into the yard of the inn across the alley. The yard was crowded with women cooking on outdoor hearths. Wet laundry draped over clotheslines. Sano smelled charcoal smoke, fermented tofu, and sewage. Many people whose homes had been destroyed by the earthquake now resided, for exorbitant prices, at the inns that had reopened. Sano listened to the women argue. Two hours passed before a man appeared at the door.

"Come in, Ishida-*san*," Sano said.

Ishida was a tall, powerfully built samurai. His wicker hat shaded features that looked chiseled from wood. He wore garments with no identifying crests. He looked nervously outside before he shut the door. "I'm sorry to be late."

Sano picked up a sake decanter from the table and poured a cup for his guest. "You're paid generously to show up on time when you're called."

"I know, but I was on duty," Ishida said. "If Yanagisawa catches me sneaking away, I'll lose my post." He was one of Yanagisawa's personal bodyguards. He drank the sake, then rubbed his mouth. "If he finds out that I'm spying on him for you, I'm dead."

"All right, never mind," Sano said. It had taken ages to find someone close to Yanagisawa who was willing to inform on him. "What's Yanagisawa been up to lately?"

"He's being more careful than usual about talking in front of his own people."

"How are he and Yoshisato getting along?" Sano asked, thinking of his extraordinary conversation with Yoshisato last night.

Ishida fidgeted with his hands. "Fine, I guess."

The trouble with spies was that they didn't always see, or tell Sano, everything. Sano broached the important question. "Did they mention that the shogun's daughter was pregnant?"

Ishida's stiff, wooden features slackened with surprise. "Was she really?"

It was obvious that he hadn't heard the news from Yanagisawa, Yoshisato, or anyone else. Sano said, "Can you ask around and find out if they knew?"

The door scraped open. Sano looked up to see Yanagisawa and Yoshisato walk into the room. "Find out if who knew what?" Yanagisawa asked.

A triumphant smile twisted his mouth. Yoshisato's expression was tight, controlled.

Dismayed, Sano turned an accusing gaze on Ishida. "You let him follow you here?" Ishida's expression was simultaneously brazen and sheepish, as if he'd pulled off a dirty practical joke. "You told him you're my spy?" Sano demanded.

Ishida moved to stand beside Yanagisawa. "Yes. He's known all along."

"He's been feeding you false intelligence about me," Yanagisawa said placidly.

Sano knew the risks of employing spies, but the betrayal angered him nonetheless. He glanced at Yoshisato, who stood an arm's length from Yanagisawa. It apparently wasn't all peace and harmony between the two.

"What were you and Ishida talking about?" Yanagisawa asked.

"The shogun's daughter was pregnant," Ishida said. "He wants to know if you knew."

Sano saw Yanagisawa's brows fly upward and lips part. A split instant later, when Sano shifted his gaze to Yoshisato, the youth wore an identical expression of shock. Their reaction was so immediate that Sano didn't think it could have been faked.

"This is the first we've heard of it. All these years, everyone thought

Tsuruhime was barren, and now, surprise." Yanagisawa spoke as if he'd narrowly escaped a fatal accident. He said to Ishida, "Wait for us outside."

Ishida left the teahouse without looking at Sano.

"It's good for you that the child died with her and can never compete with Yoshisato to be the next shogun," Sano said, glancing at Yoshisato again.

Yoshisato was regarding Yanagisawa with dismay, which he wiped off his face as soon as he saw Sano's attention on him. Did he suspect that Yanagisawa had known about the pregnancy and ensured that it never reached fruition? Maybe Yanagisawa had. And maybe Yoshisato didn't have any part in Tsuruhime's murder.

"Come, come, Sano-*san*," Yanagisawa said. "It wouldn't have made any difference to me if Tsuruhime had lived to bear the child. It couldn't have supplanted Yoshisato. He's the shogun's acknowledged son."

Maybe the death of the child was just a lucky break for Yoshisato and Yanagisawa and neither had engineered it. Sano couldn't dismiss the possibility, but he wanted Yanagisawa, if not Yoshisato, to be guilty.

"A grandson with an undisputed pedigree could very well have been a threat to a son of dubious origins," Sano reminded Yanagisawa. "You don't need another potential heir for your enemies to rally around." *Especially when your own protégé is balking at your control.* Sano doubted that Yanagisawa had any inkling of the proposition Yoshisato had made him. He threw a quizzical look at Yoshisato.

Yoshisato gazed impassively back at him. Sano was of two minds about mentioning the proposition and seeing how Yanagisawa reacted. Was there more advantage in keeping it secret or in trying to drive a wedge between Yanagisawa and Yoshisato? Caution held Sano's tongue.

"We didn't know Tsuruhime was pregnant. You're stupid if you think we risked killing the shogun's daughter on the off chance that she might be a threat someday," Yanagisawa said.

"You're ruthless enough," Sano said.

Yanagisawa said with growing vexation, "For the last time, I didn't kill Tsuruhime."

"Neither did I." Yoshisato's calm demeanor hid whatever he thought of Yanagisawa's claim of innocence. "You might as well stop trying to prove we did." As far as the murder investigation went, he and Yanagisawa were united against Sano.

"I won't stop trying to get justice for the shogun's daughter. If you did it, you'll pay." Sano looked pointedly at Yoshisato, for whom his words carried a double meaning: If Yoshisato proved to be guilty, he could forget about an alliance with Sano.

Yoshisato nodded in curt acknowledgment. Yanagisawa noticed the exchange; he frowned slightly, puzzled, then said, "There's a rumor that Tsuruhime isn't the shogun's blood daughter."

"Oh, and if the shogun isn't Tsuruhime's father, then he won't care about her pregnancy or murder," Sano retorted. "I think you just started the rumor yourself."

Yanagisawa shrugged. "It doesn't matter what you think. What matters is whether the shogun believes the rumor."

Knowing how gullible the shogun was, Sano felt his spirits sink. But he said, "Go ahead, manipulate His Excellency. In the meantime, I'll continue my investigation."

Displeasure showed on Yoshisato's face. Yanagisawa said with a malevolent smile, "I gave you a chance to cooperate. You're going to wish you'd taken it." He added, "It would be a pity if the same thing that happened to Tsuruhime's child happened to Lady Reiko's."

娘 *21*

IN HER ROOM, Reiko knelt before an open chest. She smiled as she lifted out a tiny pink kimono printed with white clover blossoms. Thinking about the baby and preparing for its birth was a happy respite from her troubles. She couldn't wait to hold her newborn child. She hadn't decided on a name for a boy, but if it was a girl, she would name it Yuki—snow.

Akiko, standing beside her, said, "What's that?"

"This is what you wore when you were a baby." Reiko had saved some of Akiko's and Masahiro's nicest baby clothes. She laid out a row of colorful garments.

"They're pretty. Can I have them for my doll?"

"They're for your new baby sister or brother," Reiko said.

Akiko's face bunched into a pout. "I said I don't want a new baby."

"You'll feel differently when it comes," Reiko said, trying to convince herself as well as Akiko. "A live baby is more fun than a doll."

"No, it's not." Akiko looked ready to cry.

Distressed by her daughter's unhappiness, Reiko said, "All right, you can have this one." She held out the pink kimono.

Akiko slapped it out of her hand. "I don't want it anymore." She stomped out of the room. Reiko sighed. This was a pattern for them. Akiko got upset; Reiko tried to console her; Akiko rejected Reiko.

A maid came to the door. "There's a visitor to see you. A Lady Someko."

Reiko was astounded. She hadn't expected Lady Someko to accept the invitation she'd sent this morning. Wild with curiosity, she hurried to meet the mother of the shogun's heir.

Two of Sano's guards stood outside the reception room where Lady Someko sat by the alcove. She wore a reddish-bronze silk kimono. Her spine was straight, her chin lifted proudly. A cinnabar comb anchored her smooth, upswept black hair. Reiko entered the room and knelt opposite her. They bowed solemnly, like rival generals facing each other across a battlefield.

While Reiko offered refreshments and Lady Someko politely refused, they engaged in mutual scrutiny. Lady Someko was very attractive, her skin smooth across her wide face, her hair untouched by gray. But her body, although sleek and firm, lacked the softness of youth. Her tilted eyes had a hard, mature glitter. Reiko saw them note her beauty, her pregnancy.

"I didn't think you would come," Reiko said.

Lady Someko's lips curved in the condescending smile with which Reiko had seen other older women express their envy of her. "Life is full of surprises."

"Why did you come?"

"One reason is that I've heard a lot about you, and I'm curious."

Reiko could imagine what Lady Someko had heard. Tales of her exploits in the service of Sano's investigations had long fed the high-society gossip mill. It was probably still churning with the story of how she'd killed a criminal outside the palace last year.

"The curiosity is mutual," Reiko said. "Many thanks for accepting my invitation."

Mirth briefly dimpled Lady Someko's cheeks. "You're not what I expected."

"What did you expect?"

"Someone bigger and tougher and less feminine," Lady Someko said. "You don't look strong enough to lift a sword."

"You're not what I expected, either," Reiko said.

"What did *you* expect?"

"Someone weak and easily dominated."

That was the stereotype of concubines. Reiko thought Lady Someko would react with scorn at this notion of herself, but Lady Someko looked faintly distressed, as if Reiko's judgment had hit too close to home.

"Another reason is that we have a lot in common," Lady Someko said. "We're both mothers of sons."

"Our men are on opposite sides of a feud," Reiko said. "I suppose you could call that something else in common."

Lady Someko smiled as if mischievously pleased to be consorting with the enemy. Reiko did feel a certain comradeship with her. The feud between Sano and Yanagisawa must be affecting Lady Someko's life as well as Reiko's.

"Won't Chamberlain Yanagisawa mind your talking to me?" Reiko asked.

"Of course. But he doesn't control everything I do." Lady Someko gave a husky laugh. "Does your husband tell you to go out and kill people, or do you take it upon yourself?"

Reiko wasn't about to discuss her marriage with a stranger who might tell tales to Yanagisawa. "Are there any more reasons why you came?"

For the first time Lady Someko seemed less than confident. She said in a falsely casual tone, "I heard that your husband is investigating the murder of the shogun's daughter."

"You mean, you want to know if Yoshisato is a suspect and whether my husband has evidence that he's guilty?"

"If it were your son whose half sister had been murdered, wouldn't you want to know whether someone had evidence against him?" Lady Someko retorted.

Despite her prickly manner, Reiko sympathized with her. She must be terrified that Yoshisato would be implicated in and punished for Tsuruhime's death. She obviously didn't think he was safe just because he'd been accepted as the shogun's son. The shogun had never been tested to see if he would let his son get away with killing his daughter. This was an unprecedented, volatile situation.

"I'll make a bargain with you," Reiko said. "I'll tell you what's happening in the murder investigation, if you'll answer a question for me."

Distrust narrowed Lady Someko's eyes.

"Who is Yoshisato's real father? The shogun or Yanagisawa?"

Lady Someko let out a puff of laughter. She didn't seem surprised or offended that Reiko would try to trap her into a compromising revelation. She seemed amused, as if by the antics of a clever child. "The shogun, of course. Now it's your turn."

"Not yet. Did you really sleep with the shogun? He prefers men."

"He preferred me for long enough to impregnate me."

"You lived with Yanagisawa while you were pregnant. Were you sleeping with him, too? Couldn't Yoshisato be his?"

"I was pregnant by the shogun before Yanagisawa took me in." Lady Someko said suddenly, "Who's the father of the child you're carrying?"

Startled, Reiko said, "My husband."

"If it wasn't him, would you tell me?" Lady Someko read Reiko's face. She smiled meanly. "I didn't think so. You wouldn't want me blabbing it around and your husband finding out you'd cheated on him. He would divorce you. So why would you think I would tell you that the shogun isn't my son's father even if it were true?"

Reiko believed as wholeheartedly as Sano did that Yanagisawa was Yoshisato's father. But she knew that if Lady Someko confessed her fraud, she would face much worse consequences than divorce. The shogun would have her and Yoshisato put to death.

"That's a good point," Reiko said. "But I figured I might as well try."

"You can stop trying my patience. Tell me about the investigation."

Reiko watched Lady Someko closely as she said, "My husband thinks the shogun's daughter was deliberately infected with smallpox."

Lady Someko looked disappointed. "Tell me something I haven't already heard."

"A witness found a sheet stained with blood and pus hidden in Tsuruhime's room."

"Who is the witness?" Caution crept into Lady Someko's voice. "Where is this sheet?"

"I'm not at liberty to say." Reiko didn't want to admit that the sheet was missing or reveal the witness's identity.

"Ah." Lady Someko's expression suggested that the evidence was fabricated. She relaxed slightly.

"Have you heard that Yanagisawa is a suspect?"

"Yes. Did your husband whip up the murder investigation just to get him in trouble?"

Reiko was angry that Lady Someko dared accuse Sano of such a reprehensible motive. But of course Lady Someko needed to believe Yanagisawa was innocent. Her fate and Yoshisato's were tied to his. Reiko said, "Yanagisawa had good reason to kill Tsuruhime. She was pregnant when she died."

Lady Someko's painted eyebrows flew up. "How do you know?"

"I'm not at liberty to say. Did Yanagisawa know?"

Lady Someko was silent. Reiko couldn't read the thoughts behind the glitter in her eyes, Had Lady Someko known about Tsuruhime's pregnancy? "What's the matter? Are you upset by the idea that Yanagisawa killed a pregnant woman, for political reasons?"

"You're the one who ought to be upset," Lady Someko said, recovering her sly humor. "Your husband probably murdered Tsuruhime himself, in order to frame Yanagisawa."

The accusation was so ludicrous that Reiko didn't bother replying to it. "Did Yoshisato know?"

"No. He couldn't have. He never even met Tsuruhime. He certainly didn't kill her." The white makeup hid the angry rush of blood to Lady Someko's face, but the bare skin on her bosom reddened above the neckline of her kimono. "He's not capable of murder."

"A lot has happened to him during the past few months," Reiko said. "All of a sudden he has power. That can change a man, especially one so young and impressionable."

"Not Yoshisato. He's a good boy," Lady Someko declared. "I know my son."

"Not as well as you think." Reiko hated to disillusion a mother about her child; but she must, for the sake of her own children. "Yoshisato did meet Tsuruhime. He went to visit her shortly before she came down with smallpox."

The anger on Lady Someko's face froze. The skin on her bosom went white. "No. He never told me." Reiko realized she'd been suspicious and afraid all along that Yoshisato was involved in Tsuruhime's death. "You're lying."

"I'm sorry, I'm not," Reiko said, genuinely contrite. "Yoshisato admitted it to my husband when they spoke yesterday. He had a chance to plant the sheet."

"There must be some other explanation for why he went." Lady Someko sounded uncertain yet eager to convince herself. "He didn't kill Tsuruhime."

"You think he might have," Reiko pointed out. "You suspected it even before you found out that he'd visited Tsuruhime. That's another reason you wanted to talk to me. Why did you suspect him? Was it something he did or said?"

"I didn't! There was nothing!" Lady Someko's chest rose and fell with quickened, anxious breaths.

"He may have started out good, but he's been under Yanagisawa's influence. Yanagisawa has had people assassinated. He wouldn't stop at murdering the shogun's daughter to put Yoshisato at the head of the regime."

"Yoshisato isn't like him!" Aghast, Lady Someko sprang to her feet.

"Then again, maybe Yanagisawa didn't have to kill Tsuruhime," Reiko went on, merciless in pursuit of the truth, "because Yoshisato did."

As a child Reiko had gone to the city with her grandmother and they'd seen a woman tied to a stake, about to be burned as punishment for arson. Her grandmother had pulled her away before the fire was set, but Reiko had never forgotten the woman. Now Reiko saw the same wild, desperate expression on Lady Someko. She'd voiced Lady Someko's worst nightmare—that Yoshisato would turn into Yanagisawa, his real father. A draft stirred Lady Someko's robes. The reddish-bronze silk glowed like flames consuming her body.

"I've begun to think Yoshisato is guilty," Reiko said, "and so have you."

The thought that she was getting close to solving the murder gave her pause: Sano wouldn't welcome evidence against Yoshisato.

Lady Someko said in a low, venomous voice, "Tell your husband to leave Yoshisato alone." The glitter in her eyes concentrated into two brilliant pinpoints of hatred. "If he doesn't, he'll answer to Yanagisawa. And you'll answer to me."

22

ACROSS THE RIVER, Hirata spied on Deguchi through the concealing foliage of the trees. More than three hours had passed while they sat on the roof of the barracks. Deguchi hadn't moved, hadn't taken his gaze off the garden inside the estate across the street. The garden was deserted, peaceful in the hazy afternoon sunlight. Then a man shuffled out of the mansion and down the steps of the veranda. A hump on his back distorted his stunted figure. It was Lord Ienobu.

As Ienobu slouched along the garden path, Deguchi leaned forward. His right hand held a small object, which he rubbed between his fingers. It looked like a pebble. Deguchi lifted his hand, sighted on Ienobu, drew back his arm. Hirata acted instinctively. He sprang, burst through the tree branches, and landed with a loud thump beside Deguchi at the same moment Deguchi hurled the pebble.

The pebble flew so fast that it made a whizzing sound, glowed white like a comet, and trailed a thin orange flame. It zoomed close by Ienobu's head and struck the wall of the mansion with a thud. An instant later, a loud boom rocked the sky. Particles of plaster sprayed around a wisp of smoke. Ienobu looked around. He frowned in confusion. He didn't see the hole where the pebble had embedded itself in the wall. He didn't know that it had been meant to pierce his skull and kill him. Shaking his head, he ambled around the corner of the mansion.

Deguchi swiveled toward Hirata. Astonished and furious, he mouthed the words, *You made me miss! What are you doing here?*

"Why did you just try to kill Ienobu?" Hirata asked.

As they stared at each other in mutual bewilderment, Hirata realized he'd lost his chance to kill Deguchi. The priest now knew Hirata had been following him. He would be on his guard. Hirata also realized why General Otani had ordered him to kill Deguchi. General Otani knew Deguchi would try to assassinate Ienobu. Hirata had been sent to stop Deguchi.

"I think we both have some explaining to do," Hirata said.

They jumped off the roof and walked to the townspeople's quarter near the river. They sat on the bank of a stagnant canal. Hirata asked, "Why did you do it? You know General Otani wants Ienobu to be the next shogun. Why did you go against him and Tahara and Kitano?" Hirata was astounded by his discovery that he wasn't the only member at odds with the secret society.

Deguchi reached over and took his hand.

"Hey!" Hirata flinched from the intimate gesture.

Deguchi waggled his finger to express that he wasn't making sexual advances. He closed his hand around Hirata's, and Hirata heard a quiet male voice that traveled along the nerves in his arm, up into his head: *Can you hear me?*

"Yes." Hirata shivered at the eerie sensation of Deguchi's thoughts invading his mind. "Can you hear my thoughts, too?"

No. Not unless you learn how to send them.

Relieved, Hirata said, "I'm ready for your explanation."

WHEN SANO ARRIVED at the rebuilding magistrates' headquarters, he met Moriwaki in the hall. "While you were gone, a message came for you, from the shogun," Moriwaki said, flashing his bright smile. "He wants to see you at once."

Sano rode to the castle. In the palace, the shogun sat in his study. Scrolls were heaped on the gold-inlaid, black lacquer desk. The shogun was stamping them with his signature seal without reading them. He frowned as if the job were taxingly difficult.

"Ahh, it's you," he said. "Come in."

Sano knelt and bowed. "Your Excellency summoned me?"

"Yes." The shogun's frown deepened. "It has come to my attention that, ahh, instead of rebuilding Edo, you have, ahh, been snooping around, making inquiries about my daughter."

There went Sano's hope that the shogun wouldn't find out about his investigation until he'd solved the crime. And the shogun was clearly displeased. "May I ask who told you?"

"No, you may not."

Sano mentally ran through the list of people who knew about the investigation. Yanagisawa and Yoshisato wouldn't have told. Or would they? Although they didn't want the shogun suspecting them of foul play, they might have enlisted him to order the investigation stopped. Lady Nobuko had agreed that the investigation should be kept secret, but Sano still didn't trust her. Sano didn't think Lord Tsunanori would tell, but who knew for sure?

"Just tell me," the shogun said. "Why are you investigating my daughter?"

Sano owed the shogun the truth. If the investigation had involved his own daughter, he would want to know. And now that Yanagisawa knew, it might as well come out. "Because I believe she was murdered."

A familiar, queasy expression came over the shogun's face: He didn't understand, and he was afraid to ask for clarification and risk looking stupid. "But, ahh . . . Didn't she die of smallpox? My memory isn't, ahh, what it used to be."

Sano explained about the infected sheet.

The shogun gasped in horror. "Merciful gods! If it happened to her, it could happen to me!" He hurried to the door, summoned his servants, and said, "Inspect my chambers. Look for things with blood or pus on them. If you find any, then burn everything!" The servants ran off. He collapsed behind his desk and held up his hands, afraid to touch anything.

"I don't think Your Excellency is in any danger." Even as Sano spoke, he couldn't quite dismiss the idea that Tsuruhime's murder was part of a larger plot against the Tokugawa clan and the shogun was next.

Calmer but not totally reassured, the shogun asked, "Who killed Tsuruhime?"

Here was Sano's opportunity to implicate Yanagisawa in the crime. If he succeeded, the shogun would put Yanagisawa to death and Sano would be rid of Yanagisawa for good. The opportunity shone like an oily, dirty rainbow floating on clean water. Sano didn't have any evidence against Yanagisawa. Honor forbade him to incriminate someone who might be innocent. Sano did have evidence against Yoshisato, but he was loath to hurt Yoshisato, even though Yoshisato was a party to an outrageous fraud. And Sano knew better than to suggest that Yoshisato had killed Tsuruhime. Casting aspersion on the shogun's heir would be treason. Furthermore, Sano hadn't forgotten Lord Tsunanori and the nurse. They were still suspects, too.

"I don't know who the killer is yet," Sano said. "My investigation hasn't progressed that far." Opportunity drained away like water down a gutter.

"Why not?" The shogun glowered. "And you call yourself a detective?" He'd obviously forgotten that Sano wasn't one anymore.

"I've had to fit my inquiries in between my duties as Chief Rebuilding Magistrate."

"Those duties aren't as important as finding out who killed my daughter and, ahh, protecting me." The shogun pointed his finger at Sano. "You will, ahh, dedicate yourself to your investigation until the murderer is caught."

"Yes, Your Excellency." Sano bowed, rose, and escaped before the shogun could tack a threat onto his order.

That he now had time and official sanction for his investigation was a mixed blessing. Duty to the shogun put him further at odds with Yanagisawa, who wouldn't let the fact that their lord wanted the investigation prevent him from trying to stop it. And if Sano couldn't solve the murder, he would be put to death regardless of what happened with Yanagisawa.

HIRATA AND DEGUCHI sat by the canal, holding hands like lovers while Deguchi told his tale. *When I was eight years old, my parents died. I lived on the streets. I ate garbage. I begged. Sometimes I went with men. They would have sex with me and pay me a few coppers.*

Hirata remembered Tahara telling him that Deguchi had been an orphan and child prostitute. Tahara had lied about many things, but at least this was apparently true.

Some of the men liked to hurt me. Ienobu was one of those.

Hirata was surprised. "I've never heard that Ienobu has sex with boys."

He keeps it secret. He doesn't want people to know he's like his uncle the shogun. He wants them to think he's pure and noble. Disdain turned the voice in Hirata's head into acid. *I've been spying on him. He travels in a closed palanquin, to inns outside town. His valet is there with a boy for him. That's what happened to me. A man picked me up on the street and left me in a room at an inn. Then Ienobu came. He beat me and choked me while he raped me.*

Anger burned in Deguchi's eyes. Hirata felt his hand trembling. *When he finished, I was bruised and covered with blood. I hurt so much I couldn't move. Ienobu left. His valet dumped me in an alley. He thought I was dead. But I managed to stand up. I started walking. I kept going until I reached Zōjō Temple. Then I collapsed. The priests took me in. They nursed me until I was well. I became a novice. I had food and clothes and an education and a place to live. But I couldn't forget the men who'd hurt me. I swore that someday I would kill them. But I didn't know how I would do it. Until one day when an itinerant priest and his disciple came to visit. It was Ozuno and Tahara.*

So this was how and where the seeds for the secret society had been planted. The canal, the ruins, and the hot sun faded from Hirata's consciousness as he listened in fascination.

Ozuno gave a martial arts lesson for the novices. I was the best pupil. He invited me to go with him and Tahara. I was twelve. He said he would turn me into a great fighter. And I saw that if I went, I could learn everything I needed.

He and Deguchi had both had personal reasons for studying the mystic martial arts, Hirata realized. He'd wanted to recover his strength after his injury; Deguchi had wanted the skills for murder.

At first Tahara was jealous because he had to share Ozuno with me, but we became friends. I studied with Ozuno for six years. Then I left to wander the country and practice my skills. Tahara had already gone by that time. After a while I came back to Edo. I became a priest. And I went looking for those men. One was a rich moneylender. I climbed in his window at night while he was sleeping, and I strangled him.

The voice in Hirata's head was chillingly matter-of-fact as it described four other murders Deguchi had committed. Deguchi apparently saw no conflict between his actions and the Buddhist prohibition against taking lives.

In the meantime, I met up with Tahara again. We met Kitano. He'd studied with Ozuno before we started. A few years later we formed the secret society. Deguchi turned to Hirata. *You know most of what happened next.*

"Why didn't you kill Ienobu first?" Hirata asked.

I couldn't find him. I didn't know his name. I didn't see him until after the earthquake. I was at the castle for a religious ceremony, and there he was, the shogun's nephew.

"By then you'd sworn to put the secret society ahead of everything else. You'd agreed to help the ghost make Ienobu the next shogun." Hirata was stunned by Deguchi's dilemma, which he'd never imagined. "If you killed him, you would be breaking your oath to the society."

Deguchi's expression was obstinate. *I swore revenge on him before the secret society was formed.*

Hirata saw that he and Deguchi both had preexisting commitments from before they'd joined the society. Hirata's was his loyalty to Sano; Deguchi's, to the wounded child he'd been.

"How were you supposed to get away with killing Ienobu?" Hirata asked. "Didn't you think Tahara and Kitano would find out?"

Deguchi shrugged. *They trust me.*

"When they heard how Ienobu died, wouldn't they have suspected you?"

I threw a bullet at him. He'd have looked like he'd been shot. It even made a noise like a gun. Things do when they move faster than sound travels. Tahara and Kitano wouldn't have connected his death with me.

"You had everything figured out, didn't you?"

Not everything. Deguchi looked mournful. *General Otani will know what I just did. Nothing can be hidden from him. I wish Tahara and Kitano and I had never killed Ozuno and stolen the magic spell book! I don't want to follow a ghost's orders anymore!* The passion in his words burned Hirata's mind with a sizzle of nerve impulses. *Tahara and Kitano used to be my best friends, but they changed. All they want is to learn new powers. They care more about pleasing the ghost than they care about me!* Hirata saw the lonely orphan in Deguchi, angry because his friends had let him down. *I wish I could get out of the secret society. If they find out I'm going against them, they'll kill me. Or Otani will, the next time I go into a trance.*

It was the same punishment with which the ghost had threatened Hirata.

That's the price I'll pay for revenge on Ienobu. My own life. Deguchi gave Hirata a quizzical look. *Why were you following me?*

"When I went into a trance during the ritual, General Otani ordered me to kill you."

Deguchi flung Hirata's hand away from him. Shock and fear were written on his face.

"Wait! I'm not going to do it!" Hirata saw a solution to his problems—and Deguchi's. "I think we can help each other."

Warily hopeful, Deguchi gestured for Hirata to explain. Hirata said, "I don't want to be a slave to a ghost, either. I want to get out of the society, too. I decided I had to kill the other members. Someone had to be first. That was you. But now I don't have to kill you." Happier than he'd been in ages, Hirata extended his hand to Deguchi. "Let's team up together. We'll kill Tahara and Kitano before they can kill us."

Deguchi stared at Hirata's hand as if it were a blade that would slice him. Hirata knew that asking him to turn on his friends was asking a lot of Deguchi. And they both knew that killing Tahara and Kitano would be no easy task.

"It's the only way we'll ever be free," Hirata said.

A long moment passed. Hirata exerted all the force of his mental powers, willing Deguchi to see reason. In the distance, a temple bell tolled the hour. Then, with an air of resignation, Deguchi grasped Hirata's hand. *How would we get rid of General Otani?*

An iron band around Hirata's heart loosened. He wanted to jump up and down and laugh with exultation. He had an ally against Tahara and Kitano! But it was too early to celebrate.

"We burn the magic book so that no one can learn the rituals and General Otani's ghost can never come back," Hirata said.

That's not good enough. Ozuno said there are other copies of the book. Somebody else could summon the ghost. Who knows, it could come after us. Before we destroy the book, we have to learn the reverse spell that sends the ghost back to the world of the dead forever.

"Then that's what we'll do."

Together they would vanquish Tahara, Kitano, and the ghost. Before his five days were up, Hirata would be free. He could reclaim his honor and his rightful place at Sano's side.

23

AS SANO WAS leaving the palace, a page came up to him, said, "Here's a message," and handed him a scroll container.

Sano opened it and unfurled the scroll. He read calligraphy as crooked as the man who'd written it: "Please meet me at the forest preserve, to discuss a matter of urgent importance to both of us. Ienobu."

The forest preserve was a carefully maintained wilderness inside Edo Castle. In the early days after the earthquake, Sano had once gone to the preserve to escape the devastation and have a solitary rest from his constant toil. He'd found it overrun by other men there for the same purpose and servants sawing up fallen trees for firewood. Now the preserve was quiet, the foliage golden green where the late afternoon sun shone on it and black under the clouds. The only blight was Ienobu and two bodyguards, seated on a blanket spread on the grass, amid empty lacquer lunch boxes, below a canopy.

"I had a bet with myself that you would get here by the time we finished our picnic," Ienobu said as Sano approached. The guards went to stand by the gate in the wall that surrounded the preserve, within clear sight of Ienobu and Sano but out of earshot. Ienobu extended his gnarled hand to Sano. "Please, join me."

Sano knelt under the canopy. He and Ienobu exchanged bows.

"Did you have a good talk with my uncle?" Ienobu asked.

At first Sano was surprised that Ienobu knew he'd seen the shogun;

then enlightenment struck. "It was you who told him I'm investigating Tsuruhime's death."

Ienobu grinned; his lips pulled farther back from his teeth. "Very astute of you."

"You suggested that the shogun should ask me why I'm investigating," Sano deduced. "You sent a page to waylay me outside the palace after I left."

Ienobu nodded.

"How did you manage to get to your uncle? You were banned from court."

"Oh, I still have friends inside the castle. They sneaked me into the palace. My uncle was a bit reluctant to see me, but when I told him that you're investigating his daughter's death, he listened."

"How do you know I am?" Sano asked.

"I have friends in Lord Tsunanori's estate. They said you'd been asking questions."

"Who are they?"

Ienobu touched his finger to his lips. "A wise man repays favors with discretion."

Sano had an image of an octopus with Ienobu's face, sitting in a dark, underwater cave, its long tentacles rippling outward, their suction cups attaching to anything or anyone it thought useful. "Why did you tell the shogun?"

"I think he deserves to know what's going on behind his back," Ienobu said with a sanctimonious air.

"Forgive me if I don't believe you're that altruistic. Are you using me to attack Yanagisawa and Yoshisato? It would please you to have the shogun suspect them of killing his daughter."

Ienobu laughed, a wheezy sound like stiff leather bellows pumping. "I can't put anything over on you, can I, Sano-*san*?"

"Not when it's obvious that you'd like Yoshisato to fall out of favor with the shogun so you can inherit the dictatorship. How did you know Yoshisato and Yanagisawa are suspects?"

"I figured you wouldn't have convinced yourself that Tsuruhime was murdered and run a secret inquiry, except to get at them."

Sano wondered whether Ienobu knew about Lady Nobuko, Korika, and the infected sheet. He didn't ask lest he give away information that Ienobu would put to bad use. "I didn't tell the shogun that they're suspects."

Ienobu frowned in disappointment but said, "It's just as well. No use throwing around accusations until you can make them stick."

Disconcerted, Sano said, "How do you know I haven't found any proof that Yanagisawa or Yoshisato is guilty? Do you have 'friends' in my house, too?"

Ienobu repeated his wheezy laugh. "Don't worry. I simply figured that if you had, they would have been charged with murder already."

Sano wasn't reassured; Ienobu hadn't denied spying on him. "Why did you want to see me? Just to find out what the shogun said?"

"Let's start with that."

"He ordered me to take time off from my other duties and catch the killer. What's the 'important matter' that you mentioned in your message?"

Ienobu brought his fingertips together, as if collecting his thoughts between them. Sano was struck by the difference between Ienobu and Yanagisawa. Since that day when Ienobu had been thrown out of the court, Yanagisawa had grown reckless, taken over by his emotions; Ienobu had cooled down. Once Sano had thought Ienobu didn't stand a chance against Yanagisawa. Now he wasn't so sure.

"Suppose you manage to incriminate Yanagisawa and Yoshisato," Ienobu said. "Maybe that will take them out of the picture; maybe not. Yanagisawa is good at getting around the shogun. He's also good at covering his tracks. It's probable that you'll fail to pin the murder on Yanagisawa, and he and Yoshisato will go on their merry way toward ruling Japan. In that case, what would you do?"

Downcast by the bleak scenario Ienobu described, Sano was silent. He thought it better not to disclose his intention—destroying Yanagisawa—to a man he distrusted more and more as time went on.

Ienobu smiled with satisfaction, as if he'd divined Sano's thoughts and Sano had played into his hands. "Here's what I wanted to discuss: I'm going to make you a proposition."

I'm attracting propositions like spilled honey attracts flies, Sano thought. "What is it?"

"Join forces with me." The mocking humor fell away from Ienobu. His voice turned rough, urgent. "I help you destroy Yanagisawa and his bastard. Then you support my bid for the succession."

Sano was still conflicted about destroying Yoshisato, but the prospect of help with Yanagisawa was alluring. Sano hadn't realized until this moment how isolated and vulnerable he felt, how exhausted from fourteen years of battling Yanagisawa and never gaining any permanent ground. All of a sudden Ienobu didn't seem so repulsive. Nor did the idea of Ienobu as the next shogun.

"Destroy them, how?" Sano asked.

"I have friends, remember. They'll supply evidence that Yanagisawa murdered the shogun's daughter. All you have to do is pretend to find it. They'll pressure Yanagisawa's allies to change sides. We'll try him for murder and convict him. The shogun will have to put him to death or lose face. And once Yanagisawa is gone, Yoshisato will be a lamb among wolves." His teeth glistened with saliva in his grin.

Sano knew he should be revolted by this scheme. "That's fighting dirty." But somehow he wasn't, and protecting Yoshisato suddenly seemed less important than a chance at a permanent victory over Yanagisawa.

Ienobu's hunched shoulders rose in a shrug. "No dirtier than Yanagisawa fights. If you want to win this war, you have to be willing to roll in the mud. Are you?"

"WHAT DID YOU say to Ienobu?" Reiko asked Sano at dinner that night, after he'd told her and Masahiro about the proposition.

"The same thing I said to Yoshisato. That I would think it over."

Reiko was so surprised she almost dropped her rice bowl. "You're not serious?"

"I am." Sano's face was drawn with fatigue and unhappiness. "You'll have noticed that I'm not exactly in a position to turn away potential allies. By the way, I had a confrontation with Yanagisawa and Yoshisato. They may not see eye to eye on how to run the government, but it's in their mutual interest to destroy me before I can prove that one or both of them murdered the shogun's daughter."

"But Ienobu is essentially offering to help you frame Yanagisawa."

"If Yanagisawa is guilty, which I believe he is, what does it matter how I go about delivering him to justice?" Sano said with a bitter twist of his mouth. "Genuine evidence hasn't been as plentiful as ruined houses after the earthquake. Fake evidence may have to suffice."

Reiko was frightened by his cynicism, which was so unlike him. Had his constant struggle to survive in the cutthroat world of politics finally changed the husband she loved into a stranger willing to compromise his principles?

"Father, how can you say that?" Masahiro asked. "I hate Yanagisawa, too, but it would be dishonorable to frame him." Reiko saw that he, too, was afraid Sano had changed. "And you've always taught me that honor is more important than anything else."

Sano responded with a wry smile, ashamed of his own blasphemous words yet proud of Masahiro for setting him straight. "Of course it is. I would never want to do what Ienobu suggested. I just had to argue in favor of it and hear how bad it sounded."

Masahiro sighed with relief, but Reiko's fear lingered. When put under enough pressure, anyone could be corrupted, even Sano. She hated seeing him pushed toward decisions he wouldn't ordinarily make.

"It's odd," Sano said thoughtfully. "When Ienobu was telling me his proposition, it sounded perfectly reasonable, somehow. It was as if he understood what I wanted, and when he offered to help me get it, I was blind to the reasons why it was bad. I could almost taste the reasons why it was good. Does that make any sense?"

"No," Reiko said, puzzled. "Of course Ienobu knows you'd like to defeat Yanagisawa. Everybody does. You've had other chances to compromise your honor for the sake of political gain and refused them. Why jump at this one?"

"Maybe because I realized that honor probably won't win my battle against Yanagisawa. I can't explain it. Ienobu had a strange effect on me."

"Ienobu has an effect, all right. Being around him feels like touching a slug." Masahiro made a disgusted face.

Reiko laughed, protesting, "You shouldn't say that about the shogun's nephew."

"I feel like that about him, too," Sano confessed. "And that's another reason I didn't accept Ienobu's proposition, aside from the fact that it's dishonorable. Because a samurai shouldn't make deals with people he instinctively dislikes and distrusts." He bent a stern, affectionate look on Masahiro. "If I ever forget that, be sure to remind me."

But Sano hadn't exactly said he was going to turn down Ienobu's proposition. Mixed feelings troubled Reiko. On the one hand, she didn't want Sano entering a dishonorable alliance. On the other, her family needed any port in a storm. "What will Ienobu do if you refuse?"

"He won't say 'no hard feelings' and let me go about my business. He said that if I'm not with him, I'm against him. Meaning, he and his allies will run me out of the regime. Unless Yanagisawa does it first."

These consequences were as bad as Reiko had thought. "Exactly who are his allies?"

"Several major *daimyo* clans," Sano said. "They're Tokugawa hereditary allies, who are enemies of Yanagisawa. Their combined armies have hundreds of thousands of troops."

"Who are our allies?" Masahiro asked.

Sano was silent. Reiko and Masahiro already knew the disheartening answer: There was no one powerful whom they could rely on to fight for them. Sano said ruefully, "Remember, Ienobu's proposition isn't the only one in front of me. There's Yoshisato's."

"You're still considering it?" Reiko asked in surprise.

"Being around him isn't like touching a slug," Sano said. He and Masahiro smiled at each other.

Reiko frowned. Yoshisato was coming between her and Sano again. "I don't understand your attachment to Yoshisato."

"You would if you met him."

"Does he have an effect on you, too?"

"Not like Ienobu's. Yoshisato gives the impression of honor and integrity."

" 'Honor and integrity'? I think he conspired to murder Tsuruhime," Reiko said, frustrated by Sano's bias.

"I don't think he did," Sano said, frustrated by her lack of understanding. "Yanagisawa could have had Tsuruhime killed without Yoshisato's knowledge. And I don't think that either Yanagisawa or Yoshisato knew Tsuruhime was pregnant."

"I'm afraid I have evidence against Yoshisato." Reiko was reluctant to fuel her conflict with Sano, but she had to tell him what had happened. "Lady Someko came to see me today."

Sano almost choked on a mouthful of grilled prawn. Coughing, he said, "I'd thought you had a better chance of getting a visit from the Buddha."

"So did I." Reiko summarized her conversation with Lady Someko. "Yoshisato's own mother suspects him of murder. You shouldn't keep making excuses for him."

"You're right," Sano said, vexed by her insistence yet chastened. "I shouldn't accept his proposition, either."

But he didn't say he wasn't going to, Reiko noticed. And she was glad of that, in spite of herself. Yoshisato represented another port in the storm.

"If you turn down Yoshisato and Ienobu, where does that leave us?" Masahiro asked.

"Out in the cold and wide open to attack," Sano said with brutal frankness.

Reiko crossed her arms over the baby. "What are we going to do?"

"Continue with the investigation. Keep trying to prove Yanagisawa is guilty. Let whatever happens, happen." Sano added, in a brighter tone, "There's good news. Ienobu told the shogun about the investigation. The shogun made it official. I won't have to sneak around or fit it in between my duties as Chief Rebuilding Magistrate."

"Thank the gods for that, at least," Reiko said. "What's the next step?"

"Tomorrow I'll pay another visit to Lord Tsunanori. I'll take troops from the army. He can't refuse to talk or let me interrogate his people this time." Sano's mood darkened. "I'll find out whether he knew his wife was pregnant by another man. I hope he didn't and I can clear his name. Because if he killed his wife and Yanagisawa had nothing to do with her murder . . ."

Despair encroached on Reiko's own hopes. "Then we've lost our chance to defeat Yanagisawa."

24

IN THE HEIR'S residence, Yoshisato prepared for bed. For most of his life he'd liked daytime best, preferring sunlight to darkness, but since he'd come to court, late night was his favorite time. Nobody made demands on him. He didn't have to play up to the shogun or worry about people thinking he was a fraud. Best of all, he didn't have to deal with Yanagisawa.

Now it was near midnight. Fresh from a hot bath, dressed in a cotton robe, Yoshisato sat on the floor of his chamber and did stretching exercises. When his muscles released their tension, he could sleep before facing another day as the future dictator of Japan. Yoshisato pretended he was back in his old home, with nothing more difficult to look forward to in the morning than martial arts lessons. He yearned for the peace he would probably never have again.

A light tapping rattled the door. It slid open. Yoshisato frowned at Lady Someko, who stood at the threshold. "Mother. What are you doing here?"

Lady Someko glided into the room. Her face wore the expression that it usually did when she looked at him—fond, worried. "I wanted to see if you were all right."

"I'm fine," Yoshisato said curtly as he stretched his arms over his head and leaned sideways. "I'm just about to go to bed."

Instead of taking the hint, she knelt near him. "It's been a long time since we had a chance to talk, just the two of us."

Yoshisato loved her dearly, but he hated having his only private time interrupted. "What do you want?"

She gathered the folds of her brown cloak around her red-orange kimono. She looked anxious and unhappy. Yoshisato recalled the day when he'd been eight years old and he'd begged her to ask his father to come to his first sword-fighting tournament. She'd had to tell him that Yanagisawa wouldn't come. Her manner was the same now.

"I want you to stop pretending to be the shogun's son," she said.

Yoshisato was astonished, and not just because she was asking the impossible. "I thought you thought it was a good idea."

"I did when Yanagisawa proposed it. He said it was the only way to save your life."

Five months ago, Ienobu had devised a scheme to have Yoshisato put to death. Yanagisawa had countered by passing Yoshisato off as the shogun's son. Yoshisato said, "It worked, didn't it?"

Lady Someko shook her head. The ornaments in her hair jangled. "He convinced me that it would give you a chance to become as important as you deserve to be." Her eyes shone with her hope and love for Yoshisato. "You would rule Japan someday! Of course I went along with him."

"Of course. You always do." Yoshisato tasted bitter rancor. "You hate him, but you make love to him. How can you let him touch you?"

They'd never discussed her relationship with Yanagisawa. Shame clouded Lady Someko's face as she realized that Yoshisato had heard her with Yanagisawa, during the time they'd all lived together in the palace guesthouse. Yoshisato had been glad to escape the sound of their passionate, violent sex.

"That's none of your business," she snapped, pulling the cloak tighter around herself. "Don't change the subject."

"All right." Yoshisato didn't really want to talk about her and his father. He hated the fact that she and Yanagisawa had come together again, after seventeen years, because of him. He told himself that if she let Yanagisawa degrade her, it was her own fault. But he couldn't help thinking that if he'd never been born, she wouldn't be a slave to Yanagisawa. "Why have you changed your mind about me pretending to be the shogun's son?"

"Because it's dangerous."

"You knew that at the start. Yanagisawa warned us that there were people who wouldn't believe the shogun was my father."

"I didn't know anybody was going to die!"

"Do you mean Tsuruhime? She died of smallpox. She would have, even if Yanagisawa had never thought up his idea, even if I'd never come to court."

Lady Someko regarded him with disbelief. After a moment's pause she said, "You never told me you went to visit Tsuruhime."

A trickle of fear chilled Yoshisato's heart. Sano wasn't the only person who suspected him of murdering the shogun's daughter. His own mother apparently did, too. "Why should I have? I don't tell you everything."

"But you used to." She smiled, sorrowfully nostalgic for their small, private world.

"I'm grown up now." Yoshisato hid his fear behind impatience. "Things are different."

Leaning closer, Lady Someko said, "What do you and Yanagisawa talk about, during all those hours you spend alone together? What has he been teaching you?"

"He hasn't been teaching me to murder people. Nor convincing me that I should get rid of anyone who might interfere with my becoming the next shogun." Yoshisato spoke sarcastically, concealing the fact that Yanagisawa's tutelage had covered those very topics.

Her stricken expression said that Lady Someko saw through his lies. "I knew he would be a bad influence. Damn him! I wish he'd never come back!"

"Oh, Mother," Yoshisato said, irritated because she thought he was so malleable. "Just because he has a spell on you, doesn't mean he has one on me."

Lady Someko averted her gaze. "Why did you go to visit Tsuruhime?"

"To pay my respects to my half sister. How do you know I went?"

"Lady Reiko told me."

Yoshisato started. "You talked to her? Why?"

"I heard that her husband is investigating Tsuruhime's death. I had to find out what he's discovered. Nobody I know can tell me anything except rumors."

"Yanagisawa won't like it." Yoshisato was glad she'd defied him in at least this one matter, yet dismayed. "He doesn't want you speaking to anyone, let alone Sano's wife."

"What can he do to me? Kill me?" Lady Someko said scornfully. "No, he needs me alive, to say I slept with the shogun and conceived you."

"He'll punish you some other way." Yoshisato had seen bruises on her, after her nights with Yanagisawa.

"That's my problem. Why didn't you tell me you went to see Tsuruhime?"

Yoshisato could see how badly she wanted him to convince her that he wasn't responsible for Tsuruhime's death. "I didn't think it was important. I probably wouldn't have kept up an acquaintance with her. I forgot about it until Sano mentioned it."

With each reason, Lady Someko looked less convinced and more despairing. "If I were Sano, I wouldn't believe your feeble excuses."

"Then it's a good thing you're not him! I seem to have a better chance of convincing my enemies than my own mother!" Yoshisato rose and glared down at her. "Do you really think I'm capable of murder?"

She stood; her anger matched his. "I don't know. I don't know you anymore!"

"Well, I'm not," he said, hurt by her lack of faith in him. "I didn't infect Tsuruhime with smallpox. I'm telling you, and I've already told Sano. What more can I do?"

"Quit pretending. Tell the shogun you're not his son." She was breathless with urgency. "I'll say that I made a mistake, that I got the dates wrong, that you were conceived before I slept with him. He'll disinherit you."

Yoshisato stared, flabbergasted. "What good is that supposed to do?"

"You won't be a target for Yanagisawa's enemies." Lady Someko eagerly grabbed his arm. "Sano will leave you alone. Don't you see?"

"I see that you're not thinking straight," Yoshisato said as he shook off her hand. She didn't understand Sano any better than Yanagisawa did. "If Sano thinks I killed the shogun's daughter, he'll never let it go. And what do you think the shogun will do if you say you made a mistake about my being his son? He'll say, 'Fine, good-bye and, ahh, good riddance'?" Yoshisato laughed in derision. "No—he'll be furious. All these years he's been wishing for an heir, and you give him one, and then you take him away? It won't matter then whether I'm innocent or guilty of murdering Tsuruhime. The shogun will put me to death, and you, too!"

Lady Someko listened with stunned comprehension. "You don't want to quit. You want to be the next shogun and rule Japan, no matter what the risk or the cost." She backed away from him, hobbling as if he'd dealt her a physical blow. "You *are* like Yanagisawa."

"No!" Yoshisato shouted. "Never say that!"

He involuntarily raised his hand. She gasped, burst into tears, and rushed out of the room.

Guilty and ashamed because she'd thought he was going to strike her—and he almost had—Yoshisato staggered to the bed. He lay on his back, arms and legs spread, buffeted by a storm of tumultuous feelings. He hated Yanagisawa, didn't want to be like him. Yanagisawa had hurt his mother, belittled Yoshisato himself. His father was a corrupt, dishonorable man. And yet . . .

Saving his life wasn't the only reason Yoshisato had agreed to the audacious plot to take over the regime. For as long as he could remember, his father's absence had felt like a big, raw hole in his spirit. His father had visited him exactly once, soon after his birth, his mother had said. It was strange that he could miss someone he couldn't remember, but he did. As a lonely child he'd dreamed that someday his father would come for him, and they would have wonderful adventures together. He'd eventually learned, by listening to his guards talk, that Yanagisawa was a powerful politician, feared for his cruelty. He'd realized that Yanagisawa didn't care about him and wasn't coming. He'd decided to hate Yanagisawa. But when Yanagisawa had unexpectedly shown up many years later, Yoshisato discovered that the hole had never healed. Although he constantly rebelled against Yanagisawa, punishing him for his neglect, Yoshisato loved him and craved his approval.

If he became the next shogun, maybe his father would love him in return.

But as Yoshisato reflected on his own motives, he knew they weren't as pure as a son's wish to please his father. He wanted to be shogun. He wanted to try his hand at ruling Japan. And he wouldn't say no to the power of life and death over everyone.

Maybe he *was* like Yanagisawa.

The idea terrified him. The stress of carrying on a charade, of bracing for attacks from his enemies, of resisting Yanagisawa's influence, seemed unbearable. But it was too late to quit. And although he wanted to kill Yanagisawa for hurting his mother and belittling himself, he couldn't. Yanagisawa was right—they needed each other. They were locked in a bond of love, hatred, and conspiracy.

Yoshisato prayed that he could build the coalition he'd mentioned to Sano. It was his only hope of countering Yanagisawa, of living long enough to become shogun and of keeping the regime under his control when he did. Such a fragile straw to grasp! Yoshisato wanted to curl up under the quilt and cry; he felt so young and helpless and alone.

Instead he laid his hands on his diaphragm, closed his eyes, and began a deep-breathing meditation. After a lengthy struggle to banish his troubling thoughts, he began to feel calmer, drowsy.

Sudden noises jarred him. His eyes snapped open. He heard stealthy footsteps and muffled cries from outside.

WIND SWIRLED AROUND the black hulk of Edo Castle. Jagged clouds raced across the night sky, sliced the moon. The trees around the heir's residence swayed and rustled. Under the building, smoke wafted out from the lattice that enclosed the foundations. The diamond-shaped spaces between the lattice's wooden slats glowed orange with firelight. Footsteps pelted the ground as a shadowy figure fled into the darkness.

25

A LOUD, INSISTENT clanging awakened Sano. The smell of smoke invaded his drowsy consciousness. He and Reiko bolted upright.

"That's the fire bell," Reiko exclaimed. She scrambled out of bed and ran to the door, calling, "Masahiro! Akiko!"

Sano was already up, flinging open the cabinet. He pulled out leather fire gear, threw Reiko hers, then put on his own.

"Fire! Fire!" Masahiro and Akiko shouted as they ran into the room.

They were already dressed in their fire gear—long capes, hoods with visors and face shields, and knee-high boots. Fires were the most dreaded natural disaster, common in Edo. Fires that had started during the earthquake had caused much of the damage. Everyone was prepared, including children. Sano heard guards and servants shouting. He sent his family to join the stampede from the mansion while he made sure nobody was left inside. When the mansion was evacuated, he met Detective Marume on the veranda.

"The fire's up there." Marume pointed.

On the second highest tier of the castle, the western fortress was engulfed in smoke that glowed with a terrible orange radiance and billowed up the hill. The bell clanged continuously. Shouts and running footsteps echoed through the castle as the fire brigades mobilized. Ash drifted. Airborne cinders glinted like fireflies.

"It's the heir's residence," Sano said.

He organized one team of men to go with him to help put out the fire, and another to protect the estate. Reiko called, "Be careful!" as Sano, Marume, Masahiro, and their team rushed out the gate.

The passage was crowded with troops clad in fire gear, speeding uphill to rescue the shogun's heir. They carried buckets and hatchets, and long poles with a hook on the end. Sano's party joined the rush. When they arrived in the walled compound, the residence was a mass of roaring, crackling flames. Smoke billowed from windows. Tiles spewed from the roof like missiles. Smaller fires kindled in trees, bushes, and grass. The compound was full of people milling around, watching the inferno.

"Why aren't they putting it out?" Masahiro asked, only his eyes visible between the visor and face shield of his leather hood.

Sano and Marume pushed their way through the crowd. "What's wrong?" Sano shouted over the noise of the clanging bell.

"The well is plugged," someone said. "There's no water."

"Damn it to hell!" Marume said.

Sano ran to the residence and accosted a fireman. "Did Yoshisato get out?" he asked.

"We haven't seen him. The house was in full blaze when we got here. He must still be inside."

Sano's heart sank. It didn't matter that Yoshisato was a fraud and the son of his enemy. Yoshisato was a human being whose life was in danger. Lowering his visor over his eyes, pulling on leather gloves from the pocket of his cape, Sano ran to the entrance. Fireman armed with hooked poles had pulled off the door. They shouted, "Don't go in there!"

Beyond the doorway, flames licked the corridor. Pillars toppled; walls caved in. Smoke and heat blasted Sano. He leaped backward. Desperate to save Yoshisato, he ran back to the well to see if he could help unplug it. Four firemen bent over the circular, stone-rimmed hole in the ground. A head emerged from the well. The fireman pulled their comrade up. He came out hauling a large, drenched white quilt. "This was down there."

Someone had deliberately plugged the well. Sano had no time to wonder who or why. Men quickly formed lines between the well and the residence. Sano, Marume, and Masahiro took their places. Filled buckets passed from hands to hands. The men at the front of the lines flung water on the burning building. The water sizzled in the flames. Steam hissed in smoke. Empty buckets moved back down the line and full ones moved up in an endless cycle. Marume looked as if he could work forever, but Sano was sweating under his leather garments. His arms began to ache. He and Masahiro had to step out of the line; others took their places. The inferno raged on. The roof collapsed with a mighty crash and a fountain of embers. Firemen began pulling the structure down, hacking it apart. The bell stopped clanging as the flames died.

Sano's ears rang in the sudden quiet. Everyone stood still, exhausted and speechless, gazing at the ruins. Wisps of steamy smoke rose from piles of blackened timbers. Cinders still glimmered. The grounds were awash in soot-blackened puddles, the air acrid with smoke.

The fire brigade captain and his assistants waded into the ruins to look for survivors. Marume muttered, "There can't be anyone alive in there."

Although Sano thought the same, he joined the search. Tossing aside beams, planks, and tiles that were still hot, he found the first body. It was burned black. The bones showed through scraps of flesh. In the abdominal cavity, organs had cooked into a foul mass. Eye sockets gaped in the skull; teeth were exposed in a horrible grin. A wave of nausea assailed Sano. He sucked air under the face shield of his mask. He gagged on the smell of charred meat.

Firemen called out as they found other bodies. There were four total. The captain said, "Yoshisato lived here with three bodyguards. This is everybody."

Silence descended on the compound. The wind keened, blowing ash on the rescuers, who bowed their heads in despair. Sano thought of Yoshisato at the martial arts tournament, so alive and agile and idealistic. He wouldn't have to decide whether to accept Yoshisato's proposition. Yoshisato would never build the coalition he'd described.

Sano's wish had been granted in dreadful fashion. Yoshisato wasn't going to be shogun.

Although glad that the regime was safe from fraud, Sano was also horrified. He would rather have Yoshisato be shogun than die so terribly. He grieved for the youth he'd liked and respected in spite of himself. He wished with all his might that events had taken a different turn.

Where was Yanagisawa?

At this moment Sano couldn't be glad that Yanagisawa had just lost his hold on the regime. A father himself, he couldn't rejoice in another father's losing a child, no matter that Yanagisawa was his enemy or that Yanagisawa had given his son over to the shogun.

The firemen stood talking amid the ruins. "Why didn't the night guard notice the fire and get everybody out?" "How did it burn the house so fast?" "Did somebody just happen to throw a quilt down the well tonight?"

An awful suspicion sent Sano running to the firemen. Marume and Masahiro joined him. Sano said, "Do you think the fire wasn't an accident?"

The captain said somberly, "It looks like arson."

Sano, Marume, and Masahiro exchanged alarmed glances. If it was arson, Yoshisato's death was murder. The repercussions would be enormous.

Sano looked around. The men in the crowd had removed their hoods. Their sweaty faces were visible in the light of dawn. Sano recognized army officers and castle functionaries; no one outranked him. The higher officials had probably stayed away from the fire because they didn't want to risk their lives or be held responsible if Yoshisato died. Sano was in charge.

"Before you tell the shogun the fire was arson, we need evidence," he told the captains. "You look for witnesses. I'll search the area."

The captain headed toward the crowd. Sano began exploring the grounds with Marume and Masahiro. "What are we looking for?" Masahiro asked

"Anything that doesn't belong," Marume said.

Sano searched the singed bushes near the ruins. From under the third bush he pulled out a metal basket, the kind used to hold coals for lighting tobacco pipes. The basket was empty, the inside coated with ash. Sano also retrieved an empty brown ceramic jar and a bundle of rags. He sniffed them. They smelled of kerosene.

He'd often been ecstatic to find clues during murder investigations. Now he couldn't have been more disturbed as he gathered up the basket, jar, and rags to show the fire brigade captain.

"Yoshisato! Where is he?" Yanagisawa shouted, barreling through the gate with a squadron of troops. His lavishly patterned silk robes were a colorful, glaring contrast to the bleak scene. When he saw the burned wreckage, he stumbled to a halt. Terror blanched his face. "What happened?"

NO ONE ANSWERED. Yanagisawa saw men in fire capes staring at him. Their features were carved in lines of exhaustion and despair. Yanagisawa roamed through the crowd, searching.

"Yoshisato! Yoshisato!" he cried with increasing urgency.

Only the echo of his own voice replied. He read the terrible news in the other men's eyes. He staggered toward the ruins, his high-soled sandals slipping in puddles. Grief began to rise in his spirit, like a tidal wave forming under water when a volcano explodes the ocean floor. He clambered among charred boards that tore at his robes. The night was eerily quiet. The wind had died down. The crowd watched him in silence. He almost stepped on the first corpse.

He screamed as he reeled away from the grinning, broken skeleton covered with blackened flesh. Crawling over broken tiles that cut his hands and knees, he found three more burned, curled-up bodies. None were recognizable. None even looked human. Yanagisawa desperately resisted believing that one was Yoshisato, but his mind did the dire calculation. Four corpses. Yoshisato and his bodyguards. They were all accounted for. Yoshisato was dead.

A dizzying, crushing sensation came over Yanagisawa as he knelt amid the wreckage. Fifteen months ago, Yoritomo had died a violent death. Tonight so had Yoshisato. Yanagisawa had already lost one son. Now he'd lost another, his better chance at complete domination over the regime. His hope of ruling Japan through Yoshisato had gone up in the smoke he'd seen while riding back to Edo Castle. But the demise of that hope seemed trivial. The anguish that flooded him was all for Yoshisato.

His insolent, contrary, tough-minded son!

His son that he loved despite Yoshisato's efforts to punish and alienate him, despite his knowledge that love made him vulnerable.

Yanagisawa hadn't thought that anything could hurt as much as

Yoritomo's death, which had dropped him into an abyss of mourning. But Yoshisato's death was the greater tragedy. The sweet, obedient, devoted Yoritomo was nothing compared to Yoshisato. Yoshisato was special. He could have been a great man someday. Wracked by grief, Yanagisawa wept.

He could never make peace with Yoshisato. Yoshisato had died hating him.

Each sob tore a bleeding gash in Yanagisawa's viscera. He didn't care who saw. He cursed himself. If only he hadn't gone to that banquet tonight, to socialize with his allies, to strengthen their political support. If only he'd persuaded Yoshisato to come with him! But Yoshisato had insisted on being left alone at night. If only Yanagisawa hadn't let him be! How he wished he'd been here to protect Yoshisato!

The thought of his own culpability was too agonizing to bear. Yanagisawa also couldn't bear to think that Yoshisato or his guards had carelessly left a lamp burning too close to a paper wall, that Yoshisato was a victim of a stupid accident.

Yanagisawa stood, glaring at the men in the crowd. "Who let this happen?"

No reply came. Yanagisawa smelled fear, as pungent as the smoke in the air. His sobs stopped as his instincts whispered that when a controversial person died violently, assassination was a likely cause. Yanagisawa wiped his eyes with his sleeve. His gaze skipped over face after face, then stopped at three people standing together by a bush.

Sano, with his bodyguard Marume and his son, Masahiro.

Yanagisawa beheld Sano as if through a scrim of leaping flames. He stalked toward the trio. Sano and Marume stepped forward, their expressions wary.

"What are *you* doing here?" Yanagisawa said, his voice thick with hatred.

"We came to help put out the fire," Sano said, "but it was too late. I'm sorry."

"How dare you pretend you're sorry Yoshisato is dead?" Yanagisawa didn't give Sano time to answer. "What's that in your hands?"

Looking down at the objects he held, Sano seemed surprised, as if he'd forgotten them. The crowd waited. The silence was so complete,

Yanagisawa heard faint, distant shouts and the clacking of sticks from a brawl in the city.

"The fire was arson. I found these under a bush." Sano held up a metal smoking basket, some rags, and a ceramic jar. "The jar and rags smell of kerosene. The arsonist must have left them behind."

Yanagisawa was horrified by the thought of Yoshisato innocently sleeping while someone set his house on fire. He was so furious that he could hardly speak. "You can't fool me! You brought them yourself. You were trying to take them away before anyone else could find them. You're the arsonist!"

"I'm not. That's ridiculous!" Sano looked stricken, confused.

"You didn't want Yoshisato to be the next shogun. You tried to prove he wasn't the shogun's son, and you failed, so you killed him!"

"I didn't set the fire. I'm not trying to fool you," Sano said, angry now. "For once in your life, realize that everything bad that happens to you isn't my fault! I didn't get here until after it was already burning."

"That's right," Marume said angrily. "I was with him."

"Shut up!" Yanagisawa was certain Sano was guilty. Sano had resorted to murder to thwart Yanagisawa's quest for power, and Yoshisato was the casualty.

"The well was plugged," Sano said. "The firemen suspected arson. I started an investigation. This is the evidence I found."

"No more lies!" Yanagisawa snatched the basket, rags, and jar from Sano's hands. He called to his troops, "Arrest him!" He said to Sano, "You got away with Yoritomo's death. I won't let you get away with Yoshisato's!"

SANO WAS ASTOUNDED by the sudden reversal of his position and Yanagisawa's. A moment ago Yanagisawa had been his primary suspect in Tsuruhime's murder. Now Sano was the suspect in Yoshisato's. He'd been searching for proof that Yanagisawa was guilty. Now he'd been caught holding the evidence left by the arsonist. Sano realized how guilty he looked. He also realized that the crime he was accused of was much more serious than the one he believed Yanagisawa had committed.

Infecting the shogun's daughter with smallpox was picayune compared to burning the shogun's heir to death.

Sano's past troubles were nothing compared to those he now faced.

As the troops advanced on Sano, he said to Yanagisawa, "You're making a mistake. If you blame me for the fire, the real arsonist will go free!"

"I've got the real arsonist," Yanagisawa said with vengeful satisfaction.

He really believed it, Sano was disturbed to see. As the troops seized Sano, an uproar rose from the crowd: Everyone was thrilled to see the feud between Sano and Yanagisawa finally culminate. Sano struggled, angrily resisting arrest.

"Let my father go!" Masahiro cried, throwing himself on the troops.

Marume rushed to defend Sano. So did Sano's other men. None of them had brought their swords, which would have gotten in the way of putting out the fire. They wrestled the troops. Masahiro punched and kicked. Sano, caught in the middle, saw Yanagisawa's troops brandishing swords.

"Go ahead, Sano-*san*!" Yanagisawa called, hysterical with grief and rage. "Fight. Give me an excuse to kill you and your son right now!"

"Stop!" Sano yelled. He ceased struggling. "I surrender!"

"No!" Masahiro protested.

Groans came from the crowd. Surrendering was the most disgraceful thing a samurai could do. Surrendering deeply shamed Sano. But he must surrender rather than fight a battle unarmed and see his son killed.

"Do as I say," he ordered Masahiro, Marume, and his troops.

They reluctantly fell back.

"Go home," Sano called to Masahiro as Yanagisawa's troops dragged him away. "Tell your mother what happened. Tell her not to worry." He said what he hoped was true and knew wasn't: "Everything's going to be all right."

26

YANAGISAWA'S TROOPS LOCKED Sano in a guard tower. He waited alone in the bare, stone-walled room. Rain began to clatter on the roof tiles. A chill in the air turned Sano's sweat cold under the leather fire cape he still wore. He stood at the window and watched morning break over Edo.

Was this his last morning?

What would happen to his family?

He tried to think of how to get himself out of his predicament, but behind his stoic façade, his mind was a cyclone of desperation. All he could do was wait.

Finally, Yanagisawa's troops escorted him uphill through the covered corridors. They marched him through lashing rain to the palace. In the reception chamber, the shogun knelt on the dais with Yanagisawa seated at his right. The four old men from the Council of Elders knelt in two grim, silent rows opposite one another on the upper level of the floor below the dais. Soldiers stood against the walls. The troops pushed Sano to his knees on the lower level of the floor. Drenched and shivering, he faced his superiors.

"There had, ahh, better be a good reason for calling a meeting at this early hour," the shogun said.

"There is." Yanagisawa's voice was ragged from weeping, his blood-shot gaze as hard as if his tears had solidified into red-hot iron. "Sano will tell you what happened last night."

Sano looked at the elders. They gazed at the floor; they already knew. Yanagisawa had designated Sano as the unfortunate messenger of the bad news that nobody else wanted to break to the shogun. Sano couldn't resent the unfairness of it. Guilt weighed heavily upon him. He'd been Yoshisato's detractor; he'd failed to rescue Yoshisato. The least Sano could do for Yoshisato was to report the fact of his death.

"There was a fire at the heir's residence," Sano said.

The shogun's eyes widened with fright. "Yoshisato . . . ?"

"I'm sorry, Your Excellency," Sano said. "Yoshisato . . . didn't survive."

The shogun recoiled from Sano in horror. An ugly, satisfied smile appeared on Yanagisawa's face.

"No. It can't be." Trembling and frantic, the shogun looked around the room. When nobody contradicted Sano, he wailed, "The poor, dear boy!" and burst into tears. "Ahh, how terribly he must have suffered!"

Even while distressed by the misery his words had caused and in fear for his life, Sano marveled at how Yoshisato's death had affected the shogun.

"He was such a wonderful young man! That he should be cut down in the prime of his life! What a tragedy!" The shogun prostrated himself on the dais as he wept.

Sano had expected the shogun to be strictly concerned about himself, as he'd been after his daughter's death. This time he lamented Yoshisato, not the disruption of his own world. Yoshisato had been, as Sano had begun to think, a truly special person.

"My son! I loved him so much!" The shogun sobbed so hard he gasped for breath. "I only had him for, ahh, such a short time. And now he's gone!"

Sano had never known the shogun to love anybody. His sincere grief made Sano feel even guiltier. Yanagisawa watched it with perverse pleasure. The shogun raised himself on his elbows. Anger surfaced through his grief. His wet gaze raked Sano's leather garments.

"Why didn't you put out the fire? Why didn't you save Yoshisato?"

"I tried." Sano felt the hot roar of the flames blasting out the door. "It was too late."

"He set the fire," Yanagisawa said, his voice loud with indignation.

"Can this be true?" The shogun gaped at Sano. "You murdered my son?"

"No," Sano said vehemently. "Chamberlain Yanagisawa is wrong."

"He's lying. Here's the evidence he left." Yanagisawa reached behind him and brought forth the smoking basket, the jar, and the rags.

"It's not mine," Sano said.

The shogun handled the ash-coated metal basket with finicky fingers, wrinkling his nose as he smelled the rags. "What are these?"

"The jar that Sano used to carry the kerosene to the heir's residence," Yanagisawa said. "He brought hot coals in the smoking basket. He lit the rags to start the fire." Conviction rang in Yanagisawa's voice. During the past few hours he'd become entrenched in his belief that Sano had murdered Yoshisato.

"I never saw them until after the fire was out," Sano insisted, glancing at the elders. They eyed him dubiously. Either Yanagisawa had persuaded them that Sano was guilty or they were afraid not to go along with him. "I was investigating the fire. I found them under a bush."

"You were sneaking them away, so that nobody else would find them. But I caught you." Yanagisawa said to the shogun, "Sano didn't want Yoshisato to inherit the dictatorship. He tried to discredit Yoshisato, but he failed. So he burned him to death."

"No!" Sano shouted in desperation. "It's not how it looks!"

"It looks to me as if you killed my son!" The shogun's voice was shrill with hysteria. Clutching the metal basket, he clambered to his feet, fell off the dais, then staggered over to Sano. "Why? Why did you do it?"

The shogun had wrongly accused Sano of many evils but never something as serious as this. Sano spoke with urgent passion. "I did not set that fire. Your Excellency has known me for fourteen years. You know in your heart that I would never do such a heinous thing!"

"Don't believe him!" Yanagisawa shouted. "Sano was envious of Yoshisato. He wants to rule Japan himself. Yoshisato was in the way. Sano got rid of him by killing him in cold blood!"

"Murderer! Traitor!" The shogun swung the basket at Sano. Its sharp metal corner gouged Sano's temple. "A curse on you!" He struck Sano again and again.

Blows hit Sano's cheekbones, nose, and mouth. Sano remembered striking Hirata, who'd stood there unresisting. Now Sano endured the abuse and pain while the shogun beat his back and chest. It was Sano's duty to take the punishment, no matter how undeserved, without striking back.

Through the blood that ran into his eyes Sano saw Yanagisawa watching him with avid glee. The Way of the Warrior demanded courage while under attack. Sano would not shame himself by pleading for mercy.

Finally the shogun backed away from Sano. He dropped the basket, crawled onto the dais, and sat, gasping and spent. Sano's head throbbed. The skin on his face felt numb, stretched across the pain underneath, as if his whole face were one big blister. The elders' alarmed faces were like mirrors that told him how bad he looked. Yanagisawa gloated over Sano's injuries but seemed disappointed that the shogun had quit so soon.

The shogun flicked his hand at Sano. "Get this piece of, ahh, garbage out of my sight."

Something broke inside Sano. It was the dam that held in his most private thoughts and feelings. Now they came pouring out in a poisonous black flood. He'd often been angry at the shogun's foolishness, selfishness, unfairness, and weakness, but that anger paled beside the fury that Sano felt now. He'd often disliked the shogun for insulting, threatening, and mistreating him. But now his wounded body rebelled against all the punishments that his mind had forced him to accept for the sake of Bushido. All his compassion toward the shogun vanished as he was finally pushed beyond the point where he could endure the constant testing of his honor or justify the shogun's violence toward him. A savage hatred fought to explode out of Sano, like a wild animal from a cage.

"I'll take Sano to the execution ground." Yanagisawa sounded exultant that after so many years he'd finally bested his enemy, yet regretful that there was nothing more he could do to Sano except deny him an honorable death by ritual suicide. He rose, beckoning to the troops. "I'll have him decapitated and his head mounted by the Nihonbashi Bridge."

Sano knew this was his last chance to defend himself, but he couldn't. He was too consumed by his hatred of the shogun, which was magnitudes greater than what he felt toward Yanagisawa. Yanagisawa had mightily abused Sano but only gotten away with it because the shogun let him. If Sano spoke, he wouldn't say something brilliant that would exonerate him. His mutinous body would seize control of the tongue that his mind had always managed to hold. He would say exactly what he thought of the shogun.

You limp little man, waving your limp little hand to condemn your innocent, loyal retainer and send other people to do your dirty work!

The troops started toward Sano. Their usually impassive faces twitched with excitement. They knew this was a historic event and were thrilled to take part in it. The shogun watched, his mouth open and eyes vacant. Sano knew what that look meant: The shogun suspected that something was amiss, but he didn't want to deal with it and so decided not to understand. Sano gazed at him with bitter loathing.

You're not really that stupid! You choose to be stupid! It's easier than exerting yourself instead of letting Yanagisawa usurp your power!

"Wait," said one of the elders. It was Kato Kinhide. He had a flat, leathery, masklike face, the eyes and mouth like slits cut in it. The troops paused. "Let's not be too hasty."

"How could we be too hasty to punish the criminal who killed the shogun's heir?" Yanagisawa sounded outraged that his crony would try to postpone his victory over Sano.

"We need to be sure Sano-*san* is guilty," Kato said.

"Merciful gods, I caught him with the evidence."

Another elder spoke up. "Did anyone actually see him set the fire?"

"I know he did it," Yanagisawa said angrily. "How dare you go against me?"

Sano knew he should jump at the chance of turning the elders into his allies, but his attention focused on the mute, seemingly oblivious shogun. *Wake up, you lazy excuse for a dictator!*

"We're not going against you," a third elder hurried to say. "We just think you should exercise a little caution."

" 'Caution'?" Yanagisawa spoke as if it were a foreign, dirty word. "Why?"

"Later," Kato said with a warning glance at the shogun.

Sano knew that the elders didn't want to talk political strategy in the shogun's presence. The shogun chose that moment to burst into a fresh spate of weeping. His sobs drowned out the conversational undertones he didn't want to hear. Sano didn't care that the elders were afraid that Yoshisato's death could shift the balance of power in his favor and that was surely why they hesitated to take action against him. He was too embroiled in his contempt for the shogun. His loyalty toward the shogun crumbled. Up from its ruins surged a compulsion bred in his samurai blood, the passion for vengeance.

"I want to execute Sano now!" Yanagisawa thumped his fists on the dais.

Not even the immediate prospect of his own death could distract Sano from his desire to redress the wrongs the shogun had done him. His right hand clenched under his leather cape. His fingers itched for the sword he'd left at home.

"We're overruling you," Kato said. He and the other elders looked scared but determined.

Sano also knew that the elders were threatening to break their allegiance to Yanagisawa unless he cooperated with them. He ignored another opportunity to win them over to his side as he gauged the distance between himself and the dais. Could he get to the shogun before the guards stopped him?

Yanagisawa shook his head, as if he couldn't believe what he was hearing. He flung up his hands. "What would you have me do?"

"Follow standard procedure," Kato said, and the other elders nodded. "Put Sano on trial, just like any other accused criminal."

It wouldn't take much effort to strangle the shogun. Sano's fingers flexed. He could almost feel the withered flesh of the shogun's neck, its fragile bones snapping.

Yanagisawa stared at the elders, his eyes fierce. "Damn you." He looked torn between his need to retain his friends and his need to shed Sano's blood right now. He said to the troops, "Put him under house arrest."

Samurai charged with crimes were imprisoned at home instead of at Edo Jail, a privilege of their class. Sano couldn't appreciate the reprieve, the chance to save his life. As the troops led him from the room, he realized how blasphemous his thinking was. If he murdered his lord, he would no longer deserve to be called a samurai. Honor could never be reclaimed after such a violation of Bushido. Yet the raging creature that was his body still lusted for vengeance.

He looked backward at the shogun, who wept with loud, oblivious abandon. Two soldiers held Sano's arms in such a tight grip that their fingers dug painfully into his flesh. Sano was glad of the restraint. It was the only thing keeping him from killing the shogun.

娘 27

AT SANO'S MANSION, Reiko stood on the veranda with Masahiro and Detective Marume. They'd been waiting there for hours since Masahiro and Marume had brought her the news that Yoshisato had died in the fire and Sano had been arrested. Now the temple bells tolled noon. Reiko watched the rain drip from the eaves and puddles spread in the courtyard. She clasped her arms around her belly, protecting the child within, and shivered.

"You should go in the house, Mother," Masahiro said.

"No, I'm all right." Praying for Sano to come home, Reiko felt her terror increase with every moment that passed. She knew he hadn't done this terrible thing, but would anyone else believe he was innocent? Had he already been put to death? Reiko tried to calm down for the baby's sake, but her heart beat so fast that she felt dizzy and faint.

"Your husband will get out of this," Marume said uncertainly.

Masahiro said, for the tenth time, "I'll go out to the street and see if he's coming." He ran through the rain, splashing across puddles.

Akiko came out onto the veranda. "Mama, what are you doing?"

"Waiting for your father," Reiko said.

"Why?"

"To greet him when he comes back." Reiko didn't want to upset Akiko.

"Where is he?"

"He's working," Marume said cheerfully, rumpling Akiko's hair. "Young lady, you ask too many questions."

Reiko had a sudden terrible vision of Sano's dead body being carried to the house. "Akiko, go inside."

"Mother!" Masahiro came running, his expression filled with anguish.

Reiko's breath caught; her heart seized. Five soldiers marched after Masahiro. They accompanied a man dressed in a grimy leather fire cape, whom she at first didn't recognize as Sano. Her relief at seeing him alive immediately gave way to horror. His face was a mass of welts, darkening bruises, and blood. His eyes were swollen shut. Two soldiers held his arms while he hobbled. Akiko screamed.

Reiko grabbed Akiko and called to Masahiro, "Take your sister to her room!"

Masahiro dragged the screaming, crying little girl into the house. Reiko rushed to Sano, heedless of the rain that drenched her. "Merciful gods, what happened?"

Sano turned his head toward her. He didn't speak. The soldiers shoved him at Reiko. He stumbled. His weight unbalanced her. Marume caught her and Sano.

One of the soldiers said, "He's been charged with murdering Yoshisato. He's under house arrest until his trial."

Most trials ended in convictions, and because the victim was the shogun's heir, this one surely would. Reiko forbade herself to think about that. Tending to Sano was her first concern.

"Let's go inside," she said in the gentle, calm voice she used when the children were sick and she was worried and trying to hide it. Sano leaned against her. She could feel his body shaking. She and Marume had to help him up the stairs; he couldn't see.

"Get lost," Marume told the soldiers.

Some accompanied Reiko, Marume, and Sano into the house. The leader said, "Guard him. Make sure he doesn't run away. Lock up his troops. Confiscate all the weapons and money." Troops swarmed the estate, herded Sano's men toward the barracks.

Marume glared at their captors as he and Reiko led Sano down the passage. Servants gaped at their injured master. Reiko called to them, "Lay out our bed. Bring hot water and clean cloths. Fetch the physician."

They rushed to obey. In the bedchamber, Reiko and Marume eased

Sano onto the futon. She told Marume, "Go keep an eye on those soldiers."

Marume left. Reiko said to Sano, "Who did this to you?"

Sano didn't answer. He sat there, shaking violently.

Reiko's anxiety spiked higher. "Where else are you hurt? Take off your clothes so I can see."

He began to undress, but his hands shook so much that Reiko had to help him. She was glad to see only minor bruises on his shoulders and torso. The leather fire cape had protected him. But his trembling rattled the house. His breath came in gasps.

"Is something else the matter?" Reiko's voice quavered with fear that his injuries had affected his mind. "Can't you speak?"

Sano mumbled through cut, bleeding lips, "The shogun. Did this." Tremors jolted the words out of him. "To me."

Reiko's relief plunged into horror.

A maid came to the door and said, "Excuse me, I'm sorry, the physician won't come."

The news about Sano was already spreading, Reiko understood; the physician didn't want to help an accused traitor. At least she had the experience of watching him treat Sano after other battles. She bathed the cuts on Sano's head, applied healing balm, and fastened cotton bandages over the worst—one on his left cheek, the other on his brow. She gently pulled up his eyelids.

"Can you see?"

Shaking, Sano nodded.

Reiko held up three fingers. "How many?"

". . . Three."

"What's your name and rank? Who am I? Name your children?"

Sano gave the correct answers, punctuated with tremors. His brain didn't seem injured. Reiko asked, "Why are you shaking?"

He didn't answer. It must be a reaction to the trauma. Reiko made him lie down with a pillow under his neck, covered him with a quilt, and put herbal poultices over his swollen eyes. His situation was far worse than his injuries.

The shogun, who abhorred violence, had savagely beaten Sano. He must believe Sano had murdered his heir.

Reiko knelt beside Sano. "What happened?" She had to know everything, no matter how terrible it was.

Sano haltingly told the story. Reiko listened, outraged by the false accusation, distraught about Sano's predicament. The only ray of hope came from the elders' insistence on following legal procedure before executing Sano.

"We have a chance to save you," Reiko said. "Let's figure out what we're going to do." Sano relapsed into muteness. She seized his hand. "I know you're hurt, but we must think of something fast! Yanagisawa will hurry up the investigation. We've no time to lose!"

"I hate him." Sano spoke with a rabid vehemence that Reiko had never heard in his voice. Now she realized why he was shaking. It was from anger and the effort to control it.

"I know. I hate Yanagisawa, too." All her own fury toward their enemy rose up in Reiko like a hot bile. "After all these years of attacking us, he's finally got us where he wants us."

"Not Yanagisawa," Sano said. "I hate the shogun."

Reiko was shocked. She stared at Sano's bandaged, poulticed face. "How can you say that? He's your lord." To a samurai his lord was his god, his reason for existence.

Sano uttered a sardonic, humorless laugh. "A fine example of a lord he is. He was only brave enough to hit me because I couldn't hit him back."

For years Reiko had harbored critical thoughts about the shogun, but she'd never heard them from Sano. She was a mere woman, free to think whatever she liked as long as she kept it to herself. Sano was obligated to respect the shogun. "What about Bushido?"

"What about it?" Sano's tremors had ceased; he'd given up trying to control his emotions; his body relaxed. "After all my service to the shogun, after everything I've gone through to satisfy him, this is what it's come to." His hand gestured at his face. "The Way of the Warrior is just an excuse for the shogun to treat his retainers however he wants. We're all fools for swallowing it and letting him get away with abusing us!"

Reiko realized that the shogun's assault had changed her husband. Sano had tolerated threats and insults before, but this injury was more personal. Loss of face was the worst thing that could happen to a proud samurai, and Sano had been literally defaced.

"I wish I hadn't bothered investigating Tsuruhime's murder," Sano said bitterly. "I didn't manage to prove Yanagisawa is guilty, and I never will. But to hell with it!"

The change in Sano terrified Reiko as much as the fact that he was under arrest for the murder of the shogun's heir.

"I wish I'd never opposed Yanagisawa's schemes and tried to prevent the shogun from leaving the dictatorship to Yoshisato," Sano said. "If I hadn't, things might be different now; Yoshisato might still be alive, and I wouldn't be charged with his murder. I'd be better off if I'd just left the shogun to his own weak, gullible devices!"

Panic shot through Reiko. Where was the honorable samurai she'd married? Evidently, the shogun had pushed Sano too far. "Be quiet!"

"Why? Because someone might hear me and report me to the shogun? Who cares?" Sano laughed again. "I'm already as good as condemned to die."

"We're not giving up," Reiko said, alarmed by his fatalism. In the past, whenever trouble had plagued them, Sano had been the one to reassure her, to keep up the family's morale. "We're going to fight this."

Sano lay there, stiff and unmoving as wood. The poultices over his eyes oozed fluid onto his cheeks. It looked as if he was crying. Reiko remembered the morning after the earthquake, when she'd first seen the wreckage of the city. She felt the same devastation now. In the past, she and Sano had always been partners, their individual strength multiplied by their togetherness. But now the husband who once would have risen valiantly to any challenge was breaking down before her very eyes. The earthquake was partly to blame. Sano had worked day and night for months, helping the survivors, rebuilding the city. He'd also solved a difficult murder case in order to prevent a civil war.

No man could take all that strain without consequences.

His beating from the shogun had been one too many traumas for Sano.

Reiko had never felt so scared or alone in her life. Sano, the foundation of their family, had collapsed like the city during the earthquake.

She heard Masahiro's footsteps in the corridor. Gripping Sano's hand, she whispered, "Not one word of this to Masahiro!"

Masahiro entered the room; he looked worriedly at Sano. "Father? Are you all right?"

Reiko pinched Sano's hand to prevent him from speaking. "He will be. He's resting." With an effort, she kept her manner calm. "How is Akiko?"

"She's all right. I took her to the kitchen and the cooks gave her some cakes." Masahiro asked, "What are we going to do?"

Reiko took the heavy responsibility for the fate of their family upon her own small shoulders. "We investigate Yoshisato's death."

"I see. If we find out who really killed Yoshisato, then Father won't be punished for it." Masahiro sounded not entirely relieved. "I can look for clues, but Father is under house arrest, and you're not supposed to go outside."

The constraints on them made it even more difficult to save themselves. "Things have changed," Reiko said. "We must exonerate your father. If we don't, then we'll all die, including the baby. I'll try not to do anything physically strenuous."

Masahiro nodded, thought for a moment, then said, "Both of the shogun's children have been murdered within such a short time. Could the two murders be connected?"

"Maybe." Proud of his intelligence, Reiko felt better. Although Sano lay as still as if he were already dead, she had Masahiro to stand in as head of the family. She also had Detective Marume. Her fear receded enough that she could apply her mind to the new investigation. "There may be different suspects, however."

"Who could have wanted to kill Yoshisato?" Masahiro asked.

Combing through the tangle of politics and alliances, conflicts and motives, Reiko said, "I can think of at least two people."

"If the murders are connected, then maybe we can solve Yoshisato's by solving Tsuruhime's," Masahiro said.

28

TAEKO SLID THE door of her room open and saw Masahiro hurry down the corridor. When she started following him, her mother's voice stopped her in her tracks.

"Taeko! Where do you think you're going?"

"With Masahiro," Taeko said.

"Oh, no, you're not," Midori said. "Get back in your room."

"But, Mama, don't you know that Sano-*san* is under arrest?" Taeko couldn't believe that her mother would continue punishing her at a time like this. "They say he killed the shogun's son."

"Who are 'they'?"

"The maids. They were talking outside my room."

Midori frowned in annoyance. "I've told them not to gossip." Seizing Taeko by the arm, she said, "Come with me."

"But Mama, they said Sano-*san* is going to be put to death and so is everybody else in this house. I heard Masahiro and Lady Reiko say they have to find out who really killed the shogun's son and daughter and prove Sano-*san* is innocent. I have to help them!" The world was falling apart, and her mother pretended everything was normal. "Don't you understand?"

"You're the one who doesn't understand." Midori dragged Taeko into her room. "You're going to stay here."

"Please!" Taeko had to help Masahiro, and not just because she wanted him to like her. That seemed silly now. She must do whatever she could to save her family and his.

"If you leave this house, there's nothing you can do but drive me mad with worrying about you!"

"But I helped them before. I found a clue!"

"That was just a lucky accident."

"But, Mama—"

Midori crouched in front of Taeko, put her hands on her shoulders. "Look at me." Taeko gazed into her mother's eyes, which were filled with worry, frustration, and love. "I know how bad things are. I'm not trying to ignore it. But I will not let you chase around the city and put yourself in danger." She hugged Taeko fiercely. "I've lost your father. I'm not losing you!"

AT THE PALACE the wake for Yoshisato began. The reception chamber was crowded with government officials, court ladies, *daimyo*, and prominent merchants. They waited in line to offer condolences to the shogun, who sat weeping on the dais. Beside him was Yoshisato's coffin, an oblong wooden box wrapped in white cloth, mounted on a stand. An altar in front of the coffin held lit candles, smoking incense burners, a wooden tablet with Yoshisato's name written on it, and a painted portrait of Yoshisato. Below the dais, priests dressed in saffron robes and brocade stoles knelt, beating drums and chanting prayers.

Yanagisawa and Lady Someko walked toward the palace. She leaned on his arm, stumbled, and sobbed. When he'd told her that Yoshisato was dead, she'd screamed and fallen on the floor. That had been more than eight hours ago. She'd been crying ever since. Yanagisawa couldn't bear her grief on top of his own. He forced himself not to rage at her. She was Yoshisato's mother and deserved sympathy. She also required careful handling.

Her maids had dressed her and put on her makeup, but her hair was already messy from her clawing at it. Tears had already streaked her white face powder and red cheek rouge, which stained her dark gray kimono. As she and Yanagisawa entered the reception chamber, she sobbed louder. Everyone turned to stare.

"Be quiet!" he whispered.

Many people stood in a line that led to the shogun on the dais but more loitered by the walls. Yanagisawa knew they were waiting for him, to see his reaction to Yoshisato's death. Lady Someko blubbered, heedless of their attention.

"Pull yourself together," Yanagisawa ordered as he led her toward the dais.

The crowd parted to let them pass. Yanagisawa saw the coffin. His eyes burned, but the tears didn't spill. His knees wobbled, but he marched forward. Yoritomo's death had knocked him flat. Yanagisawa was even more devastated by Yoshisato's, but he would not fall into a pit of mourning, not shut himself away from the world. When Yoritomo had died, he must have sensed that he could fall apart and make a comeback later. This time he knew that if he let grief carry him away, there would be no returning. This time he must stay strong enough to gain power over the regime and avenge both his dead sons.

Lady Someko broke away from him, ran, and flung herself on the coffin, shrieking, "Yoshisato! Yoshisato!"

The shogun gaped fearfully at her. Yanagisawa grabbed her arm. "Don't," he said in a low, stern voice.

"I want to see him! You wouldn't let me see him!"

"I already explained to you—his body was too badly burned."

"I have to see him!" Lady Someko tore at the coffin's white cloth wrappings, exposing the plain wood underneath.

"Stop that!" Yanagisawa struggled to restrain her.

The shogun scooted away from them. Murmurs of discomfort swept through the room. Lady Someko heaved up the lid of the coffin. She exclaimed in disappointment and outrage. The coffin was empty. No one had been able to identify which of the four corpses belonged to Yoshisato. All had been so fragile that they'd crumbled when taken from the ruins; all reeked of smoke and charred meat. Yanagisawa had ordered that no remains should be inside the coffin during the wake; they would be put in before the funeral, which would take place in two days, then cremated, and all the ashes buried in the Tokugawa clan tomb.

Lady Someko wrenched free of Yanagisawa. She clawed the bottom of the coffin, as if digging for Yoshisato.

"Get her out of here!" the shogun ordered.

Yanagisawa hoisted Lady Someko over his shoulder. As he carried her from the room, she screamed and pounded his back. He was panting by the time he got her outside. He carried her past the sentries at the door and down the path. Furious at her because she was making everything harder, he also felt sorry for her. He'd only known Yoshisato for five months. She'd loved him for seventeen years.

"I can't carry you any farther." Yanagisawa set Lady Someko on her feet. "You'll have to walk home."

She collapsed onto the grass beside the path. She cried so hard she began to choke.

Officials strode along the path, heading for the wake or leaving it. They gawked at Lady Someko. Losing his patience, Yanagisawa said, "Get up! Do you want the whole world to see you like this?"

"I don't care who sees me! My baby is gone. Nothing else matters!"

"Well, I care. For Yoshisato's sake, show a little dignity!"

"Don't you criticize me, you bastard! It's your fault he's dead!"

"How is it my fault?" Yanagisawa demanded.

"If you'd left him alone, if you'd never introduced him to the shogun, he wouldn't have been inside the heir's residence when it caught fire. He would be alive!"

She was right. Yanagisawa felt a sickening guilt, which fueled his anger at her. "Face the facts, woman: Sano set the fire. He's to blame for Yoshisato's death."

"Oh, yes, you told me." Scorn showed in Lady Someko's drenched eyes. "But I don't believe you. You tell so many lies. Like the one about Yoshisato being the shogun's son."

"Keep your voice down!" Alarmed, Yanagisawa saw two officials coming up the path.

"Why does it matter if the world finds out that you made up the astronomer's story and that you're Yoshisato's real father?" She was doing what Yanagisawa had feared—exposing their deception. Grief had driven her mad.

"Because it was part of a plot to trick the shogun," Yanagisawa whispered furiously. "That makes it treason. And treason is punishable by death."

"Well, the plot didn't work, did it?" Lady Someko laughed through her sobs. "Yoshisato won't inherit the dictatorship. And unless you can trick the shogun into thinking he's the father of one of your other sons, then you'll never rule Japan."

The officials were dangerously close. "Shut up before you get us both killed!" Yanagisawa lunged at her and clamped his hand over her mouth.

She squealed, clawed at his hand, and kicked. The officials stared as they passed. Yanagisawa hauled Lady Someko to her feet. She bit his palm. He cursed and let go.

"I don't care what happens to me!" She alternated sobs with wild laughter. "Now that Yoshisato is gone, I have nothing to live for. I'll gladly die if I can take you with me!"

Yanagisawa glanced at his bitten hand as he dragged her toward the gate. Blood oozed from deep tooth marks. She hated him enough to sacrifice her own life to deprive him of his. "Fine, punish me, but wait until I've punished Sano. In your mind I may be guilty of a million crimes, but it's Sano who burned Yoshisato to a crisp while he slept."

Lady Someko moaned at his brutal description of Yoshisato's death. "You are guilty!" Her voice was hoarse from screaming. "Guilty of killing my baby. Guilty of making me go along with your scheme to rule Japan. But that's not all. You killed the shogun's daughter!"

A spear of dread pierced Yanagisawa. He'd forgotten about Tsuruhime. The shogun probably had, too. But eventually the ado about Yoshisato would dwindle and somebody was bound to remind the shogun that his daughter, too, had been murdered. Yanagisawa would fall under suspicion again, and although Sano wouldn't be around to persecute him, other enemies would. Yanagisawa needed to shore up his defenses, and one of the weaknesses in it was Lady Someko. He had to shut her up.

"Oh, come, now." He mustered a gentle, joking manner. "You're just out to blame me for every evil under the sun. I didn't kill the shogun's daughter."

They reached the guesthouse. He towed her through the door into her chamber. When he let her go, she faced him, her eyes glittering with vindictive malice. "Don't try to fool me. Before Tsuruhime got smallpox, you knew she was pregnant. You knew that if she lived to give birth, and she had a son, it could have ruined your plans for Yoshisato to be the next shogun."

"How did you find out she was pregnant?" Yanagisawa said, startled.

"Lady Reiko told me."

"You spoke with Sano's wife? I told you to stay away from everyone associated with Sano."

"I went to see her," Lady Someko said, brazenly proud of her disobedience. "Because nobody else will tell me anything."

Yanagisawa dragged his bleeding hand down his face. This woman would be the death of him. "What else did Lady Reiko say?"

"She asked if Yoshisato knew Tsuruhime was pregnant. She tried to make me say he killed Tsuruhime. But I know he didn't. He would never kill anybody." Lady Someko's hoarse voice was replete with conviction. "Unlike you." She jabbed her sharp fingernail at Yanagisawa. "I know you knew she was pregnant."

"You don't know any such thing," Yanagisawa said, urgent with his need to convince her. "Because I didn't know until Sano told me yesterday."

"I don't believe you. You must have known. Because you have a spy in Lord Tsunanori's estate. It's the housekeeper. You were paying her to tell you if Tsuruhime missed any monthly courses."

Yanagisawa deduced how Lady Someko had learned of his spy. His chief retainer served as liaison between him and the housekeeper, whom he'd never met. Lady Someko must have coaxed the man into telling tales. Yanagisawa was dismayed that she knew. The information was useless to Sano, but it could still be lethal in the hands of Yanagisawa's other enemies. Ienobu could use it as evidence that Yanagisawa must have known Tsuruhime was pregnant and therefore must have had her killed.

Lady Someko began laughing hysterically. "You went to all the trouble of murdering the shogun's daughter. And now, with Yoshisato dead, a lot of good it did you!"

29

"THE SHOGUN'S SON has been murdered!"

The words, shouted outside his window, awakened Hirata. He sat up on the bed in his room at the inn. Alarm cleared the fog of sleep from his mind. He threw on his robe and ran barefoot into the rainy street. The news-seller was standing under the eaves of a teahouse across from the inn. Hirata gave him a coin, snatched a broadsheet, and anxiously read the story. It said Yoshisato had died in a fire at Edo Castle, and Sano was under arrest for arson.

Hirata was horrified yet elated. Yoshisato's murder changed everything. Hirata ran to his room and unpacked a silk kimono, surcoat, and trousers. They were wrinkled, but he put them on; then he looked in the mirror. A face with long, shaggy hair and patchy whiskers gazed back at him. He couldn't go to Edo Castle looking like a bum. He hung his swords at his waist, donned a wicker hat and straw rain cape, and went to a nearby barbershop.

The barber shaved his face and crown, oiled his hair, tied it into a neat topknot, trimmed the end, then held up a mirror for Hirata. Hirata's skin was brown where the sun had tanned it, pale where hair had covered his scalp and face. His cheekbones were sharper. New wrinkles bracketed his mouth. His eyes had a hunted, haunted expression. Hirata winced. He paid the barber, ran outside, mounted his horse, and galloped through the rain to Edo Castle.

He had a new chance to help Sano and win his forgiveness.

SANO LAY IN bed. The cold, damp poultices weighed upon his closed eyelids. His face throbbed. The skin was numb where Reiko had applied balm, sore underneath. The bruises on his body ached. His mind roiled with guilt caused by his disgraceful thoughts about the shogun, fear that he was in trouble he couldn't get out of, and the anguish of knowing that his family was in it with him.

Rain clattered on the roof. Reiko moved about the chamber. Garments rustled as she dressed. Sano said, "Where are you going?"

"To find out who killed Yoshisato. What are you going to do while I'm gone?"

"I don't know." Sano felt too inert to take any action.

"Well, I'll tell you. Stop wallowing in misery and save yourself!"

Reiko had never spoken to him so harshly. Sano involuntarily turned toward her. The poultices fell off his eyes. The swelling had gone down; he could see Reiko kneeling by the bed.

"Please," she said, distraught. "Masahiro and I can't do it alone. We need you."

Sano felt even guiltier for letting his emotions paralyze him, leaving his wife and son to struggle on their own. He sat up. It took a gigantic effort. "You're right. I'm being unfair to you." His cut lips felt thick and sore.

Reiko smiled tremulously. Sano had to look away from her. Something else besides his samurai discipline, his sense of honor, and his loyalty to the shogun had broken. It was his faith that his actions mattered. He couldn't believe that investigating Yoshisato's murder would do any good. He tried to remember that he'd solved difficult cases and gotten himself out of jeopardy many times, but he couldn't help thinking his luck had finally run out.

He'd also lost his faith that the universe favored those who tried to do right over those who deliberately, blatantly did wrong.

"What are you going to do?" Reiko's tone anticipated a better answer than before.

Sano couldn't tell her how he felt. She was depending on him. His mind groped for some source of strength or guidance, like a lame, blind man gropes for a cane. He found it in a memory from his childhood.

He'd been seven or eight years old. He and his parents had been walking to a funeral. Sano had hated funerals. The people crying made him sad, the smell of cremation made him sick, and all the praying didn't bring back the dead. He'd told this to his parents. His father had said, "The ancients said that a journey is hardest when it's to somewhere you have to go and you don't want to because you doubt that it's worthwhile. But you must put your doubts aside, set your course, and follow it by putting one foot in front of the other until you get there."

Sano didn't know if the ancients had ever said that. His father had often put his own words in their mouths. But the advice suited this occasion. Sano would put his doubts aside and focus on solving Yoshisato's murder. He would take one step after another, and maybe the results would be worthwhile.

"I'll invite my new favorite suspect over to talk about Yoshisato's murder." To assure Reiko that he was all right, Sano added with forced humor, "Maybe my face will scare him into confessing."

THE RAIN HAD lessened by the time Hirata dismounted outside Sano's estate. Cool mist hung in the air. The sky brightened to a murky silver, but thunder rumbled. A Tokugawa army soldier was guarding the gate. "What do you want?"

"To see Sano-*san*," Hirata said.

The soldier obviously recognized Hirata and knew his reputation as a great fighter; he understood that trying to keep Hirata out would be as dangerous as letting him in. "All right. Just behave yourself."

Walking toward the mansion, Hirata looked around furtively. He longed to see his wife and children, but he was nervous about how they would react. He didn't want to run into Sano's other retainers. His heart pounded as soldiers guarding Sano let him in the door. In the private chambers he came upon Sano and Detective Marume. Sano's face was cut and bandaged, the skin around his swollen eyes turning purple. He handed Marume a scroll container and said, "See that it gets into his hands."

"I'm on my way." Marume scowled at Hirata. "What are you doing here?"

Sano's aura was even more disturbingly changed than his appearance.

Once it had pulsed with a strong, steady glow and rhythm. Now the glow was veined with darkness that bled out of him. Appalled, Hirata said, "What happened to you?"

"None of your business," Marume said.

Sano put a hand on Marume's arm. "Go deliver that scroll."

Marume shot an ominous glance at Hirata as he departed. Sano didn't seem surprised to see Hirata. He didn't seem glad, either. He said, "I had a bad encounter with a smoking basket," and stepped into his chamber. Uncertain about whether Sano wanted him to come in, Hirata followed.

"What are you doing here?" Sano asked.

"I heard you were arrested for killing Yoshisato," Hirata said.

"I suppose everybody has heard by now."

Sano's voice frightened Hirata. It had a wooden quality, as if the black veins in his aura had drained away his spirit. Hirata said, "I know you didn't do it."

"Thank you for your faith in me." Sano spoke without sarcasm or sincerity.

"I came to see if I could help." Hirata realized that there was something seriously wrong with Sano, something that went deeper than the cuts on his face and beyond the fact that he was accused of murder.

"That's good of you," Sano said.

He was in shock, Hirata supposed. Although Hirata hated to see Sano like this, maybe now he could make up for the wrong he'd done Sano and reconcile himself with his master. "I'll find out who really killed Yoshisato. I'll exonerate you."

"Well. I appreciate the offer." The first sign of emotion inflected Sano's voice. It was doubt.

Shame flushed Hirata's cheeks. Sano hadn't forgotten the times Hirata had promised to do things for him and let him down. Hirata thought of Tahara, Kitano, and Deguchi. If he didn't show up at the canal, Tahara and Kitano would get suspicious. And he mustn't let them get suspicious before he and Deguchi could kill them. Hirata didn't have time to hunt Yoshisato's murderer. He had to do something faster and more spectacular for Sano.

"Is Yanagisawa responsible for your arrest?" Hirata asked.

"How did you guess?" The usual wry humor was absent from Sano's tone.

"I'll assassinate Yanagisawa. Then he can't get you convicted."

Hirata braced himself for an angry reaction. Sano had never been willing to kill Yanagisawa because Yanagisawa was the shogun's delegate and Sano's loyalty to the shogun extended to him. Hirata prepared to convince Sano that lowering his standards was necessary and that if Hirata did the deed, Sano's hands would be technically clean.

"No," Sano said. "The shogun thinks I killed his son, and he's set on killing me. He doesn't need Yanagisawa to egg him on." Sano fingered the bandages on his face. "Killing Yanagisawa wouldn't solve my problem. But thank you anyway."

Hirata was shocked. Sano had rejected the idea because he didn't think it would work, not because he thought it was wrong. "I'll kill the shogun, too, then," Hirata said. "If he and Yanagisawa both die, nobody else will care much about Yoshisato. You'll be safe."

It was a blasphemous idea. Even to speak it was treason. But Sano didn't revile it as he once would have. His aura turned darker as the black veins swelled. It was like watching a healthy animal consumed by a fast-growing cancer. It made Hirata sick, but he hastened to nudge Sano toward the decision he seemed ready to make.

"I'll make it look like a natural death." Hirata looked beyond the simple act of eliminating Sano's adversaries. "The government will be in chaos. You can take advantage of it. You'll have a fresh start." *And so,* Hirata thought, *will I.*

"A fresh start," Sano echoed, and Hirata heard another tinge of emotion in his voice. This time it was yearning.

"Well?" Hirata said. "Should I go ahead?"

Sano pondered. His aura was almost completely black. Hirata held his breath against an onslaught of exhilaration and fear. *Merciful gods, Sano was actually going to say yes!*

A spasm shuddered through Sano. His bloodshot eyes filled with horror. The black veins in his aura constricted, as if he'd sucked the darkness back inside him.

"I can't believe we're talking like this," Sano said in a tone of wonder.

He shook his head violently. "No. I'm not that far gone. I forbid you to kill the shogun!"

Hirata started to argue, but Sano raised his hand and demanded, "Where are your secret society friends? Is this their plan—for you to assassinate the shogun and make me a party to it?"

A terrible realization struck Hirata: If he killed the shogun, Ienobu would surely inherit the dictatorship. Hirata would have played right into the ghost's hands.

Sano backed away from Hirata. "I can't listen to any more of this! Get out!"

HIRATA WAS SO shaken that he stumbled through the corridors. By offering to assassinate the shogun, he'd tempted Sano to join him in a treasonous conspiracy. Sano, in a moment of weakness, had almost stepped into the pit of disgrace that Hirata had dug. Hirata was so angry at himself that he wanted to strike his own face until it was as damaged as Sano's. He'd almost corrupted Sano, the most honorable samurai he knew. Sano would never forgive him. Even if he shut down the secret society, he'd permanently ruined his relationship with Sano.

Hirata belatedly noticed he wasn't alone. A boy stood in the corridor, watching him. His heart gave a painful thump. "Tatsuo?"

His son had grown taller since Hirata had been away. Tatsuo took a step backward. His solemn eyes widened in fear.

Dismayed, Hirata said, "It's Papa." Five months must seem a long time to a child. "Don't you remember me?"

A door down the hall opened. A girl came out. Hirata was surprised to recognize his daughter. How grown up and beautiful Taeko was! She eyed him warily. Tatsuo ran to her. They stood together, speechless. Tears burned Hirata's eyes. He'd missed his children so much, and they were looking at him like two fawns cornered by a hunter.

He heard a gasp. He turned. There was Midori, holding their baby, her eyes filled with amazement. Seeing his wife and youngest child, Hirata felt a joy like an updraft of warm wind that lifted him out of his misery.

"*You.*" Midori's cold voice brought Hirata down to earth. "Why did you come back?"

Hirata didn't want to lie to her; he'd done it too many times, and she hated it. He'd already blown his relationship with Sano; now his marriage was at stake. But if he told her what had happened between him and Sano, she would be even madder. And if he told her anything about the secret society, she would be in danger.

"I missed you and the children," Hirata said.

Skepticism and her need to believe him warred in Midori's eyes. "Go play outside," she told the children.

She didn't want to quarrel in front of them, and neither did Hirata, but he said, "Please don't send them away." He smiled at Tatsuo and Taeko. "Would you like to play a game?"

They shrank from him. Midori laughed, a sharp, bitter sound. "Do you think you can just walk back into their lives? They're afraid of you."

"Why are they afraid? Have you been telling them bad things about me?"

Midori put herself between him and the children. "I've only told them the truth—that you left us because you don't care about us."

"That's not true," Hirata protested. "I love them. I love you. I didn't want to leave. But I had to."

"I can't listen to any more excuses!" Midori said. The baby in her arms started to cry. "I can't take any more of your coming and going and lying! Go away!" She burst into tears. "Never come back again!"

30

SANO KNELT AT Reiko's dressing table and looked in the mirror. His reflection belonged to an alien that wore white cotton bandages on its cheek and brow. The rest of its face was a bloated mask of garish purple bruises and red cuts, shiny with medicinal balm. Sano swallowed hard. He watched his hand rise to touch the alien's split, puffy lips. He'd never been vain about his looks, but the extent of his injuries was appalling. His face seemed an ugly manifestation of his wicked thoughts about the shogun, his lapse of honor.

He abruptly turned away from the mirror as Detective Marume entered the room and said, "Lord Ienobu is here."

Less than an hour had passed since Sano had sent Marume to ask Ienobu to visit him. "That was fast." Sano was surprised that his voice sounded so normal when nothing else about him was.

"I didn't have to go to his house. I met him inside the castle as I was leaving."

Walking toward the reception room, Sano tried to chart his conversation with Ienobu, but his thoughts kept raging around the shogun, like a storm around its eye. He felt like a broken jar that had been put together without glue. A slight tap could shatter him and let out the storm.

In the reception room, Ienobu's hunchbacked figure knelt by the alcove. When he saw Sano, his eyes bulged with shock.

"Thank you for coming, Honorable Lord Ienobu." Sano knelt and bowed.

"My heavens," Ienobu said. "Does it feel as bad as it looks?"

"More or less." Sano forced himself to think of his family, to discipline his emotions for their sake. Ienobu seemed plump with contentment, like a maggot that had just fed. "Are you as happy as you look?"

"Oh, not happy at all." Ienobu put on a reproachful expression. "It's terrible, what happened to Yoshisato."

Sano wasn't deceived. Ienobu was obviously thrilled that Yoshisato was dead. "Have you seen the shogun today?"

"Yes, I just went to the wake."

"How is he?" Sano knew he should feel compassion for the shogun, but he hoped the shogun was drowning in misery.

"Oh, he's devastated by Yoshisato's death." Ienobu couldn't control the grin that peeled his lips farther back from his teeth. "He begged me to move into the palace with him. I was just going to my house to fetch my belongings when your man gave me your invitation."

"So Yoshisato has been dead less than a day, and you're already back in the shogun's good graces."

Ienobu shrugged off Sano's hint that he'd capitalized on Yoshisato's death. "The shogun needs comfort and counsel, which I'm certainly glad to provide."

"He also needs a new heir," Sano said. "You must be glad to provide that, too."

"Someone has to plan for the future."

"A future in which you're at the head of the regime?"

"I was the shogun's heir apparent five months ago. I'm now the heir apparent again." Ienobu spoke as if Yoshisato's rise and his own fall from favor were but a brief kink in his schemes. "Nothing could be more natural."

"Nothing could be more natural than enjoying the murder of one's rival," Sano said.

Hostility hooded Ienobu's eyes. "Why did you want to see me?"

Sano hated to grovel to Ienobu, but he must, for his family's sake. "A few days ago you made me an offer. Is it still good?"

"That's what I thought you wanted to ask. Things have changed. You need me to help you fend off the murder charge that Yanagisawa has slapped on you. But I no longer need your help. An alliance with you could only hurt me. Therefore, I'm rescinding my offer."

This was what Sano had expected, but he argued, "You're in no position to turn down help. Yanagisawa is still your enemy."

"He's finished," Ienobu said disdainfully.

"Don't underestimate him. If you think he'll lie down and let you inherit the dictatorship, think again. I've survived his schemes before. I'll survive this one." Sano spoke with more conviction than he felt. "And when I do, you'll want me on your side."

Pity tinged Ienobu's disdain. "I don't see you surviving."

Sano saw his port in the storm close; he was more alone in the cold than ever. His rage toward the shogun spilled over onto the shogun's nephew. "You knew I would mention your offer, and you knew you were going to rescind it. So why did you come?"

"To see how you were."

Sano pictured Ienobu poking a dead snake with a stick, to test if it was really dead. "Well, I'm glad you came. Because there's something else I want to ask you. Did you have Yoshisato's house set on fire?"

"Certainly not." Vexation disrupted Ienobu's complacence. "Your question is not only ludicrous, it's insulting."

Sano hadn't expected Ienobu to confess to the murder, but an overemphatic denial was often an indicator of guilt. "What's so ludicrous? You're the one who benefited the most from Yoshisato's death. He was blocking your path to becoming the next shogun. Now he's gone. Your path is clear."

"I beg to differ, Sano-*san*. *You* set the fire because you wanted to destroy Yanagisawa and Yoshisato. *I* only benefited from your actions." Ienobu added smugly, "*I'm* not the one who was caught holding the rags, the kerosene jar, and the smoking basket."

Sano recalled Masahiro asking if Yoshisato's and Tsuruhime's murders could be connected. Now he saw reason to think so. "Did you have the shogun's daughter infected with smallpox?"

Ienobu laughed his dry, wheezy laugh. "Really, Sano-*san*, you're the most single-minded man I know. First you accuse me of murdering Yoshisato. Then Tsuruhime. But you may as well give up. Nobody is going to believe your irrational allegations."

"What's so irrational about the idea that you killed Tsuruhime? Yoshisato wasn't the only one who could have prevented you from becoming the next shogun. So could she have."

"How?" Scorn rasped in Ienobu's tone. "As a woman she wasn't eligible to inherit the dictatorship."

"A son of hers would have been. More eligible than you, in fact. He would have been the shogun's direct descendant."

"He didn't exist," Ienobu said impatiently.

"Tsuruhime was pregnant when she took ill."

"Pregnant?" Ienobu looked as startled as when he'd seen Sano's face. But Sano wondered if he'd anticipated that the subject of her pregnancy would arise and prepared his reaction. "How do you know?"

"That's not important." Sano knew how flimsy the evidence sounded, a pouch of herbs and a servant girl's story. He wasn't going to give Ienobu a chance to poke holes in it. "What matters is whether you knew. Did you?"

"No. Because you're making it up." Ienobu clamped his lips shut between his teeth.

Sano tried to read Ienobu's thoughts. Had Ienobu known Tsuruhime was pregnant? Was he uncertain as to whether Sano was bluffing?

"What's the matter?" Sano asked. "Are you worried that other people will hear about her pregnancy and realize that you benefited from her death as well as Yoshisato's?"

"My uncle must have hit you hard enough to jar your wits loose, Sano-san. You've mixed up the timing of events." Ienobu sounded cautious, as if groping through unmapped terrain. "When Tsuruhime got smallpox, Yoshisato was alive and well and set to become the shogun's heir. Killing her wouldn't have put me first in line for the succession."

"Perhaps not right then. But I think you decided that she and Yoshisato both had to go before you could feel secure about inheriting the dictatorship." Sano groped his own way toward a new theory of why Tsuruhime had been murdered. "It was only a matter of which to kill first. And you've admitted to having friends in her house."

Ienobu's face grew uglier with rage. "How dare you even think I'm capable of such cold-blooded calculation?"

"You waited decades for the best time to make your appearance at court. It was after Yanagisawa had gone into seclusion, after the earthquake. The shogun's usual attendants were busy working to restore the city. He needed company. And there you were." Sano warmed to his own theory. "You're the kind of man who would take the precaution of eliminating Tsuruhime even though she wasn't an immediate threat. And now that Yoshisato is dead, you can relax because she's already been dispatched."

"Is this how you intend to defend yourself? By splashing mud on me?" Ienobu's voice vibrated with fear that the shogun might be convinced that Ienobu had murdered his children.

"You once asked me if I was willing to fight dirty," Sano said. "I am."

The beating he'd taken had changed more than his attitude toward the shogun. In the past he'd risked his life to serve justice, but now he would gladly sacrifice Ienobu, even if Ienobu was innocent, to save himself and his family. He was alarmed to find the change liberating.

Ienobu eked out a chuckle. "It's a pity we can't be allies. I could use a man as ruthless as you've apparently become. But since we can't, hear this." He thrust his finger at Sano's face. Once more Sano was reminded of an octopus uncoiling its tentacle. This tentacle had a curved, yellow, sharp nail at the end. "If you publicize your theory about me, I'll make you regret it."

Sano ceased regretting that he couldn't ally with Ienobu. Ienobu was now his primary suspect in Tsuruhime's and Yoshisato's murders. Even his new, broken self couldn't have stomached joining forces with a killer. He had some vestige of honor left. But he did regret that he was now pitted against Ienobu as well as Yanagisawa. One powerful enemy had been bad enough.

Hiding his despair, Sano resorted to bravado. "Give me your worst. And I'll give you mine."

GROUPS OF LADIES, chaperoned by guards who wore the crests of *daimyo* clans, walked up the path to the palace. Reiko tagged along behind them. Loath to be recognized, she wore a cloak that concealed her pregnancy and a silk drape that veiled her face. She was shaky with nerves, uncertain about the wisdom of attending the vigil for Yoshisato. The wife of the man accused of murdering him could hardly be welcome.

Reiko followed the ladies into the reception chamber, which was crowded with people and abuzz with polite conversation. When she saw the soldiers stationed along the wall, her heartbeat quickened with panic. The baby pressed against her bladder. She needed to urinate, but she couldn't leave. Courageous for Sano's sake, she kept her head down and stayed close to the ladies so that anyone who saw her would think she was one of them. Casting furtive glances around the chamber, she located Lady Nobuko and Korika near the dais, with other women from the Large Interior. One half of Lady Nobuko's face was distorted by her headache. The other half wore a secretive smile as she contemplated the coffin.

As Reiko edged alongside the line of people waiting to offer their condolences to the shogun, Lady Nobuko met her gaze but offered no acknowledgment. She averted her eyes. Korika smiled an apologetic smile before she, too, turned away from Reiko.

The snub hurt, but Reiko didn't stop. The other women saw her. They began whispering and pointing. The crowd turned toward Reiko. The object of all censorious eyes, Reiko felt fear as well as mortification. Would the soldiers throw her out?

Lady Nobuko winced with displeasure but gave Reiko a brief nod. She and Korika moved toward the back door. Reiko hurried outside after them, grateful to avoid a dangerous scene. The rain was coming down hard again, cascading off the eaves, deluging the trees. She joined Lady Nobuko and Korika under a narrow roof that sheltered the path through the garden.

"I'm surprised to see you," Lady Nobuko said in an unfriendly voice. "I didn't think you would have the nerve to come."

"I need to speak with you, and I thought you might be here," Reiko said. "But why are you? You had no love for Yoshisato."

Lady Nobuko frowned at Reiko's suggestion that her attendance at the wake was hypocritical. Korika looked insulted on her mistress's behalf. "Yoshisato was my stepson," Lady Nobuko said. "My attendance was obligatory."

"It looked like you were enjoying the fact that he's dead," Reiko said.

"Your impertinence is offensive," Lady Nobuko snapped. "So is your intruding where you must certainly know you are not wanted. I will take this opportunity to tell you that I wish to have no further contact with you or your husband."

Anger flared in Reiko. "You were happy to have contact with us when you wanted my husband to prove that Yanagisawa murdered Tsuruhime."

"Circumstances have altered."

The alliance between Sano and Lady Nobuko had been a matter of mutual convenience rather than friendship, but Reiko could hardly believe the woman would be so cold. "You mean, because my husband isn't useful to you any longer, you're severing your ties with us."

"There's no need for you to put it so bluntly," Lady Nobuko said in a pitying tone. "The only person you're hurting is yourself. But since you insist on being blunt, I will tell you that I cannot associate with a traitor or his wife."

People associated with an accused traitor risked being implicated in his crime and sharing his punishment. Not even the shogun's wife dared maintain a connection to Sano. But Lady Nobuko's repudiation still rankled. Reiko despaired at how alone she and Sano were. She was also furious at the injustice of their plight.

"Now, if you'll excuse us, we must return to the wake," Lady Nobuko said. She and Korika started up the path.

"No." Reiko blocked their way. "We're not finished talking yet."

"What more is there to discuss?"

"Where were you last night when Yoshisato's residence caught fire?" Reiko asked.

Affronted, Lady Nobuko said, "That is none of your business."

"I say it is. Because my husband didn't set the fire, and I have to clear his name by finding out who did."

Lady Nobuko's expression turned incredulous. "And you think it was me?"

"She didn't do it!" Korika blurted. Horror sharpened the perpetual anxiety on her face. "Why would she?"

"She hates Yanagisawa," Reiko said. "She thinks he killed Tsuruhime, who was like a daughter to her. What better way to get revenge on him than by killing Yoshisato?"

"For all we know, Yoshisato may be the shogun's son and Yanagisawa really is only his adoptive father," Lady Nobuko said. "If so, his death doesn't compensate me for Tsuruhime's."

"Don't play games with me," Reiko said hotly. "*You* believe Yanagisawa is Yoshisato's father. You didn't want Yoshisato to be the next shogun or Yanagisawa to rule Japan through him. And now that Yoshisato is dead, you've gotten double the value for the price of one murder. You don't need my husband to prove that Yanagisawa is responsible for Tsuruhime's death because you think Yanagisawa has already gotten his comeuppance."

Lady Nobuko permitted herself a smug little smile. "Yoshisato's death was merely good luck for me. I didn't set the fire. Maybe it was an accident. Most fires are."

"Not this one," Reiko said. "My husband found a smoking basket, a jar of kerosene, and some rags hidden at the scene."

She saw uncertainty disturb Lady Nobuko, who obviously hadn't heard about everything that had happened last night. Then Lady Nobuko's composure returned. She said, "Even if the fire was arson, why are you accusing me? Other people besides myself probably didn't want Yoshisato to inherit the dictatorship or Yanagisawa to control the government."

"You have a personal grudge against Yanagisawa. He had you kidnapped and raped. My husband tried to prove it and couldn't. Then Yanagisawa infected Tsuruhime with smallpox, according to you." Reiko moved closer to Lady Nobuko. "What happened? Were you afraid my husband wouldn't be able to prove Yanagisawa was responsible for that crime, either? Did you take matters into your own hands?"

Arms folded, Lady Nobuko stood her ground. "Your suppositions are ridiculous." Her voice could have frozen boiling lye. "I did not kill Yoshisato. The very idea of my creeping around at night, setting a fire!"

She seemed to think she should be absolved of the crime because the practicalities of it were beneath her. Reiko did have difficulty picturing Lady Nobuko pouring kerosene under the heir's residence and throwing in rags lit from the coals in the smoking basket, but she'd encountered other unlikely murderesses in the past.

"Then answer my question," Reiko said. "Where were you last night?"

"In my bedchamber, asleep," Lady Nobuko said.

"She was," Korika hastened to say. "I have the room next to hers. She never left."

"Of course you would vouch for her," Reiko said. "She's your mistress."

"She's telling the truth. I was awakened by the fire bells. The noise made my head ache terribly. I called Korika. She spent the rest of the night nursing me," Lady Nobuko said. "This conversation is finished."

She and Korika started up the path. This time Reiko stepped aside. It was no use trying to badger a confession out of Lady Nobuko. The frail old woman was too strong-minded. And she might be innocent.

But Reiko perceived that Lady Nobuko was ruthless and clever enough to have hired someone to set the fire. A wild, helpless fury seized Reiko as the wind blew rain on her. She called after Lady Nobuko, "I will exonerate my husband—I swear. You'd better hope you never need another favor from us."

娘

31

YANAGISAWA STOOD OUTSIDE Lady Someko's chamber. Her sobs quieted to whimpers. The physician came out with his medicine chest and said, "I gave her a potion. She'll be asleep soon."

"Good." After the physician left, Yanagisawa lingered in the corridor. Moments passed before he realized what he was doing. He was waiting for Yoshisato.

He had a strange, irrational notion that Yoshisato was still alive. Maybe it was because he hadn't actually witnessed Yoshisato's death. He couldn't believe that one of those grisly corpses was Yoshisato. A stubborn part of him thought Yoshisato was coming back.

Yanagisawa shook his head at himself. He couldn't hang around wishing for the impossible. He had to go back to the funeral, put up a strong front, and make sure his faction didn't desert him. But as he walked through the empty guesthouse, he slowed outside Yoshisato's room. He experienced an overpowering sense that Yoshisato was there. His heart leaped. He looked through the doorway. The room was empty, but the atmosphere vibrated with Yoshisato's presence, as if Yoshisato had just left. Yanagisawa could almost smell his fresh, youthful scent and hear the echo of his sardonic voice. Joy gave way to consternation.

Was Yoshisato's death driving him mad?

At the sound of footsteps in the corridor, hope resurged. Yanagisawa rushed out of the room and bumped into Kato Kinhide from the Council of Elders. He shouted.

"Sorry if I frightened you," Kato said.

Yanagisawa could barely contain his disappointment. "What are you doing here?"

"I saw the scene Lady Someko made at the funeral." Apprehension tinged the disgust on Kato's flat face. "Is she under control?"

"For the time being."

"That's not good enough. You should get rid of her."

Kato was right, but Yanagisawa balked at the idea of killing Lady Someko. He hated her viciousness, and at this moment he couldn't even imagine desiring her sexually, but she was Yoshisato's mother. She was his only connection with Yoshisato.

"I can't," Yanagisawa said. "She's the only person who can say for sure that the shogun is Yoshisato's father. That still matters even though Yoshisato is dead." Again he had that irrational feeling that Yoshisato was nearby, alive. He couldn't breathe a hint of it to Kato, who would think he was losing his mind. "If the shogun stops believing Yoshisato was his son, he'll be furious, and you and I and all our friends had better prepare to die."

"She's the only person who can say for sure that the shogun isn't Yoshisato's father." Kato obviously suspected the truth. "She's dangerous."

"I can take care of her," Yanagisawa assured himself as well as Kato.

"You'd better take care of Sano, too. As long as he's alive, he'll cause you trouble."

Yanagisawa responded indignantly. "I tried to take care of him. You and the other elders stopped me. Why? Don't tell me you really think Sano might be innocent and he should get a fair trial."

"Some people are still sympathetic toward Sano. You don't want them to think you're rushing to frame him."

"Not many. They can't hurt me," Yanagisawa scoffed.

"You're wrong. The political situation has changed drastically since yesterday," Kato said. "Ienobu is the heir apparent again. The next battle will be you fighting him for control of the regime. You can't afford to offend Sano's friends. You need to get them on your side."

Vexed because Kato was right again, Yanagisawa said, "How would you have me do that?"

"When Sano goes to trial, make the case against him so conclusive that everybody will believe he's guilty. Then nobody will take offense at his death. His former allies will join your camp. Ienobu has the advantage of being the shogun's nephew, but he's repulsive. You aren't. Never underestimate the power of good looks."

Yanagisawa hesitated, torn between his craving for immediate revenge against Sano, his need to shore up his political position, and his urge to search for Yoshisato.

"You lost a war ten years ago," Kato reminded him. "You should strengthen your forces as much as possible for this one." The slits of his eyes gleamed with fear for himself. "Do you really want your hatred for Sano to push you into hasty action and then gamble that you'll be able to pull off another comeback?"

Yanagisawa sighed, conceding to reality.

"Look at it this way," Kato said. "You can make Sano suffer for a little while longer before he dies. Pile the mud on his name. He'll be the most despised criminal in Japan."

"WELL, LOOK WHO'S here, right on time," Tahara said to Hirata.

"We thought you wouldn't show up," Kitano said.

They and Deguchi sat on the bank of a canal in the Kanda district, under an overturned wooden boat that sheltered them from the rain. Kanda had been hit hard by the earthquake. Houses, embankments, and bridges had collapsed. Ruins still lay everywhere. Rebuilding had barely started. Tahara, Kitano, and Deguchi were the only people Hirata saw.

"Why wouldn't I show up?" Dismounting from his horse, Hirata avoided looking at Deguchi, who avoided looking at him. They mustn't let Kitano and Tahara guess that they were now in league against the secret society.

"You haven't exactly been enthusiastic about working with us," Kitano said. He and Tahara and Deguchi crawled out from under the boat.

"I've decided to quit fighting you and enjoy the benefits of being in the society," Hirata said as nonchalantly as he could.

"Will wonders never cease?" Eyes twinkling, Kitano clapped Hirata on the back.

The four men walked to the canal's edge. The government had cleared most of the waterways, but this was a narrow branch in what had been a poor neighborhood. It was a swamp clogged with broken boats, a fallen bridge, collapsed houses, and other debris, all blanketed by a green scum of algae. Gnats and mosquitoes buzzed. The men began to breathe in slow, deep rhythm. Mystical powers started to flow. Hirata's lungs expanded his ribs; his heartbeat accelerated to a thunderous drumming. The blood in his veins swelled with invigorating forces. He chanted an ancient Chinese magic spell. His nerves and muscles tingled. He felt a stiffening sensation as the physical, mental, and spiritual energies within him gathered and aligned. He and Deguchi, Tahara, and Kitano extended their hands toward the canal.

Invisible rays of energy shot from their fingertips. The air around the rays shimmered; raindrops vaporized. Jolts shook Hirata as his power locked onto objects in the canal. He and the other men slowly raised their hands. Boards and stones levitated. They hung in the air, dripping water. The men gestured, wafting the debris toward the opposite bank. They cut off the flow of power long enough for the debris to fall on the ground. They brought up furniture and pieces of the bridge. They gasped as fatigue began to set in. Levitation required a lot of energy. Up came more debris. The water level dropped. Something big was hidden below the surface. As Hirata and the other men strained to lift it, his fingertips burned as if they were on fire. The thing slowly rose.

It was an oxcart filled with water that streamed out of cracks in the bottom. Ropes tied to the yokes stretched under the heavy weight of two dead oxen. Decayed meat clung to the skeletons. The men let the whole mess drop on the bank. The spell broke. Panting, they collapsed. Sweat poured from Hirata. He and the others lay still, their eyes shut, their mouths open, swallowing rain to cool their parched throats.

"I hope General Otani has a good reason for putting us through that," Tahara said.

"Maybe he'll tell us what it is at the ritual tomorrow," Kitano said.

Alarm snapped Hirata's eyes open. He raised himself on his elbow. The other men sat up. He smelled the stench of the ox carcasses. "Another ritual? Tomorrow?"

"Yes," Tahara said. "Something wrong?"

Hirata glanced at Deguchi. The priest was looking at him in naked horror. "No," Hirata said, trying to sound unconcerned. "I'm just wondering why so soon."

Tahara and Kitano didn't catch Deguchi's expression. Kitano said, "It's time."

Neither Hirata nor Deguchi could risk going into a trance. General Otani would know they'd banded together against him and Tahara and Kitano. He would kill them both. But they had to pretend to go along with Tahara and Kitano and not arouse their suspicion.

"All right," Hirata said. Deguchi nodded. "When tomorrow?"

"The hour of the snake," Tahara said.

"In the morning?" Hirata said, alarmed because he and Deguchi had less than a day to prepare for killing Tahara and Kitano.

"There's no rule that says all rituals have to be done at night," Tahara said.

"Let's go back to town and have a drink," Kitano said. He and Tahara stood.

Hirata glanced at Deguchi, then groaned and lay down again. "I'm not ready to move yet." Deguchi lay down, too, shutting his eyes.

"See you tomorrow morning," Kitano called as he and Tahara rode away on their horses.

Hirata and Deguchi waited until the sound of hoofbeats faded. They sat up and turned to each other. Deguchi raised his eyebrows, spread his palms, and opened his mouth in a mute demand: *What are we going to do?*

"We'll kill them when they come for the ritual," Hirata decided.

How?

They needed more than will or luck to kill Tahara and Kitano. Hirata dragged himself to his feet. "We'd better go make some preparations."

THE HEIR'S RESIDENCE was a pile of blackened timbers, cracked roof tiles, and cinders drenched by the rain. Masahiro walked through the grounds, which were awash in sooty puddles. He smelled burned meat under the odor of smoke. He held his nose, trying not to throw up. He didn't want to go where he'd seen the corpses of Yoshisato and the other men. But he must look for clues. This was the most important investigation ever, no time to be a sissy. Unless he and his mother found out who'd set the fire, his father would be convicted of arson and put to death.

Masahiro stopped at the edge of the wreckage. Despair crept through him. What clues could possibly not have burned up?

Three oxcarts rolled through the gate. Laborers jumped out of the carts as the drivers halted near the wreckage. They began picking up burned debris and tossing it into the carts. Masahiro hurried toward them, to tell them to wait until he finished searching for clues. Then two men came into the compound. They were high-ranking officers from the Tokugawa army, with elaborate armor and helmets. Masahiro instinctively knew they wouldn't be pleased to find him snooping around. He scampered to a grove of pine trees and hid.

"What are we looking for?" said one of the officers.

"Evidence to use at Sano's trial," said his comrade.

They looked at the ruins, then at each other. "It seems hopeless," the first man said. He had a squat body and thick jowls. Masahiro recognized him. His name was Okubo. He and his comrade were Yanagisawa's friends.

"I agree, but we'd better go through the motions of searching." The other man was named Kitami. His armor hung on his bony figure like hide on a skeleton. The features under his helmet were gaunt, pinched. "If we don't, somebody might say the investigation wasn't thorough enough and raise a stink."

Masahiro was horrified. That his father's fate depended on a lazy investigation by men who worked for Yanagisawa!

The laborers heaped the oxcarts with debris. Kitami said, "Let them do the dirty work. We'll see if they turn up anything interesting."

He and Okubo watched the laborers. Masahiro knew that if he interfered, they would only laugh at him and throw him out. He waited helplessly, trembling with rage.

Okubo coughed. "Ugh, the smell is making me sick."

"Me, too," Kitami said. "Let's go stand over there."

They headed straight for Masahiro's hiding place. He scuttled backward, farther into the trees. He crouched behind the biggest one.

"Hey, what's that?" Okubo said.

Masahiro thought he'd been spotted, but the men weren't looking at him. Okubo pointed at something caught on a stub of branch that protruded from a pine tree. Kitami pulled it off, held it up, and said, "It looks like a fire hood."

Masahiro saw that it was indeed a fire hood, made of pale leather, shaped like a cone with a blunt tip. It had a hole cut out for the eyes and a flap that tied over the nose and mouth with ribbons.

"Whoever was wearing it must have got caught on the tree and it came off," Okubo said.

"It's a woman's," Kitami said. "See the flowers." He touched the pink cherry blossoms embossed in the leather.

Masahiro pictured flames licking at the heir's residence while a woman dressed in a leather cape and flowered hood ran away through the trees. He saw the branch snag the hood and tear it off her head. His heart raced with excitement. Here was evidence that someone other than his father—a woman—had set the fire.

"What are we going to do with this?" Kitami asked. "Bring it to Chamberlain Yanagisawa?"

Okubo said, "It doesn't belong to Sano. No man would wear this."

The men looked at each other. Masahiro read their shared thought: Yanagisawa only wanted evidence that incriminated Sano.

Kitami carried the hood to an oxcart that was almost full of debris. He threw the hood in. Masahiro watched, dismayed, as the laborers dumped burned planks on top of it. The driver cracked his whip at the oxen. They began hauling the cart away. Masahiro wanted to run after the cart, but Kitami and Okubo stood between him and the gate through which it disappeared. He clenched his fists and jittered, silently begging them to leave. He had to get that hood. It was proof of his father's innocence.

32

SANO PACED THE floor in his chamber. The wounds on his head and face hurt, and he was exhausted because he'd hardly slept last night, but he was too restless to lie down. The house felt like a cage that shrank with every passing hour. Whenever he left his chamber, his jailers followed him around. Now it was late afternoon. He hadn't seen anybody else all day except the servants who brought his meals. He'd sent Detective Marume to find out how a fire could have been set in a heavily guarded section of the castle. He'd never felt so trapped, isolated, or powerless in his life.

Yoshisato's murder was his biggest case, the one in which he had the most at stake, and he had to depend on his wife, his twelve-year-old son, and his chief retainer to solve it. He was alone with his hatred of the shogun, which preyed on him like wolf's teeth gutting a live deer. His mutinous thoughts and desire for revenge multiplied. He dreaded his impending trial.

Marume came into the room, saying, "I tracked down the guards who were on duty around the heir's residence last night. That's three in the watchtower that overlooks the residence, three in the nearest checkpoint, and three on patrol. One of the watchtower guards is a friend of mine. He said they were called away from their posts."

"Called away, how?" Sano was intrigued. "By whom?"

"A message from the captain of the night watch. It ordered them to come to a meeting at headquarters, which, as you know, is on the other side of the hill and two levels down."

"When was this?"

"A little less than an hour before the fire started."

"So nobody was watching the heir's residence at the critical time," Sano deduced. "Which explains how the arsonist entered the compound and left without getting caught."

"Listen to this: When the men got to headquarters, there was no meeting."

"The message was a ruse to get them out of the way, then. Who delivered it?"

"A page," Marume said. "He brought it to their supervising lieutenant at the watchtower. My friend doesn't know the boy's name, never saw him before. He also told me the night watch captain says he never sent any message. Maybe the page was an imposter sent by the arsonist."

"Or by the person the arsonist was working for. This crime required careful planning."

Marume followed Sano's line of thought. "It sounds too sophisticated for someone who does dirty work like setting fires. The arsonist must have been the hands. Who was the mind?"

"Lord Ienobu," Sano said. "If not him, then Lady Nobuko."

"Any word about her from your wife?"

Sano shook his head. "None from Masahiro yet, either. That was good work, Marume. Thank you." Words were inadequate to express his appreciation for his retainer's competent, loyal service.

"I hope to do even better," Marume said, cheered by Sano's praise. "I've launched a search for that page. Somebody must have seen him. Or seen something at the heir's residence before the fire started. I've called in every favor. If there are any witnesses, I'll dig them up."

"That will take time. Yanagisawa isn't going to wait for me to find evidence to clear my name. I need some sort of defense. Will your friend testify for me at my trial?"

The cheer drained from Marume's face. "I asked him. He said no. The lieutenant ordered him and the other guards to keep quiet about what happened. They'll get in trouble if it comes out that they left their posts. If they'd been there, they might have rescued Yoshisato. They could be put to death for letting him burn."

"Whoever lured them away knew they would be afraid to talk," Sano said, disappointed but not surprised. "Where's the message they received?"

"It was verbal, not written."

"And he was careful not to leave tracks."

"Don't lose hope," Marume urged. "Our luck is bound to change."

Without warning, soldiers invaded the room. The leader said to Sano, "It's time for your trial. Come with us."

Sano felt as though he'd been standing at the edge of a cliff and a thunderbolt had suddenly fractured the ground under his feet. He was falling away from everything solid and safe, into the abyss. "But I have to wait for my wife and son." They might have evidence that could save him. Even if not, Sano couldn't leave without seeing Reiko and Masahiro. He might be put to death immediately after the trial.

"You can't. We have orders to bring you to the palace now."

The bottom of the abyss came rushing up to meet Sano. Cut loose from all loved ones and all possibility of rescue, gripped by panic, Sano backed away from the troops.

"Come peacefully, or we'll take you by force," the leader said.

There was no use delaying the inevitable. Instinct and training took over. A wise samurai knows not to waste energy on undignified, futile struggling when the decisive battle is yet to come. Sano had to keep his strength for the trial, his last chance to save himself. He held up his hands, yielding.

"I'm going with him," Marume said, "to testify on his behalf. He couldn't have set the fire. He was at home asleep when it started."

"He's not allowed to bring any witnesses," the leader said.

"That's against the rules!" Marume protested.

"Chamberlain Yanagisawa sets the rules." The leader shoved Marume aside.

Marume shoved him back. Suddenly the troops were all shouting, yanking at Marume, grabbing at Sano. Marume roared, throwing punches. Cries rang out as his fists connected with flesh. Steel rasped as the troops drew their swords.

"No!" the leader said sharply. "We're supposed to bring him alive!"

Sano, caught in the scuffle, yelled, "Stop, Marume-*san*! Don't get yourself killed."

Marume ceased fighting. Two guards seized him and held his arms. He panted, his eyes hot and his teeth bared, like a wild horse restrained. The troops surrounded Sano so closely that he could smell the animal scent of the leather that covered the metal plates of their armor. As they nudged him toward the door, Sano said to Marume, "Take care of my family."

The bluster leaked out of Marume. His big face filled with anguish. He knew this might be the last order Sano ever gave him. Sano felt a swelling in his throat. Marume nodded. This was their only tribute to the years that they'd been master and retainer. They both hoped this wasn't the end. Neither could bear to say good-bye.

The troops marched Sano down the passage. His home felt strangely impersonal, like a way station on a journey from which there was no return. When he emerged from the mansion, his few retainers were in the courtyard. Army troops guarded them. As Sano walked down the steps, they bowed with solemn dignity. The gesture touched Sano's heart. They must be afraid for themselves—if he were convicted and put to death, they could be executed as associates of a traitor. But they paid him what might be their last respects.

"Papa!" Akiko came running onto the veranda. Midori, Taeko, and Tatsuo followed her. She bounded down the steps, raced to Sano, and threw her arms around his legs. She cried, "Don't go, Papa!"

Sano's heart clutched painfully. She was too young to understand why he was leaving, but she knew it was bad. The troops shuffled to a halt. The leader said, "Keep moving." He grabbed Akiko's arm and pulled.

Akiko wailed and held on. Stroking her hair, Sano said gently, "Akiko, you have to let me go." The leader pulled harder. Her little fingers gripped Sano's trousers, then came loose. Sano felt as if a part of his own body were being torn away. Akiko shrieked. She turned on the leader, yelled, "You're not taking my father away!" and clawed his face.

He recoiled, cursing, his cheeks marked by bloody scratches. Sano rushed Akiko toward the house. Midori hastened down the steps to meet them. Taeko and Tatsuo were crying. They were old enough to understand. Sano turned to Akiko. She wasn't crying. Her little face was savage with rebellion.

"Listen to me, Akiko," Sano said. "You have to be a good girl while I'm gone."

"When are you coming back?" Akiko said.

He hated lying to his child, but the truth was worse. "Soon."

"Do you promise?"

"I promise." Sano hugged Akiko, hiding his tears against her soft hair. Then he gave her over to Midori.

As the soldiers led him away, he couldn't look back. He kept his gaze trained straight ahead while he marched through the passages inside Edo Castle. Soldiers peered at him from watchtowers, from windows in the covered corridors atop the walls. He felt as if he were enclosed in a bubble of putrid slime. But the slime didn't keep spectators at a distance. As his procession moved uphill, it attracted followers. By the time it reached the palace, its ranks had swelled to hundreds of soldiers, officials, pages, and servants. Sano thought of the parades during religious festivals, when crowds followed men carrying portable shrines through the streets. But here there was no loud, gay reveling. Everyone was quiet, befitting a grave moment in history. Instead of a shrine that housed the holy spirit of a god, the parade followed the lowest form of life, an accused traitor.

Flames guttered in the stone lanterns that flanked the path to the palace, even though the gray sky was still light. Palace sentries opened the door. It gaped like the maw of hell. As Sano neared it, the crowd dropped back. Pigeons fluttered in the eaves as he passed under them. The sound of hammering drifted up from the city. Life was going on, indifferent to his plight. The palace swallowed him up. Inside, officials, troops, and attendants lined the hall. They mutely watched him and his escorts enter the large reception chamber.

A narrow aisle divided a silent crowd that occupied the lower level of the floor. The troops ahead of him blocked Sano's view of the chamber's far end. All he could see was the ochre glow of lanterns burning on the dais. The crowd watched the troops march Sano up the aisle. Glancing from right to left, Sano saw rows of unfriendly faces that belonged to officials and *daimyo* who were cronies of Yanagisawa.

Anyone who might have come to Sano's aid had been banned.

Sano stepped onto the higher level of the floor. In its middle, a small square of white sand covered the wooden boards—the *shirasu,* the white sand of truth, symbol of justice. The troops pushed Sano to his knees onto a straw mat in the center of the *shirasu.* Irony twisted Sano's cut lips. A short time ago he'd been conducting trials, dispensing justice. If justice were served here, it would be a miracle.

The troops retreated. Now Sano saw the three judges seated at his right, in a row angled to face him and the dais. One was Kato Kinhide from the Council of Elders. The other two were also Yanagisawa's cronies. Inspector General Nakae audited government operations, which meant he kept a lookout for misbehavior done by everyone except Yanagisawa. Broad of girth, he reminded Sano of an overripe pumpkin—he'd lost most of his teeth, and his face had caved in. Beside him was old, white-haired Lord Nabeshima, *daimyo* of Saga and Hizen Provinces, whose skin and eyes were yellow with jaundice.

Sano had run afoul of Inspector General Nakae and Lord Nabeshima when they'd been judges in a controversial murder trial. They beheld him with dirty pleasure, anticipating revenge. Sano looked toward the dais. Yanagisawa sat at its center, dressed in a formal black robe with glittering gold crests. The shogun was absent, and Sano knew why: Yanagisawa didn't want him to talk the shogun into letting him go free. Yanagisawa's handsome face was theatrically shadowed by the lanterns. His eyes were so rimmed with red and so underscored with dark shadows, his complexion so pale and so carved by lines of grief, that he looked like he was wearing stage makeup. He regarded Sano with a hatred as rigidly cold as chain mail in winter. The pity Sano had felt for this father who'd lost two sons vaporized in the heat of his anger.

There was no place on the battlefield for compassion toward one's opponent.

"I hereby commence the trial of Sano Ichirō," Yanagisawa said in a voice hoarse from weeping and raging.

A smile shimmered upon his mouth, its message as clear as if he'd shouted it: *All scores between us are about to be settled. For all the wrongs you've ever done me, you will pay.*

33

AT SANO'S ESTATE, his few retainers were locked inside their barracks with the army guarding them. Servants stampeded out the gate. They knew their master was on trial for the murder of the shogun's heir, and they were leaving before he could be condemned and his household rounded up to share his death sentence. Inside the mansion, Taeko huddled with her mother, brother, baby sister, and Akiko. Midori hugged the children close. Her eyes were filled with fear.

"Mama, what are we going to do?" Taeko asked.

"I don't know." Midori's voice trembled.

"Everybody's leaving," Tatsuo said. "Should we leave, too?"

"No. Maybe. I don't know," Midori said, frantic with confusion.

"I'm scared," Tatsuo said. "Can we go to our grandfathers?"

Midori's father, Lord Niu, had an estate in the *daimyo* district. Hirata's parents lived in the *banchō,* an area populated by hereditary Tokugawa vassals. "I don't know," Midori wailed.

Her mother's indecisiveness scared Taeko. She said, "We can't leave without Masahiro and Lady Reiko."

"Yes, you're right." Midori eagerly snatched at any guidance. "We'll wait for them. They'll know what to do."

"My father will be home soon," Akiko said. "He promised." She was serene in her faith in Sano. "He'll fix everything."

Nobody had the heart to contradict her. Taeko wished she could help

Masahiro solve the murder and save them all. But even if she could bear to leave her mother and the other children, how could she get away?

Midori stood up suddenly. "Maybe we should pack some things, in case Reiko and Masahiro say we have to leave. Tatsuo, Taeko, get some clothes, enough for a few days. Come, Akiko, I'll help you pack." Carrying the baby, she hurried Akiko away.

Tatsuo began pulling clothes out of the cabinet. Taeko saw her chance. There was no time to think. Impulse sent her running out the door.

"Hey!" Tatsuo called. "Where are you going?"

Taeko joined the servants fleeing the estate. Following them downhill through the passages inside Edo Castle, she was thankful for the company. She'd never left the castle at night by herself, and it was strange and scary. Lanterns cast shadows in which monsters seemed to lurk. Taeko cringed from mounted patrol guards, their faces dark under their helmets. They looked like suits of armor with invisible ghosts inside. Finally Taeko exited the main gate. It slammed shut behind her. She fought the urge to run back and pound on it. The maids scurried off in different directions. Taeko was alone.

On the avenue outside the castle, the friendly priests and nuns who begged for alms during the day were gone. Soldiers were chasing away other beggars, yelling threats and waving swords at a family camped on a blanket. The man had no legs. He and his wife scrambled to gather up their belongings as their little boy and girl cried.

Taeko hurried toward the *daimyo* district. The long, broad streets were like dark tunnels enclosed by the walls of the estates. The only light came from lanterns at the gates, where the *daimyo*'s guards stood watch. The guards called to passing troops. Masculine laughter echoed up and down the tunnels. Few other people were about. The side streets were even darker than the main ones. Taeko turned corners, lost. After what seemed like hours, she arrived breathless at the back gate of Lord Tsunanori's estate.

"What do you want?" the sentry asked.

"To go in," Taeko stammered through her fear. "I work in the laundry."

"Oh, you're the missing maid." He opened the gate. Taeko scurried in before she could lose her nerve. He called after her, "Housekeeper's been looking for you."

Taeko's heart sank. She'd forgotten the mean old housekeeper. She tiptoed around the outbuildings to the laundry courtyard. It was dark except for moonlight reflecting in puddles. The tent flaps were closed. Taeko cautiously lifted one and peered inside.

Warm air exuded the smells of lye, mildew, and stale breath. Taeko heard snoring, saw bodies lumped on the ground. The tent was too dark for Taeko to see very far. She took a step into the tent and trod on a foot.

The person it belonged to said in a cross voice, "Hey, be careful." The girl was Kiku, who'd chased Taeko yesterday. "Taeko? What are you doing here?"

"Shh!" Taeko glanced at the other women. "I have to talk to Emi."

"I'm going to tell Housekeeper you're back."

"No, please, don't," Taeko whispered.

A small figure rose inside the tent. Women grunted as Emi stumbled over them. Emi reached Taeko and pulled her outside. They ran together across the courtyard, between buildings, and crouched in the manure-scented shadows behind the stables. Horses neighed.

One side of Emi's lovely face was white in the moonlight, the other dark with the bruise where the mean woman had hit her. "I'm glad to see you, but why did you come back? You're going to be beaten for running away."

"You helped me once," Taeko said. "I need you to help me again."

Emi drew a sharp, frightened breath. Taeko hated to press Emi, but she was desperate. She said, "I know you didn't tell me everything last time. What else do you know about Lord Tsunanori's wife?"

"I can't tell you," Emi whispered. "I'll get in trouble."

"Please." Taeko grabbed Emi's hand. "It's important. If you don't tell me, my family and friends will die!"

Emi's eyes, immense and black in the moonlight, filled with confusion. "You're not really a poor orphan, are you? Who are you really? What do you want?"

"No, I'm not," Taeko confessed, sorry she'd deceived Emi. "My father is a samurai. His master is in trouble. I have to find out who killed Lord Tsunanori's wife."

"Why?"

Aware that she wasn't making much sense, Taeko said, "Because." She gripped Emi's hand tighter. "Now tell me!"

Emi's hand wilted as she gave in to the habit of following orders. "I saw Namiji."

"Who is Namiji?"

"She took care of Lady Tsuruhime when Lady Tsuruhime got small-pox," Emi explained. "But this was maybe six or seven days before then."

Taeko struggled to be patient. "What was Namiji doing when you saw her?"

"She was in Lady Tsuruhime's room," Emi said. "She was scrubbing the bed."

Puzzled, Taeko said, "Scrubbing, how?" Beds weren't usually scrubbed. The mattresses were hung outside to air, and the linens washed.

"With a dirty sheet. It looked like there was blood on it. And yellow stains. She rubbed it all over the mattress and the quilts and the pillow."

"Why?" Using a dirty sheet to scrub a bed made no sense to Taeko.

"I don't know. I was afraid to ask. She stuffed it in the cabinet."

Taeko felt sick with disappointment. She'd disobeyed her mother and come back to this scary place to hear about a servant acting strangely?

Emi chewed her lip, then said, "I just thought of something else."

"What?" Taeko's hope resurged.

"I saw Namiji with that sheet again later," Emi said. "She was in the back courtyard. It was the night after Lady Tsuruhime got smallpox."

Taeko pretended to be interested because she didn't want Emi to think her information was worthless. "What was Namiji doing?"

"She was burning the sheet."

Quick footsteps approached. The girls looked at each other in fright. Emi rose and said, "You'd better go."

Angry voices called, "Emi! Taeko!" It was Kiku and the housekeeper. Emi seized Taeko's hand. "Come with me!"

They ran past buildings, through grounds and passages. It was so dark that Taeko couldn't see where she was going. She blindly trusted Emi. They came to a compound that was under construction, deserted. Piles of lumber and roof tiles waited by the wall. Taeko spied a gate and started toward it, but Emi held her back.

"No! There's a guard outside." Emi pointed to a lumber pile. "Climb on that. Jump on top of the wall and go over the side."

The pile seemed as tall as the sky. Taeko gulped. She was afraid of high places.

"Hurry!" Emi whispered as the footsteps and voices came closer.

Taeko began to climb. Her heart beat so hard, it felt like it would jump out her throat. She crawled on top of the pile and stood on the uneven planks. The short distance to the wall looked as wide as the Sumida River, the gap bottomless. Taeko breathed so fast, she felt dizzy. With a wordless prayer on her lips, she jumped.

She flew through the air for an instant that lasted forever. Landing on the wall, she teetered, waving her arms. She crumpled, clutched the rough surface, and gasped.

"Go!" hissed Emi.

Taeko sat with her legs dangling over the wall. She shut her eyes and dropped far, far down to the street.

34

"THE COURT WILL now hear the evidence against Sano."
Yanagisawa spoke from the dais. "I call the first witness."

The three judges sat silently in their row, Sano on his knees on the
mat on the *shirasu*.

"Aoki Kenzan, step forward," Yanagisawa said.

Sano frowned, recognizing the gray-haired samurai who rose from
the audience, walked up the aisle, and knelt near him to his left.

"State your position," Yanagisawa ordered.

"I'm a retainer to Sano-*san*," Aoki said. "I'm captain of the night watch
at his estate."

Sano stared at Aoki in disbelief. The man had served him for fourteen years. "You're testifying against me?"

"You'll have a chance to speak later," Yanagisawa said coldly. "Until
then, be quiet or forfeit your chance to defend yourself."

Captain Aoki cast a miserable, pleading gaze at Sano. "I'm sorry,
master."

Sano supposed Yanagisawa had threatened Aoki into betraying him,
but the betrayal still hurt. Yanagisawa said, "Captain, please describe
what happened last night."

"I was at my post in the barracks. It was about half an hour before
midnight." Aoki's voice quavered. "Sano-*san* came and asked me to fetch
a smoking basket with hot coals, a jar of kerosene, and some rags."

"Aoki-*san*, you know I never did that!" Sano burst out.

"I'm warning you," Yanagisawa said. "Continue, Captain Aoki."

Tears of shame glistened on Aoki's face. "I put the things in a bag and gave them to Sano-*san*. He took the bag and left the estate."

Sano realized that although Yanagisawa truly believed him to be guilty, Yanagisawa hadn't enough evidence, so he'd fabricated some.

"That will be all, Captain Aoki," Yanagisawa said.

Captain Aoki's shoulders sagged as he left the room, a broken man who'd committed the worst violation of Bushido.

"I call the next witness," Yanagisawa said.

This was a man wearing the armor tunic and metal helmet of a castle guard. He had a square jaw, a nervous pucker between thick eyebrows, and a thick neck. He knelt without looking at Sano. He identified himself as Lieutenant Hayashi.

"Where were you on duty last night?" Yanagisawa asked.

"In the watchtower outside the heir's residence."

He was one of the guards who, according to Marume's friend among them, had left their posts to respond to a fake message, Sano realized. Hayashi had told the others to keep quiet about it.

"What happened?" Yanagisawa asked.

"Sano-*san* went to the heir's residence," Lieutenant Hayashi said in a small voice.

"Was he carrying anything?"

"Yes. A bag."

Yanagisawa aimed a significant look at the judges. "The bag that held the items Sano had obtained from Captain Aoki." His gaze dared Sano to say the lieutenant was lying, to forfeit his right to defend himself. Lieutenant Hayashi raised his shoulder, as if warding off heat from Sano's outraged stare.

"What happened next?" Yanagisawa said.

"I didn't see Sano-*san* go inside the building—it was too dark." Hayashi's speech sounded wooden, rehearsed. "A little while later, he came hurrying back down the passage."

"Did he still have the bag?"

"No." Without further prompting, Hayashi said, "Then the fire started."

The judges nodded at one another. Sano was furious because they were accepting the evidence without question, but he hadn't expected otherwise of Yanagisawa's cronies.

Yanagisawa dismissed the lieutenant. "Now I will present the physical proof of Sano's guilt." He beckoned a guard stationed along the wall.

The guard brought the metal smoking basket, the jar, and the rags. He set them on the dais by Yanagisawa, who held them up one by one. "This jar contained the kerosene Sano-*san* poured under the heir's residence. This is the basket in which he carried the burning coals he used to start the fire. The rags are leftover kindling. When I arrived at the scene, after the fire, I caught Sano trying to remove them. But that's not the most conclusive proof."

What now? Sano thought with disgust. *A forged confession supposedly written by me?*

Yanagisawa held up a large scrap of cloth. It was dark red silk, the edges torn. A design embroidered on it in gold thread glinted like flames. The design was a flying crane.

"The flying crane is Sano's family crest," Yanagisawa said. "This scrap was found stuck in a bush near the burned building. It was torn off Sano's robe while he set the fire."

It hadn't been torn off any of Sano's clothes. Yanagisawa had probably had the crest copied long ago and saved it until he needed it. But the judges seemed ready to believe anything Yanagisawa said.

"That concludes my evidence against Sano-*san*. Now you may speak." Yanagisawa's expression told Sano not to waste his breath; he was already defeated.

Sano faced the judges. Denials wouldn't do him any good. Neither would accusing Lord Ienobu or Lady Nobuko. He had no evidence against them and no witnesses to testify to his innocence. The only weapon he had was words. They had better be spectacular.

"I did not set the fire," Sano declared in a voice that resounded through the chamber. "I did not murder Yoshisato."

That was the only unadulterated truth he intended to tell.

Truth, which he'd always valued dearly, along with justice and honor, wouldn't save his life. His honor had already been trampled in the dirt, and so had justice. Pushed to the extremes of desperation, Sano kicked away truth, the third, obsolete pillar that had once constituted the foundation of his life.

The judges looked bored, unimpressed. Sano was about to change that. "All the evidence you've heard is false, except one piece." He told his first lie. "I did go to the heir's residence last night."

The lie tasted bitter, but like the right medicine for a disease.

Low, uneasy murmurs arose from the audience, as if the floor had tilted under it. Surprise wiped the boredom off the judges' faces. Yanagisawa twitched involuntarily. He said, "Don't be fooled. He's about to feed you a fairy tale."

Sano said blandly, "I'm just confirming what Lieutenant Hayashi said. Are you contradicting your own witness?"

Yanagisawa's mouth fell open. Lord Nabeshima said, "I want to hear this." His yellow eyes gleamed with interest. "Sano-*san,* why did you go to the heir's residence?"

"To visit Yoshisato." Sano tossed his next lie on top of the first two. Lying was getting easier. "Because Yoshisato invited me."

"He didn't," Kato Kinhide said. His scorn, and Yanagisawa's, didn't hide their effort to figure out where Sano was going with this. "Why would he have?"

"He wanted to finish a conversation we started at the tournament," Sano said.

"A conversation about what?" Inspector General Nakae asked.

"Yoshisato made me a proposition." Sano mixed a dash of truth into his story. "He wanted to build a coalition to clean up corruption in the government, end the political warfare, and bring peace and harmony to the regime. He asked me to join his coalition."

Outrage shattered Yanagisawa's control. "Yoshisato did no such thing!"

"How do you know?" Sano said. "You weren't there."

"A *coalition?* With *you?* That's ridiculous!"

"That's why Yoshisato wouldn't let you purge me from the regime or kill me," Sano said truthfully. "Because he wanted me to help him run the government when he became shogun."

Yanagisawa's eyes widened: He realized Sano couldn't have known

Yoshisato had saved him unless Yoshisato had told him so. The judges seemed shocked into believing Sano, amazed to learn that the youth they'd counted on to cement their power over the regime had had his own plans.

Sano wished he'd made Yoshisato's proposition public earlier. It might have changed everything. At any rate, it was a card he could play now. "I told Yoshisato I needed to think about his proposition. He invited me to visit him last night. When I got there, he asked what my answer was." Sano paused. The room was hushed with suspense, Yanagisawa too flabbergasted to speak. "I said yes."

Sano beheld the stricken faces of the judges and Yanagisawa as they absorbed the possibility that if Yoshisato had lived, the world would have seen a new day. Sano wondered whether, if he really had accepted the proposition, Yoshisato would be alive and himself not charged with arson and murder.

"I had no reason to kill Yoshisato," Sano concluded. "We parted as friends."

"That's a blatant lie!" Yanagisawa's passionate, angry voice rang with conviction. "Yoshisato never mentioned this coalition to me. Sano is just trying to save his despicable skin."

Sano thought that Yoshisato couldn't have been eager to reveal his plan to Yanagisawa and probably hadn't done so. But Yanagisawa never sounded more convincing than when he was lying. Sano saw the same thought occur to the judges. Disbelief tinged the gazes they bent on Yanagisawa.

"Yoshisato did tell you about his coalition. He said so last night," Sano lied. "He also said you were furious because he told you he didn't want you in the coalition. He thought you would only make trouble. He was going to cut you out of the regime." Sano pointed at Yanagisawa. "I'm not the one who had reason to murder Yoshisato. You are."

Yanagisawa's eyes filled with enlightenment and indignation. The judges' mouths dropped as they perceived the point of Sano's testimony. Mutters from the audience sounded like grudging cheers. Sano had turned the tables on Yanagisawa.

"You went to the heir's residence after I left," Sano said, embellishing his tale. "You set the fire. You showed up afterward and pretended to be upset that Yoshisato was dead." His tale could very well be true. Yoshisato's plans for the future gave Yanagisawa an excellent motive for murder. "And you put the blame on me." Sano turned to the judges. "Yanagisawa burned Yoshisato to death."

They looked to Yanagisawa, as if hoping he could brush off Sano's charges and fearing they'd cast their lot with the real murderer of the shogun's heir.

A change came over Yanagisawa. He relaxed, smiled, and began to applaud. The sound was like the clappers used at Kabuki plays, to herald a new development in the plot.

"That's a good story, Sano-*san*." Yanagisawa was never a better actor than when he was under pressure, Sano remembered. "But have you evidence to back it up?"

Here was the weakness in Sano's ploy. "You didn't give me enough time to find some."

"I'll take that as a no," Yanagisawa said. "How about witnesses?"

"I wasn't allowed to bring any."

"Well, I have one more." Yanagisawa signaled to a guard.

The guard went out and returned with a woman. It was Lady Someko, Yoshisato's mother. Her makeup was perfect, her deep red kimono opulent, but her features seemed oddly flaccid. She tripped on her skirts as she walked toward Sano. The guard held her up. When he lowered her to her knees, she seemed unaware of her surroundings, of the other people in the room. Her eyes had a dark, unnatural shininess.

"You said you were finished presenting evidence," Sano objected.

"I changed my mind." Yanagisawa had apparently saved a surprise witness in case Sano made too good an impression on the judges. He wasn't letting himself be cornered into confessing he'd murdered Yoshisato. He said to Lady Someko, "What happened yesterday?"

". . . Yesterday," Lady Someko echoed. Her voice was sleepy, her expression vague.

"She acts like she's been drugged," Sano said. "She's in no shape to testify."

The judges regarded her doubtfully. Yanagisawa ignored Sano. He asked Lady Someko, "You went to Sano's house, didn't you?"

"I went to Sano's house," she murmured.

"You're coaching her." Sano was dismayed but not surprised that Yanagisawa knew about Lady Someko's visit.

"Do you want me to bring in your guards to confirm that she was in your house?" Yanagisawa retorted, then turned back to Lady Someko. "What did you hear there?"

"I heard . . ." Confusion wrinkled her forehead.

"You heard my wife tell you that Yoshisato went to visit the shogun's daughter," Sano said. "You were upset because you realized he could have put a smallpox-infected sheet in her room. You think he killed her." It was true, and if Sano couldn't get rid of Lady Someko, at least he could cast aspersion on Yoshisato and distract the judges.

Lady Someko seemed oblivious to Sano. The judges' attention was on her. "I heard Sano talking to his wife and son." Her eyes were half closed.

"I wasn't there," Sano said hotly to Yanagisawa. "Go ahead, bring in my guards—they'll tell you that."

"What did Sano and his wife and son say?" Yanagisawa said, impatient for Lady Someko to finish the story before Sano debunked it or she fell asleep.

"Sano said Yoshisato had to die," Lady Someko murmured. "His wife suggested setting his house on fire. His son said to make it look like an accident. Sano agreed."

The judges blinked in surprise. Horror launched Sano to his feet as the point of Lady Someko's testimony became clear. Yanagisawa wasn't content to persecute Sano. He was after Reiko and Masahiro, too. "We never said that! She couldn't have heard it!"

Guards ran to Sano, pushed him down on the mat. Yanagisawa said, "So Sano didn't conceive the murder alone. His wife and son conspired with him." He added triumphantly, "They're as guilty as he is."

"No!" Sano struggled against the guards. White sand scattered.

"They deserve to be convicted along with Sano," Yanagisawa told the judges.

"You invented the whole story for Lady Someko to tell!" Sano shouted. "It's a lie!"

Yanagisawa ordered, "Silence him!" The guards pinned Sano on the floor, tied a kerchief around his mouth, and twisted his arm behind his back.

Lady Someko slumped, dozing. Yanagisawa said, "The trial is concluded. Judges, render your verdict."

Immobilized, Sano looked pleadingly up at the judges. They exchanged perturbed glances. Sano felt them weighing their choices. They could convict Sano, whom they weren't sure was guilty, and please Yanagisawa; or they could give Sano the benefit of their doubt and enrage Yanagisawa, whose retaliations were brutal.

"Guilty," they chorused. Lord Nabeshima brushed particles of white sand off his robe.

Yanagisawa's chest inflated with satisfaction. "What about his wife and son?"

Inspector General Nakae spoke with confidence now that he'd made his decision about Sano. "Both guilty of treasonous conspiracy to commit arson and murder the shogun's heir."

The other two judges nodded adamantly. Sano shouted protests through the gag.

"Your sentence is as the law requires." Yanagisawa's smile was cruel, exultant. "You and your wife and son are sentenced to death. So is your daughter. Also your father-in-law Magistrate Ueda, and your other close relatives, and top retainers and their families. You will all be burned at the stake tomorrow, after Yoshisato's funeral."

35

THE CLANK OF a shovel digging rocky soil echoed through the hills outside Edo. Their steep, forested terrain was dark except for the clearing, where lanterns surrounded a deep, round pit. Using a pulley hung from a branch that extended over the pit, Hirata hauled up a bucket full of dirt on a rope. He dumped the dirt in the woods, then said, "That's deep enough."

Far below him, at the bottom of the pit, Deguchi leaned on his shovel. His face was grimy; his shaved head glistened with sweat. He tossed his shovel to Hirata. Hirata caught it in hands that were sore and blistered. He and Deguchi had taken turns digging for more than two hours. Even with their supernatural strength it was hard work.

Deguchi climbed up. He and Hirata overlaid the pit with branches they'd cut, then covered the branches with leaves and twigs.

"That trap is set," Hirata said. "Let's do a final inspection on everything else."

They walked around the clearing. Hirata held a lantern up to the trees. Ropes, tied to strong boughs, were camouflaged with vines coiled around them. Hirata shone the light into a clump of bushes that hid extra swords. He examined a patch of open ground and rearranged the leaves that he and Deguchi had scattered over the forty sharp blades they'd planted upright in the earth. "And in case all else fails—"

He lowered the lantern; the light touched the thick base of an oak tree. Tucked inside a hollow was a small paper bag.

Hirata collected equipment and blew out the flames in all the lanterns except the one he held. Deguchi unrigged the pulley and coiled the rope. They sat on the flat altar stone in the center of the clearing and gazed around the battlefield they'd prepared for their confrontation with Tahara and Kitano. Deguchi mouthed, *Won't they notice that something's different?*

Mystic martial artists were hypersensitive to changes in the environment. Hirata said, "We won't give them time to react."

Worry dimmed the glow in Deguchi's eyes. *Is this enough?*

"We've done the best we can." Hirata was worried, too. He and Deguchi couldn't defeat Tahara and Kitano in a fair fight. He hoped their preparations would give them enough of an extra advantage. "We should go back to town and get a good rest, so we'll be ready for tomorrow."

They had to win, or they were dead.

WHEN REIKO ARRIVED home, she saw the army standing outside the walls, encircling the estate. Her heart began to pound with fear. She faltered up to the gate. Soldiers wordlessly opened it for her. She found the courtyard occupied by more troops guarding the barracks. Sano's retainers peered out the barred windows like caged animals.

Panic weakened Reiko's legs. The baby inside her seemed suddenly heavier. She gripped the railing as she mounted the stairs. Inside the mansion, she called to Sano. Her own voice echoed. She hurried through empty corridors. The chamber where she'd left Sano was also vacant. She clutched the walls, faint with terror.

"Mama!" Akiko cried. She and Tatsuo came running.

Reiko gasped, bent, and embraced Akiko. "Where is your father?"

"The soldiers took him," Akiko said.

Horror clenched icy tentacles around Reiko's heart. Sano had gone to his trial. "When?"

"A long time ago."

Had he already been convicted and put to death? Reiko shut her mind against the thought. "Where is Masahiro?"

"He hasn't come home yet," Akiko said.

"Where are your sister and mother?" Reiko asked Tatsuo.

"Taeko sneaked out. Mama went to find her." Tatsuo's face was woeful.

"Where are the servants?"

"They left."

Because they thought Sano was done for, Reiko realized. They wanted to avoid being punished along with him. Reiko's self-control eroded like cliffs lashed by a stormy ocean. But the children needed her; she mustn't fall apart.

"Come with me." She put her arms around them and hurried them along the corridor.

"Where are we going?" Tatsuo asked anxiously.

Reiko didn't know, but she couldn't bear staying in the deserted house. It was too full of Sano's absence. Outside they found Detective Marume arguing with one of the soldiers in the courtyard.

"Go back in the barracks," the soldier ordered.

"I have to talk to my master's wife," Marume said angrily.

The soldier saw Reiko and the children on the veranda. "Oh, all right. Just stay outside where I can see you."

Marume bounded onto the veranda, muttering, "When this is over, I'm going to slice off your fat rear end and you'll never be able to sit down again."

"Where did they take my husband?" Reiko asked urgently.

"To the palace," Marume said. "Less than an hour ago."

Masahiro rushed across the courtyard and up the steps. "I have evidence that could save Father!" Dirt and sawdust coated his hair, his clothes, and his sweaty face.

Alarmed, Reiko said, "Where have you been?"

"The dump." Masahiro pulled a wad of leather from inside his kimono, unfolded it, and waved it at Reiko. It was a leather hood with flowers painted on it. "Yanagisawa's investigators found this near where the fire was. The arsonist must have left it."

"It's a woman's," Reiko said, elated. "Lady Nobuko did set the fire."

"They threw it in an oxcart that was going to the dump. When I got there, I had to dig through mountains of trash. But I found it!" Masahiro smiled triumphantly.

"I haven't found out anything." After confronting Lady Nobuko at the wake, Reiko had spent the day loitering near Lord Ienobu's house, hoping to ask his maids about his and his retainers' movements the night of the fire. But no maids had come out. Reiko seized Masahiro's hand. "We must go to the palace at once and present your evidence to the court."

"You won't be able to," Marume said unhappily. "I tried to go with Sano-*san,* to testify for him. The soldiers wouldn't let me. They said he wasn't allowed to have witnesses."

"But the fire hood says he's innocent and Lady Nobuko murdered Yoshisato!" Reiko protested.

"It's the kind of evidence Yanagisawa is keeping out of the trial," Marume said.

Midori trudged into the courtyard, dragging Taeko by the hand, saying, "If we get out of this alive, you will never, ever leave home again, do you hear me?" When Taeko saw Masahiro, her dejected expression turned into a radiant smile.

Reiko was horrified by what Marume had said, but she was relieved to see Midori and Taeko. "Did she go back to Lord Tsunanori's estate?"

"Indeed she did," Midori said grimly.

Taeko pulled free of her mother. "Masahiro, I found the witness again. She told me a story." Her eyes brimmed with hope that it would please him. "She saw the nurse who took care of Lady Tsuruhime scrubbing her bed with dirty sheets."

Masahiro's jaw dropped. "So the nurse gave her smallpox."

Astonishment flooded Reiko. "Taeko, you found out who killed the shogun's daughter!"

"I did?" Taeko looked delighted and confused.

Midori looked dumbfounded. Reiko beat her fists against the veranda railing in helpless frustration. Taeko had solved the murder, but it was the wrong one, not Yoshisato's. If only Masahiro had come home earlier! Sano might have used the evidence against Lady Nobuko as his defense during his trial. But the fire hood was useless now. It was too late to save Sano.

TROOPS ESCORTED SANO downhill through the dim passages of Edo Castle. A buzz of excited chatter in the watchtowers and covered corridors followed them as soldiers spread the news about his conviction. Sano was too stunned to care that soon everyone in Edo would know. An awful verse pounded repeatedly through his mind.

Yanagisawa won.

This is the end.

Sano felt insubstantial, as if he'd already begun crossing into the netherworld of the dead. The hardness of the pavement under his feet, the painful throbbing of his cut face, and the breaths that his lungs drew seemed a mere illusion that he was still on earth among the living. Tomorrow he would be tied to a stake and set on fire. But that wasn't the worst.

What Sano dreaded more was telling Reiko, Masahiro, and Akiko that they would be burned with him. What he dreaded the most was watching them suffer and die.

His procession reached his estate. For the first time Sano felt no happiness, only sorrow, at the thought of his family. His escorts walked him to the courtyard, where army troops were massed. Reiko and Masahiro stood on the veranda with Akiko, Midori, and her children, and Detective Marume. The distress on Reiko's and Masahiro's faces turned to surprise, then joy.

Akiko clapped her hands and laughed. "See, it's Papa. He promised he would come home, and he did."

She and Masahiro ran toward Sano and hugged him. Reiko staggered down the steps, crying as she asked, "Were you found innocent?"

Sano couldn't answer. The lump in his throat was too big. He could only watch Reiko read his expression. Horror dried up the tears in her eyes. She whispered, "No."

The leader of his escorts told Sano, "Get in the house." He pointed at Reiko, Midori, and the children. "You, too. You're all under house arrest."

"What?" Reiko said. She and Masahiro were obviously stunned. "Why?"

Sano couldn't let them learn their fate from hostile strangers. He had to be the one to tell them, in privacy. "Come with me." He hurried Reiko and Masahiro up the steps. He herded Midori, Akiko, Taeko, Tatsuo, and Detective Marume into the mansion along with them and shut the door. In the entryway he said to Midori, "Take Akiko and your children to your room."

She obeyed. Marume said, "What happened?" He looked more scared than Sano had ever seen.

"I'll tell you in a moment. Wait here." Sano took Reiko and Masahiro into the nearest room, a reception chamber.

They gazed fearfully at him. There was no delaying any longer. Sano said, "There were three judges, all Yanagisawa's cronies. I defended myself as best I could, but it was no use."

He felt physically ill with a catastrophic sense of guilt as well as defeat. "They convicted me, based on fake evidence presented by Yanagisawa." Reiko and Masahiro listened in horror. "But I'm not the only one who was convicted. Lady Someko testified that she heard both of you conspiring with me to murder Yoshisato. Yanagisawa sentenced all of us to death by burning." He told the rest while trying not to cry. "That includes Akiko, and your father, and our other close relatives, and my top retainers and their families."

His failure had doomed them all.

REIKO'S FRAGILE SELF-CONTROL gave way before an avalanche of horror.

They were all going to die.

Loud, piercing screams burst from her. They blared in her ears, savaged her throat, plundered air from her lungs. The strength drained from her legs; they buckled. Sano caught her and eased her to the floor. Masahiro looked terrified. Still Reiko screamed. She couldn't stop. It was as if her spirit were having a delayed reaction to terrible things that had happened in the past. The earthquake. A near-fatal attack on her father. Masahiro's kidnapping, and her own. The occasions when she or Sano had almost been killed by criminals. This latest, worst disaster had let out all her buried emotions. Reiko screamed until she was breathless. She sobbed until she was nauseated. She retched, but nothing came up; she hadn't eaten since morning. The baby inside her rolled. A painful contraction hardened her stomach. She clutched it and panted.

Sano held her shoulders and spoke urgently, trying to calm her. But Reiko was so lost in agony that she couldn't listen. As she began screaming again, Masahiro grabbed her shoulders and shook her violently. "Stop it, Mother!" When she didn't, he slapped her face.

A gasp sucked the screams into Reiko. Abruptly quiet, she stared at Masahiro, shocked. He'd never hit her before.

"We're not really going to die." Masahiro sounded as if he thought things would turn out all right because they always had. He had faith in his own, and his mother's and father's, invincibility. He appealed to Sano. "We'll get out of it, won't we?"

Sano's bloodshot eyes were dark with despair. Reiko saw the confidence and faith seep out of Masahiro. "Won't we?" he repeated in a plaintive, suddenly childish voice.

Reiko and Sano looked at each other. This was the worst moment of their lives as parents.

Another contraction seized Reiko. She moaned. Sano looked around for help. Reiko saw him realize, at the same moment she did, that no doctor would come to the aid of a woman who was a condemned criminal.

"Here, lie down." Sano pressed her gently onto the floor.

Reiko told him about the evidence that Masahiro and Taeko had gathered. "But it was all for nothing!"

"Never mind," Sano said. "Breathe. Relax. Masahiro, bring your mother some water."

What did it matter if she lost the baby? She was going to be burned to death, and the baby with her, tomorrow. Reiko thought of the woman she'd once seen tied to a stake. It had been a glimpse of her own future. She began trembling. More screams threatened to burst from her. Masahiro knelt beside her, a cup in his hand, his face white with fear. She forced herself to drink and smile. He and Sano looked momentarily relieved. The contractions stopped, but Reiko was too devastated to do anything except lie there while tears spilled from her eyes.

"How long do we have?" Masahiro said.

"Until tomorrow, after Yoshisato's funeral," Sano said.

Detective Marume came in. "Let's hope it's a long one." His wretched expression said that he'd overheard everything. Nobody laughed at his attempt at a joke.

"Are we just going to sit here and wait?" Masahiro said.

"I guess so," Sano said, then shook his head emphatically, pointing to the door through which the troops might eavesdrop. He put his finger to his lips, then whispered indignantly, "Of course not. Does our family ever give up without a fight? No! I have a plan."

He was taking on the burden of upholding morale, as Reiko had done when he was downcast and weak. Love for him made her cry harder. She sensed that he didn't have much faith in this plan of his, but he would pretend he did, to raise her and Masahiro's spirits.

"What is it?" Masahiro said eagerly.

Sano whispered his plan. It seemed the product of desperation rather than sane, practical thinking. But Reiko, Marume, and Masahiro nodded. They had nothing to lose. And the best Reiko could do was support Sano in his impossible plan.

"We'll have to wait until morning," Sano said.

36

THE RISING SUN spilled a golden glow over Edo. Townspeople massed along the main street, waiting to see the procession that would accompany the shogun's dead heir to Zōjō Temple. Troops kept the space outside the castle gate clear of peddlers hawking tea and rice crackers to the throngs. Nuns and monks sold incense, prayers printed on wooden tags, and amulets for the biggest funeral in recent memory.

Inside the castle, samurai and ladies dressed in white, the color of mourning, emerged from their mansions. They streamed uphill through the passages to the palace. There, priests in saffron robes, equipped with drums, gongs, bells, and cymbals, were gathered. Troops held white lanterns, and banners emblazoned with the Tokugawa crest, on long poles. Servants lit incense burners. Maids brought huge bouquets of flowers. White doves fluttered in bamboo cages. Bearers stood by the funeral bier—a miniature house that contained Yoshisato's remains, decorated with flags and gilded artificial lotus flowers, mounted on two horizontal wooden beams. Everyone waited for the shogun and his entourage.

Sano's estate was the only one in the castle from which nobody went to join the funeral procession. Inside the mansion, Sano stood by the front door. His bandaged face felt like raw, stiffening leather. The cuts burned as if carved with a hot knife. They throbbed in a warning rhythm.

In his lifetime he'd engaged in many subterfuges but never considered himself a good actor. Now he must act the role of a condemned man resigned to dying.

Sano opened the door and said to the two soldiers on the veranda, "I must speak with the officer in charge." He hoped his voice was loud enough to cover any noise from inside the house. He didn't have to fake his exhaustion or misery. "I have a last request."

The soldiers looked at each other, then back at Sano. Their pity served his purpose. One fetched an older samurai who had a florid, pleasant face. Sano walked across the courtyard to meet him. The fewer guards near the house, the better.

"I'm Captain Onoda," the officer said. "What is your last request?"

The last request of a samurai sentenced to death was a serious matter. Sano could see that Captain Onoda wanted to grant his, if possible. "Please allow me to fulfill my last duty to the shogun before I die. I want to solve the murder of his daughter."

The last thing he really wanted was to serve the fool who'd defaced him and let him and his family be condemned to death. Yet Sano really did want to finish the investigation. If things went wrong today, he wouldn't like to die with the case unsolved. He did want justice for Tsuruhime, whom everyone else seemed to have forgotten.

Captain Onoda looked impressed. "I'd like to help you, but I can't let you leave the premises."

"I'm not asking to leave. I think I already know who killed Tsuruhime. It's the woman who nursed her when she had smallpox. Her name is Namiji. If I can just talk to her, I'll find out whether she's guilty. Will you bring her to me?"

Captain Onoda considered. "I don't see how it could hurt." He sent a soldier to fetch Namiji. He whispered to Sano, "I always thought you were the most honorable samurai in the regime. I can hardly believe you killed Yoshisato. It was wrong of you, but I know you must have meant well."

"A thousand thanks." Sano bowed, touched by these kind words, hating to trick the man.

INSIDE THE MANSION'S private chambers, Masahiro pulled out a section of drawers in the cabinets built against the wall. It rolled out on oiled wheels. He bent, inserted his fingers into a groove in the floorboards, and pried. A large, square panel popped up. The hole it had covered gave access to the space under the building.

Taeko, Tatsuo, and Akiko took turns jumping down the hole. They crouched beneath the house. Midori lowered herself into the hole while Reiko held the baby. Reiko handed the baby down to Midori, then awkwardly followed the others. They waited in the earth-smelling darkness until Masahiro joined them. Then they began crawling.

Masahiro led. Reiko had forbidden the children to play under the house because it was dirty and inhabited by poisonous spiders, but now she was glad he'd disobeyed. Despite the meager light coming through the lattice panels that covered the building's foundation, he moved swiftly between the stone posts that supported the mansion. The other children and Midori, the baby riding on her back, kept pace with him as he angled under wings and corridors, around courtyards and gardens. Reiko lagged behind. Her heavy belly dangled. She felt the twinge of a contraction, but she didn't stop until she caught up with the others at the back of the mansion. Through the diamond-shaped openings in the lattice Reiko saw the sandaled feet and armored legs of troops outside. She and the others huddled together, waiting.

SHOUTS BLARED. A soldier ran into the courtyard, where Sano stood with Captain Onoda. "That big fellow has gone crazy! We need help!"

Calling troops to accompany him, Captain Onoda followed the soldier. Sano trailed them to the yard where he and Masahiro practiced martial arts. Marume knelt on the ground, clutching a kitchen knife, surrounded by troops.

"Go away!" he yelled. An empty wine jar lay beside him. "Leave me alone!"

"He's going to commit *seppuku*," said the soldier who'd called for help.

"He can't," Captain Onoda said with concern. "Chamberlain Yanagisawa said that all Sano's retainers are to be kept alive, so they can be executed after he's dead."

"Let me take my life honorably." Marume's eyes were red and teary from the vinegar he'd splashed in them. He reeked of the liquor he'd poured on himself.

"Seize him," Captain Onoda ordered.

The soldiers moved in on Marume. He waved the knife at them. They leaped back. He tore open his kimono and held the knife to his belly.

"Surrender, Marume-*san*," Sano said. "It's the law." He hoped his words didn't sound phony and rehearsed.

"Please don't make me," Marume blubbered. "I don't want to die in disgrace!" He was a much better actor than Sano.

They argued back and forth, deliberately wasting time. Marume grew louder, wilder. More troops rushed over to watch. When they stopped coming, Sano said, "Marume-*san*, this is my last order to you: Give me that knife!"

Weeping dramatically, Marume handed the knife to Sano. The troops rushed Marume, grabbed him, and dragged him to the barracks.

REIKO HEARD MARUME bellowing. She peeked through the lattice. The troops had gone to see what the commotion was. Reiko, Masahiro, and Midori tore off their outer robes and the younger children's. They all wore white silk garments underneath. Reiko and Midori draped their heads with white shawls. Masahiro pushed the lattice panel. It popped loose. He scooted out from under the house, looked around, then beckoned. In the distance, Marume cursed. Midori handed the baby to Masahiro and crawled out next. She and Masahiro helped Reiko out.

The younger children scrambled after her. Tatsuo and Akiko suppressed giggles. This was a game to them. Taeko was as somber as Masahiro and the women. Reiko took Akiko's hand and Taeko's. Midori wrapped the end of her shawl around the baby and took Tatsuo's hand. Everyone ran for the gate.

Masahiro opened it a crack. Reiko saw a flurry of white garments and heard the clap of sandals on the pavement as people going to the funeral walked past. Masahiro slipped out the gate first. Blending with the white-robed people, he ambled down the street. Reiko shooed Midori and Tatsuo out, then followed with Akiko and Taeko, closing the gate behind her. Draping her shawl over her face, she glanced anxiously backward.

Would Sano get out alive?

She swallowed her fear for him and concentrated on her surroundings. Although there were other children of Masahiro's age in the crowd, Taeko, Tatsuo, and Akiko were the youngest. Nobody except Midori had an infant. Nobody except Reiko was pregnant. She felt dangerously conspicuous. Ahead, Masahiro loitered in the passage. Midori and Tatsuo caught up with him. Hurrying Akiko and Taeko through the crowd, Reiko joined her group.

"You go on ahead," she whispered to Midori. "Take Akiko with you and Taeko and Tatsuo."

"Aren't you and Masahiro coming?" Midori said, startled.

"We'll come later."

"But Sano-*san* said we're supposed to sneak out of town with the funeral procession and go to his mother's house in Yamato." That village was a few days' journey from Edo. Heaven knew how they would manage the journey without money or help, but they must try; it was better than staying home and waiting to die. "Sano-*san* will meet us there. That was the plan."

"We're going to exonerate him," Reiko whispered.

Midori frowned, uncomprehending. "Does he know?"

"No," Masahiro said. "If we'd told him, he never would have agreed to it."

Reiko hated to deceive Sano, but she had to make one last attempt to prove his innocence. Even if they all managed to escape, the murder and treason conviction would stick to them. They would always be hunted. And Sano wouldn't be able to endure the disgrace.

"But what if you're caught before you can get out of the castle?" Midori demanded. "That's not what Sano-*san* would want!"

Reiko knew that Sano wanted most of all to save her and the children. But she and Masahiro would gladly risk themselves for a chance to save him. "This is what we're doing."

Panic shone in Midori's eyes. "I can't go by myself!"

"There's no time to argue! Pretty soon the guards at home will notice we're missing. Just go!" Reiko pushed her daughter at Midori.

"Mama," Akiko protested.

"Go with Midori," Reiko said.

"I want you to come!" Akiko sucked in her breath, opened her mouth wide.

She was about to have a tantrum. Reiko quickly put her hand over Akiko's mouth and squeezed hard. Akiko yipped in pain.

"Be a good girl and go," Reiko said in a firm voice. "Or you'll get us all killed!" She dropped her hand.

Akiko stared at her, furious yet shocked silent because Reiko had never treated her so harshly. Her cheeks had red marks from Reiko's fingers.

The stream of white-robed people going to the palace had thinned. Soon there wouldn't be crowds to hide among. Masahiro whispered, "Mother, hurry!"

As she and Masahiro joined the march uphill, Reiko couldn't look backward. She'd left Akiko again. Akiko wouldn't forget this time. If Akiko escaped safely and Reiko didn't, Akiko's last memory of her mother would be Reiko walking away from her. Reiko blinked away tears as she trudged behind Masahiro.

They didn't see Taeko run after them or hear Midori frantically calling her daughter.

HIRATA AND DEGUCHI stood in the hillside clearing, by a bonfire they'd built. They lifted their chins, their bodies still, all their senses alert. Hirata exerted all his mental discipline to keep calm. Tahara and Kitano would arrive soon. He mustn't let emotions impair his judgment or his reflexes. He mustn't lose the slightest advantage.

He looked sideways at Deguchi, whose expression was inscrutable. But Hirata knew Deguchi was feeling the same doubts about the wisdom of their plan. They stood without speaking or touching, united by their terror, chained to a course from which they couldn't deviate.

The familiar aura pulsed distantly, ominously, in the cool morning air. "Here they come," Hirata said.

37

AT THE PALACE, Masahiro gaped at the hundreds of white-robed mourners, the priests with their musical instruments, the troops with their lanterns and banners. "How are we going to find Lady Nobuko in all this?"

"Maybe she's still in her quarters," Reiko said.

She and Masahiro hurried around the palace to the separate wing of the Large Interior, where Lady Nobuko lived. They dodged patrolling troops. They didn't knock on the door of the little house attached to the main building. They had no time for formalities, and Reiko wasn't giving Lady Nobuko the chance to refuse to speak to her. She and Masahiro needed a confession fast. They walked right in.

The entryway and the parlor were deserted. Reiko heard a soft rustling sound. She and Masahiro followed it to an inner chamber. There Lady Nobuko lay in bed. Her gray silk night robe rustled as she tried to make herself comfortable. Reiko stalked into the room, Masahiro behind her. Lady Nobuko rolled over to face them. Her complexion was gray, without makeup, her hair straggly from tossing in bed. She was apparently too ill to attend the funeral. The spasm on the right side of her face pulled the muscles so tight that the eye was screwed shut in pain. Her left eye stared indignantly at Reiko.

"I thought you were under house arrest," she said.

"Not at the moment," Reiko said.

Lady Nobuko drew a breath to call for help. Reiko snatched a bamboo hair spike off the dressing table and held the sharp tip to Lady Nobuko's withered throat. "Don't." Never mind that Lady Nobuko was the shogun's wife; Reiko hadn't the patience to be respectful.

"What do you want with me?" Lady Nobuko lay on her back, palms pressed against the bed, her good eye rolling as she tried to see Reiko and the spike at the same time.

"I want you to admit that you know my husband is innocent and my son and I didn't conspire with him to murder Yoshisato," Reiko said.

"I don't know anything of the sort!"

"Yes, you do," Masahiro said. "You're the arsonist. You let my father be blamed." He was shaking with fury, his fists clenched. Reiko was afraid he would hit Lady Nobuko, even though Reiko and Sano had taught him never to hit a woman. "You were going to let our family be killed for what you did!"

"I didn't—" The spasm around Lady Nobuko's eye tightened.

"Show her," Reiko said.

Masahiro reached inside his kimono, whipped out the fire hood, and shook it in Lady Nobuko's face. "This is yours. Yanagisawa's men found it by the burned building."

"It's not mine." Lady Nobuko spoke vehemently, but recognition opened her eye wider.

"Don't lie to us!" Masahiro shouted. "You wore it while you set the fire, so you wouldn't get burned. It got caught on a bush when you ran away."

"No." Shrinking from the hairpin, Lady Nobuko said to Reiko, "I didn't set the fire. That's the truth. If you'll take that thing away, I'll tell you what happened that night."

Against her will, Reiko began to think she and Masahiro had been wrong about Lady Nobuko. Her intuition said so.

"Mother, don't let her fool you," Masahiro said.

Reiko shushed him. She retracted the hairpin slightly. "Tell me."

Gasping, Lady Nobuko said, "The fire bells woke me up. My headache was terrible. I called Korika. She brought my medicine and put a wet cloth over my eyes. She was out of breath, as if she'd been running." Lady Nobuko finished in a low, sorrowful voice, "She smelled like smoke. That hood isn't mine. It's Korika's."

"Korika set the fire, then." Reiko wasn't entirely surprised. The devoted lady-in-waiting had fulfilled her mistress's wish for revenge on Yanagisawa.

"She's just trying to shift the blame," Masahiro scoffed.

"I don't think so," Reiko said, although reluctant to absolve Lady Nobuko. "Korika vouched that Lady Nobuko was at home when the fire started, but if Lady Nobuko was asleep, Korika hasn't anyone to vouch for her. Korika could be guilty. Where is she?"

"She went to the privy," Lady Nobuko said.

"Let's hear what she has to say." Reiko knew time was speeding by; every moment they remained in the castle increased the chances that she and Masahiro would be caught. But they needed the truth about Yoshisato's murder and a valid confession that would leave no doubt in anyone's mind that Sano was innocent. Reiko told Masahiro, "Get Korika."

WHILE THE TROOPS were busy taking Marume to the barracks and settling him down, Sano ran to his private chambers. He saw the bank of drawers pulled away from the wall. The floor panel lay by the hole that led to the space under the house. Reiko, Masahiro, Akiko, and Midori and her children were gone.

Sano let out his breath in relief that immediately gave way to apprehension. Would someone recognize them and stop them before they got out of the castle? Would the troops discover they were missing before they could leave town? Was anywhere safe from Yanagisawa's long reach? Sano closed his mind to those questions. It was too late to stop the plan he'd set in action or feel ashamed because running away seemed cowardly. Sano told himself that this was like a warlord retreating from the battlefield to live and fight for his honor another day. For now he must conceal his family's absence for as long as possible.

He fitted the panel over the hole in the floor. He shoved the bank of drawers over it just as he heard soldiers tramping toward him along the corridor.

"Be a good boy, Masahiro. Don't cry, Reiko," he said, as if his family were with him.

The troops moved on. Sano tore off his surcoat, kimono, and trousers.

He pulled his white funeral garments and a hidden dagger out of a cabinet. He donned the garments, put his other clothes on over them, and strapped the dagger to his calf under his trousers. Then he knelt and prayed for his family's safety. He hadn't told Reiko and Masahiro that he didn't think he could escape. But he'd let them think so; otherwise, they wouldn't have left him. And he would try his best.

Moments dragged with painful slowness, as if each one drove a needle into Sano's nerves. At last temple bells tolled the hour of the dragon. Shouts and thumps came from the barracks as his men started a riot, the diversion he'd told Marume to create. Sano heard troops hurrying to quell it, leaving the house. He jumped to his feet. As he pulled out the bank of drawers, there came a knock at the door. He shoved the drawers back in place.

"Sano-*san,* that nurse is here," said Captain Onoda's voice.

Sano couldn't say he didn't want to talk to her, not after he'd made a big production about his final request. Onoda would get suspicious, look in the room, and see that his family was gone.

"All right." Sano opened the door just enough to slip through. He called over his shoulder, to his absent family, "I'll be back soon," and shut the door.

Captain Onoda led him to the reception room. The noise from the barracks got louder. Sano hoped his men would keep it up long enough. In the reception room, he sat stoically on the dais, the condemned man ready to tie up the loose ends of his life.

Troops brought in Namiji. She was dressed in white cotton robes; she must have planned to attend the funeral with Lord Tsunanori's household. Her gloved hand held her white head drape over her face. She knelt on the floor in front of Sano. The troops and Onoda stood along the walls. Sano wanted them away from the house, so that he could sneak out after he talked with Namiji, but if he asked them to leave, they might decide to check on his family.

He said to the nurse, "I brought you here for you to confess that you infected Lady Tsuruhime with smallpox."

Her eyes gleamed with fear and insolence. "I'm innocent," she said in her husky voice. "I already told your wife."

"You're guilty. Don't bother denying it." Sano had spent a lifetime having lies poured into his ears. He was sick of people who tried to avoid the consequences of their actions.

"I didn't—"

"You scrubbed her bed with a contaminated sheet." Fear for his family and his need to join them drained Sano's well of patience dry. From outside came the sound of crashes as the men in the barracks hurled wine jars out the windows. He'd never conducted an interview while under such pressure. "You thought nobody saw you. You were wrong."

Namiji gasped, sucking the fabric of her drape against her mouth. But she was too smart to ask who'd seen her, to admit that she'd done just what Sano said she had.

"Stop wasting my time." Sano couldn't leave until he was finished with her. "Confess."

"I won't. Because I didn't do it." She knew that denial was her only recourse.

"We'll see about that." Sano rose and stepped off the dais.

The hand that wasn't holding her drape over her face went up in self-defense. "You can't touch me."

"Why not?"

"Lord Tsunanori won't stand for your hurting me."

"Lord Tsunanori isn't here." Sano ordered, "Confess that you killed Lady Tsuruhime by giving her smallpox."

"He'll send somebody to rescue me."

"Why would he bother?" His impatience growing by the moment, Sano was curious in spite of himself.

"Because he takes care of me." Namiji spoke with smug confidence.

Sano's anger toward the shogun was like a fire that burned anyone else in its path. It incinerated whatever pity he might have felt toward this pariah of a woman. She'd coughed on and mocked his pregnant wife. Hiding her face, hiding the truth that she was a murderess, she was obstructing justice and delaying his flight from a death sentence.

"Why would Lord Tsunanori take care of this?" Sano grabbed her scarf and yanked.

Namiji shrieked as if he were peeling off her skin. She hung onto the scarf, but he tore it away. She covered her face with her gloved hands. Sano seized them by the wrists, pulling them down. Her face was a mass of puckered, pitted, circular scars. They disfigured her nose, lips, and ears. Her hair was wispy, her scalp bald where scars had proliferated.

The troops groaned in revulsion. Sano didn't hide his own reaction or temper his cruelty. Thrusting Namiji away from him, he said, "Have you never looked at yourself in the mirror? How can you think that your master would protect a woman as ugly as you?"

"I wasn't always ugly." Tears of shame oozed from her eyes, the only features left unspoiled.

Sano saw that her body was slender but voluptuous, her neck long and graceful, her breasts full above the sash that circled her small waist. If not for the smallpox, Namiji would have been attractive.

"Lord Tsunanori knew me before." Having lost her veil, she'd also lost her guardedness. Vulnerability replaced insolence. "He's never forgotten what we were to each other."

"What were you?"

"I was his mistress."

"There's nothing special about that," Sano said. "Men sleeping with their servants—it happens all the time."

Protest burst from Namiji. "We were in love!"

"Women fooling themselves. That happens all the time, too." Sano said, "Let me guess: Lord Tsunanori ended the great love affair as soon as you got smallpox."

"I didn't want him to catch it," she said, rushing to defend Lord Tsunanori. "But he still loved me." Breathless with her need to convince Sano and herself, she said, "He could have thrown me out on the street to die. That's what other masters do with servants who get sick. But he sent me to a convent. He paid the nuns to nurse me. When I recovered, he let me come back to his house, even though I looked like this." She spread her arms in a gesture of triumph.

The vain, selfish Lord Tsunanori had more character than Sano had thought. But Sano kept goading Namiji. "So Lord Tsunanori let his former mistress empty his chamber pot. How generous."

"He gave me a home when no one else would have!"

"What other dirty work did you do for him?" Sano turned the conversation back to the most important issue. "Kill his wife?"

"No! I would do anything for him but that!"

"Why not that?" Sano recalled what Reiko had said the nurse had told her. "You knew he hated Tsuruhime. She treated you like filth. You decided to give her the same disease that made you ugly. You accomplished two things at once—you got Lord Tsunanori out of his bad marriage, and you got your revenge on Tsuruhime."

"I didn't kill her." Namiji regained some of her insolence. "It was Yoshisato."

"Yoshisato wasn't seen scrubbing Tsuruhime's bed with a contaminated sheet," Sano pointed out. "Or burning the sheet after Tsuruhime came down with smallpox."

"Whoever says they saw me is lying."

Sano reversed course. "Maybe you're right. Maybe you didn't infect Tsuruhime. If not you, it had to be Lord Tsunanori."

Namiji looked startled, as if she'd been following a road she'd thought was straight and it had taken a steep, downward turn. Her expression turned aghast as she realized that she had to choose between confessing to the murder or incriminating her beloved master.

"I did it," she said with pride and resignation. "I confess."

Captain Onoda signaled the troops to take her away. Sano said, "Wait. Did Lord Tsunanori ask you to infect Tsuruhime with smallpox?"

"No. I did it on my own." Namiji sounded dismayed that her confession had damned her but hadn't put Sano off Lord Tsunanori.

Sano heard his men rioting; he felt time slipping away. But he wanted the complete solution to his last case. "Why are you still protecting Lord Tsunanori? He won't protect you. He'll let you take the whole blame for Tsuruhime's murder."

"He'll take care of me." She sounded desperate to believe it. "He always does."

"Not this time," Sano said. "Tsuruhime was the shogun's daughter. He can't save you. He can only save himself by letting you take the whole blame. You'll be put to death. And he'll take as many new mistresses as he wants."

Namiji whimpered as she absorbed the truth about her fate.

"Don't let him get away with it." Sano couldn't care that he was breaking a vulnerable woman. He needed this business done with. "Make him take his part of the blame."

She curled forward, put her scarred face against the floor, and dissolved into agonized weeping. "It was his idea. He asked me to do it. He knew I couldn't say no."

Sano nodded to Captain Onoda. Onoda told the troops, "Take her to Edo Jail. Tell army headquarters what happened. They'll issue an order for Lord Tsunanori's arrest."

The troops carried Namiji from the room. Sano felt none of the satisfaction he usually did when he finished an investigation. Success in the past had improved his fortune, but it wouldn't this time. This time he was still a man condemned to die, never mind that he'd solved the murder of his lord's daughter. He had yet to make his escape, his only chance of living to see another day and reuniting with his family.

"That was impressive," Onoda said with sincere, regretful admiration. "It's too bad things went so wrong for you, Sano-*san*. I hate to lose a good man."

"Thank you." Knowing he'd better get lost soon, Sano edged toward the door.

A guard ran into the room. "Captain Onoda, have you seen Sano-*san*'s wife and children?"

Alarm struck Sano's heart like a ramrod.

"No," the captain said. "Why?"

"I can't find them. They're not in the house."

Sano's nerves zinged with tension; his thoughts raced. "My wife probably took the children outside to play."

"Search the grounds," Onoda said.

"It's being done now."

Sano slipped out the door; he eased down the corridor.

Captain Onoda came after him. "Weren't they with you a little while ago? I thought I heard you talking to them."

Sano forced himself to stay calm. "Yes, they were. I'll go see if they've come back."

Captain Onoda regarded him with growing distrust. "I'll go with you."

At that moment Sano knew what he would have to do. "All right."

They walked to his room. The door he'd shut was open; someone had already searched it. Onoda looked inside, turned to Sano, and said in a grieved tone, "They weren't there, were they? You were pretending."

His eyes widened as he saw Sano holding the dagger he'd pulled from under his trouser leg. Before he could move, Sano stuck the blade in his throat. Blood gushed. As Onoda fell, Sano caught him. Sano dragged the corpse into the room and laid it on the floor. He heard troops shouting, "They're not anywhere! The other woman and children are gone, too!"

Sano had no time to regret killing a man who'd been kind to him. He ran to the cabinet, pulled out the bank of drawers, and pried up the floor panel. He stole Onoda's long sword, tucked it under his own sash, then squeezed through the hole. He dropped into the space under the house and crawled. Running footsteps shook the floor above him. Soon the troops would discover Onoda's corpse and the secret exit. Sano had to get out of the estate fast.

He'd practiced using the secret exit before and familiarized himself with the escape route in case he ever had to use it. Bursting through the gap in the latticework, he found himself face to face with two soldiers in the back courtyard. Their faces registered surprise for an instant before Sano drew the stolen sword and slashed them across their throats. Sano heard the other troops running toward him, yelling. He tore off his outer garments. Then he was out the gate.

38

"DIDN'T YOU SUSPECT that Korika killed Yoshisato?" Reiko asked.

"I suspected," Lady Nobuko said bleakly. "I didn't know until you showed me that hood."

They sat in Lady Nobuko's chamber, waiting for Masahiro to bring Korika. Reiko thought that by now the troops at home must have noticed that seven of their prisoners were gone. There couldn't be much time left before they went hunting for Reiko, Masahiro, and the others. Reiko forced herself to sit still and wait for Korika, her sole hope of exonerating Sano.

"Why didn't you ask Korika if she set the fire?" Reiko asked.

Lady Nobuko sighed. "Because I didn't want to believe it." Reiko recalled that Lady Nobuko had been disconcerted to learn that the fire was arson and that evidence had been found. That information had fed her suspicions about Korika. "I didn't want to know."

Had Sano managed to escape yet? Were Midori and the children on their way out of town? Anger toward Lady Nobuko displaced some of Reiko's anxiety. "You did it again. You withheld information." This time the consequences were more serious than ever. "Why didn't you tell somebody about Korika?"

"I wasn't sure she did it. Weren't you listening when I said so?"

"I think you were sure enough. Why didn't you come forward and testify at my husband's trial? How could you sit back and let him be convicted?"

"Do you think Yanagisawa would have let me testify?" Lady Nobuko chuckled through her grimace of pain. "Even if he had, what would I have said? 'My lady-in-waiting killed Yoshisato for me'? Yanagisawa wouldn't believe I had no part in it. He'd have made it look as if you and your husband and son and I were all in league with Korika. He'd have burned us all to death."

Although Reiko knew Yanagisawa would have done just that, she was bitter. "So you kept your mouth shut. You'd have let my family die while you lived happily ever after."

"Wouldn't you have done the same?" Lady Nobuko asked.

"I would try to save everyone who was innocent and deliver the guilty person to justice."

Lady Nobuko smiled pityingly. "Young women are so idealistic until their own little necks are threatened."

Masahiro ran into the room. "I can't find Korika. She wasn't in the privy."

Surprise lifted the brow over Lady Nobuko's good eye. "That's where she said she was going. She said she would be right back."

"Well, she's not anywhere around here," Masahiro said. "I looked. Everyone's gone."

"She must have come back while we were talking," Reiko said. "She must have overheard."

"Then she knows we know that she set the fire." Masahiro exclaimed, "She ran away!"

"We have to catch her! We need her to confess that she murdered Yoshisato. The fire hood isn't enough proof." Reiko couldn't expect Lady Nobuko to testify that it belonged to Korika and that Korika had come home on the night of the fire smelling of smoke. Lady Nobuko had already made it plain that she didn't want to implicate herself in the crime.

"I'll go after her." Masahiro ran out of the room.

"Maybe a confession from Korika won't be enough proof, either." Lady Nobuko said acerbically, "Yanagisawa will dispute it for all he's worth. He'll make sure no one else believes she is guilty and not your husband."

Reiko wouldn't concede defeat. "It's our only chance."

THE FUNERAL PROCESSION advanced down Edo's main street. Mounted troops cleared the way through the crowds of spectators. First in the cortege walked Kato Kinhide from the Council of Elders. He headed banner bearers and thousands of troops carrying white lanterns on poles, and servants carrying the cages of birds and the huge bouquets of lilies, irises, and peonies. Next came the priests, like an army uniformed in saffron robes and glittering brocade stoles. They thumped drums, beat gongs, rang bells, and banged cymbals while they chanted prayers. Chamberlain Yanagisawa, the designated chief mourner, walked alone. His expression was rigid as he held the funeral tablet, a wooden placard that bore Yoshisato's name. Behind him, the pallbearers shouldered the poles of the bier that carried Yoshisato's coffin inside the miniature mansion decorated with gold lotus flowers. Spectators crowded closer to see the bier. Troops riding alongside the procession pushed the crowd back as a fleet of palanquins followed. The palanquins contained the shogun, his mother, and other members of the Tokugawa and branch clans. Everyone else followed on foot—hundreds of officials, court ladies, and attendants. The procession stretched all the way back to Edo Castle, whose main gate discharged more white-robed mourners.

Sano hid among the mourners still filing down through the castle. They were minor officials and their attendants. Some wore white-painted wicker hats to shield them from the sun. Sano stole a hat and put it on his own head. He pushed through the crowd of people that clogged the passages from wall to wall. The guards at the checkpoints didn't stop or search anyone. They didn't recognize Sano. But even with the hat tipped over his face Sano noticed people eying him strangely as he squeezed past them. He reached the gate. Crossing the moat with the procession, he saw a gigantic throng in the avenue. People craned their necks to see the procession; men sat on other men's shoulders; women held up their children. Beggars scrambled for coins that servants in the cortege tossed. Sano thought he could easily disappear into the crowd.

Before he stepped off the bridge, a stir rippled through the people behind him. He glanced backward, saw his guards pushing mourners out of their way as they ran. They yelled to the troops riding with the procession. "Sano has escaped! He's somewhere in the procession. Catch him!"

The mounted troops nearest Sano lined up along both sides of the procession. To flee into the crowd, he would have to get past them. He stayed in the middle of the procession, with two men walking on either side of him, screening him from the troops. The men were palace officials he knew. Keeping his head down, he felt their gazes on him. He walked faster, hoping to outpace the troops.

They called to others along the route. The others also fell into line, continuous barricades that stretched as far as Sano could see. He heard a cry: "There he is!" A backward glance showed him the guards weaving through the mourners, gaining on him. They shouted his name, ordered him to stop.

Sano bolted. He had a lucky break in the *daimyo* district. *Daimyo* and their huge entourages streamed out of their gates. The part of the procession that was behind Sano had to stop and let them in. They separated his guards from him. People who couldn't have heard the guards stared intently at his chest as he hurried past them. He glanced down at himself. His white robe was stained red with Captain Onoda's blood.

Dismayed, Sano ran faster. The *daimyo* estates on either side of the avenue sealed him in. When he reached Nihonbashi, crowds at every intersection cut off his escape. He heard his name repeated throughout the procession, faintly at first, then louder. Troops squeezed through the narrow streets, alongside mourners who walked two abreast. Sano ran from pointing fingers while his name echoed above the priests' distant chanting, drumming, and bells. Along the country road that led to Zōjō Temple, troops on horseback formed a moving cordon that flanked the procession, all on the lookout for Sano. He couldn't break through it to hide in the forest. As his hope of escape died, he prayed that the hunt for him would buy his family extra time to flee.

The procession crossed the bridge over the Sakuragawa Canal. Ahead, the cordon accompanied the mourners along the main approach to the temple. Sano was a fish swimming up a narrow channel. All the troops had to do was wait for him to swim out the end and net him. All he could do was keep moving.

The temple's two-story gate engulfed him in shadow for a moment as he passed under it. The bells, chanting, and drumming grew louder. Sano smelled sweet, pungent incense smoke. The procession wound around to the area of the temple that contained the Tokugawa mausoleum.

Entering through a black-lacquered gate emblazoned with gold Tokugawa crests and flanked by statues of guardian deities, Sano saw banners and lanterns waving on poles above the mourners' heads. He was nearing the front of the cortege. The mausoleum entrance was a long, covered corridor raised on a stone foundation, roofed with tile, its windows covered with ornate latticework, its wooden walls decorated with carved flowers and painted brilliant red. A flight of stone steps led to the door, which was shaded by a heavy, curved roof supported on pillars encrusted with gold dragons. Beyond the corridor rose the lavishly decorated roofs of the tombs where past shoguns and important Tokugawa clan members were interred. Completely renovated since the earthquake, the mausoleum shone with unreal splendor, as if it inhabited a dimension between this world and the next.

It was the end of Sano's journey.

Pallbearers stood at the base of the steps, holding Yoshisato's bier. A somber Yanagisawa waited by it. The priests had congregated on one side; on the other, the people with the flowers, birdcages, and incense burners. Troops and mourners filled the courtyard. Sano recognized top army officers and government officials, the most powerful *daimyo,* and important Tokugawa clan members. There wasn't enough room for the rest of the procession, which must wait outside during the funeral. The shogun, his mother, Lord Ienobu, and other relatives climbed out of the palanquins. Attendants led them to the bier. The priests chanted, drummed, and rang bells. Incense smoke clouded the air. The crowd around Sano shifted as troops quietly worked their way toward him. They meant to capture him without making a scene and disrupting the funeral.

Breathless, drenched in sweat that stung the cuts on his face, Sano desperately looked around. Walls and the crowd hemmed him in. Troops blocked the gate. There was no place to run or hide. People around Sano noticed the troops homing in on him, the blood on his robes. They receded from him until he was standing alone in the middle of an empty space. The chanting, drumming, and bells faded to murmurs, taps, and jingling, then died. Voices buzzed outside the compound as people there realized something extraordinary had happened. Sano heard people inside whisper back his name. Disgust appeared on the faces turned toward him, the loathed object of all attention. He'd never felt so shunned or in so much despair. This was worse than all the bad times in the past, when he'd still believed salvation was possible.

As his time left on earth dwindled, every detail of the scene around Sano took on a crystalline, unnatural clarity—the outline of the mausoleum's roofs against the blue sky; the snarls on the statues at the entrance; the gleams of reflected sunlight in the other men's eyes. His vision fragmented; he saw everything simultaneously—the mute, immobile priests; the troops faltering because there was no protocol for arresting a criminal at a state funeral; the desert of paving stones around his solitary self. He watched the shogun and Ienobu slow their pace toward the mausoleum entrance, Yanagisawa pause on his way to meet them, and Lord Tsunanori step forward from the ranks of the dignitaries. Sano's vision narrowed. Everything on its periphery lost definition as he focused on those four men.

The shock on their faces quickly altered. The shogun's expression reverted to his customary stupidity and bewilderment, Ienobu's to his usual canny caution. Lord Tsunanori looked irate. Yanagisawa's face went dark. Sano focused on the shogun. He experienced a rage so powerful that his whole body engorged with hot blood and the cuts on his face throbbed. Here was the weak, selfish, frivolous fool who had brought him to this.

But the same clarity that affected his vision took command of Sano's mind. His thoughts detached from his emotions. He saw the remainder of his life laid out before him, a short road with four branches. All led to death. But he had four choices of what to do next.

He could let himself be arrested and burned.

No.

He could draw his stolen sword, seize his last chance to fight for his life, and be massacred by the troops in an ugly, dirty, public spectacle.

No again.

He could seize his last chance for revenge on Yanagisawa and the shogun. Since he couldn't kill both before the troops killed him, it would have to be the shogun. Even as Sano's emotions demanded blood, his mind calculated the consequences. If he killed the shogun, he would become the murderer and traitor that the court had decided he was. That would permanently besmirch his honor, compromise the legacy he would leave for Reiko, Masahiro, and Akiko. He could forget his hope that after he was dead the regime would spare them. As the kin of the man who'd killed the shogun, they would be hunted down and slaughtered.

Sano mentally erased those three branches of the road. The crowd stirred restlessly. Ienobu scowled. Confusion appeared on Lord Tsunanori's face. The shogun looked timidly to Yanagisawa, who opened his mouth to speak. Troops hastened toward Sano. Sano contemplated his last choice.

He could finish the investigation. The murderer he'd sought was here. Now it seemed inevitable that circumstances should have brought Sano and Lord Tsunanori together today. The fourth branch of the road glowed with a mystical light in Sano's mind. He'd begun his career as a detective. He could die a detective who had managed to solve his last case. He could deliver one last murderer to justice.

That would be a legacy his family could cherish for however long they lived.

Honor steered him down the fourth branch of the short road to death.

As the troops closed in on him, Sano spoke. "Lord Tsunanori!"

His voice sounded clearer, louder, and more resonant than usual, amplified by his conviction that the choice he'd made was the right one. It silenced the crowd. Calmed by his sense of inevitability, Sano raised his hand and pointed at the *daimyo*.

"You murdered the shogun's daughter," Sano said.

39

TAHARA AND KITANO appeared at the top of the trail that led downhill from the clearing. "You two are early," Tahara said cheerfully. His smile slipped as he became aware of the changed atmosphere between Hirata and Deguchi.

"Something's different." Kitano sniffed the air, as if he smelled danger.

As much as Hirata wished to delay the confrontation, he said, "You're right. There aren't going to be any more rituals. It's over."

Deguchi nodded. Tahara turned an incredulous gaze on him. "You've turned against us? *Why?*"

Deguchi's expression was apologetic but resolute. Hirata answered, "He's as sick of conspiracies as I am."

"How could you?" Kitano asked Deguchi in a hard, angry voice. "After all we've been through together?"

"You murdered our teacher and stole his magic spell book," Hirata said. "Why should you expect loyalty from a fellow criminal?"

"You defected to *him*?" Tahara pointed at Hirata.

Deguchi stared at the ground, miserable.

Fury strengthened Tahara's and Kitano's aura, deepened its pulse. Tahara said, "Whatever Hirata-*san* has told you, ignore it. He's leading you astray."

"Remember who your friends are," Kitano said.

Deguchi's aura shrank under pressure from the other men's. He set his jaw.

"Then remember what we have on you." The twinkle in Tahara's eyes were chips of ice. "Those men who tortured you when you were a child? We know you tracked them down and killed them. We could turn you in."

So they knew at least part of Deguchi's story, Hirata realized. Deguchi beheld them with shock. Hirata understood that Deguchi had told his two friends about killing his abusers but never expected them to use it against him. Not all had been cozy and secure within the trio. Tahara and Kitano hadn't taken their mutual loyalty for granted. They probably had goods on each other, too.

Deguchi stepped farther away from them and closer to Hirata, furious at their attempt to blackmail him. Tahara and Kitano couldn't hide their dismay. They weren't afraid of Hirata by himself, but Hirata plus Deguchi was a different matter.

"All right, I shouldn't have said that. I'm sorry. Let's talk about this." Tahara gave a strained version of his roguish smile. He and Kitano obviously didn't want a two-on-two fight. "Hirata-*san* has mixed up your mind. You've forgotten what we've accomplished together."

"Without us—without the rituals and the ghost of General Otani— you would be nothing special," Kitano said. "Just another piddling martial artist priest."

"I've brought him to his senses," Hirata said. "He realizes that he should quit before General Otani gets us all in trouble."

Deguchi nodded, but Tahara said adamantly, "Nobody quits our secret society."

Hirata didn't mention the former member he'd met. "There is no more secret society. Deguchi-*san* and I are dissolving it."

"Oh, really?" Tahara laughed with sardonic humor. Kitano's eyes crinkled in his paralyzed face. Their aura boomed; the sky shook. "How, pray tell?"

"You're going to cooperate with us." Although prepared for battle, Hirata wanted to avoid it if he could. "Give us the magic book. We'll work the spell that will send General Otani's ghost back to the netherworld for good. Then we'll burn the book. We'll go our separate ways and never interfere with the Tokugawa regime again."

"We won't." Kitano's voice was insolent.

"Then I'm sorry," Hirata said, truly regretful. He didn't want anyone to die, least of all himself, and Tahara and Kitano were fellow disciples of his teacher, his brothers. He longed to resolve matters peacefully. But he'd known they would never agree to banish the ghost, their source of supernatural powers they had yet to attain.

They went still and somber as they realized that Hirata and Deguchi meant to kill them. Now came the showdown Hirata had been dreading, the fight to the death.

Hirata and Deguchi drew their swords so fast that their hands and arms were blurs of motion. Blades exited scabbards with such speed that the shrill rasp was barely audible. Energy currents sizzled through Hirata. Every muscle swelled with power, every nerve tingled with exhilaration. All his training had prepared him for this. In the same swift, fluid motion, Hirata and Deguchi lunged at Tahara and Kitano. Their bodies and their swords whizzed through air that flattened the skin of their faces against the bones. Hirata's roar distorted into a deep groan. Heat shimmered off him and Deguchi as they lashed out with their swords.

Their blades carved empty space.

Tahara and Kitano disappeared in the same instant Hirata and Deguchi attacked.

A boom rocked the hills, louder than the one after Deguchi had thrown the bullet at Ienobu. Landing on their feet, Hirata and Deguchi circled, their backs to each other, preventing an attack from the rear, as the boom echoed.

The clearing was empty.

An updraft of warm wind raised Hirata's eyes skyward.

TAEKO CROUCHED OUTSIDE Lady Nobuko's quarters. Hidden behind a bamboo thicket, she'd watched Masahiro run out of the house, then come back. She hadn't let him see her because she was afraid he would scold her for staying in the castle. She didn't know why Masahiro and Reiko had stayed, but if they found out that Taeko was here, they would be angry.

Her mother would be angry, too, and worried. Running away from her mother had been a bad thing to do. Maybe her mother was still inside the castle, looking for her, instead of taking the other children away. If so, Taeko had put Tatsuo and Akiko and the baby in danger. If anything happened to them or her mother, it would be her fault. Tears welled in her eyes. But crying wouldn't change what had already happened. She was stuck with her decision. She somehow had to make it right.

Masahiro raced out of the house. This time Taeko followed. He ran too fast through the palace grounds; she lagged behind. Nobody else was there. Everybody had gone to the funeral. Masahiro slipped through a gate in the wall that surrounded the palace. Taeko sped after him. The passage was empty, but she heard voices, bells, and drums. Rounding a curve, she saw a straight stretch of the passage below her, jammed with people dressed in white. They stood behind a group of saffron-robed priests. The funeral procession was stalled inside the castle.

Taeko didn't see Masahiro, but the crowd stirred, like water when a fish swims just below the surface. People shifted around whatever was causing the disturbance. Taeko glimpsed the top of a head with a long forelock tied at the top, bobbing along. It was Masahiro.

She plunged into the crowd and followed in his wake.

"EXCUSE ME," MASAHIRO said, pushing his way through the passage.

"Don't be in such a hurry," a priest said. "We're not going anywhere until the line ahead of us starts moving."

"It must be stretched out all the way through Edo," someone else said.

Masahiro had to catch Korika. He'd already checked the other passages that led downhill and not found her. If she was trying to leave the castle, this was the only other route. Masahiro stepped on someone's foot, said, "I'm sorry," and squeezed between the crowd and the wall.

"Hey! There goes Sano's son!" came a shout from above.

Masahiro saw a guard leaning out of a watchtower, pointing down at him. Alarm clenched his stomach. The guards at home had discovered that he and the others had escaped. Footsteps pounded down the passage behind him. He wriggled faster through the crowd. Troops called from the covered corridor atop the wall, to guards accompanying the procession. "He's headed toward you! Don't let him out of the castle!"

Talk buzzed as people realized that a fugitive was in their midst. Shoving and jostling, Masahiro felt someone grab his collar. He tore free. He had to get Korika before he was caught. The guards pushed toward him, coming closer. As Masahiro squirmed through the procession, the passage gradually sloped downward. On the right side of the mourners and priests, the hill soared vertically to the retaining wall and covered corridor that encircled the castle's uppermost tier. On the left was a section of wall that had collapsed during the earthquake. Reconstruction had begun. A dirt foundation, faced with flat stones, climbed in irregular steps to the high, square base of a new watchtower. The tower was wide at the bottom, tapering upward. From its base rose a wooden framework. Below the new wall, the hill dropped off steeply. Folks ahead of Masahiro, on the lower stretch of the passage, turned to look for him. Some twenty paces distant he glimpsed a woman's broad face with a low forehead beneath a round puff of hair.

It was Korika.

Masahiro fought his way toward her. Troops yelling at him drowned out the bells and drums. He caught up with Korika. Her shiny black eyes goggled with fear. He seized her arm.

"Stop him!" called the troops behind Masahiro.

"My father didn't kill the shogun's son!" Masahiro yelled. "She did!"

Korika screamed, "Let me go!" She tried to jerk loose.

Masahiro held on. People shrank from them. They stood in the only empty space in the passage. "You set the fire. Admit it!"

"No!" Korika clawed at his hand, digging bloody gouges in his skin.

Furious at her for the trouble she'd caused his family, Masahiro grabbed her other arm. "Your fire hood was found on a bush. I showed it to Lady Nobuko. She said it was yours."

"Leave me alone!" She was breathless, frantic, trembling.

The crowd quieted. Priests stopped their drumming and bell-ringing; troops leaned out the windows of the towers and corridor to listen.

Masahiro shook Korika. Lacquer combs fell from her hair, clattered on the paving stones. "She said you went out that night and came home smelling like smoke."

Korika abruptly ceased struggling. Her mouth hung open, mute. Her eyes filled with woe because she'd been betrayed by her mistress.

"You murdered Yoshisato!" Masahiro said. "There's no use denying it. You're guilty!"

His words rang out loudly in the silence. Mutters swept through the procession. "Who's that woman?" "It's Lady Nobuko's lady-in-waiting." "*She* killed Yoshisato?"

Masahiro looked around. Priests, mourners, and troops massed above and below him in the passage, gaping at him and Korika in surprise. The mutters continued up and down the line, echoing through the castle. The sound of bells and drums in the distance gradually faded as the news spread outside. Masahiro kept his grip on Korika.

Hunching her shoulders, she offered him and the spectators a sickly version of her usual, ingratiating smile. She looked guiltier than anyone Masahiro had ever seen. The people nearest them saw her guilt, too. Skepticism in their expressions gave way to belief. The troops stood dumbfounded.

"Everybody can see that you did it," Masahiro told Korika. "You might as well confess."

Huge sobs wracked Korika, as if she would vomit up her guilt. She doubled over, leaning on Masahiro. "I'm glad I did it!" She seemed as much relieved to give up her secret as she was distressed at being caught. "He was a fraud! I couldn't let him be the next shogun!"

Voices babbled as people farther down the procession asked what was happening and spectators closer to Korika told them.

"His real father hurt my mistress," Korika wailed. "My mistress and I were afraid they would get away with it. We wanted them both to suffer. So I burned Yoshisato's house." Tears streaked her makeup. They trickled over the self-righteous smile she gave the spectators. "Was I so wrong to make them pay when nobody else would?"

Masahiro was astonished. He'd feared that his mother's plan to exonerate his father would fail; now Korika had confessed in front of hundreds of witnesses.

"Was the fire Lady Nobuko's idea?" he asked.

". . . No. It was mine," Korika said.

Her pause raised doubts in Masahiro. "Did she ask you to kill Yoshisato?"

"No, she didn't." Korika called to the crowd, raising her voice above the hum of voices reporting her confession. "I acted alone! Lady Nobuko didn't know I was going to do it!"

If she was telling the truth, then Lady Nobuko had done nothing wrong. If she was lying, then she was protecting her guilty mistress. But that didn't matter. Masahiro called to the troops, "Here's the arsonist. Take us to the shogun, so she can confess to him and I can tell him that my father and my mother and I are innocent."

The troops that had been guarding his family were standing close to Masahiro and Korika. The leader said, "Let's take her to Chamberlain Yanagisawa. He can sort things out."

"Not Yanagisawa!" Masahiro was horrified. Yanagisawa would kill Korika, ignore her confession, and put Masahiro's family to death anyway. "We have to speak to the shogun." That was his only chance of overturning the court's verdict.

"It's not up to you," the leader said. "You're going back under house arrest, and you're going to tell me where your mother and sister and friends went."

He seized Masahiro by the arm. As they tussled, Korika broke loose from Masahiro, stumbled a few paces down the passage, and halted at the crowd blocking it. Soldiers advanced on her. Whimpering, she turned to her right and looked up at the vertical hillside. On her left, the unfinished wall was waist-high. She awkwardly heaved herself up on it. The soldiers grabbed for her legs. She squealed, kicking at their faces. They leaped backward. She crawled onto the surface of the wall's dirt foundation.

"Get her down!" the leader ordered while he struggled with Masahiro.

Korika staggered up the foundation, which ascended above the downward-slanting passage beside it. Masahiro punched the leader's nose. The leader yelled. Blood poured from his nostrils. He lost his grip on Masahiro. Masahiro climbed onto the foundation, which was some ten paces wide. Eight troops were already bounding up it after Korika. She looked over her shoulder, saw them, and screamed. Tripping on her white skirts, she veered toward the sheer drop on the other side of the wall.

"Look out!" Masahiro cried, hurtling up the slope.

Spectators groaned in consternation. Korika teetered at the edge, arms flapping. The soldiers were almost upon her when the foundation began to move. Their feet sank into the dirt as they ran. Masahiro felt the packed earth under him loosen and slide sideways. He heard clunking, skittering noises. On the wall's other side, stones fell off and bounced down the slope. The builders of the wall had done a shoddy job, hurrying to finish it. The weight of people running on it had destabilized the structure. The whole foundation canted toward the sheer drop.

"The wall is collapsing!" someone in the procession exclaimed.

Korika screamed as the ground gave way under her, Masahiro, and the troops. She ran toward the unfinished watchtower. As the foundation spilled over the drop, Masahiro fell on his stomach. The soldiers, higher on the foundation ahead of him, went down, too. They all crawled frantically against the flow of earth, toward the side of the wall that bordered the passage. A sound like a waterfall thundered as the foundation cascaded down the slope. Masahiro reached the rim of facing stones. But the soldiers slid faster than they could climb.

"Help!" they shouted as the avalanche swept them downward.

Terrified, Masahiro flung his arms over the stones' jagged edges. They held firm while the foundation collapsed and the crowd moaned. At last the thunder faded. The world went still. Masahiro could hear his heart pounding. His breath pumped so hard he thought his chest would burst. Glancing over his shoulder, he saw that he was lying on a long, narrow ridge of flat earth—all that remained of the foundation. Below him, dust swirled from a swath of dirt, rock, and sand that covered the hillside all the way down to a retaining wall on the lower tier of the castle. Nothing moved. The avalanche had buried the soldiers and apparently killed them all.

Masahiro turned to the people staring at him from the passage below. The angry leader with the bloody nose said, "Come down from there!"

The rest of the foundation could collapse and kill him, Masahiro knew. But he couldn't go back under house arrest. He had to take Korika to the shogun. Alarm struck. He'd lost sight of her after the avalanche started. Had she been killed?

He looked up to his left. Korika stood on the base of the watchtower, holding onto the wooden framework and crying.

Masahiro scooted up the ridge toward her. The troops shouted at him to stop, but they didn't come after him. They were afraid to climb onto the unstable wall. Masahiro kept going. The ridge crumbled. Sand slithered downhill. Masahiro crawled through a gap in the framework onto the tower's base. It was solid, level. The wall foundation that extended from the tower's other side was also intact, too high for the troops to scale. Masahiro lay there a moment, panting with relief, then rose.

Korika sobbed, pressing the knuckles of one hand against her mouth. Masahiro glanced down into the passage. The foreshortened figures of priests, mourners, and troops stood with heads tilted, raptly watching him and Korika. The leader called, "Somebody fetch a ladder!"

"You have to come with me. You have to tell the shogun that you set the fire," Masahiro said, even though he didn't know how he would get Korika to the shogun.

"I can't." She shook her head violently. "I'm afraid."

She sidled between the wooden posts of the framework, to the edge of the base that overlooked the hillside. Masahiro gazed down the vertical stone surface. Below was the castle's official district. The houses on the street directly under Masahiro had been crushed when the old tower fell during the earthquake. The debris had been cleared; a new retaining wall braced the slope. On either side of the street were mansions under construction. Beyond them, the tile roofs of finished mansions extended to a breathtaking view of the city below the hill. Masahiro didn't know how far above the street the tower base was—maybe five or six stories. But he was up high enough that waves of fear rippled from his toes to his chest.

Standing at the edge, gazing down, Korika said forlornly, "I'd rather die here, now."

40

"YOU MURDERED THE shogun's daughter."

Sano's accusation sent a flurry of excitement through the crowd outside the mausoleum. Lord Tsunanori's face showed the chagrin of a man who'd thought he'd gotten away with murder and just realized he hadn't.

"You have no business interrupting the funeral!" Yanagisawa said, furious that Sano had managed to slip from his control, had intruded on the rites for his son. "Your days of conducting investigations are over!"

"This isn't the time or place to be flinging around accusations," Ienobu huffed.

Yanagisawa ordered the soldiers, "Put Sano back under house arrest. Keep him there until it's time to burn him and his family to death."

The soldiers moved in on Sano. Lord Tsunanori blew out a breath of relief. The shogun nodded, glad to be spared more unpleasantness. Sounds of disappointment issued from people in the crowd who wanted to learn whether Lord Tsunanori was indeed the murderer. Sano experienced a despair more complete than he'd thought possible. He'd walked the last branch of the road, lost his chance to finish his last investigation and bring one last criminal to justice.

But even though he was trapped at a dead end, pushed to the limits of his resources, another course of action occurred to him. He could do something he'd been wanting to do for fifteen years. He had nothing left to lose.

Sano called out, "Tokugawa Tsunayoshi!"

The shogun jerked, startled by the sound of his name spoken without the customary honorifics. The crowd buzzed. The soldiers paused, disconcerted.

"What do you think you're doing?" Sano asked the shogun.

The shogun's mouth pursed. His eyebrows rose quizzically. He pointed to his chest.

"Yes, you," Sano said. "Why are you standing there like a wax dummy?"

The buzz from the crowd turned to groans. Nobody ever talked to the shogun like that. Ienobu and Lord Tsunanori gaped. Even Yanagisawa was dumbstruck. The shogun, who had the power to order Sano killed on the spot, seemed too flummoxed to speak.

"How typical of you," Sano said scornfully. "You would rather be passive than act. You let other men tell you what to think and lead you around by the nose. You sit idle while they run the government. What's the matter with you? Are you too lazy, or weak, or stupid to take control yourself?"

It felt so good to speak his mind, to express his anger at the shogun, to vent the frustration bottled up inside him for so long. The shogun bit his lips, like a child trying not to cry. Sano pitied him not at all.

"Or maybe you're lazy, *and* weak, *and* stupid. You certainly give that impression." Sano supposed he would pay for his rant, but he didn't care. He would be dead at the end of the day. Then, nothing would matter. For now, the release was supremely worth it.

"Look what's happening," Sano said. "You're letting him get away with murdering your daughter." He pointed at Lord Tsunanori, who flinched. "And you let *him* protect Tsuruhime's killer by silencing me before I can make him confess!" Sano pointed at Yanagisawa. "Is it too much trouble to stand up to other people? Are you not smart enough to realize they're manipulating you? Or are you just too scared?"

The crowd gasped. That someone would openly accuse the shogun of cowardice! It was unheard of, blasphemous. Ienobu sputtered, offended on behalf of his uncle. Sano saw a familiar, hooded expression on Yanagisawa: He was letting the scene play out while scrambling to determine where it was going and how to turn it to his advantage.

"Yes, I think you are a coward." Sano gloried in recklessness. "Why else would you stand there and let me insult you?"

The shogun's face was white except for his pink-rimmed eyes and red, bitten lips. He did look like a wax dummy. The bearers set down Yoshisato's bier. Nobody else moved. Nobody tried to stop Sano. He was saying what many secretly thought about the shogun and wanted somebody else to voice.

"It's hard to believe you're descended from the great Tokugawa Ieyasu, who founded the regime. He fought the Battle of Sekigahara against powerful warlords and their armies, and he won. What would he think of you?" Sano asked with biting contempt. "Your conceited ass of a son-in-law murders your own daughter, and instead of getting revenge for her, you stick your head up your behind!"

The fluttering of the birds in their cages was the only noise. Ienobu, with his bulging eyes and livid complexion, looked ready to explode. Yanagisawa wore a faint, curious smile. Sano rushed on, heedless.

"You let Chamberlain Yanagisawa condemn me for Yoshisato's murder even though I'm innocent and you know it in your heart. You should make Lord Tsunanori confess to his part in Tsuruhime's murder and put him to death. If you don't, you're the sorry, disgraceful dupe that Tokugawa Ieyasu would think you are!"

Sano stopped, out of breath. He'd thought he could go on forever, but he'd distilled all his grievances into one short, devastating speech. His reservoir of anger and hatred toward the shogun was empty. He felt cleansed, shaken by catharsis, and as light as air.

A hush filled the atmosphere, as if the world were holding its breath. The shogun stood speechless, blank-faced and shrunken by Sano's invective, the temper and pettiness flayed out of his fragile body.

"Well," Yanagisawa said. "You must feel better now that you've gotten that out of your system." He sounded disgusted by Sano's tirade yet gleeful. "Enjoy it while you can. You've just put the seal on your own doom."

Even as exhilaration wore off and reality sank in, Sano held his head high. He didn't regret what he'd said. It was true and just, and he'd dedicated his life to the pursuit of truth and justice, his personal code of honor. He hadn't violated Bushido by telling off the shogun. A samurai's duty included telling his lord things he didn't want to hear and alerting him to mistakes he was making. Sano had performed his last, best service to the shogun. He could go to his death, not happily but with a sense of completion.

Yanagisawa nodded to the soldiers. "Take him."

Ienobu's concave chest and Lord Tsunanori's muscular one expanded with relief. Excited whispers hissed through the crowd. People were already discussing what had transpired, passing the news to people outside the mausoleum compound.

"No," the shogun said. "Wait."

The whispers faded; the audience realized the show had a second act. "Why, Uncle?" Ienobu said, as surprised as Sano was.

Ignoring Ienobu, the shogun addressed Sano. "You're right. I am a lazy, weak, stupid, cowardly dupe." His voice trembled, and his face was wet with tears, but his speech impediment had vanished. "Everything you've said is fair, even though it hurts. I've always revered Tokugawa Ieyasu, but he would be ashamed of me." Sano had unwittingly touched his most tender spot, his wish to deserve his ancestor's respect. "Thank you for making me look at myself through his eyes. I don't like what I see, but I must face it."

This can't be happening, Sano thought. He couldn't believe what he, or the shogun, had just said. Now it was his turn to gape in shock.

Yanagisawa and Ienobu reacted with horror. "Don't swallow that tripe Sano threw at you!" Yanagisawa said.

Ienobu said, "He's trying to dupe you into sparing his life."

"Quiet!" the shogun said with more force than Sano had ever heard. "I have to think for myself, instead of, ahh, being led by the nose." Out of habit he lapsed into faltering speech, but recovered. "I must do what I, not other people, think is right."

"Your Excellency," Yanagisawa and Ienobu began.

The shogun waved, hushing them. "I always wanted to be my own man. But it was easier not to." Shame lowered his voice. The spectators pressed closer to hear. "Being led by the nose became a habit. I thought it was too late to change." A smile brightened his face. "But recently a wise young man told me that it's never too late. He said, 'As long as we're alive, there's a chance to do the things that are important.'"

Sano was amazed to hear his own words coming out of the shogun's mouth. That was what he'd told Masahiro whenever Masahiro complained that he wanted to be good at many things but didn't have enough time to practice them all. Masahiro must have talked to the shogun and passed on the sayings he'd heard at home. He was the shogun's wise young man.

"He was right, too," the shogun said. "I vow to change, starting today. I'm going to study the Way of the Warrior, and make my own decisions, and take my own actions. Even if other people don't like it. Even if I make mistakes. 'Mistakes are our best teachers.'"

Sano's lips involuntarily formed these words he often said to both his children.

The shogun swelled with ardor. Color flooded back into his face. "I'm going to be like Tokugawa Ieyasu instead of a wax dummy."

Sano saw the horror in Yanagisawa's and Ienobu's expressions worsen, and a lack of enthusiasm on the faces in the crowd. Nobody welcomed the shogun's transformation. But Sano wanted to applaud the shogun. For the first time Sano had ever seen, the shogun was demonstrating humility. He sounded ready to make good on his vow. Sano forgave him fifteen years of maltreatment. His own forgiveness made Sano feel even calmer, lighter, and more at peace with the way he'd chosen to spend his last moments.

"I shall start by seeking justice for my daughter." The shogun pointed to Lord Tsunanori. A tremor in his hand betrayed his fear of taking the first step, of opposing his subordinates, of confronting a murderer. "I order you to tell me: Did you kill Tsuruhime?"

Lord Tsunanori put his hand over his heart. He oozed sincerity. "I swear on my honor, I did not."

Sano said, "You have no honor to swear on. I just talked to Namiji. She confessed that you asked her to infect Tsuruhime with smallpox. She betrayed you when she realized that she would take the whole blame for the murder and you would let her die rather than share the punishment. She's under arrest."

Lord Tsunanori's loose mouth sagged. Terror enlarged his bold eyes. "That's not true! I never asked Namiji to kill anybody! If she said I did, she's lying."

"No, *you're* lying!" the shogun exclaimed. "I see your guilt written on your face. You're responsible for my daughter's death!" He looked frightened but determined to challenge the younger, stronger man instead of backing down. His cheeks reddened with anger. "Why?" he said. "Why did you do it?"

Lord Tsunanori hesitated, balanced between his tendency to do whatever he felt like, no matter how inappropriate, and his inkling that a wise man in his position would stand his ground. The shogun's demands and his own impulsiveness tipped him over the edge.

"How would *you* like being married to a homely, vain, silly cow who constantly criticizes you?" he burst out. "How would *you* like to pay through the nose for the privilege, just because she's your lord's daughter? And she couldn't even give me an heir. You of all people should know what a pain that is!"

The shogun frowned at the insult to Tsuruhime, the rudeness to himself. Lord Tsunanori went on, as if unable to stop. "Could you stand to be stuck with an ugly, barren, tiresome wife for the rest of your life? Well, I couldn't. She kept pushing me and pushing me until she finally pushed me too far. And I couldn't divorce her! So I told Namiji to give her smallpox. It was supposed to look natural, except that bitch Lady Nobuko got involved. She put Sano on to me. The way everything turned out, it's all her fault."

Sano had heard many self-justifying confessions but none as brazen. The shogun regarded Lord Tsunanori with loathing. He believed the confession.

Lord Tsunanori looked around at the spectators. He obviously realized he'd doomed himself. Tears blotched his face, but he smiled; his broad chest inflated his white robe. The man who stripped while playing *hanetsuki* enjoyed the attention. He said with pathetic triumph, "I'm not sorry I killed Tsuruhime. I'm just sorry I got caught."

The audience beheld him with the vacant aspect of people who'd already used up their capacity for surprise.

"Uncle, you must—" Seeing the shogun glower at him, Ienobu said, "If I might make a suggestion—your law requires that since Lord Tsunanori is guilty of murder, he must commit *seppuku*."

"Thank you, Nephew, I wouldn't have thought of that myself," the shogun said with atypical sarcasm. He turned to Lord Tsunanori. "Because you're a *daimyo* and you have much business to put in order, I give you, ahh, three days until your ritual suicide." He signaled the soldiers with a firm hand. "Put him under house arrest at his estate."

The soldiers moved away from Sano, toward Lord Tsunanori. Lord Tsunanori gazed at the shogun and Ienobu with sudden confusion and anger. "Hey, wait."

The shogun shook his head. The soldiers kept coming. Lord Tsunanori backed away from them, his hands raised. "I'm not finished confessing."

"I've heard enough from you," the shogun said.

Sano was surprised that there could be more to the crime than he'd thought. "Please let him finish, Your Excellency."

"I said, that's enough!" Now that he'd decided to think for himself, the shogun was as touchy about taking direction from Sano as from everyone else.

Lord Tsunanori drew his sword. "If I have to go down, I'm not going alone!"

TAHARA AND KITANO hung in midair, higher than the treetops, their knees flexed, arms spread, swords in hand. They began to spin as they plummeted, like twin tornados. Wind from them buffeted Hirata and Deguchi. Staggering, Hirata beheld them with frightful awe. They seemed made of air, as if speed had dissolved their substance. Above them, tree branches tossed. Under them, columns of dust swirled. As they touched ground, invisible blades lashed out of the tornados. The tornados separated. Kitano's circled Deguchi. Tahara's assailed Hirata.

Hirata's mind vaulted to a higher level of consciousness. Thought and emotion were jettisoned like obsolete cargo. Mind and body united on a plane where training and instinct melded seamlessly. Reflex commanded his muscles. Hirata dodged blades he couldn't see. They whistled past his face. His sword, an extension of his arm, flashed in all directions, like a crazed lightning bolt. His blade parried Tahara's with clangs that sounded like the heavens shattering. Booms caused by their fast motion rocked the hill. Collisions melted steel surfaces. The smell of vaporized metal laced the air. Hirata barely felt the impacts. Mystical forces within him carried their energy from his body like harmless gases.

Deguchi and Kitano battled with equal, superhuman power. Hirata was simultaneously aware of them, Tahara, and everything else around him. He effortlessly avoided trees and rocks. As he pivoted and whirled, his speed caught up with Tahara's and Kitano's. He could see the shapes of their bodies and the movements of their limbs. Their faces came into focus, grimacing monstrously as they fought. The landscape blurred into a smear of green, brown, and blue. The fighters existed in a vacuum created by their own motion.

Hirata anticipated Tahara's next actions right before they happened. A faint, luminescent image of Tahara, like a twin specter joined to his body, preceded him by an instant, whatever he did. The specter dodged to the right. Hirata swung at it, but his blade passed through vacant space. Tahara had changed course. He could see Hirata's own specter revealing Hirata's intentions. They feinted, ducked, and leaped within the hissing patterns carved by their swords. Kitano and Deguchi were caught up in the same contest. Despite fast, vicious slicing, no one could score a strike. The men battled furiously in the murky glow from their specters. The air filled with sweet chemical fumes from the energy their bodies burned.

There was a loud crack of steel fracturing.

Deguchi's broken blade flew spinning into the woods.

The priest jumped into the air and somersaulted backward as Kitano lunged at him. Landing, he reached into the bush where Hirata had cached spare weapons. His hand came out holding another sword. He went at Kitano with undiminished vigor. But Hirata felt himself tiring. His wounded leg began to ache, a sign that he couldn't keep this up much longer. He launched a dizzying spate of maneuvers at Tahara, forcing him onto the field of swords. Tahara jumped to elude a low strike Hirata. As he came down on the strewn leaves, a blade sliced up the inner side of his right foot and calf. Slashing at Hirata, he started to fall facedown onto the deadly blade tips.

Sword gripped in both hands, Hirata bellowed as he swung downward at the neck of Tahara's specter. Tahara curled his body in midair, knees to his chest. Hirata's strike, which should have decapitated him, grazed the top of his head. Blood spilled from the shallow cut on his crown, but he landed on his feet like a cat. He seemed not to feel the blades slash his ankles. Suddenly he was gone.

Hirata felt Tahara behind him, found himself in the sword field, hopping frantically to avoid the blades as Tahara swung at him. Sweat streamed from his pores, draining away precious water, salt, and elixirs. The battle had begun only moments ago, but it had already lasted for as long as many grand tournaments in martial arts legend.

Nobody had ever lasted much longer.

As Hirata's movements slowed, Tahara's and Kitano's figures began to blur again. Deguchi's was clearly visible: He was slowing down, too. The lights from the specters made Hirata dizzy. Aches burned his muscles. While he fought, Tahara's blade licked his arms like sharp tongues of fire. Blood flew from him and Deguchi as the battle raged on. With an effort that wrenched a yell from him, Hirata jumped. He grabbed a vine-covered rope. Deguchi jumped, too. They swung high through the air on the ropes, away from their opponents.

Caught by surprise, Tahara and Kitano slackened their speed. Their figures came into focus, then halted. They stared upward.

Swinging down, Hirata and Deguchi slashed at Tahara and Kitano. Tahara dove to the left, Kitano to the right, too late. Hirata felt his blade hew flesh. He heard a cry from Tahara, then Kitano. They fell. Clinging to the ropes, Hirata and Deguchi swung upward again. As they descended, Tahara and Kitano stood. Blood stained Tahara's surcoat, Kitano's leggings. If their injuries were painful or serious, their enraged faces showed no sign. They leaped as Hirata and Deguchi hurtled toward them. Tahara caught Hirata's rope. Chest to chest, they swung. They kicked and butted heads, punching with the hands that held their swords while their left hands gripped the rope, trying to throw each other off it. Kitano swung with Deguchi. The two pairs crisscrossed wildly, like spiders fighting on airborne webs.

Hirata felt his hand on the rope slipping. His nose bled from a blow from Tahara's forehead. Tahara's clenched teeth were bloody. Hirata kneed Tahara in the crotch. When Tahara recoiled, Hirata sheathed his sword. He reached down and grabbed the length of the rope that dangled under them. He flung the loop over Tahara's head as he coiled the end around his right hand. Then he opened his left hand, releasing its grip on the rope.

His weight yanked the loop tight around Tahara's throat. Tahara squealed as his air was cut off. His legs flailed above Hirata's head. Hirata drew his sword for the killing stroke.

Tahara slashed the rope above him. The tension broke. He and Hirata plunged to the ground. Hirata landed on his back. Tahara crashed onto him. Hirata felt his ribs crack. Stunned by both impacts, he couldn't breathe.

Tahara staggered upright. His face bright red, he gasped. A purple bruise circled his neck. He raised his sword in a trembling hand.

Sheer terror pumped energy through Hirata. Wheezing, he drew his sword. Tahara hacked at him. He parried while lying on the ground like a piece of meat on a chopping board. Tahara's blade was a swishing silver whir directly over him. Through the whir Tahara's red face grinned, its mouth drooling blood. Hirata didn't have room to stand up. His arm tired from fending off Tahara, who battered him relentlessly.

Far above him, Deguchi and Kitano swung from their rope, tangled in furious combat. They fell together. Their tangled bodies crashed through the branches and leaves spread over the pit. The pit swallowed them up. A thud shook the earth. Hirata was exhausted. His sword grew heavier every moment. Tahara seemed determined to kill Hirata. He'd either forgotten that General Otani needed Hirata alive or he didn't care. Enraged by Hirata's betrayal, fixated on retaliation, he circled around to Hirata's left side as he slashed.

Hirata spun on the dirt like a broken pinwheel, keeping his head as far from Tahara's blade as possible. Digging his heels into the ground, he scooted backward so fast that the friction burned his spine. Tahara chased him. Hirata couldn't look where he was going. He didn't dare take his eyes off Tahara, who towered at his feet, or the silver maelstrom of their blades clashing. Instinct guided him toward the edge of the clearing, to the hollow tree. He flung his sword at Tahara.

Tahara batted it away with his own blade. Hirata kicked with both feet at Tahara. They grazed Tahara's trousers. Tahara leaped back, toward the bonfire behind him. Hirata reached into the hollow tree, pulled out the paper bag, and hurled it at the bonfire. Confused, Tahara began to turn, following the motion of Hirata's arm. The bag, which contained explosives, plopped into the bonfire. Hirata saw the paper go up in flames, saw Tahara recognize the trick.

Roaring with anger, Tahara lunged at Hirata. A tremendous boom lifted Tahara off his feet. A brilliant orange sun exploded in the clearing. Tahara flew toward Hirata, arms spread, sword in hand, his face snarling, like a winged demon. Behind him, white, green, and red fountains of stars detonated and boomed within the sun. Hirata rolled over, pushed himself onto his hands and feet, and sprang.

The blast hit him with searing heat and propelled him like a human rocket toward trees lit by the explosion. The collision wiped out his senses. He plunged into blackness.

41

INSIDE LADY NOBUKO's chamber, Reiko paced the floor.

"Stop that." Lady Nobuko put a hand to her temple. "You're making my head worse."

Reiko was too restless to sit. "I'm worried about Masahiro. He should have come back by now." She wrung her hands, fearful that he'd been captured.

The sound of the door opening halted Reiko. A young woman dressed in white burst into the chamber. She was a maid from the Large Interior. Panting with excitement, she said, "Korika is up on a watchtower! I thought you'd want to know. She's going to jump!"

Reiko's breath caught. If Korika killed herself before she confessed that she'd set the fire, then all hope of exonerating Sano was lost.

Lady Nobuko demanded, "What? Why?"

"She said she killed Yoshisato. Right in front of everybody! Then she climbed up on the wall, and the soldiers went after her, and it collapsed, and now she wants to jump off the tower so she can't be burned to death!"

Korika had confessed in front of witnesses. She'd publicly exonerated Sano! But Reiko's joy immediately turned to anxiety. Would the news reach the shogun in time for her family's death sentence to be cancelled? And where was Masahiro?

"Isn't anybody trying to stop her?" Lady Nobuko asked, incredulous.

"Yes," the maid said. "There's a boy on the tower with Korika."

The news sent Reiko flying out the door. The boy had to be Masahiro.

The soldiers would be after him. And if the wall had collapsed, the tower could, too. Fearful for the baby but frantic to rescue her son, Reiko ran through the deserted palace grounds. She was winded by the time she reached the gate. Her back ached as she hobbled down the passage, toward a babble of voices. Around a curve, priests and mourners jammed the long, straight, descending passage. They faced away from her, looking up. Reiko's gaze followed theirs along the jagged, ascending line of the wall on their left. All that remained of it was a narrow ridge. The tower rose dark against the blue sky. Its skeletal wooden framework enclosed two small figures dressed in white. Masahiro and Korika stood near the sheer drop.

Fright spurred Reiko down the passage. She drew a breath to cry, *That's my son! Let me through!* Then she saw troops in the procession, among them men assigned to guard her family. They massed below the tower, shouting at Masahiro and Korika. They apparently didn't want to risk climbing up what was left of the collapsed wall, and the wall on the other side of the tower was too high. If they saw Reiko, they would arrest her. She turned and ran in the opposite direction. She must find a way to make Korika surrender, to save Masahiro.

A strong contraction cramped her belly. Wincing, she followed the passage around the hill to a plank gate set in a partially restored wall. This was one of several temporary shortcuts through the castle, which the workers used during the construction. Reiko pushed open the gate. She limped down a flight of wooden stairs that led between trees and rocks. Through another plank gate she entered a passage on the lower level. A painful twisting, sinking sensation in her belly frightened her. She had to stop and rest; her heart was beating so hard. She was so weak, she fell through the gate to the official district.

Trudging along the main street, past new mansions and some half built, past closed gates and empty guardhouses, Reiko met no one. Everybody had gone to the funeral. The wall on the hillside above her came into view. The section to her left was tall, clad with stone, intact. The section to her right was a spill of earth topped by a rim of stones. Above the rim Reiko saw the heads of people standing in the passage. The tower base rose between the intact and collapsed walls. Its wooden framework resembled a giant birdcage. Masahiro and Korika stood at the edge of the base. He extended his hands to her while she gazed down at the ground. The tower was even higher than Reiko had thought.

Lungs heaving, heart pounding, Reiko held her belly while she trudged toward the tower. A contraction came upon her, more painful than the last. She bent over, moaning.

"PLEASE DON'T JUMP!" Masahiro begged.

"Why not?" Korika sobbed. "It wouldn't hurt as much as burning."

Not only did Masahiro need her to confess to the shogun, but his impulse was to save her even though she was a murderess. He had to keep her too busy talking to jump. "How do you know it won't hurt as much?"

Korika shook her head. She wiped her hand across her wet eyes. She gazed longingly at the street below. "It would be quicker."

Unable to dispute that, Masahiro said, "If you come with me and talk to the shogun, I'll tell him you didn't really mean to hurt Yoshisato, you set the fire by mistake. He'll pardon you."

His words sounded unconvincing to himself. Korika's woeful glance said she didn't believe them, either. Desperate, Masahiro appealed to her mercy. "Unless you talk to the shogun, I'll be burned to death. So will my father, and my mother, and my little sister."

The thought of Akiko screaming while she went up in flames upset Masahiro more than the thought of his own death. "Please!" he said, extending clasped hands to Korika. "We'll all die unless you help us!"

"I don't care." Korika stepped so close to the edge that the toes of her white socks and thong sandals hung over the drop.

OUTSIDE THE MAUSOLEUM, Lord Tsunanori brandished his sword at the soldiers. They drew their swords. The people in the crowd gasped. Sano shouted, "Lord Tsunanori! Put down your weapon!"

Lord Tsunanori and the soldiers sprang into frenzied motion. Their yells were drowned out by screams from the crowd. It was so swift, Sano couldn't tell who'd attacked first.

An instant later the soldiers stepped back, looking stunned. Lord Tsunanori lay bleeding from cuts all over his body, the largest on his midsection. His sword was by his hand, its blade clean. His eyelids stretched so wide that his pupils looked like black dots painted on round white pebbles. His mouth gaped in a wordless howl.

The audience moaned. The shogun turned, ran from the gory sight, bent over, and spewed vomit. Yanagisawa and Ienobu rushed to his aid. Ladies fainted. Servants fussed over them. Sano rushed to Lord Tsunanori. Kneeling, he pressed his hands against the *daimyo*'s stomach, trying to stanch the flow of blood. His fingers slid into a cut so deep that he felt hot, slippery innards. The wound was beyond repair, mortal.

"What else do you want to say?" Sano asked urgently. Neither Lord Tsunanori nor he had long to live. He grabbed Lord Tsunanori's hand.

It was cold from shock and blood loss, but the fingers clenched Sano's with fierce strength. Lord Tsunanori gurgled as he breathed. His eyes communicated his agony and terror. His face was already white. His lips, grayish blue, moved in a wordless plea.

"I can't help you, I'm sorry." Sano didn't like to pressure a dying man, but he wanted the whole truth about the crime. "This is your last chance to finish your confession."

Lord Tsunanori wrung out his voice between gurgles. "Wouldn't have . . . thought of it . . . myself."

"Thought of what?"

"Smallpox." Lord Tsunanori grimaced; his body stiffened in a spasm of pain.

"Who gave you the idea, then?"

Lord Tsunanori moaned. His robes and the ground under Sano's knees were soaked with blood, which still poured from his gut. "Ienobu."

Shocked, Sano looked toward Ienobu. The man hovered by the shogun. The crowd assailed the gate, trying to flee the carnage. Yanagisawa shouted angrily. Troops ran about, trying to restore order. Nobody was listening to Sano and Lord Tsunanori.

"Ienobu gave you the idea of infecting your wife with smallpox?" Sano asked.

The grip on Sano's hand loosened. Lord Tsunanori whispered, "He knew about Namiji. He said she could do it and not get sick. He said . . . if Tsuruhime were to die of smallpox, nobody would ask questions.

Once he gave me the idea, it wouldn't go away, it sounded so good." His eyes burned briefly with indignation as he gazed up at Sano. "Nobody was supposed to know!"

Just as Sano had suspected earlier, Ienobu had been involved in Tsuruhime's death. He'd exercised his strange effect on Lord Tsunanori. Although Ienobu hadn't touched the smallpox-infested sheet, he was just as guilty as Lord Tsunanori and Namiji. Now Sano understood the true scope and monstrousness of Ienobu's crime.

In order to clear his path to the head of the dictatorship, Ienobu had had Tsuruhime murdered. It wasn't much of a mental stretch for Sano to believe Ienobu was also responsible for the fire that had killed Yoshisato. He'd eliminated Tsuruhime first, because although he'd perceived her as less of a threat, she'd been the easier target. Ienobu had engineered each death, benefited from both, and done the dirty work for neither.

Lord Tsunanori's face relaxed. His eyelids half closed.

"You can't die yet!" Sano cried. "You have to tell the shogun that his nephew killed his daughter and his heir!"

Lord Tsunanori was also Sano's only chance at exoneration.

One last spasm wracked Lord Tsunanori. He emitted one last, weak moan, one last gout of blood. Sano felt the animating spirit fade from his body.

"Come back!" Sano dropped Lord Tsunanori's hand, shook him, and pounded his chest in a futile attempt to revive him. But Lord Tsunanori was gone.

No one except Sano had heard his last testimony.

Drenched in blood, Sano rose. Yanagisawa pointed at him, shouting, "Arrest him!" Soldiers rushed in his direction. Sano's reprieve was over, the machinery that would destroy him set in motion again. Hopelessly seeking an escape, he heard a roar of voices outside the walls. It came from a great distance and grew louder, like a tidal wave coming. The flow of talk along the funeral procession had reversed direction. The roar burst into the mausoleum compound.

"The shogun's wife's lady-in-waiting confessed to setting the fire!"

"Sano is innocent!"

Yanagisawa listened, his expression filling with horror and rage. The soldiers paused, looking to him for new orders. The shogun raised his green, befuddled face. The mourners stared at Sano.

As his mind reeled with astonishment, Sano ignored the crowd, the shogun, and Yanagisawa. His eyes sought one man. He met Ienobu's deliberately bland gaze.

42

A HIGH-PITCHED RINGING, like wind chimes, roused Hirata. Lying on his stomach, he felt cold, jagged rock pressed against his cheek. Breathing sulfurous fumes, he coughed. His body was a constellation of pains, the worst one in his right arm, which was twisted under his chest. Rolling over, Hirata opened his eyes and saw only blackness.

For a terrifying instant he thought he was blind. Then light paled the black after-image of the explosion. Vision returned. The woods surrounded him. His head pounded. He lifted his right hand to it, then yelled and stopped because of the pain in his arm. He felt the arm with his left hand. Jagged bone poked through the skin above the wrist. It must have broken when he fell. He touched his head and found a plum-sized knot. Blood wet his fingers. He looked toward the clearing.

Sunlight filtered through smoke. Scattered green flames burned fallen leaves on the ground. Where the bonfire had been was a black crater ringed with charred sticks and earth clods. Between Hirata and the crater, a human shape lay facedown.

Tahara.

His clothes were burned to smoking tatters. His exposed back, legs, and neck were red, blistered, and studded with black cinders and twigs from the bonfire. His topknot was burned to a frizzle. His hand still clutched his sword. He didn't move.

Cautious relief trickled through Hirata, but he mustn't assume Tahara was dead. He sat up, swaying dizzily. The deep exhaustion that always set in after strenuous combat permeated him. Cramps contracted every muscle. Pain vibrated every nerve as his body purged the poisons that had accumulated inside it. Gasps pumped chemical fumes from his lungs. Foul sweat leaked from his skin. He crawled, right knee, then left knee, then left hand, holding his broken arm against him. He inched toward his sword, which lay between him and Tahara. The ringing in his ears faded. As he struggled to lift the sword, he heard rustling noises from the pit.

Kitano and Deguchi.

Hirata walked on his knees toward the pit. He dragged the sword, which felt as heavy as if made of stone. Thrusting one leg after the other took all his strength. Each time his kneecap hit the ground, his arm and the knot on his head throbbed. When he reached the pit, a hand slowly rose from inside it and clamped onto the edge. Another hand followed suit. A face appeared between them. Blood and grime overlaid its mesh of old scars. Kitano gasped out, "I killed Deguchi."

Hirata looked into the pit. At the bottom Deguchi lay amid blood-soaked leaves and sticks. His eyes, their glow extinguished, stared vacantly. His throat was cut.

"Too bad for you," said a voice from behind Hirata.

Hirata looked over his shoulder. Tahara struggled to his feet; his legs buckled, but he remained upright. His face was bruised, his nose bleeding.

"That didn't go quite the way you planned." His swollen lips managed to smile.

Horror worsened the weakness that crippled Hirata. His ally was dead. His last trick had failed. He was alone with his two enemies.

Kitano groaned, pulling himself out of the pit. He collapsed with his legs inside it and his upper body flat on the surface. Tahara moved toward Hirata, wobbling as if swamped by ocean waves. The effort pulled his smile into a grimace. His arm trembled as he brandished his sword. This was the weakest condition in which Hirata had ever seen Tahara and Kitano, his best chance to kill them. But Hirata was even weaker. Swinging at Kitano, he toppled on his stomach. Kitano crawled from the pit. Tahara fell. They lay gasping on the ground. Hirata hoped they were too exhausted to kill him. Then Tahara lifted his shaking hand and pointed.

Across the clearing, a lumpy cloth sack levitated. It flew jerkily to Tahara. Hirata exerted his mind against it, in vain. Tahara fumbled the sack open, pulled out an oil lamp and incense burner. He lit them with a flame he rubbed up between his finger and thumb. He and Kitano began chanting.

Hirata whispered, "Stop. No."

Tahara and Kitano chanted louder, faster, gaining strength from the spell. Hirata tried to block the sound from his mind and hold his breath. But their combined will overpowered his. The sweet, rank incense smoke penetrated his lungs. His voice involuntarily uttered the chant. He found himself on the Sekigahara battlefield, kneeling among the corpses. Ravens swooped down from the mountains, lured by the stench of death. General Otani materialized in front of Hirata. He wore his horned helmet and black armor. His face was disfigured by leprosy sores, fierce with rage.

"You disobeyed me," he said in his booming voice. "You betrayed your comrades. Now you will suffer the consequences."

Terror bit deep into Hirata. General Otani must have no further use for him, no reason to spare him. If he was killed while in a trance, he would die for real. He groped for his sword. His hand touched mud. The sword hadn't accompanied him into the trance, but his physical infirmities had. The pain in his arm doubled him over. He was too feeble to stand.

General Otani raised his armor-gloved hand. Distant hoofbeats thundered. Two mounted soldiers galloped across the battlefield, one from either side of General Otani, heading straight for Hirata. As they drew near, Hirata recognized Tahara and Kitano. They wore armor that matched General Otani's. Poles on their backs flew banners that bore his crest. They raised chain-mailed arms and waved swords. They howled as their horses trampled corpses.

Hirata uttered an incoherent plea for mercy, a cry of despair.

Tahara and Kitano converged upon him. General Otani dropped his hand. Their blades came slashing down.

Hirata's cry was lost in the cawing of ravens that fluttered up from the battlefield, into the sky that turned as black as their wings.

TAEKO WRIGGLED HER way through the funeral procession. Frantic to reach Masahiro, she dropped to the ground and burrowed through a forest of women's white kimono skirts, men's flowing white trousers, and priests' saffron robes. She crawled out between the armored legs of a soldier. She scrambled to her feet on a dirt ridge alongside the passage, where the foundation for a new wall had been. Looking down the hill, she saw the landslide. Surprise opened her mouth. Her gaze moved up the ridge. Two people stood on the base of a tower inside wooden beams and posts. One was a lady. The other was Masahiro.

"Little girl, come away from there before you fall!" someone called.

Heedless, Taeko began walking up the ridge. Her love for him pushed her toward Masahiro. She didn't dare glance down the steep, frightening hillside. The ridge crumbled under her feet. Dirt slid. People in the passage raised their hands to her and begged her to let them lift her down. Taeko walked faster. The ridge narrowed as it rose. She crawled the rest of the way to the tower, grasped the wooden framework, and pulled herself inside, onto the stone-paved floor.

Masahiro stood, turned away from her, at the edge of the tower. He leaned toward the plump woman with the puffy hairdo, who stood beside him on his right. His hands were clasped. Taeko heard him say, "Please don't jump." He sounded as if he were going to cry. Taeko had never seen Masahiro cry.

The woman sobbed and gulped. "I have to."

Something told Taeko to keep quiet. She crept toward Masahiro until she was close enough to touch him. He and the woman didn't notice her. She looked over the edge and saw the long drop to the ground. Her stomach plunged. She felt as if she were falling. Wind whistled in her ears. Her heart banged. She clutched a low crossbeam on the framework and turned away from the terrifying view.

There was a clatter behind her. A wooden ladder leaned against the side of the tower that was above the passage. It shook as someone climbed up. Anxious voices racketed from below. Masahiro and the woman turned toward the ladder. Masahiro's back was to Taeko, but she could see the woman's face. It was a gray, red, and white mess of makeup and tears. It bunched like a crying child's. The woman wailed, turned back to the edge, and stepped off.

Taeko gasped. Masahiro yelled. He snatched at the falling woman.

.   .   .

PANTING WITH EXHAUSTION, Reiko arrived at the base of the tower just as Korika jumped. She saw Masahiro reach for Korika. His hand caught her skirts. Her weight pulled him with her. Reiko stared in disbelief as he toppled. Horror consumed her with its awful, breathtaking, heart-stopping sickness. A fall from that height would be fatal.

The baby inside her writhed, as if with her agony, as Reiko screamed, "Masahiro! *No!*"

TAEKO ACTED WITHOUT thinking. Her left hand locked onto the beam while her right hand flashed out and grabbed Masahiro's ankle. He fell. She heard him shout. A huge tug stiffened her arm as it took his weight and the woman's. The joint in her shoulder popped. Pain shot down her arm. Taeko screamed.

IT HAPPENED SO fast, Masahiro didn't have time to be afraid. He saw the ground rush up to meet him. For the first time he realized that he could die.

Then something clamped tight around his ankle. A wrenching jerk on his leg arrested his fall. He slammed flat against the side of the tower. The impact jarred his chin, knocked the breath out of him. Masahiro gasped. He was suspended by his leg, pulled downward by Korika, whose skirts he clutched in his hands. Dangling upside down against the tower, high above the ground, she shrieked.

BELOW THE TOWER, Reiko sobbed. She flung out her arms to catch Masahiro when he fell. She braced herself for the terrible moment when he and Korika crashed upon her, killing her as they died. Blinded by tears, at first she didn't see what had happened.

The crash didn't come. Reiko heard shrieking above her. Masahiro and Korika dangled from the tower. She exclaimed in astonishment. A small person clutched Masahiro's ankle with one hand and the frame-work with the other. It was Taeko.

TAEKO WAS STRETCHED between the framework and Masahiro like a rope about to snap. Groans came from the procession. Taeko looked over the edge at her hand holding Masahiro's ankle, and Masahiro and the woman dangling. The long drop made her dizzy. She sobbed with terror. The pain in her shoulder was so bad, she thought she would vomit. Reflexes almost sprang her fingers open. She wasn't strong enough for this. Her arm would tear off. But she held on to the beam. She held on to Masahiro.

HANGING BY HIS leg, Masahiro felt Korika's robes slide through his fingers. The silk was slippery, her weight pulling hard. Her hem slithered from his grip. He saw the soles of her sandals, saw her arms spread in a vain effort to fly while she plummeted. She screamed, then landed with an awful thud. Masahiro saw her body crumpled on the street. Another woman dressed in white stood by her, gazing up at him and crying. It was his mother. He twisted around to see what had kept him from falling.

A small hand clung to his ankle. It belonged to Taeko. Her face was wild with fear, her teeth clenched. Masahiro felt her trembling with the strain of bearing his weight.

Three soldiers bounded up the ladder behind Taeko. They seized Masahiro by his leg and pulled him up onto the tower. Masahiro sat speechless while they pried Taeko's hand off his ankle. His foot was numb from the pressure, his ankle ringed with fingernail gouges. Taeko cradled her right arm, looking as shocked as he was.

"Taeko!" Midori came bounding up the ladder. She knelt beside the girl. "Thank the gods you're safe! I'm going to kill you!" She reached for Taeko.

Masahiro heard Akiko and Tatsuo screaming his name. He figured out what had happened: Taeko had run away from her mother to follow him. Midori, and the other children, had stayed in the castle to look for Taeko instead of escaping.

As her mother hugged her, Taeko began to cry.

REIKO WATCHED THE troops carry Masahiro and Taeko off the tower. She fell to her knees and sobbed with gratitude. Taeko had acquired the superhuman strength that people sometimes do during a crisis. Masahiro was safe. Reiko didn't know for how long, or what would happen next, but she didn't care. This relief, this joy, was enough.

Hearing a groan, she looked down at Korika. Korika lay in a tangle of white robes and broken limbs, her neck twisted, her cheek against the paving stones. A red pool of blood, mixed with gray brain tissue, circled her head. Despite her mortal injuries, she was still alive.

Reiko felt an unexpected sympathy for this woman who'd burned a young man to death, whose crime had led to the downfall of Reiko's family, whose suicide attempt had almost killed Masahiro. Taeko wasn't the only one who'd acted out of selfless loyalty. Korika had murdered Yoshisato for Lady Nobuko, and she'd delivered herself to justice.

Reiko held Korika's limp, moist hand and murmured soothingly, "You gave Lady Nobuko her revenge. She appreciates your sacrifice. You can die in peace."

Korika's neck muscles tensed. Her body was paralyzed. She groaned; her eyes blinked. She whispered, "I lied. To the boy. It wasn't. My idea."

Puzzled, Reiko said, "What wasn't your idea?"

"The fire."

Reiko realized that someone else had been involved in Yoshisato's murder. The crime wasn't yet solved, all culprits not brought to justice. Reiko demanded, "Whose idea was it?"

"Lord Ienobu." Korika's voice was as soft as dry grass rustling in the wind. "He came to see me. He knew I would. Do anything for. Her." A smile twitched her lips. "And I did."

Reiko's heart gave a thump of astonishment. "Ienobu put you up to it? He was involved in Yoshisato's death?"

The shine in Korika's eyes dulled. A last breath sighed from her. Reiko was holding the hand of a dead woman.

A tremendous contraction squeezed Reiko like a cruel fist inside her. She doubled over, hugging her belly, gritting her teeth in pain. Warm liquid oozed between her legs. The baby was coming.

43

THE MORNING AFTER the funeral was gray, windy. Clouds shadowed the castle. In the palace, an assembly convened. The shogun sat on the dais, flanked by Ienobu on his right and Yanagisawa on his left. "I have two announcements," he said to the government officials packed into his reception chamber.

Sano and Masahiro sat together in the front row, on the higher of the two floor levels below the dais. Sano's cut, bruised face was stiff with his effort to conceal his astonishment. He couldn't believe he'd lived to see this day.

The shogun held up his index finger. "I have heard a full report about the confession made by that woman Korika. I am satisfied that she set the fire and killed my son." Grief momentarily halted him; he swallowed. "Sano-*san,* I hereby void the charges against you and your family. I declare all of you innocent of murder and treason."

"Many thanks, Your Excellency." Sano bowed. Waves of disapproval emanated toward him from the silent, motionless audience. He remembered the previous assembly, the purge, General Isogai, and Elder Ohgami. He had no friends here.

He looked at the men beside the shogun. Ienobu met his gaze calmly. Yanagisawa's face was as white and rigid as an ice sculpture. Only the molten heat in his eyes hinted at how furious he was that Sano had survived against all expectation. If the death of his son's murderer gave him any satisfaction, Sano couldn't tell.

"I also excuse you for killing three of your guards when you escaped from house arrest," the shogun said. "You can keep your post as rebuilding magistrate. And Masahiro, you are reinstated as head of my private chambers. That should suffice as reward for, ahh, solving the murders of my son and daughter."

Masahiro glowed with jubilation. Sano was glad, too, but he felt bad about killing the innocent men. He also felt a bad sense of unfinished business. He couldn't consider the crimes solved. Ienobu's role in them had yet to be exposed. Sano and Reiko were the only people who knew about it so far.

"Today begins a fresh start for me." Determined to follow the course of action into which Sano had pushed him, the shogun cast a baleful gaze around the assembly. "None of you will twist me around your fingers again."

The disapproval aimed at Sano grew stronger. These men, who'd been his enemies to begin with, blamed him for the shogun's fresh start, which would diminish their power. Sano himself wasn't sure he liked it. Had he created a monster that not even he could control?

"Now for my second announcement," the shogun said. "I am adopting my nephew, the honorable Ienobu, and naming him as my heir."

Ienobu bowed to the shogun, then the assembly. He acted as humble as if inheriting the regime were a duty for which he must nobly sacrifice himself. Nobody seemed surprised. Sano wasn't. The shogun had had his face rubbed in his own mortality twice. He needed more than ever to choose a successor. Ienobu, his closest surviving relative, was the logical choice. Sano suspected that many people weren't happy about it, but they didn't object and test the shogun's new temperament. Neither did Sano.

He and Reiko were the only people who'd heard Korika's and Lord Tsunanori's full confessions. Last night, when they'd talked over what had happened, they'd agreed not to tell anyone, not even Masahiro. It was too dangerous to accuse Ienobu of multiple treasonous crimes when the only evidence against him was the words of two witnesses who were now dead.

Yoshisato the fraud wouldn't inherit the dictatorship. Ienobu the double murderer was set to be the next shogun.

"Consider this a warning," the shogun said. "You know what happened to the person who murdered my previous heir. Harm this one at your own peril."

All attention swiveled to Yanagisawa, the most likely threat to Ienobu. A muscle in Yanagisawa's rigid jaw twitched. He didn't look at anyone. Nor did he reveal his disappointment that instead of being the adoptive father of the shogun's heir, he was the enemy of the next shogun. Sano could only imagine how Yanagisawa would react if he knew Ienobu was partially responsible for Yoshisato's death. He wondered whether, or when, to tell Yanagisawa.

"In view of new circumstances," the shogun said, "some changes in the government are necessary."

Yanagisawa stood. He didn't wait for himself and his allies to be purged and replaced by men friendly to Ienobu. His back straight, his eyes ablaze, he walked out of the room.

"HERE'S YOUR MEDICINE," Midori said, handing Reiko a ceramic cup.

Reiko sat up in bed. She drank the potion of lotus seeds, ginseng, cassia twig, ginger, and beef heart that the doctor had brewed. Then she lay back, clasping her hands over her flat, tender stomach. Blood oozed into the cloth pad between her legs. Her eyes were sore from weeping.

"You can have another baby," Midori tried to console her.

A sob caught Reiko's breath. No child could replace this one that she'd spent five years hoping to conceive.

"I know this is terrible," Midori said, "but remember, you're lucky to be alive."

"I know." But nothing could assuage Reiko's heartbreak. Nothing could change what had happened yesterday.

When the troops had come to remove Korika's body, they'd found Reiko lying beside it, in the throes of labor. They'd carried her home, where she'd delivered a stillborn baby boy. Reiko had cried while she held him. He was hardly bigger than her hand. His pink skin was wrinkled and blue-veined and translucent, his eyes closed as if in sleep. Reiko loved him as immediately and powerfully as she'd loved Masahiro and Akiko when they were born. But he would never grow up, never know her or his father or his brother or sister. This was a loss whose magnitude she'd never comprehended, a grief worse than any she'd experienced.

"Your family is lucky to be alive, too." Midori spoke as if she knew her words were no comfort to Reiko, but she had to keep trying. "It's a miracle, how everything turned out."

Moments after the baby had been born, Sano had come home. He'd told Reiko that the news of Korika's confession had reached the shogun at the mausoleum. Reiko tried to be happy that she'd exonerated him and her family was safe. With Sano's reputation cleared, the servants had returned. But good fortune didn't abate Reiko's immense sorrow or guilt.

She'd known she was overexerting herself. No matter that she would do it again given the same circumstances. She'd saved her family but sacrificed her baby.

Midori said, "Look who's here," and left.

Akiko stood in the doorway, her face tight and unsmiling. "That old lady is here to see you." She turned to go before Reiko could say she wasn't receiving visitors.

"Wait, Akiko." Reiko hadn't seen her daughter since they'd separated in the passage yesterday. "Come here."

Tears glistened in Akiko's eyes. "You left me." Her angry voice wobbled. "You went away and left me."

"I know. I'm sorry." More guilt pained Reiko. Not only was the baby's death her fault, but she'd hurt her daughter. "Let me explain." She extended her hand. "Sit with me."

Akiko looked at Reiko's hand as if it held dung that Reiko was trying to pass off as candy. But she came, against her will, and knelt by Reiko.

Reiko exerted herself to choose words that a child would understand. "I didn't want to leave you. I never do. But there will be times when I must. Yesterday I left because I needed to do things to save your life." She spoke with all the sincerity and gentleness that her grieving spirit could muster. "You're my little girl, and I would do anything for you because I love you."

Akiko's face worked. She was obviously torn between wanting to believe Reiko and not wanting to be placated so easily and hurt again. Then her tears spilled. "It's my fault the baby died," she blurted out. "Because I didn't want it."

Surprise and alarm stunned Reiko. While she'd been feeling guilty about Akiko, her daughter had been harboring an unfounded guilt about her. Reiko gathered Akiko in her arms. "No, it's not your fault. Just because you think something, that doesn't make it happen."

Stiff and resisting at first, Akiko relaxed as she sobbed. Reiko soothed her with pats and murmurs. Soon Akiko pulled away, uncomfortable with too much closeness. But she skipped out of the room, light enough to fly.

Reiko was glad that the baby was the only child she'd lost.

A servant ushered in Lady Nobuko, the last person Reiko wanted to see. Lady Nobuko knelt, bowed, and offered Reiko a gift-wrapped box. "I've brought you some herbs from my doctor. They're good for women who have miscarried."

Reiko made no move to take the box. "Why are you here? Our business is finished."

Lady Nobuko raised her eyebrows at Reiko's discourtesy. She set the box by the bed. "I wanted to express my condolences and to thank you and your husband for bringing Lord Tsunanori to justice." She looked extraordinarily well. The spasm around her eye was slight today. "When he commits *seppuku,* I shall be there to watch." Her gaunt face seemed fuller, with satisfaction. "My only regret is that he won't suffer for as long as Tsuruhime did. All in all, things couldn't have turned out better."

Reiko couldn't believe what she was hearing. "A young man was burned to death. You call that good?"

"Yoshisato deserved to die," Lady Nobuko said, unfazed by Reiko's repugnance. "And Yanagisawa deserves to be punished for his plot to take over the regime. The loss of his pawn was divine retribution."

"There was nothing divine about it," Reiko said. "Korika murdered Yoshisato. She's dead, too. Don't you care? Or are you just glad that the shogun decided she was solely to blame and he's not punishing you?"

Lady Nobuko smiled condescendingly. "You young women think the world should dance to your whims. When you're my age, you'll understand that everything has a price, and sometimes one must pay it and be glad to take whatever one can get."

Reiko thought her innocent baby had paid the ultimate price of everything that had happened since she and Sano had agreed to investigate Tsuruhime's death. She hated Lady Nobuko for her selfish, cynical attitude.

"Ienobu is going to be the next shogun," Reiko said. "Is that a price you're glad to pay?"

"Ienobu is a legitimate Tokugawa."

Reiko couldn't reveal that Ienobu had put Korika up to murdering Yoshisato and Lord Tsunanori up to murdering Tsuruhime, exercising his strange, manipulative effect on both. She'd promised Sano that she would keep it secret. Lest she yield to the temptation to blurt it out and smack the contentment off Lady Nobuko's face, Reiko said quietly, "Please go."

OUTSIDE THE PALACE, Yanagisawa stormed through the grounds. Buried up to his chin in the ruins of his hopes, suffocating in anger, he could hardly breathe.

He'd lost his chance to rule Japan. He couldn't make up a new prophecy and style one of his other sons as the shogun's offspring. The shogun wouldn't fall for that again.

Sano had lived to plague him another day. And with Ienobu ensconced as the shogun's heir, Yanagisawa's days were numbered.

How could this have happened? What in hell was he going to do?

Terror sped Yanagisawa along the paths. There was no place safe to go. Aimless flight took him to the garden behind the palace. Ienobu shuffled toward him, accompanied by two guards. Yanagisawa's anger blasted at Ienobu, like a torch flame blown by the wind. Ienobu had exploited Yoshisato's murder. Ienobu had won.

Yanagisawa stalked over to Ienobu. "I'll see that you never become shogun."

Ienobu grinned. "On the contrary—you're going to make sure I do."

Yanagisawa stared, incredulous. "Are you insane? I'll kill you first."

The guards reached for their swords. Ienobu said to them, "Let us have a private word." After they'd moved out of earshot, he said, "You'll change your attitude when you hear the news I have for you." He spoke in a dramatic whisper: "Yoshisato is alive."

Surprise momentarily tied Yanagisawa's tongue. Then he laughed in derision. "Don't talk nonsense." But Ienobu's words gave credence to his secret, irrational notion that Yoshisato wasn't dead, that Yoshisato was coming back.

"Yoshisato didn't die in that fire. He wasn't murdered." Ienobu's bulging eyes gleamed. He knew he had Yanagisawa as surely as if he'd closed his fist around Yanagisawa's heart.

Resisting the desire to believe a man he hated and distrusted, Yanagisawa turned away.

"Don't you want to know what really happened the night of the fire?"

Yanagisawa kept his back to Ienobu, but he was immobilized.

"I became privy to certain conversations between Lady Nobuko and her lady-in-waiting. I deduced that Korika wanted to harm Yoshisato because of what you supposedly did to her mistress. I recognized an opportunity."

Smug pride inflected Ienobu's tone. Yanagisawa listened in spite of himself as Ienobu said, "The next day I paid Korika a visit. I suggested that fire was a good way to kill someone and make it look like an accident. I said that if she went out that night, she would be able to move freely without being observed. That night I arranged for the castle guards to be absent from their posts. Korika went to the heir's residence. Five of my men got there first. They plugged the well. They killed Yoshisato's personal bodyguards. Then they went after Yoshisato. He put up quite a fight, but they tied him up and drugged him. Then they waited."

Yanagisawa envisioned his son struggling as the intruders overpowered him. He turned to stare, eyes wide with shock, at Ienobu.

"Soon Korika arrived. She set the fire and ran away. Before the fire bells started ringing, before the house burned down, my men dragged the dead guards inside. Then they carried Yoshisato out. During the uproar when everyone was rushing to put out the fire, nobody paid attention to my men carrying a trunk out the back gate of the castle."

Yanagisawa's wish to believe the story was so fierce, it felt like a wild beast wrestling with the rational part of him that doubted Ienobu's scenario. "There were four corpses in the ruins. Everybody was accounted for. Yoshisato didn't get out alive."

"The arithmetic was a slight problem." Ienobu chuckled. "I solved it by having my men kill one of their comrades. They left his body in Yoshisato's chamber. He was the right size."

This ruthlessness sounded just like the man Yanagisawa had always suspected Ienobu to be. This detail fed the beast in his mind that fought to convince him that Ienobu was telling the truth. The politician in him scorned the story as pure fabrication.

"Why would you save Yoshisato?" Yanagisawa demanded. "If he's alive, he's the shogun's first choice for an heir. He's a threat to you."

"Because I need him," Ienobu said. "He's not the only threat. There are people who don't want me to be the next shogun. I want you to help me neutralize my opposition. You're good at that kind of thing. When I'm shogun, you can have Yoshisato back."

The cruel manipulation, the nerve, the self-delusion of the man! "I was right. You are insane. I would never lift a finger to help you. And I won't listen to any more of this." Yanagisawa vehemently denied his own cherished delusion. "Yoshisato is dead. You can't trick me into thinking otherwise."

"Here's proof that he's alive." With a sly smile, Ienobu reached under his sash and pulled out a sheet of white paper, which he offered to Yanagisawa.

Despite his better judgment, Yanagisawa snatched the paper and opened it. He saw black characters written in Yoshisato's bold, graceful, yet precise hand. The letter was dated the day after the fire. Even as tears of yearning stung his eyes, Yanagisawa said, "This is a forgery."

"Don't be so quick to debunk it. Read it first."

Against his will, Yanagisawa read:

Honorable Adoptive Father:
You've really outdone yourself this time. You got me kidnapped by your en-
emy Ienobu! I never imagined that anyone could match you in ruthlessness,
but he does. If you ever want to see me again, you'd better cooperate with
him. On second thought, it would be better for you if you didn't cooperate.
Because if I get out of here alive, I'm going to kill you. After all the trouble
your schemes have caused me, and my poor mother, you deserve to rot in hell.
Yoshisato

Yanagisawa could almost hear Yoshisato speaking the words. Ienobu couldn't have written them. Ienobu couldn't have known how Yoshisato and Yanagisawa talked to each other.

"Handwriting is easily faked, but the voice is more difficult." Ienobu clucked his tongue. "Yoshisato doesn't like you very much, does he?"

Yanagisawa wanted to bury his face in the letter and weep with the joy of a father who finally believes that his dead child has been miraculously resurrected. Instead he glared at Ienobu, who'd made him suffer the anguish of thinking Yoshisato had been murdered and now sought to use him. He grabbed the front of Ienobu's robe.

"Where is he?"

"In a safe, secret place, with my men," Ienobu said. "Take your hands off me."

The guards started toward Yanagisawa. He flung Ienobu away from him. "The shogun will be overjoyed to hear that his son is alive. He'll make you tell me where Yoshisato is."

"You won't breathe a word of this conversation to him or anyone else." Ienobu's eyes gleamed; he enjoyed Yanagisawa's distress. "If you do, I'll have Yoshisato killed. You'll never see him again."

Yanagisawa boiled with fury and hatred. "I'll kill you!"

"If anything bad happens to me, or if you refuse to support me as the next shogun, Yoshisato dies," Ienobu said.

In spite of himself Yanagisawa felt a grudging esteem for Ienobu, who'd bettered him in imagination and audacity. Yanagisawa had never dreamed of, let alone attempted, such a move.

"If you cooperate with me, you get him back safe and sound." Ienobu smiled expectantly, confidently. "Well? Do we have a deal?"

The wild beast inside Yanagisawa thrashed and bellowed. Yanagisawa desperately wanted Yoshisato to return. Rationality screamed at him not to be deceived. "You've no reason to bring Yoshisato back. If you do, the shogun will disinherit you in favor of him. You're going to string me along, while I dispatch your enemies for you, until you're shogun. And then you'll kill Yoshisato so that he can't raise a revolt against you."

"That's a definite possibility," Ienobu agreed. "But remember: Unless you cooperate, Yoshisato dies. For real."

All his life Yanagisawa had taken pride in his ability to find a way around a problem. Now he found none, saw no choice but the bargain offered by Ienobu. Desperation pushed him to accept even though he didn't trust Ienobu to uphold his part of the bargain, even though it was so humiliating. He would accept for Yoshisato's sake.

"All right." The words tasted as foul as excrement in Yanagisawa's mouth. "You win."

Ienobu nodded as if he'd never doubted he would. "By the way, you can keep your post as chamberlain. It will give you the authority to do what you need to do for me. Oh, and when you dispatch my enemies, start with your friend Sano." He turned and shuffled over to his guards. They accompanied him into the palace.

Yanagisawa stood alone in the garden, consumed by rage yet less bereft and lost than when he'd walked out of the assembly. "You win for now," he said to the absent Ienobu. "But I'm going to find Yoshisato. And I swear that as soon as he's safe, I will kill you, you bastard."

STILL GROGGY FROM the medicine the doctor had given her, Taeko sat on the veranda, her right arm in a sling, watching the ducks swim in the pond. Yesterday seemed like a dream. Her shoulder had hurt so bad that it had blanked out her memory of much that had happened. She did recall her mother crying over her, the doctor saying her shoulder had been dislocated, and fainting because of the awful pain when he reset it in the socket. The rest was hard to believe.

Masahiro came out of the house. Taeko snapped fully alert. He looked as shy as she felt with him. He crouched near her and asked, "How's your shoulder?"

Looking sideways at him, Taeko said, "Better."

He nodded, then frowned. "You shouldn't have climbed up on the tower. It was stupid and dangerous. When you caught me, we could have both fallen and been killed!"

Taeko was relieved as well as saddened by his scolding. The scene on the tower really had happened. She glanced at Masahiro's ankle. Just above the top of his white sock was a purple bruise that encircled his ankle, dotted with raw, red gouges from her fingernails.

Masahiro sighed. "That's not what I meant to say." He said gruffly, "You saved my life. Thank you."

She heard new respect in his voice. It gave her the confidence to look directly at him. Their eyes met. His were serious, without the usual annoyance, teasing, or condescending affection.

"Why?" Masahiro sounded puzzled. "Why did you risk your life to save me?"

Taeko didn't have the words to express her feelings, but she couldn't hide them, either. As she gazed at Masahiro, all her love shone out from her eyes.

His eyes darkened with astonishment. A shadow of fear crossed his expression. This boy Taeko had thought wasn't afraid of anything was afraid of how much she cared for him, how much she was willing to do for his sake. Something in the air changed. The garden shimmered and flowed, like a painting with water poured on it. Masahiro's image blurred. Taeko had a sense that years had passed in an instant. She knew, without knowing how she knew, that she was seeing the future. Someday, when she and Masahiro were older, they would be much more to each other than they were now. Their fates were connected.

Clarity returned to the world. Masahiro abruptly stood up. He looked confused, as if he'd experienced something he didn't understand and didn't know whether he liked. His trousers covered the bruise around his ankle, but Taeko knew it was there. She had the strange, comforting idea that she'd put her mark on Masahiro.

Without a word he went into the house. Taeko had no urge to run after him. She smiled.

He could leave, and she didn't mind, because he would come back to her. He would always go, but he would always have to come back.

SANO HESITATED AT the threshold of Reiko's chamber. His wife was just as he'd left her this morning—in bed, her tear-swollen eyes gazing into space, her frail hands clasped over her empty womb. When he knelt at her side, she looked at him as if she were alone with her grief on one side of an ocean and he on the other with the rest of the world.

"Are you feeling better?" Sano asked.

The misery on her face intensified. He knew he'd said the wrong thing. Everything he'd said since he'd come home and found her weeping over their stillborn son had been wrong. He couldn't seem to find the right thing to say.

"I was just at the shogun's assembly," Sano said, resorting to conversation that was impersonal, less fraught with hazards. He told Reiko that the shogun had officially voided the charges against them and reinstated him and Masahiro to their positions. "It looks like Yanagisawa will be forced out of the regime."

"That's good." Reiko hardly seemed to care.

Sano was sorry about losing their child, but his grief couldn't equal hers. He hadn't carried it inside him for six months. It had never seemed as real to him as their other children, and he realized he'd been bracing himself to lose it; Reiko had been through so much during her pregnancy. He hated that she had paid such a high price for the solution to their problems. Her love for him and her effort to save him had cost her the child for which she'd longed.

To distract her from her grief, and himself from his guilt, Sano said, "The shogun has named Ienobu as his heir."

"Oh." Reiko's tone was indifferent. "What are you going to do?"

Once she would have said *we,* Sano thought sadly. She'd have rushed to help him prevent Ienobu the murderer from becoming the next shogun. "I'll find other proof that Ienobu had a hand in Tsuruhime's and Yoshisato's deaths. There must be witnesses or evidence somewhere. When I have enough, I'll go to the shogun."

Reiko didn't respond. Sano knew it was selfish to mind the change in her, but his heart ached with loneliness. Many times he'd tried to prevent Reiko from involving herself in things that were dangerous. Now he would give anything to restore her to her normal, feisty self.

"There's something else I have to do." Sano didn't like to bother Reiko with problems, but he had no one else to confide in about his other unfinished business, and he couldn't help trying to draw her back to him. "It's about Hirata. The time I gave him to resolve things himself is up. I have to arrest him and his friends in the secret society and prosecute them for treason."

Alarm overshadowed the misery in Reiko's expression. For the first time Sano had her full attention. "You would really do that to Hirata?"

"I don't want to." There had been few things Sano wanted less. "I have to."

"But he's been your friend for fifteen years. He saved your life."

"I know. That's what makes it so hard."

"He and his friends haven't yet done anything to hurt the regime."

"Not yet," Sano said grimly.

"Why should you care about protecting the regime?" Reiko said with a hint of her old fire. "Remember what the regime almost did to us. Look what the shogun did to your face."

"It's not about whether the shogun or the regime are worth protecting. It's about honor." Sano confessed, "I came close to throwing away mine, telling off the shogun like that." But he was too ashamed to tell Reiko what else he meant, that he'd almost tried to kill the shogun. "I have to recommit to Bushido. That means not making allowances for a friend at the expense of my duty to my lord."

One more step out of line and he wasn't a true samurai anymore.

A sob at the door startled him. Midori stood there, her hand at her throat, her expression stricken. She'd overheard everything about Hirata. "I knew he was up to something bad. I just knew it!" She rushed into the room and fell on her knees before Sano. "He didn't mean to be a traitor. It was a mistake! Please give him another chance!"

"I gave him many chances," Sano said, distressed by her anguish yet bound to his duty. "He just used up the last one."

"But what about his children? What about me?" Midori said, horrified by what she saw as Sano's cruelty. "We've done nothing wrong. Are you going to put us to death, too?"

A traitor's family shared his punishment. That was the law. Sano had avoided thinking about what would happen to Midori and the children when he prosecuted Hirata, but the issue was now as unavoidable as his course of action.

"I don't have a choice." Sano felt a despair more anguishing than he'd thought possible.

"I can't believe this." In a panic, Midori seized Reiko's hand. "Talk to him," she begged. "Make him change his mind!"

Reiko wilted, as if arguing was too much for her; she knew she couldn't change Sano's mind. She sank into deeper desolation. Sano could tell what she was thinking: First the baby was lost; now their beloved friends.

"Please!" Midori prostrated herself, her hands extended to Sano. "My husband saved your life. Our daughter saved your son's." Forsaking propriety, she called in the debts. "Have mercy!"

Sano wished with all the fervor in him that things could be different. If he'd dealt with Hirata's misbehavior earlier, he might have headed off this calamity. If only his learning the truth about Hirata's secret society hadn't coincided with his own breakdown! If he'd had no lapse in honor to atone for, he might have been able to bend the law.

His wishes were in vain. Bushido and conscience pressured Sano to take the high, difficult road.

"I can't." At this moment Sano hated himself more than he'd ever hated Yanagisawa or the shogun. But he'd gone after Yanagisawa because he and Yoshisato were committing treason. He couldn't look the other way for Hirata any more than he could let Ienobu inherit the regime after setting up two murders. "I have to treat Hirata like the criminal he is."

HIRATA OPENED EYES crusted with dried tears and blood. Flat on his back, he gazed up at a low ceiling studded with rocks. Haloes of light rimmed lanterns mounted on stands around him. Slow, raspy breaths filled his dry nostrils with the smell of dank earth and pungent chemicals. His body felt stiff and numb, his mind fogged with a sleep too heavy to be natural. A droning sound filled his ears. Hirata tried to sit up.

Tight cuffs around his wrists and ankles bound him to the padded surface on which he lay. Panic dispelled some of the sleep-fog. Hirata raised his head. He saw his torso and limbs encased in white cloth bandages stained with green ooze. On his left, a ceramic bottle hung upside down on a pole. The bottle had a long, thin metal tube inserted in its stopper. The tube's other end was stuck in his arm and tied in place with string. The place seemed to be an underground cave. Tahara and Kitano bent over a hearth on which an iron pot simmered. Their lips moved. The sound was their voices chanting.

"Where am I?" His voice was a feeble croak.

Kitano continued chanting as he stirred the pot. Tahara came to stand over Hirata. "In a safe place where no one will bother us." His unfriendly face was still bruised from the battle. Not much time had passed since then.

"What happened?" he asked.

"General Otani punished you," Tahara answered.

"What are you doing to me?"

"Secret medical treatments and mystical healing spells. Your wounds are pretty bad."

Still chanting, Kitano pushed a strange apparatus on wheels toward Hirata. It was a bellows connected by a metal tube to the neck of a large ceramic jar. Kitano fetched the pot from the hearth. His scarred face was covered with raw, stitched-up gashes from his fight with Deguchi. He poured the pot's contents into the jar, corked it, and inserted another, thinner tube through the cork. Tahara connected the end of the thin tube to a leather mask, which he pressed over Hirata's nose and mouth. Kitano pumped the bellows. Hirata moaned as steam laced with sweet chemicals invaded his lungs.

"Why . . . ?" The mask muffled his voice. The fog of sleep thickened.

"Why are we healing you instead of letting you die?" Tahara said, his hostile voice echoing in the cave. "Because General Otani has further use for you."

With his last waking thought Hirata wished he were dead. That was better than being saved in order that he could continue his treasonous collaboration with Tahara, Kitano, and the ghost. Worse trouble was coming. But a glint of hope eased his anguish, illuminated the noxious black sleep that overtook Hirata's consciousness.

As long as he was alive, he had a chance to destroy his enemies, make amends to his family and Sano, and restore his honor.